The Tree Museum

Kathleen Kaufman

The Way Things Are Publications
Los Angeles

For Mark and Robby
You are my sun, my moon and all my stars

A special thank you to Nicole Priesmeyer and John McLean for your unending patience and efficiency. Any errors that exist in this book are my doing and the direct result of not following your good advice.

Thank you also to my family. I am grateful everyday for your faith in me and
your unwavering support.

The Tree Museum

The actual tragedies of life bear no relation to one's preconceived ideas. In the event, one is always bewildered by their simplicity, their grandeur of design, and by that element of the bizarre which seems inherent in them.
-Jean Cocteau

1

To Whom It May Concern:
It has come to our attention that boats belong in water.
Therefore, in order to correct the error that was made here, the area formally
known as "Priceplan" will be permanently removed.
This correction will take place in one day's time.

The new sign appeared on a Tuesday. Rosemary was unexpectedly
pleased with the development, since she was in complete agreement: boats belong in water. The truth was the aged wooden houseboat hadn't touched water
in years, not since Priceplan built a supercenter over the marina. At the time, it
was considered a small sacrifice to ground the marina, especially since the community would be receiving a supercenter that would save its citizens hours of
driving to town. Now they could shop for groceries, car batteries, bottled water,
flashlights, and cold medicine in one convenient spot, which just happened to be
located on what used to be the marina. It was a small sacrifice.

Of course, that was the opinion of the Priceplan people. The boat owners found themselves grounded. Those who could, left town, sailed down the
coast, and docked in Francine Bay. Rosemary liked Francine Bay; it was quiet,
lots of khaki and flannel shirts. It was the best part of every college town—
without the college. The blocks were dotted thoughtfully with coffee shops
and pubs. Despite its proximity to San Diego, the air had a mysterious bite that
guaranteed it was never too hot or cold. It was the kind of place you could walk
for hours, staring at the beach cottages, musing about the lives that went on
inside.

Rosemary assumed that she and Nate would be joining everyone else, so
she packed up their breakables and began collecting bottled water and canned
goods for the trip. She found herself pulling Nate a little closer to her at night;
he'd sleepily take her hand and place it on his chest, covering it with his own.
She'd sleep, breathing in his night scent, bobbing on the water, dreaming of a
beach cottage.

There was, of course, an expectation of protest. The initial rallies on the marina planks, the endless petitions and letter writing campaigns. A local representative with the unfortunate last name of Shmutty even came to the marina and attempted to deliver a less than inspirational speech. He tried, but Rosemary could see the sweat beading at the edge of his hairline, the tightness commanding his throat. She felt her stomach begin to do flip-flops just watching him. By the end of the rally, she was so nervous for him that she fled from the crowd, holing up in their boat, *Clementine*, until the crowds dispersed. These protests were expected and necessary. Every time the crowds began to gather in that first six-week period, Rosemary secretly hoped for failure. It was good to protest the corporate machine; it was healthy to write letters to your senator. But, if it worked, she would never get out of Mussel Shoals, she would never be able to convince Nate to leave the tiny nothing of a beach town that had been their home since college.

Rumor had it that Mussel Shoals was the birthplace of the west coast jazz scene. By the time Rosemary had moved here with Nate, thirteen years ago, it was pretty hard to believe that it was the birthplace of anything. It sat just south of Santa Barbara and still had remnants of the Santa Barbara wealth in some of its larger homes. Over the years, however, Mussel Shoals had fallen into disrepair, despite the desperate attempts by the city council to spark tourism. Nursing homes outnumbered the single-family houses, and restaurants like Chili's and Applebee's were crowded out by Furr's and Country House Buffet. Even the "hip" downtown stretch that was built shortly before Rosemary and Nate arrived had faded. Now it served as a walking track for the elderly population. There were some business towers, and the in and out movement of tenants and clients provided the only suggestion of a "downtown" environment. For the most part though, the town had aged with its citizens, and Rosemary felt herself aging with it, too. At thirty-five, she felt itchy; the compulsion to bolt almost overpowering her at times. If the protests worked and Priceplan was shut out, she would lose her chance forever.

She watched with growing dread as Nate befriended the conspiracy theorists in the green houseboat named *Cursory Angel*. Her heart sank a little lower when it became clear that Priceplan had no intention of saving the seal nesting beach. One morning, she watched a Priceplan executive toss his Styrofoam coffee cup into the marina water as he walked the planks with a crowd of other suits. She wanted to run after him, turn him around, and shake him.

Don't you know I want you to win! Don't give everyone such a good reason to hate you!

Still, at night Rosemary would sleep beside her husband, her hand on his bare chest, and dream about sailing out of Mussel Shoals. She dreamt of Francine Bay and its dark wooded coffee shops, she even imagined sailing further, even to Perth, New Zealand. *Clementine* would never make it that far, she'd be lucky to make it to Francine Bay, but Rosemary let herself imagine. As she felt Nate's chest rise and fall, she wondered about sailing north, stopping in San Francisco on their way to Juneau Bay. Maybe they'd even stay the summer and watch the birds migrate from the poles.

As it was, the birds still migrated, and the docks in Francine Bay filled with the Priceplan refugees. *Clementine* wasn't the only houseboat still in port when the bulldozers arrived; *Cursory Angel* stubbornly refused to budge, as did *Nancy's Hideaway*, *Last Man on Earth*, and *Lana Turner*. Rosemary pleaded with Nate to reconsider; she posted maps of Francine Bay and Juneau all over *Clementine*'s bulkheads.

"What is possibly left here for us? What are you trying to prove?"

With a growing darkness behind his eyes, Nate let her questions wash over him before finally breaking.

"Why doesn't this bother you? Are you so blind, so self-focused that you can't see the problem? This is ground zero. This is where we stand up for ourselves! I'm not taking their goddamn money; I don't want their fucking charity!"

Financial settlements were offered, but Nate took the buyout proposal and shredded it right in front of the Priceplan lawyer. Rosemary threatened to leave, even going so far as to pack her suitcase, but she couldn't convince herself to move it to their ancient car and actually drive away. Instead, she sat on the dock, feet dangling. Too tired for tears. She heard Nate approach and sensed him sit down beside her. The effort it would have taken to look at him was too much.

"Baby, look, I know this is hard. I'm doing this for us, I'm trying really hard here and I need you, I need you...."

"For what? You have everything you need right here." She said. "Your buddy from *Cursory Angel*, your bag of rotten fruit to throw at the suits."

Tentatively, Nate's hand moved to her thigh. She considered brushing it off, but allowed the warmth to spread from his hand out to her body.

"I'm gonna make this up to you. I really am," he said, softly. "We're gonna win this thing. But I—I can't do this without you; there's no point in it without you. If you leave, I might as well move into one of those freakin' nursing homes, load up on Jell-O, and watch Golden Girls all day."

Despite herself, Rosemary giggled. Nate continued, encouraged.

"Baby, you're the most important thing in the world right now. If you say go, we go. We'll push out today, and we'll go wherever you want. But I'm hoping you don't say Juneau—it's considerably less temperate, not to mention really, really far away."

Rosemary allowed herself to lean into Nate's chest, his arm curling around her.

"You're such a jackass."

Nate's arm tightened around her. "Is there a but, in that, as in, 'you're such a jackass, but....'"

Without looking at him but allowing his warmth to overtake her, she replied, "Nope, you're just a jackass."

Nate's hand twined into her hair, and Rosemary felt herself melt further

13

into him.

He lifted her face up toward him, his lips barely touching hers.

"We could go together. That place over on Third Avenue lets couples and small dogs all live together. I'll bet we could get matching hospital beds, and you could come visit me late at night when the nurse falls asleep. Whaddya say?"

So Rosemary stayed. Maybe it was the memory of that kiss on the docks, or the peace in his voice. She felt herself cave, her resolution giving way. They didn't set sail for Francine Bay, and they didn't pack up the car. Rosemary pushed her growing dread further down and clung to Nate's dream. Even when the Priceplan executives revealed their plan for the holdouts, she clung to that kiss.

In light of the boatyard residents' utter refusal of their buyout proposal, Priceplan devised a much more Machiavellian strategy. If the boats refused to leave, they would be welcomed by the Priceplan complex! By welcomed, the suits meant boxed in by concrete walls and forced to dock on the artificial gravel surface that Priceplan engineers were rapidly using to fill in the marina. In the end, no amount of picketing, screaming, or shaking of tiny fists at the sky stopped Priceplan from finishing its supercenter. The artificial gravel surface was of such a consistency that it expanded, absorbed, and hardened the entire marina into what resembled a rocky playground. The front area of the super-center was then subsequently paved and lined for parking spaces. The protesting boats were hidden away from view in the rear of Priceplan. They were still upright, but instead of floating on ocean water, they were nestled in the artificial gravel.

Clementine was on the far side of the new boatyard. She had shifted during the construction and now leaned about twenty degrees to the port, balanced against the Priceplan wall. The other houseboats were similarly positioned. *Nancy's Hideaway* and *Last Man on Earth* leaned on each other, providing their residents a slightly slanted interior. *Lana Turner* was half buried in the artificial gravel surface. Her residents were infuriated at this development, because even though they enjoyed a tilt-free existence within her walls, she would be stuck when the water returned, and would surely be destroyed. *Lana Turner's* residents were optimists. *Cursory Angel* was the saddest case. She had actually lurched forward during the construction and as a result was stuck half under the Priceplan and half out. The conspiracy theorists could no longer sit on her bow drinking imported beer and smoking dark tobacco. The bow was wedged under several tons of concrete and an assortment of discounted sporting goods.

Rosemary watched it all happen as though from a distance. She refused to listen to the internal voice that kept nagging at her, telling her that she had had a chance to get out. She could have insisted that they set sail, but she didn't, and now it was too late. She tried to push the resentment she felt toward Nate so far down that she could no longer recognize it. She became annoyed with everything he did, the way he closed the kitchen cabinets, the shirts he dropped on the floor, the way he breathed at night. She reminded herself that this was her choice, she chose to see Nate's rebellion through, and no matter the outcome, she needed to swallow it. So, Rosemary woke up every morning and headed to work. She stood in front of her classroom and tried to drive her home out of her thoughts. She dreaded the end of each day. That kiss on the dock drifted further away. Nate still pulled her to him at night, she still felt her body surge when that warm darkness surrounded her, but when the morning arrived, his joy was gone.

The first year was the hardest. Nate had lost his job at the Chronicle due to his frequent absences from work and increasing paranoia. In lieu of finding another job, Nate had devoted his energy to protesting Priceplan. The *Cursory Angel* conspiracy theorist and his roommates adopted this new profession as well. They were remarkably disciplined, rising every morning at half past six, and meeting by the steel ladder that would take them up from the gravel boatyard and onto the Priceplan sidewalk. They became adept at climbing the ladder while carrying homemade picket signs, bullhorns, and soggy produce. The purpose behind the signs and bullhorns was obvious, and the produce they lobbed at the suits who were constantly milling about. Afterwards, they enjoyed shaking each other's hands, congratulating each other on their fine marksmanship. Rosemary had joined them on more than a few excursions, and while she admitted that it was oddly satisfying to see the squishy tomatoes and peaches fly through the air and land with a splatter on the suits, it wasn't rewarding enough to convince Rosemary to make this her full time profession.

Good thing too; protesting pays very little. Rosemary taught eleventh grade History at the local high school. Most of the boatyard residents had lost their jobs during the protest, and only Rosemary and a cylindrical man from *Nancy's Hideaway* left the yard each day to go to work. The others would occasionally join Nate and the rest of the conspiracy theorists on the sidewalk for soggy fruit lobbing, but for the most part, they were content to bemoan their days and drink rum and Cokes on the decks of their stranded boats. Eventually, the bulk of the *Cursory Angel* residents lost interest in the protest, and only one other man still climbed the ladder with Nate every morning; the others stayed on the stern of the boat, drinking loudly. How they afforded the rum was a mystery to Rosemary, since she, Nate and *Clementine* were barely making ends meet on her salary. Priceplan had been kind enough to waive any kind of rent they might have exacted from the boatyard, but repairs, generator costs, and food added up quickly.

Rosemary settled into a numb kind of rhythm. At times, the boatyard was comforting, the other residents periodically bringing over drinks. On the weekends, Rosemary would cook up a giant pot of chili, one of three things she could actually cook—the other two being variations on her chili recipe—and the neighbors would stop by, eat, and together, they'd bemoan their fate. Rosemary would look over at Nate to see him smiling, even laughing. But when everyone left and it was just the two of them, he slipped into his silence. He

15

seemed to slowly shift, as though in sympathy with the boat. More and more, he seemed incapable of talking about anything but Priceplan, and more and more, Rosemary found herself beating down her conscience. Any respite she had during the day and early evening hours when the neighbors would stop in disappeared as soon as they were left alone. She wondered if he actually would have left if she had demanded it. She also questioned why she hadn't taken the chance and made them leave.

For Nate's part, he slipped back into his old habits. Rosemary watched him park himself in front of their thirteen-inch television and watch reruns until his eyes were sore and bloodshot. They never had the money for cable TV, but the bunny ear antenna still picked up a public access channel out of Santa Barbara that showed sitcoms and movies from the eighties. Rosemary would bang around the tiny houseboat kitchen, daring him to tell her to be quiet. She even took to repeating a mantra to herself every night.

"Please give me patience, please give me patience, please give me patience."

But simple patience wouldn't be enough. What she needed was something to overwhelm her growing sense of frustration. She salvaged every scrap of normalcy, forcing it to nourish her until another morsel was thrown her way.

In many ways, Nate hadn't changed at all. He was still the same guy who talked to celebrities in his sleep, snippets of dreams inspired by his hours of television watching. But he'd always done it, and the cast of characters was eerily consistent. His outbursts provided the scraps she needed. As she listened to the television in the other room, she wondered what kind of fight he was going to have tonight.

2

Nate listened to Rosemary slam the kitchen cabinets. "Beyond the Miracle" was playing on TV, Mare Winningham as a grown Helen Keller. She was at the college dance, waiting pathetically in a chair for Annie Sullivan, when Rosemary began her nightly passive-aggressive attack on the kitchen. Nate grumbled to himself and turned up the volume. He knew the television only fed his sleep disorder, but he couldn't bring himself to turn it off.

Of course, it wasn't always bad. In the past, Mare Winningham had been pretty nice; it was only recently that she'd turned on him. It was the others Nate dreaded. When he was thirteen, Nate deprived himself of sleep for five full days just to avoid a nasty run-in with Judd Hirsch. After he started seeing spots and talking to the walls, Nate's parents had hauled him off to the New Mount Sleep Clinic and Research Center. Twenty grueling days and 200 electronically charged tests later, Nate was diagnosed with a subconscious fixation with celebrities that can—and in Nate's case most certainly did—bleed into their sleep patterns and dreamscapes.

Nate never talked about the Judd Hirsch incident that sparked his breakdown, but to this day, whenever he heard the theme song to *Dear John,* goose bumps rose up on his skin. Since the Priceplan incident, Nate had woken up three nights out of the week in a heated debate with Mare Winningham, which for the most part, concerned her rather sloppy performance in a 1980s TV drama about a woman who undergoes a brain transplant.

Nate remembered the first time that Rosemary had been witness to his sleep disorder. It was about fifteen years ago, before the wedding, before any trouble at all had seeped into their lives. Rosemary had slept over, her body and scent still so unfamiliar in Nate's bed. He'd woken up to Rosemary shaking him, crying. Evidently, he'd had a screaming match with Mary Elizabeth Mastrantonio. He remembered the dream, but had no recollection of actually vocalizing the argument. Rosemary had no idea what to make of it. She was crying, frightened by the anger she'd never seen in him, thinking that Nate was dreaming about an ex-girlfriend named "Lizzy."

Nate wanted to walk into the kitchen and close the cabinet, take Rosemary into the bedroom, lie down beside her, and let the smell of her apple shampoo overwhelm him. Instead, he sat in front of the thirteen-inch television again, squinting to see Mare Winningham waltz awkwardly around the room. The sheer effort of trying to please her made him exhausted. He meant what he'd said. He would have left with her if she'd demanded it. She said no—that she'd give it a shot—but now she marched around the kitchen like a spoiled child, taking out her anger on the chipped plastic plates.

She was beautiful, and even more so when she was pissed off. Before the marina had dried up, before their ocean view was blocked by the Priceplan wall, he would have gotten up. He would have gone right to the store and bought her the vanilla-filled chocolates she loved. Rosemary swished by the kitchen entrance and glared briefly in his direction. Nate sighed and turned back to the TV. It'd only piss her off more if he spent any of their money on chocolates. He knew he should be working, but with each passing day, he found himself less able even to talk about a "boss" figure without suppressing an urge to smash a rotten pear in the person's face.

Fuck the Chronicle. Fuck 'em! He'd gotten that lousy job right out of college, and he had been the best thing they had going for them. A newspaper in Mussel Shoals was a joke anyway. Nothing happened and no one cared about the outside world. A few years ago, they'd tried to introduce a "world news" section in the paper, but they were flooded with complaints from the geezer residents. They wanted their local news, they wanted to read the menu for the Community Cafeteria Bakeoff; they did not want anything to do with Kazakhstan or Bosnia. So, now he wasted his Journalism degree editing recipe lists for banana bread and making sure the dates for the Senior Beach Walk were accurate. Fuck the Chronicle. So what if he hadn't shown up every day? He didn't need to be at work every day to typeset the "Ask Melvin" advice column. Melvin only answered one letter a week; Nate could do the Chronicle job in his sleep.

It wasn't as if Rosemary's job was any better. He watched her go to school every day and try to teach the kids that belonged to the migrants who worked the vineyards and orange groves. She taught them the history of a country they cared little about, and then they moved on; usually as soon as the harvest was over and usually before the school year was finished. Nate learned early on not to make any mention of that to Rosemary. When Nate met Rosemary, she was a writer. He had absolutely no idea why she was still in college, especially since she even had a book out, and a successful one at that. She hadn't made much money off of it, but it was just a matter of time.

He tried to read it, but it was a paperback romance. Nate made it through about thirty pages before he had to put it down. It read like one of the daytime soap operas, but of course, women loved it. Nate was almost certain he loved Rosemary by then, even though he'd never spoken to her. Back then, she sat near him in class at Santa Barbara City College. He'd tried a few dozen times to get her attention, but she'd largely ignored him. Still, she fascinated him. Her long, honey hair was perpetually pulled back from her face, she wore no make-up, and she smelled like vanilla and caramel. The other girls in their political science class whispered about her; it was from them that Nate learned about her book. Rosemary always looked distracted, and somewhat dumfounded. Most of the girls in the room thought she was snobbish, but Nate found himself spellbound by the perplexed crinkle on her forehead, the way her light brown eyes faded two shades deeper when she concentrated.

Even now, as she banged around the kitchen, he was fascinated by her movement, the way she bounced between being hyperaware of and then totally oblivious to her surroundings. He knew he should get up, go in there and stop her, but his body and mind were tired. He was tired of fighting, fighting with Rosemary, fighting with the Priceplan suits, tired of feeling so fucking ineffectual. The bone deep weariness made it impossible for him to care what got slammed around in the kitchen.

He tried not to think about what was going to happen to them. They had no money to move; they'd have no option but to stay with Nate's parents in Santa Barbara if they left now, and that simply wasn't an option. Maybe she'd been right; maybe they should've made a break for it. Nate turned up the volume and nodded off to Mare Winningham talking to Mark Twain.

3

Nate was very much the same guy he was when he and Rosemary finally met. Rosemary, on the other hand, wasn't so sure about herself. She wasn't supposed to be here, slamming kitchen cabinets and living in a parking lot. She was supposed to be on novel writing tours, or at the very least working in a cushy job in the Harlequin office in New York. She hadn't spent the bulk of her teen years memorizing Marlen's monologues from Days of our Lives for nothing. It was during her sophomore year at City College that she'd received an offer for the publication of a short story she'd written. It was about Raul, an unfortunately handsome street urchin who was forced to work nights at the panty factory. One can guess the specifics of the plot, but suffice it to say the ladies of the factory took pride in proper job training. It was good—good enough to get her noticed, anyway.

Rosemary's novel had been selling through grocery store stands by the time she was twenty, about the time she met Nate. The novel itself was typical romance novel fare, several sweaty princesses and a washer boy. She finally spied Nate one day, hunkered down under a tree on campus. He was reading her book, but it was the confused look he wore on his face that made her notice him. He said he'd read the entire thing when he finally asked her out a month later. They'd been a couple for a few months after that, when Rosemary's publisher called to give her some news about a potentially bad situation. Apparently, a group of co-eds had tried to recreate a scene from her book that involved a box of laundry powder and a loofah. The problem arose in their choice of soap. Rosemary had never thought to mention that that particular scene should only be attempted with a lye-free soap choice, and having neglected to do so, she was facing a lawsuit by the parents of the now half-blind co-eds. While the court case didn't hold any water, Rosemary's publisher got skittish and dropped her publishing deal. After that setback, Rosemary sent out manuscript after manuscript, eventually realizing that her fifteen minutes were over. Then, she had no choice but to figure out what she was going to do with the rest of her life.

Every day as Rosemary faced her eleventh graders, she wondered if she had given up too quickly. She wondered if it was still in her to write, she wondered if the light had gone out for good. She sacrificed her passion for stability.

20

At the time, it was all very exciting; moving aboard a houseboat meant never being tied to a permanent address again. Later, she and Nate would travel the world together, see the coasts of all the continents, swim with dolphins, ride on the backs of manta rays, and live off the ocean. As it turned out, with the exception of a couple of weekend trips to Irish Bend Cove, *Clementine* would remain tied firmly within the very same berth Rosemary spotted when Nate carried her over the threshold—through the hatch, Nate told her—thirteen years before.

And now, they would never sail again. Not even to Irish Bend Cove. Their home was now a parking lot surrounded by other stubborn refugees of a war resolutely lost. To add insult to injury, there was always the occasional Priceplan patron who would throw a can or a glass bottle down into the boatyard.

Rosemary felt herself shutting down, turning off the senses she couldn't manage any longer. She stopped slamming around the kitchen, left Nate alone more often to watch his television reruns while she sat on the deck of her stranded boat, wishing for a change—any change at all. Things certainly had changed, she observed, as she looked around, but not enough to free them from the artificial gravel that had become their prison and their home.

Which is why the sign that appeared on a Tuesday was particularly exciting for Rosemary. It represented freedom—*Clementine*'s release. Now, Nate couldn't come up with a reason to stay docked, he would be forced to sail them to a new place, a place without a Priceplan, or suits. Rosemary had hurried up the rickety ladder and had just swung through the decaying hatch to find Nate pacing furiously in cramped kitchenette as he lectured a *Cursory Angel* conspiracy theorist.

"What right do they have? They're messing with our civil liberties, here! I will not—I cannot stand by and watch some goddamn invader stomp on our basic freedoms. I will not have my fate decided by some kind of goddamn faceless problem solver!"

The *Cursory Angel* conspiracy theorist silently nodded in agreement.

Upon seeing Rosemary in the doorway, Nate paused, gulped, and crossed the space in two steps.

"This is it baby, this is the big fight. This is our chance to stand up for our liberties. We won't let them tell us when, where, and how we lead our lives."

Upon hearing this, Rosemary was confused.

"But, why? What are you talking about? They're removing Priceplan!"

Nate's green eyes darkened and narrowed.

"It's just like you to be complicit in this. Just let everyone do everything for you. That's what you do, isn't it?"

Rosemary felt her breath catch and a cold vacancy filled her stomach.

Nate saw her weaken and continued, his voice deadly steady and calm. "We've been here how long Rosemary? Ten years? Stuck in this pile of shit? Have you ever done anything to change it? No. You wait until some goddamn signmaker comes along and changes it for you, then you're all smiles and light."

Rosemary found her voice. "Fuck you! I've been the reason we've been able to survive! I've been the reason you haven't worked in what? Ten years now? Do you even remember having a job? You have food because I bought it; you have everything because of me!"

Nate stepped back, his hand stiff. Rosemary wondered if he would actually hit her.

"You bitch! I've given you everything you ever asked for. I gave you a chance to leave, remember that? You said no, you said stay, and now you have the nerve..."

"The what? What kind of fucking choice was it, Nate? You never would have left this piece of shit! You would have stayed here whether or not I said go!"

The conspiracy theorist squeezed past Rosemary. "That's my cue to exit, man."

Nate didn't seem to notice his leaving.

"What did you ever bring, Rosemary? You know why I stayed here, with you, why I let you stay? I felt fucking sorry for you! So pathetic. Poor little Rosemary, everyone always out to get you! You're lucky I didn't kick you out years ago. Pathetic."

Rosemary felt a sob well up from the bottom of her throat before she forced it back down. "Too much has happened for you not to accept this! You can't still fight this! It's everything, Nate! The waitresses..."

"Jesus Christ! Bring those fucking machines back into it! You'd love to see me kowtowing to some goddamn robot wouldn't you? Go ahead, Rosemary, this is your chance. Go see what they can give you, if they can fix everything, if they can bring daddy back. Go ahead, you pathetic little nothing!"

The sob finally tore free from her throat and wrenched its way into being. The Nate she married wouldn't say this. The Nate from thirteen years ago would never do this. Even the depressed Nate, who'd resigned himself to a frozen boat and lost himself in television would never say this. When she looked closer, even Nate's face seemed stunned, as if he couldn't quite believe what he'd said, either.

They'd had this fight before, four months ago. They'd fought about it when the waitresses first appeared. But even then, Nate had stopped himself. He'd stopped short of going too far and kept it to the surface. But in an instant, his look of astonishment gave way. When it did, even more words came spilling out of his mouth.

"Go ahead and leave! Go! Run away! That's what you do, isn't it? I don't want you here! Get the fuck off my boat!"

Rosemary recoiled. He might as well have gone ahead and hit her. The words she might have spoken were frozen within her throat. She stumbled drunkenly back toward the stairs that led to the deck, backing up, silently begging Nate to stop her, to ask her to stay.

4

Nate tried to stop the words even as they came flying out of his mouth. Part of him meant it. He was sick of her goddamn whining, sick of her moping around all the time, not trying to change anything, acting like a beaten puppy. Part of him wanted to help her pack up their stuff, walk away from the boat-yard, maybe catch a Greyhound to LA and find some means of starting over. It wouldn't be that easy of course. They couldn't afford Greyhound tickets any more than they could afford to move to another city. They couldn't afford to do anything, and Nate knew it was his fault.

Nate watched Rosemary back up the boat's steps, tears running down her face. He felt frozen. A voice in the back of his head kept chanting softly:

"She should apologize. Don't back down. She should apologize."

Soon enough, Rosemary's form disappeared from sight and Nate heard her footsteps cross to the ladder, and then disappear. Where the hell was she going to go? Nate knew the answer before he even asked the question. She'd run to the waitresses. The thought unfroze his feet from the spot where he was standing and he felt a surge of anger rush through his body. He charged up the steps and onto the deck, just in time to see Rosemary on the sidewalk, walking away. His head was swimming, and he heard his voice as is from a distance.

"Get the fuck off my boat! Find someone else to blame for everything!" She didn't react. Just kept walking, eyes straight ahead. Nate sunk to his knees, the anger draining, exhausted.

5

Rosemary felt numb. She walked down the street, only half-hearing Nate's voice. Why did she bring up the damn waitresses? Why was he so crazy against them? She couldn't think about the rest of Nate's words without feeling the cold spread across her stomach. Instead, she forced herself to concentrate on the waitresses. She knew what to do with that fight. That fight was safe, it wasn't about her; it could be fixed. Tuning out every word that inched toward her heart, Rosemary mumbled to herself.

"Goddamn baby, that's what he is. God forbid we have anything pleasant in our lives. He has no problem taking everything from me, God forbid it comes from them; yeah, that'd be wrong...goddamn hypocrite."

The waitresses had begun to appear about four months ago, along with the signs, and Rosemary and Nate had a similar argument back then. Rosemary refused to see how a creature that was able to supply unlimited food, drink, and medicine was a negative influence on society. Nate, however, was infuriated at what he called "their moral high horse" and "false sense of superiority." He refused to see that "their moral high horse" was simply a means of preventing drug addicts and alcoholics from going on a free bender.

Rosemary did have to admit that the means of censoring these requests was questionable at best. No one really knew what happened when you were permanently removed, except that it happened in a magnificent flash of light, and then you were no more. In the first few weeks after the waitresses were introduced, there were a lot of magnificent flashes of light. Of course, everyone knew the rules. Signs had been posted all over town outlining the services provided by the waitresses and the consequences for abusing their kindness. Dressed like fifties diner girls, their purpose was to dispense food, water, or medicine to anyone who showed a need. The rules clearly stated that requests made within reason would be granted. This included family vehicles and pet supplies, furniture items, and essentially all non-harmful means of entertainment.

As was to be expected, however, rules were disregarded and consequences were paid. The signs stated clearly that acts of unnecessary greed would be punished. Still, this didn't stop businessmen from demanding twenty-five Jaguars and a penthouse loft. The businessmen were permanently removed. Rosemary felt terrible thinking it, but she couldn't help but wonder if it served them right. Nate, however, took this action as a sign of supposed moral superiority and even broke from a day of lobbing soggy fruit at suits to pace the town's streets dressed in black mourning robes that had "Death of the Human Spirit" printed on the back. While she never told Nate, Rosemary herself had experimented with the waitresses. One day on her way back from work, Rosemary had stopped in front of one of the neatly coifed girls. Her waitress wore a black and white diner dress with buttons that ran down the front. A perfect pink apron was tied perfectly around her waist and matched the perfect pink headband that pulled the perfect beehive hair back from her face. Rosemary was greeted with a wide smile.

"Welcome. Is there anything you would like, today?"

Rosemary thought for a minute, she really wanted a soda, and it seemed small enough that it wasn't really like she was betraying Nate. As Rosemary opened her mouth, she censored the word that started to come out.

"I'd like a Co   Pepsi, please."

Censored because of the word choice, of course. In addition to the greedy businessmen, a great many others had been permanently removed for unreasonable requests that ranged from firearms to excessive amounts of alcohol to drugs. Coke seemed a little too close to cocaine, and Rosemary did not want the two confused.

The waitress blinked twice.

"Repeat that please, I'm not familiar with a copepsi."

"I meant, a Pepsi."

"Of course."

A tray hovered in front of the waitress, untouched by her perfect, smooth hands. A frosty glass filled with cola suddenly appeared. Rosemary lifted the icy glass, and the tray disappeared.

"Thanks."

"No problem. You enjoy that!"

Rosemary never told Nate about the Pepsi; she knew he would be furious. He looked at the waitresses as control mechanisms, devices the signmakers were using to lull the public into complicity. She knew that even if she explained that the Pepsi was just an experiment to test the waitresses—and really out of simple curiosity—he would shake his head and produce that low grumbling sound he always made when he was disappointed. Things would have progressed much like the argument they had about the boatyard sign. Rosemary knew instinctually that she should be outraged, but she found that she was even more outraged by living in a gravel lot.

6

Nate knew about the Pepsi. He had always known. In fact, he had seen the entire thing. It happened to be a day that he had picketed the Priceplan site in the morning and then switched to their corporate office for the afternoon. He liked to keep his approach fresh; plus, Priceplan occasionally had its security people remove him from the sidewalk in front of the store. Of course, that didn't happen very often, because public outcry about the boatyard only became more apparent when security was seen to be hassling the poor residents of the once-watery marina.

Nate had watched his wife approach the waitress, and a secret hope had risen in him that maybe she had a soggy pear or a squishy tomato in her pocket that she would launch at the waitress's airbrushed face. But instead, his wife ordered a Pepsi, and then proceeded to sit down on a park bench and drink it while looking happy. He had initially planned all the nasty words he might say to her, but the longer he watched her on the park bench, the faster his nasty words went silent. She looked happy. The vein between Rosemary's brown eyes wasn't twitching and bulging as it did anytime she sat down to write out the bills. Her eyebrows weren't knotted as they were when she was under *Clementine*, wrench in hand, trying to repair the ancient generator. Nate was overcome with a sudden sense of immense guilt when he realized that the happiest he had seen Rosemary in years was when she was drinking an artificial Pepsi, sitting alone on a bench in the middle of a crowd of strangers.

The goddamn waitresses! The signs had appeared first. Out of nowhere, they would just materialize, sometimes in the shape of stop sign, other times a yield sign. Sometimes, it was a sign that already existed, such as a restaurant sign or a road sign, but the lettering would change. But instead of the speed limit, or STOP, the sign would display some cryptic message. No one paid much attention at first. Most of the Mussel Shoals residents figured it was a prank, or didn't care to think at all. Nate figured it was some kind of publicity stunt, maybe for a new movie. As the weeks passed, the signs became increasingly serious, warning people to stop doing things.

It has come to our attention that Carol Newman
Was responsible for the traffic accident on the corner of
Blake Street and 3rd Avenue last Tuesday.
It has come to our attention that Ms. Newman drove away without
Remedying the situation.
You have forty-eight hours to make amends.

The scary part was that the signs were right. There had been a hit and run accident on Blake and 3rd Avenue. A car had run a red light, slammed into a minivan full of kids, then took off. But no one had written down the license plate; there were no leads. So how did the signmakers know it was Carol Newman? Nate didn't have any idea who she was, but sure enough, the next day's edition of the Chronicle ran a front page story on her.

"Hit and Run Driver Turns Herself In After Offering Full Restitution for Last Monday's Accident"

Carol Newman was one of the lucky ones. There were other signs, and other people who didn't take them quite as seriously as Carol had. Nate remembered the first time he'd seen someone permanently removed. He was standing on the plank walkway that led to Priceplan. Taking a break, he was leaning against a post, watching the shoppers come and go. It all happened so fast that Nate didn't quite know how to react. An elderly woman tottered out the door toward the parking lot, glossy brown purse hanging from her crooked hand. In an instant, a man, young—nearly a kid—raced in, saw the purse, snatched it, and knocked the old lady to the ground in the process. Stunned by what he'd seen, Nate started toward the man, hoping to block his path as he approached rapidly. But Nate didn't have the chance to intercede. A stop sign shot up instantly in front of the mugger. He didn't even have time to stop before he ran head first into the pole. Nate saw him scan the words and then look back at the Priceplan security officers who had started after him. Without pausing and purse still in hand, the kid dodged the sign and took off again. He didn't get five steps past the sign before a blinding flash of light erupted around him. And he was gone; just gone. Somehow, the purse remained. A crowd formed around the sign.

It has come to our attention that Darryl Mansing
Has caused grievous harm to another citizen.
Darryl Mansing has been permanantly removed.

Over time, the language of the signs became clearer. They became more cautious, and offered offenders more time to remedy their wrongs. But in the beginning, the justice was fast and brutal. The signmakers also seemed somewhat inconsistent in the attention they paid. Some people, like Carol Newman, weren't found guilty right away, but others, like Darryl Mansing, were caught immediately. Nate figured it was like the police. Sometimes, people were dumb enough to commit crimes while a cop watched from ten yards away, and some got away with murder just because they were in the right place at the right time. The thing about the signmakers that made Nate shiver was that it wasn't as clear-cut as having a cop ten yards away. No one knew where they were, what they were watching.

The waitresses were a recent addition, and they made Nate crazy. They looked like live cartoons, standing completely still, dressed in their ridiculous diner girl garb, the smile pasted on their frozen faces. It was only when someone asked for something or seemed to need something that they snapped to life. If he hadn't been afraid of getting a sign of his own, Nate would have hurled his rotten fruit at them, just so see what happened. He loathed them on every level of his being. He didn't need charity, he needed his boat back, he needed his life back, he needed the last few miserable years to disappear, and he needed a chance to start over.

But still, as much as he hated the signmakers and their goddamn wait-resses, Rosemary looked happy with her Pepsi. So, he said nothing about it. Deep inside, he felt incredibly sad about *Clementine*, but he could never express that to Rosemary. When they had bought *Clementine*, Nate had been convinced that he would be able to win over this deeply anti-social girl, in part because of the isolated life promised by the houseboat; he thought it was a perfect match.

Since childhood, Nate had a fixation on houseboats. He was from Santa Barbara, about an hour north of Mussel Shoals, and he remembered waking up on the first day of summer vacation. His parents would sometimes rent little houseboats from the Santa Barbara marina, vessels they would sail south to San Diego and dock north of La Jolla. Nate remembered jumping up from bed and diving overboard into the marina. It never bothered him that the marina water was full of gasoline and oil; to him, it felt cool and sweet.

That was what he wanted for his family; the cool sweetness of total free-dom and abandon. This was also why the Priceplan had unhinged some core element in Nate's psyche. Funny thing was, Nate knew it. He was fully aware that his behavior not only was seen as eccentric and downright irresponsible, but also that he had dropped the weight of reality squarely on Rosemary's shoulders. He knew the wrinkle that had begun to form between her eyes was largely his fault. Every day, when he rolled out of his crooked bed and stumbled down the port side ladder on his way to the Priceplan sidewalk, he felt like a little part of his soul was dying. The gravel parking lot that was now his home had become a symbol of everything he had failed to accomplish and everything that had defeated him.

The gravel boatyard was Nate's childhood Judd Hirsch, and Judd Hirsch had caused him two breakdowns. The first being the terrific incident that led to his diagnosis at age thirteen, and the second was the end result of a five-day sleep fast that nearly made Nate jump from the window of his second-story high school history class when he was sixteen. The human brain is an amazing organ, the only one capable of actuating every crank in the human body. In Nate's case, the sleep deprivation had caused him to begin hallucinating, mostly about Judd Hirsch, but it also had caused an amazing elasticity in his joints. The elasticity faded almost immediately upon recovery, but Judd Hirsch stuck around. Even though the doctors had explained to Nate that Judd Hirsch was only a figment of his sleep-starved brain, he refused to believe it. After all, it was because of Judd Hirsch that the sleep fast had begun.

Increasingly, Judd Hirsch had begun appearing in a long series of Nate's dreams involving a shopping cart, a deli counter, and an abacus. The details were hazy, but one or more of these objects threatened him through a steadily escalating series of horrors until sleep was no longer an option for him. The five-day fast was greatly misunderstood. Nate had attempted to explain that it wasn't forever, just until his tickertape number had been called and passed, and therefore erased from the deli's obligation list. Nate knew that in explaining it, he only solidified the doctor's reasons for keeping him longer in the hospital, and by justifying his decision, he was prolonging his hospital menu of Jell-O squares and dry toast.

Eventually, the week before Nate's seventeenth birthday, he finally told the doctors what they wanted to hear. He said that he had been terribly depressed and he was now aware that the deli, Judd Hirsch, and the abacus posed no threat to him. He agreed to go to sleep, and he really wanted to help himself get better. It was, of course, the exact combination of words that would release Nate from the hospital some two weeks later, after intense monitoring and a great deal more Jell-O. Since he had received absolutely no help in dispensing with Judd Hirsch, Nate could only hope that the doctor would never return and prevent him from popping NoDoz.

That was all in the past though, and Rosemary had been remarkably understanding about all of it. In fact, she found a way to talk him out of particularly bad dreams. She would simply start speaking to Nate in her producer voice, which sounded a bit like a husky drag queen.

"You! You don't talk to the stars! Wake up! Get out of that trailer!"

It not only woke him up every single time, but immediately broke the spell the dream held over him. Nate's frustration lay in never being able to remember the details. He always maintained that if he had been able to remember even a few of the details, he might be able to stop the dreams.

The boatyard situation only solidified Nate's sleep disorder. As soon as the artificial gravel had begun to absorb the marina's water, Nate heard the *Dear John* song beating in his right ear like a heartbeat. While Judd Hirsh hadn't actually made an appearance in years, Nate knew that it was just a matter of time. He knew that even Rosemary's producer wouldn't be able to stop that one; he would have to deal with the monster himself.

Nate twitched at the thought and shifted his gaze to a black and white print of Rosemary in her wedding dress that was pinned to the cupboard. It was one of the only photos they had, and Rosemary thought she looked constipated in it. Nate liked her concentration, the abstract thought that visibly showed on her face. The wedding was beautiful, but beautiful in a small and cold kind of way. Nate and Rosemary discovered soon after announcing their engagement that not everyone was thrilled that they were getting married. Nate's family immediately translated the wedding date as the time the couple would start producing grandchildren. Nate's mother even bought the couple a car seat and plush pink elephant as a wedding present. Nate's father gave them an ornately scripted family tree, which Nate wrongly assumed was intended for the living room wall. But Nate's father soon informed them that the tree was meant to be hung in the baby's room so he or she would know the significance of the McLeod name.

However baffled Nate was by his family's reaction to the wedding, he was even more confused by that demonstrated by Rosemary's family. Rosemary's mother stopped talking to her and threatened not to show up at the ceremony. Her brother and sister didn't even RSVP the invitation and skipped the ceremony and reception entirely. In fact, the only relatives that seemed happy for Rosemary were her loony second cousins from Portland. The twin sisters, Tanya and Roxie, who had spent their lives running a pet supply company, showered them with gifts that spanned the initial engagement and lasted until well after the honeymoon. They were the only relatives on Rosemary's side of the chapel with tears in their eyes.

Nate had taken it personally at first, but after he watched Rosemary's family shun her brother's subsequent wedding in the same manner, he realized it had nothing to do with him. Rosemary herself was oddly stubborn about going to her brother's wedding. It wasn't until Nate coaxed her out of her defiance with a plane ticket and a promise that they would visit Epcot Center that she relented. Nate didn't understand how Rosemary, a normally loving person, could be part of such a disconnected family. He wondered, sometimes, if the family's overall coldness was the reason for Rosemary's nasty case of social anxiety. It wasn't anything like the pharmaceutical companies tried to portray in the commercials; actually, it was more like an awkward party where the cool kids were forced to invite the class dork. While composed and appropriate most of the time she was with Nate, Rosemary turned into a stuttering, social buffoon anytime she encountered a requirement for social interaction. Nate could hardly hold it against her; after all, he was the one who was being stalked by Judd Hirsch.

On their third date, Nate made the mistake of taking Rosemary to a party being thrown by his ex-roommate from college. He saw her eyes widen in fear when she realized that they weren't simply going to a restaurant or a movie. She almost didn't get out of the car. In retrospect, Nate knew she was trying hard not to throw up because of nerves. Now if this scenario had occurred in the present, after eleven years, Nate knew that Rosemary would never have played along. Instead, she would have told him politely to take her home. But, since the incident took place in the dating stage of their relationship, Rosemary attempted to hide her anxiety from Nate and soldier through the evening.

The first social faux pas she made was grabbing a drink out of a stranger's hand as she was entering. Nate thought she might have known the girl at first, but soon realized that Rosemary had just stolen a drink from a complete stranger. Luckily, the stranger was pretty toasted by then and hardly noticed the affront. The second indication that the party was a bad idea came when Rosemary made a comment to the host. She had already begun stuttering, and in a broken and overly high voice, squeaked:

"Youurr house is realllly um, messy with pppeople."

While messy with people isn't exactly an insult, her observation was nonsensical enough that is made Nate's ex-roommate think Rosemary had been hitting the Jell-O shots. Nate proceeded to guide Rosemary through the party as she snatched bites of food and placed the remainders on other people's plates, poked her finger in the nacho dip, tripped people who were carrying drinks for no apparent reason, and called everyone she met "Frank."

It would be some time before Rosemary would admit to Nate that her social anxiety manifested itself by switching off her impulse control. The change took place because of the stress, and there was really nothing to be done about it, except avoid parties or similar social situations unless Rosemary had a chance to take her medication beforehand. After a couple of the tiny red pills, Rosemary behaved much like any shy, quiet girl would. She talked very little, and laughed appropriately. But, she didn't poke people in the forehead or introduce herself as "Slappy." Nate wasn't sure if he preferred the medicated Rosemary or the no-impulse control Rosemary. Clearly, no-impulse control Rosemary was a good time under the right circumstances. While the third date party had been baffling, it was in retrospect incredibly funny. Nate still laughed out loud when he thought about the look on people's faces as Rosemary had kissed them on the lips randomly, or had started her shopping cart dance on the lawn. The only reason he didn't object to her medication was because he knew how embarrassed Rosemary would be the next day, otherwise. Still, no-impulse control Rosemary was a rocking good time.

Lately, Rosemary had been taking the red pills nearly every day. Nate knew teaching was a terrible career choice for her, and he also knew that he needed to face the reality of the situation that confronted them. But when it came down to actually making a change, he was frozen, just like *Clementine* in her artificial marina. From the time he woke up to the time he fell asleep, his thoughts were dominated by Priceplan. He had whole conversations in his head with the Priceplan executives. He imagined himself speaking to crowds, and it wasn't until he was awake again and realized he'd been muttering to himself and staring in the distance that he knew that opportunity had passed him by. There were no crowds or executives to be harangued.

When the new sign appeared on the street entrance to the trapped boatyard, Nate felt something unwind in his heart. He heard the whir of the cable rolling within him and with a sharp tug, felt the catch clamp down just in time. The waitresses were bad enough, but now the signmakers were telling him what to do with his boatyard. The boatyard was his responsibility, and people would solve their own problems. The signmakers were ignoring their constitutional rights as boat owners to protest and control their own destiny. A wave of blind rage swept over him, and it wasn't until he heard Eli from *Cursory Angel* that he came back to his reality.

"Hey, man, isn't that something? Goddamn signmakers gonna fix all our problems now, huh?"

Nate realized he had been staring at the same spot humming the *Dear John* theme song for nearly an hour. Something had indeed snapped.

Nate saw the sign before Rosemary. He'd been stewing about it all day by the time she'd burst in the door looking flushed and excited. Eli remained in the tiny two-seater booth that served as their kitchen table while Nate ranted. Eli understood why this was so terrible. He understood why they needed to fight this! How could Rosemary come barging in, crying victory? Bullshit! Now, Eli was nowhere to be seen. He'd left sometime during the argument. Nate went back downstairs and flicked on the television to distract himself from his anger. As an LA Law episode from 1987 began, he nodded off to a dream with Harry Hamlin. Harry was confused. He was dressed in his "Clash of the Titans" armor and waved his sword around while ranting

"Isn't this what you wanted?"

It was what Nate wanted, but he didn't want or need Harry Hamlin, the signmakers or any other goddamn busybody sacrificing his last vestiges of human freedom to make him happy. He would fix this himself. He would protest until the executives realized their sins and bulldozed the Priceplan. Nate would actually deliver one of his dream monologues to a crowd that would assemble with an army of sledgehammers and jackhammers. They would tear down each and every brick that held the Priceplan together. They would distribute its reasonably priced groceries, produce, school supplies and foreign made clothing to the homeless and to the nearby Indian reservation. *Clementine* would bob back into the ocean, and the three of them would sail out—out to sea never to look back. Sadly, Harry Hamlin didn't want to hear any of it. It wasn't until Nate began taunting him about "scary scorpions" that he dropped his sword in disgust and walked away with his golden owl.

7

Rosemary found herself at the fifth avenue Walkabout. The Walkabout was a four-block open-air mall that was littered with coffee shops, martini bars and a movie theatre. Geared toward tourists, it also contained every boutique you could ever want, and several nail salons. It was presently the easiest place to find the waitresses, who stood politely on each corner waiting to fill the needs of the passersby. It hadn't always been like this. Rosemary remembered coming here with Nate right after they were married, and had moved into *Clementine*. They would easily spend $200 a night going to bar after bar, eating at the Chinese restaurant on the corner, and drunkenly watching movies. Some of the memories from that time were great, but of course, some weren't. Rosemary remembered puking in her underwear while sitting on a movie theatre toilet. That wasn't great. Fortunately, there weren't many of those exceptions. Rosemary and Nate would find a dark booth in a wine bar, order a bottle of blood red merlot, and vocalize every single dark spot, every single fear left unspoken. They made plans for things they would never do, they talked about the universe, and religion, and why their friends were acting crazy. They laughed about the stupid things Nate's buddies had done the night before. They made fun of the *Cursory Angel* conspiracy theorists, and Nate did a scathing impression of the one with an E name who always talked as though he was high.

About the time the Priceplan landed, however, the Walkabout nights ended. They tried a couple of times, but apart from the fact that Nate's unemployment made it unreasonable—impossible—to spend $200 a night, the intimacy had disappeared. Instead of talking about each other, every silence was overtaken by Priceplan. The protests, the actions, the plans to picket dominated every moment, every snippet of conversation. Rosemary became quiet and let her mind wander. Often, she would zoom out for an hour or so at a time, and set her face on auto-respond, so her light nods and "uh huhs" would cover her absence. Since then, Rosemary hadn't come to the Walkabout very often. Not only did it remind her of some embarrassing times (who could possibly forget the puke in the underwear incident) but more than that, it just made her feel empty.

As Rosemary walked away from the boatyard, the tears began streaming down her cheeks. She had nothing, save what was in the pocket of her jacket, and she didn't know where to go. So, she headed downtown. Getting there was a four-mile hike, and by the time she arrived, the sun was starting to dip in the sky. She wasn't going back; something had broken inside her. She also knew she wouldn't go back tomorrow either; school would just have to start without her. Around 7:30 in the morning, her students would mill about the hallway, stand in front of her classroom door and knock, halfheartedly and unsuccessfully. Ms. Mulroney in the room next to hers would place an urgent call to the office and soon, the assistant principal, a rat faced man named Powler, would open her door with a key. He'd let the students in, stand at the front of the room, and try to coax them into an activity that would prevent them from fighting with each other or carving up the desks. Eventually, a sub would arrive, and her students would probably spend the rest of the day watching some movie from the office, probably "Dead Poets Society."

Rosemary didn't care. The day would go on without her, and outside of a few calls to her cell phone (which she would never receive since she hadn't been able to pay the bill for five months), everyone would forget that she wasn't there. Tonight, even more than most nights, Rosemary felt the end of something. She felt heartsick about Nate, a deep gnawing grief in the pit of her stomach that had been growing for some time. She couldn't imagine life without him, but she couldn't imagine how she would stay. Rosemary was done being angry, and she had been angry for quite awhile. Not just about the boatyard sign, but so many things. She had felt the first twinges when she realized years ago that Nate had no intention of sailing to Perth or Juneau Bay, but instead planned to stay docked and motionless. She felt that disappointment compound when she realized that graduate school would have to wait until Nate was working again. She felt the gnawing chew farther into her every time she had to roll the change from the bottom of her purse and under *Clementine*'s seat cushions so she could buy groceries. Lately, the red Exanthoral she took for anxiety had numbed the gnaw enough to get through the day, but it was really only meant to be taken every once in awhile. The frequent doses had been causing Rosemary's heart to race, and her arm to feel numb. She had considered asking the waitresses for an answer, but Rosemary presumed that answers like those were not quite as accessible as Pepsi.

Sometimes, it worked. Sometimes, Nate would roll over in the night and hold her so tight she could hardly move. Sometimes his green eyes would follow her around *Clementine* while she carried out whatever task she was in the middle of, and Rosemary knew that he was there, and as soon as Priceplan was gone, things would be all right again. To leave him would be to abandon the only person who thought it was funny when her medication didn't stop her from singing the alphabet, or giving strangers wedgies. To leave him would mean abandoning the only person who ever made it okay to just be herself, and to know that without boundaries, she was okay. To leave would be to cut off a part of herself, and never have it back. It would mean becoming an amputee and knowing that she caused the break. Over time, Rosemary repeated to herself the mantra that had so far gotten her through the days and nights:

"When Priceplan is gone when Priceplan is gone when Priceplan is gone...."

But nothing really followed the when. Rosemary hoped that the when meant that Nate would return to the Chronicle, or maybe he would pack up *Clementine*, and the three of them would sail up to Juneau Bay in time to see the Northern Lights. When might mean that Rosemary would never have to see the *Cursory Angel* conspiracy theorists, especially the one with an E name, who smelled like dirt.

The sign had broken the when. The sign had meant for a minute that Rosemary, Nate and *Clementine* were free, but when Rosemary had opened the houseboat door, flushed and excited, she knew at once that you can't repair something left broken for so long. Whatever they had once was lost, and if Nate wouldn't even walk an inch in her direction, wouldn't even compromise his ridiculous pride by one morsel to achieve what it was he had insisted for ten years that he wanted; well, Rosemary knew that whoever it was that married her on a snowy day in December was gone. Rosemary couldn't move any further, she couldn't face the job that she hated or the boat that she had grown to loathe. She was done. And being done was causing the grief in her heart to spill into her stomach.

Without guilt, she asked the waitress on the corner of Watson Street for chicken nuggets, French fries and coffee. Rosemary hadn't eaten chicken in thirteen years, not since Nate decided that the meat industry was not only cruel to its animals, but also to the migrant worker population. Tonight she didn't care. She sat on a bench and dipped the crispy chicken in the ranch sauce the waitress offered. It tasted wonderful. The coffee tasted like vanilla, the French fries were just salty enough. Rosemary ate her chicken and watched people walk around her. She watched a couple of little girls order pom poms from the waitress. Children were generally granted whatever request they made of the waitresses without consequence. They were certainly not subject to the threat of permanent removal; the only negative response Rosemary had ever witnessed was an eleven or twelve-year-old boy being given the transcript of Adam Smith's second proclamation on fiscal frugality in response to his request for a brand new Porsche.

The boutiques and nail salons still had customers. The cash registers still held money, and people just like Rosemary still went to work every day to earn it. Rosemary often wondered why the signmakers hadn't just eliminated money. It seemed to her that if they were truly attempting to work with the deepest happiness of the people, eliminating money would be the first logical step. Without money, or bills, or a job, what would the people have to worry about? Conversely, she mused as she sipped her vanilla coffee, when you can eat chicken nuggets and order family cars whenever you want, it doesn't make much sense to worry about money.

Rosemary presumed that the money was still in place for those who needed it, the suits in the office buildings that outlined the Walkabout, the stock market yellers who placed their identities in their hands and numbers; the money was for them. Once, money had been for her too; the motions of normalcy had kept her and Nate together. The denial that anything had changed kept the seams from ripping for the last four months when the signmakers arrived. Rosemary realized with a heavy sigh, that if she was willing to rip the seams apart, she no longer needed the worries they were holding together.

She didn't want Juneau Bay any longer; never wanted to set foot on *Clementine* again. Rosemary wanted to leave Mussel Shoals, order a family car and a never-ending supply of chicken nuggets with ranch, and drive east. Drive somewhere with trees and quiet. Rosemary wanted to stop pretending that nothing had changed, that things still mattered when they didn't. Rosemary suddenly didn't care if Priceplan fell in the ocean or disappeared in a flash of bright light. She wanted to move forward.

The gnawing in her stomach began to grow to excitement. If she did this thing, if she had courage, maybe she could stop pretending that the Exanthoral wasn't dissolving her nervous system. Maybe she could find a place where it was okay to lose her social proprieties when she became nervous. Maybe there was a place where it was okay that Rosemary didn't have the button that stopped her from sitting on stranger's laps or taking her shoes off at inappropriate times. Maybe.

8

The new sign appeared on Wednesday morning around nine. Nate actually saw it materialize. There wasn't a light or a flash; the lettering just began to swim around in a blur until the words became a little clearer, and then cleared beyond that.

A Reminder:
The permanent removal of the area formally known as Priceplan
Is to take place today, promptly at sun setting.
Please plan accordingly.

Nate had been waiting by the boatyard entrance for Rosemary. She hadn't come home last night, and he was fighting the panic in his belly. He hadn't really expected her to come home, not right away. He kept telling himself that she was probably staying with her teacher friend, Kathy. Was that her name? Rosemary was right about a lot of things, and Nate was confused. He did want the Priceplan to disappear. He did want to have his life back and not be angry all the time. Nate really was angry all the time now. He spent most of his days being angry at the suits, the gravel, the parking lot. But he was also angry with Rosemary. He knew she was unhappy, and he could not understand why she didn't just join him and fight the Priceplan instead of silently putting up with it for eight years. He resented her overacted sighs as she turned away from him in bed at night. Nate remembered a time when Rosemary had been more than willing to stand with him in a fight. He knew she was unhappy about *Clementine* , about the boatyard, about their life, but she just didn't do anything to change it.

Standing by the boatyard entrance, Nate became agitated as he remembered what Harry Hamlin had told him last night. The guy actually had the nerve to imply that maybe it wasn't the Priceplan that Rosemary was unhappy with. He flat out told Nate that he was the problem, and not the suits. Such bullshit. Nate didn't need another Judd Hirsch jutting his way into his business, presuming to know his wife when Nate knew perfectly well that once *Clementine* was free, everything would be back to normal again. His anger would dissipate,

37

and he would have his wife back. Nate really did want Rosemary back. He wanted the girl who fell asleep in movie theatres and drooled on his shoulder. He wanted the girl who used to wind around him at night, making it impossible to move. He missed the way she smelled when she got out of the shower, and the way her eyebrows would pinch together when she was trying to work something out.

Priceplan had taken all that away, and Rosemary was right. It would be permanently removed tomorrow at sun setting, and in a flash of light, all the energy Nate had poured into being angry would be gone. What do you do with the space that used to hold anger? Nate leaned against the signpost and tried to imagine what it would be like not to feel wronged. It had become so much a part of his identity that it was nearly impossible to consider.

It was close to 9:45 now. When she finally came home, he would tell her that it was going to be okay. They would look at that map of Juneau Bay that she kept in the kitchen cabinet. Together, they would look at the route she traced with her finger when she didn't think that Nate was watching. After sunset tomorrow, all the ugly things he had said wouldn't matter. They would be washed away. She needed to come home so it could all be okay.

9

The soft hotel bed wrapped around Rosemary and the poofy comforter smelled like lemons. Rosemary stayed in bed for a good half hour just watching the light play along the windowpane. She expected that she wouldn't be able to sleep but to her great surprise, Rosemary had fallen unconscious as soon as her head hit the pillow. For the first time in several years of mornings, Rosemary felt hopeful. No one knocked on the door, and Rosemary mused that her theory about the waitresses having created this room just for her was indeed correct, which was also why the sheets and comforter smelled of lemon. The smell represented summer and lightness. Eventually, Rosemary would pull on her jeans, button up her shirt and go down to the lobby to ask the waitresses for coffee and a cream cheese Danish, but there was plenty of time. It's funny how time stretches out in front of you when you know what you have to do with it. Rosemary had decided to gamble last night. She knew she couldn't go back to the boat, and sleeping on the benches outside the Walkabout was not an option. Rosemary approached the waitress who had supplied the chicken nuggets.

"Why, hello there. Welcome back! What can I get for you?"

"I know this might, um, do you do have hotel rooms?"

The curly brown haired waitress blinked twice. "You'll have to repeat that one, and remember, try to just state the item you need."

"A hotel room."

"Why, of course, I can help you with that! Here's your key, and all the information you need is right on the back. You have a great night! Anything else before you go?"

"Can I have more coffee?"

"No need even to ask! You take care now!"

Before she knew it, Rosemary was standing on the corner holding a key to the Hyatt business tower and a steaming cup of vanilla coffee. Once she tracked down the right street, the key fit right into the door. The room was a pale pink, accented by faded pastel curtains. The window looked out over the sleepy little beach town, and in the distance was the water. It had been a long time since Rosemary had looked out a window that showed the water. It had been a long time since she didn't have to adjust for the left-hand slant. It was wonderful. Rosemary wondered briefly how the hotel worked...if the employees knew she was there, if the waitresses only had certain room that they could give away. If this room had even existed before she asked for it. Rosemary sat in the window, sipped her coffee and felt the verge of her new life beginning. She would ask for a family car and a cooler of groceries, then she would drive back to Colorado. Once there, she would drive to the little cabin that her Dad had left her years ago, the one that sat right by the Colorado River. She wouldn't need much.

Rosemary assumed that the waitresses were everywhere by now, she would ask for groceries when she needed them, Maybe the waitresses would even give the cabin electricity. If she became cold, she would ask for firewood.

She wondered if they might even send her a baby. Rosemary had heard of people being sent babies. She wasn't sure of the qualifications for babies, but the sign had appeared a little over a year ago by the freeway.

It has come to our attention
That there are a great many adults who have not yet
Picked up their babies.
If qualifications are met, your baby will be delivered

And it had happened too! Rosemary worked with a woman who had been woken up in the night by crying. When she entered the living room, she found a baby girl surrounded by brand new, unwrapped baby toys, bibs, cradles, and myriad other supplies. Attached to a gold chain around the girl's wrist was a note that read:

Delivered from China
Please enjoy.

Soon, the newspapers were reporting the dramatic reduction in the local and foreign orphanages. The signmakers had neglected to outline the qualifications, but Rosemary assumed that living in a left leaning, stranded houseboat with a fruit-throwing professional protester had to put her low on the list. But maybe in that cabin in Colorado.... It had two bedrooms, a little kitchen and den, and a deck that wound all the way around the outside. It was cut to allow the pine trees in its path to barrel through and keep rising skyward. Maybe she would finally qualify for a baby from there.

Rosemary never thought she'd ever want a baby, but now it was a constant, nagging thought, a noticeable lack that she had never experienced. She started on the pill before they were married. She and Nate would watch the people with kids, laugh at them, congratulate themselves about not having to put up with the hassle. She had also been twenty-two when they were married, and everything was different then. A baby represented the end—it represented old age, settling down, and trouble.

Trouble was exemplified by a couple of Nate's friends, Jack and Marie. Nate had known Jack since high school, Marie had come along in college. In the early days of Rosemary and Nate's relationship, they had all hung out a lot. They'd hole themselves up in the back of the campus bar and drink dark beer together, discuss politics, writing, everything. Then, it all ended abruptly. Marie found out she was pregnant during their senior year. She and Jack were married a month later, and divorced six months after the baby was born. The baby boy, who had the misfortune of suffering through those six months with them, went to live with Marie's parents. The last time Rosemary and Nate had seen Jack, he was drinking too much, working in a video store, and sending most of his earnings to his now teenage son. Trouble.

When Rosemary and Nate had been in their twenties, this seemed like the perfect reason not to have kids. Rosemary was terrified she'd become Marie, who had gone from a smart, witty girl, to a bitchy, stressed ball of nerves. She was scared Nate would turn into Jack, who tried to demand that they put the baby up for adoption three months after he was born. No way.

Now, at thirty-five, Rosemary couldn't believe she thought their experience was the norm, that all pregnancies turned out like that. Now all she thought about was holding her baby, feeling his or her little hands in her hair, smelling their sweet baby scent. It was a want that she never saw coming until it hit her like a ton of bricks. She mentioned it to Nate a few times, testing the waters. He'd alternately laughed her off or ignored her entirely. It was funny, in a way. The idea of having a baby when you were living on poverty level wages in a crooked houseboat in a stranded boatyard...was laughable. Rosemary knew it was selfish of her even to think about, but it didn't stop her from wondering what his or her voice would sound like, what the little hand would feel like in her own. Plus, it might be just the thing Nate needed to shock him back into reality. Maybe he'd get his focus back, get a job, move away from *Clementine* and find them all a nice apartment or even a house.

That was the general idea anyway. It had been over a year since Rosemary had taken her last birth control pill. And while intimacy with Nate had been lacking for the last few strained years, there had been enough that something should have happened by now. Rosemary tried not to think about it every second of the day, tried not to cry every time she got her period. She found that it was more overwhelming now than it was before, now she was constantly wondering why, if, or when. The worst part was that Nate had absolutely no idea that anything was wrong. She'd never told him, not about the bone-deep, raw desire to have a baby that had been eating her alive for the last two years, and not about the last year when she'd watched her body for any signs, any changes.

And now, Rosemary mused as she lay entangled in her lemon sheets, it was all for the best. She'd make it to her Dad's cabin, and it wouldn't matter that she wasn't pregnant, she could request a baby. They'd live there together, just the two of them.

She'd been afraid to think about requesting one before. When she first saw the sign on the freeway from the bus window, her heart had leapt, but there was also dread. A baby in *Clementine*, locked into the artificial gravel, facing the Priceplan and leaning to the left, would certainly be better off with someone else. Nate never mentioned a family; he hardly talked at all about his own parents, much less about a family of their own.

She wondered if she got to pick what kind of family car she would receive. Not that it really mattered, but she was terrible about driving a stick, surely she could be a little picky. Funny how comfortable she had gotten with the waitresses after avoiding them for so long and scraping by, but she didn't feel guilty about it at all. Rosemary mused that it must be a little like when you finally cure a chronic pain, you never realize how much energy goes into managing that pain until you don't have to anymore. All the nights Rosemary and Nate had gone to bed hungry, all the nights spent sleeping on a leftward leaning houseboat in an artificial yard; the gangrenous limb had been amputated, and instead of the phantom pain Rosemary assumed would still be there, there was nothing. And the nothing held a strange excitement.

Despite everything, Rosemary found herself wishing Nate could be in this lemon bed, full of chicken nuggets from the night before, watching the sun glint off the business towers. Not the strange, fanatical Nate of the last ten years, but the one she married. The Nate who brought her flowers every day for a week when she had the flu. When her Dad had passed, he did everything. Nate was the one who answered the phone and made the plans with her family. He made dinner and forced her to eat it, he cleaned up the plates, and he brought Rosemary enough rum and cokes to relax her into sleep. Nate was the one who behaved as she should have at the service. He greeted people as they came into the viewing room, he shook their hands and avoided words like "premature" or "suicide" or "intentional". Even when her father's new wife had passed out in the lobby from too many Valium, Nate simply ushered the guests into the other room, and carried "Mixie" to the lobby sofa as he called her doctor on the phone.

Rosemary was forever grateful for the way Nate never acted like her family was crazy, even though they were. He wasn't resentful that he had married into her estranged, deranged and over-medicated family. Rosemary's dad had been sixty-two when he died—young. He had been on his own for a few years, and everyone, even Rosemary, had begun to hope that the worst was behind them. Once out of the institution, Dad had begun to straighten out. He was placed in a group home for other functional schizophrenics, and quickly graduated to his own, well-supervised apartment, and eventually the cabin. That was where Mixie had come into the picture. Rosemary was irrationally resentful of Mixie. She knew her feelings were ridiculous, yet she couldn't stop having them. Mixie was another group home refugee, although her living on her own experience had fallen through. After Rosemary's Dad met Mixie, he somehow talked the doctors into letting her move in with him. To his credit, Mixie was still straight, holding a job, taking her medication. She had been working the bakery counter at Shopmart for the last years before the accident.

Rosemary couldn't understand why of all the things to be planning on this day, she was thinking about Mixie, she hadn't seen her in years, not since Dad's passing. It was probably because of the cabin. Before yesterday, the idea of living in the cabin was pure fantasy. It wasn't anything Rosemary thought would ever happen. Nor could she grasp how it would happen before yesterday, before the waitresses. The nearest town was over two hours away, and the cabin was completely primitive. Like *Clementine*. There was a generator out back, but that only produced enough charge to light a small room for a limited time. At best, it would be inconvenient to live there without the waitresses. She was sure they would help with the power and the groceries. She wondered what their limitations were, what was asking too much.

The first week the waitresses arrived, Rosemary saw a young man order 200 Rolex watches. The waitress had frowned at him and asked if he would like to reconsider his request. The young man laughed, and then in a flash of light . . . he was gone. Rosemary wasn't sure she wanted to know what happened to people when they were permanently removed. Although, to be honest, it was a lot nicer not having some people around. The drug dealers that hung around the Fifth Avenue Bridge, the rapists and child molesters. Anybody who was guilty of a violent offense and hadn't taken the signmakers up on their offer to make good with the family of the victim, they were all gone, too.

Of course, it wasn't quite that straightforward all the time. The warning signs that preceded the waitresses were distressing to say the least. Occasionally a rash of signs would appear out of thin air, a light would flash, and several people who had been walking down the sidewalk, sitting behind their desks, or sipping their lattes at Coffee Ruckus would simply disappear. Presumably, there was no word to their families about how or why or what it meant. One could, of course, guess why the people who disappeared had done it. They were the petty thieves, the road ragers, the guy who made cruel comments to the women at work just to see them get upset, the people who kicked their dogs when they cried to go outside, and who had somewhere along the way committed a wrong that they refused to make right. But the signmakers had eventually streamlined their system. Now, no longer were these potential victims "flashed," but more time was given to offenders to right their wrongs. It was up to the individual to either accept or change his fate.

The whole situation inspired a fierce and bizarre sense of loyalty. Rosemary remembered Nate attending a service for a man who had been permanently removed. He had even spoken briefly at the reception afterward. Never mind that Nate was getting teary eyed about the guy who had drunkenly hit Rosemary and Nate in their old tan Buick while they were driving back from the store. This, of course, had been years ago, and it was why Rosemary had been riding the bus since. The guy had slammed into their right front fender and sent the Buick spinning into the oncoming traffic. It was amazing that the cars were able to stop as quickly as they did. But not before they took off the front end of the car, leaving Rosemary nose to nose with a fender from another vehicle.

The guy who hit them was so drunk that he literally fell out of his car and collapsed on the roadway. When Rosemary and Nate tried to get their damages covered, the bastard tried to pin it on them, saying they were swerving, trying to run him off the road. He accused them of intimidating him into the legal process by posing as police officers. The entire case was a series of ridiculous lies, but nevertheless, Rosemary found herself in small claims court battling over whether she and Nate should have to pay for the drunken bastard's stitches, the ones he needed after he smashed his head on the pavement. Unreal.

Even more unreal was that Nate honestly looked sad when the drunken bastard was permanently removed. Rosemary couldn't remember how she found out; maybe she saw it in the newspaper. Back before the newspapers silently disappeared, Rosemary and Nate had pored over the long lists of people who had been removed the day before. It was chilling, and at the same time, when you ran across people like the drunken bastard, it was difficult to say that it didn't serve him right. Of course, not knowing what permanent removal actually was made it easier to be cavalier. For all Rosemary knew, the drunken bastard was eating bagel chips and drinking hefeweizen on a rooftop bar in a place where he would never required to drive again. If that was permanent removal, then maybe it wasn't so bad. Naturally, Nate didn't see it that way. He was convinced that that bright light was the end of life light, and the signmakers were instantly killing them. He thought that "permanent removal" was a sick euphemism for genocide. Maybe Nate was right; no one had come back to tell anyone else about the happenings, so you had to assume they were dead.

It was nearing ten a.m. The sun had long since traded watch with the moon, and reflected off the city, the glare barreling up like pine trees. By this time tomorrow, Nate and *Clementine* would either be halfway out to sea or *Clementine* would be stuck like a fish bowl ornament on the bottom of the new marina while Nate looked on.

Rosemary seriously didn't think that *Clementine* would sail with any reliability after the abuse that had been heaped on her by the artificial gravel. For one thing, she was half stuck in the spongy stuff, not to mention that her bow was warped from the pressure of the left hand lean. At best she would bob twice and then pitch her bow down and disappear. Hopefully, Nate would realize this and not attempt to steer her out. If he did, and she sank, hopefully he wouldn't attempt to salvage her. In retrospect, it seemed perfectly ridiculous that she had spent so many years fantasizing about what she would do when Priceplan was gone and the water returned. Up until this morning in the Hyatt, Rosemary had never even considered the possibility that what Nate had been fighting for, and what Rosemary had endured in the fight, was already lost.

10

Around eleven am, Nate went back to *Clementine*. It was dark inside the cabin despite the sunlight outside. Out of habit, he tried to switch on the light, but the generator had been out since yesterday. There was a time when he would have hooked up the clip lights and broken out the tool kit right then and there, but he wondered if he really wanted to see what this boat—this life—really looked like. The dishes were piled in the sink, and the mini fridge stood empty. Rosemary's last check had been lower than she expected and as a result, they had been rationing the last bag of egg noodles through the weekend. Now it was Wednesday, the egg noodles were gone, and Nate was left with only half a package of stale saltines and the last of the peanut butter. He could smell the barbeque from *Cursory Angel*; Eli ordered barbecued ribs from the waitresses nearly every day. He refused to see how dangerous it was to play into the sign-makers hands. Eli didn't have a defense, he simply mumbled how good it tasted, and hell, at least if he had to live half under the Priceplan, he was going to enjoy something, goddamit.

Although he had an idea of where she was, Nate felt the knot in his stomach tighten as he sat at his dark table and ate the saltines. Surely she had gone to that blond teacher friend's house. Kristi? Kathy? It was a K name for sure. Kristi/Kathy lived near the valley, in the area that borders the redwood preserve. If Nate remembered correctly, Kristi/Kathy was the one who had the baby delivered. That had been a whole different fight with Rosemary. Nate shuddered just thinking about it. Rosemary had come running in, a small, strange smile on her face.

"You'll never guess the sign on the freeway today."

Nate hadn't guessed, he couldn't conceive of something so dangerous and ridiculous. Couldn't Rosemary see that the signmakers were just imposing a new kind of morality on her? A new set of rules that weren't any different or better than the last. This wasn't the greener pasture, this was an illusion. Nate couldn't believe that based on some imaginary standards, the signmakers were just transporting babies. Imagine if the baby ended up with a child molester. Or a gang member. What if the new parents didn't want the child and abandoned it?

It wasn't until later that the signmakers posted the rules for baby delivery. Nate had seen them plastered by the entrance to the Laundromat; he hadn't told Rosemary. Something inside him knew that she would be better off not seeing this sign.

In order to have your baby delivered:
1. You must live in a reliable shelter, free from calamity.
2. You must have an uncluttered mind and a category for your purpose.
3. You must express an honest desire to our wait staff

Having a category for his purpose wasn't the problem for Nate, but the phrase, "free from calamity" kept ringing in his ears. He knew that Rosemary would take that regulation as an omen. *Clementine* had provided them with two good years of calamity free life before Priceplan landed. Anyway, Nate hadn't come this far in his fight to just abandon her. Besides, if *Clementine* didn't exist, what was his fight about?

The knot in his stomach tightened and rolled. He didn't have a phone to call Kristi/Kathy and check on his theory, but he was sure she would go there if there was ever any trouble. Even if there hadn't been trouble, Nate had no idea what her phone number was. What if she wasn't even there? Where would Rosemary have gone? Nate felt a wave of anger wash over him and dissipate. Why wouldn't she call? They can fight, but they should start to act like adults. You don't just leave a person behind; you don't just abandon your family. Nate hoped she wasn't wandering the street in the downtown area. Rosemary was really funny about that section of town. She had made a big stink about it when they stopped going there every weekend, but Nate thought it was for the best. What reason could there be to spend money they didn't have just to buy a couple of drinks that they could have at home for free. Nate yawned; he wasn't up for protesting today. And in light of recent events, it hardly seemed worth it.

Nate was fidgety, and he started packing his LPs into a flat box just for something to do. As he worked, he spied the TV and leaned over to turn it on, forgetting that it suffered from the same loss of power as the rest of the lights. He stared at the blank screen for a minute, desperately hoping for a rerun of MASH or maybe a made-for-TV movie to appear. He wanted the noise, something to distract himself. As Nate worked, he stuffed crackers into his mouth, his hands shaking from nerves as much as from hunger. The barbeque smell that wafted in from *Cursory Angel* was driving him crazy.

Nate wondered if he should tell the police. Wouldn't do any good, after all, she'd only been gone one night, and she had a pretty good reason for being gone. In any event, the police had become fairly useless anyway. They were still around, of course, but they walked the planks of the Priceplan looking a little lost. In light of the signmakers' new brand of justice, they were largely unnecessary—and unmissed.

He should go to the school and confront her, but the thought made his head hurt. Nate was tired of fighting with Rosemary, tired of making her cry.

Maybe he'd go to the school and beg her to come home. They could pack up their stuff together and figure out what was going to happen next. But she probably wouldn't see him. Nate leaned back against the wall, drained. He'd really fucked up this time, and he knew it. It wasn't going to be enough to say he was sorry; he'd broken something in Rosemary, had seen in it in the way she walked from the boatyard, her head down. She'd probably tell him to go to hell if he showed up at her school, if she was even there. Rosemary had only kept that job because she'd been supporting him, and she was probably buying an Amtrak ticket to Colorado this very minute.

No doubt, she was surviving off the waitresses, and the thought made Nate's brow itch. It was enough to propel him forward and back to work. The idea that the goddamn signmakers would take over their most basic rights by imposing these...things, was too much for Nate. He didn't need any help; he'd find a job. Except for the last few years, he'd always worked, and he wasn't about to start taking charity from some damn robot or whatever the hell it was. He earned his own way, and as soon as *Clementine* was back in the water, he would make it up to Rosemary. He would make enough money that she could stop working for as long as she wanted. She could start writing again.

Nate's mother had gotten him his first job. She worked as a manager at a gift shop in an amusement park called "The North Pole." The North Pole was nestled way back in the Santa Barbara hills, and in order to get there, you had to wind a teensy road until you began seeing little gnomes and elves holding hand painted signs that pointed to the right. The owner was a youngish looking man in his forties, who had inherited the park from his father, and grandfather before that. It was a neighborhood institution and a tourist oddity, much like the giant ball of rubber bands, or the pancakes with Jesus' face.

Nate was assigned to kitchen duty in one of the North Pole's grease pits that passed as a restaurant. It was a typical teen job, and Nate went home every night smelling of hamburgers and covered in grease—which in turn caused massive cystic acne. The only plus side to the job was the doorway to the restaurant; it had an upward blowing fan. Ordinarily this wouldn't be big deal, except that employees who happened to be sixteen to eighteen years old were required to dress up like fairy tale characters. This alone made Nate willing to put up with the grease and the ensuing acne. The boy's costumes were comically horrible, one guy even had to wear a modified bear suit, modified because he couldn't wear the bear head and still see the cash register, and the bear claws were useless. The girl's costumes, however, resembled something out of a fairy tale soft-core porno. The management had chosen such characters as Little Miss Muffet, Peter Pan, and Little Red Riding Hood, and given them all tight fitting bodices, in some cases just a little low cut, enough to show a hint of cleavage. The skirts were short and accompanied by matching hosiery. Nate was actually surprised that the outfits were allowed. Nate's mother seemed oblivious to the overt nature of the costumes, and called them "cute."

Nate's favorite was Little Miss Muffet. She was a cute brunette, with olive skin and dark liquid eyes. Or at least that's how Nate remembered her. What he remembered the most was the upward blowing fan in the doorway to the restaurant and Miss Muffet's useless attempt to keep her skirt from blowing straight up. He tried to talk to her once, sat next to her as she ate her lunch in the employee dining park. Despite the costume, and the heat, she smelled like curry spices and sweet darkness. Nate never knew if it was because of the cystic acne that covered his face, or his awkward attempt at conversation, or maybe even that she had seen him gawking at her flying skirt, but she didn't respond. In fact, she ignored him altogether, promptly turned to Little Red Riding Hood, and started talking.

At the employee Christmas party, Nate had seen Miss Muffet again, this time wearing jeans and a tight t-shirt. It was almost more than his sixteen year old mind and body. The guy who normally wore the bear suit had brought a couple of Gatorade bottles full of vodka, and Nate, and the bear sat on the edge of the party drinking until Nate found his courage.

The bear kept saying, "You just gotta do it, man. You just gotta get over there. I mean, really, she's a freakin' hotty; a god...goddamn hotteress."

The bear's words of advice and encouragement, reinforced with a good many ounces of straight vodka, breathed courage into Nate. He decided it didn't matter; he was going to tell that girl what he thought, then he was going to make out with her, and not necessarily in that order. Unfortunately though, upon standing up, Nate's courage came rushing up from his stomach fast and splattered in a fan pattern in front of him, partially on the bear's shoes, and a little on Bo Peep's pants. Nate saw Little Miss Muffet staring at him from across the room. She looked him up and down and then turned to Peter Pan and laughed. Nate knew that now, he was not only the guy with the zits, but also would forever be associated with the sickly sweet stench of courage.

Nate still cringed when he thought about that night, even though he supposed that Miss Muffet had probably erased the memory of the awkward teenager who stared at her skirt and ruined her Christmas party. His mother had told Rosemary the story on the first holiday they spent together. Nate had been mortified, and throughout the telling, had found himself subconsciously tracing the pocks left by the acne all those years ago. Rosemary had laughed so hard that wine had come out her nose. Afterward, she liked to tease him about Miss Muffet. But, not in a pornographic, offering to dress up in a sexy costume sort of way. Instead, she would wait until there was any occasion, especially around Christmastime, when the holiday cartoon programs would start to air, and then say in her most deadpan voice, "Yeah, I can see it. This is totally hot. I'm getting turned on right now." Afterward, she would laugh at her own joke until Nate couldn't pretend to be indignant any longer.

He missed that. She hadn't made the Miss Muffet joke in awhile.

Television had changed a lot since the signmakers; now, it had mainly to do with the celebrities. After all, they were a precious commodity now, since a good portion of them hadn't survived the first wave of permanent removal. At first, the papers and the television had made a big affair of it, and big, very public services were held. But by the time Paris Hilton was permanently removed, it seemed as though people were deadened enough that no service had taken place and hardly anyone cared. Nate didn't personally know why Paris Hilton had ever been famous. In fact, the only reason he knew who she was at all was because of an ex-coworker from the Chronicle. The guy in the cube next to him had spent all day on Ticketmaster.com trying to get tickets to her concert for his daughter's fourteenth birthday. He eventually had to bid for them on E-bay at $140 a pop, but he lost. Nate was glad. Tickets for $140 a pop? The guy was out of his mind to spend that kind of money on tickets to a concert given by a girl who didn't look a day over twenty.

There didn't seem to be much rhyme or reason to it. On some random day, a sign would be posted to no one in particular. They usually read something like :

To Whom It May Concern:
It has come to our attention that fill-in-the-blank
Has not provided you with a viable career path or
Skill
In order to balance this inequity, fill-in-the-blank
Will be permanently removed as of Monday morning.

Of course, fill-in-the-blank was occupied with the celebrity's name. Movie stars, pop singers, rappers, even performance artists were removed by the dozens in what the newspapers called "Hollywood Massacre." After while, people just stopped reacting; stopped reading the signs. You stopped hearing about the removals, stopped waiting for new movies to be released, stopped watching TV. The signmakers seemed all right with the newspapers, but Nate was altogether glad not to be anywhere near the media. He often wondered what constituted a "viable career path" and imagined that he might be the next fill in the blank to land on a sign. After all, if Colin Farrel could be removed, then why was Nate any more viable?

11

The waitress gave Rosemary a Pinto. A freakin' Pinto. Rosemary knew that she didn't want to be the guy who asked for 200 Rolex watches, and certainly didn't want to risk permanent removal just because her family car didn't have a CD player, but a Pinto? It was olive green and the seats were ripped and smelled vaguely of body odor and cigarette smoke. The waitress had obliged Rosemary with a cooler of groceries, but upon inspection, it was full of frozen peas and a loaf of white bread. It was true that Rosemary hadn't been specific in her request. She had simply asked for food for a road trip. At which the waitress had given her an uncomprehending blink.

"I'm sorry. You'll need to repeat that. I don't understand 'road trip.'" After several attempts and lots of blinking on the part of waitress, Rosemary had simply said, "Groceries for two days."

She figured Denver was about fourteen hours from Mussel Shoals. Her dad's cabin was even closer than that, just outside Glenwood Springs. Two days was plenty of time to get there, or at least get to another waitress. She didn't count on the waitress' incongruent choice of grocery items. The frozen peas were just comical. Rosemary couldn't imagine what the signmakers must have witnessed to think that this was a normal shopping list.

Usually, Rosemary was pretty much on board with what the signmakers did. While she obviously had no quantifiable evidence, she supposed that they had done extensive, if somewhat flawed, research before the signs appeared and things changed. For instance, the fact that the waitresses looked and acted like 1950s diner girls showed an obvious predilection for the Marilyn Monroe movies of the 50s and 60's, and the signs themselves appeared most often in the shape of a stop sign, which Rosemary figured was the only thing most people really paid any attention to. She had noticed other things as well, but so far, all she really had was a theory. Rosemary enjoyed the fact that the Pepsi was now being delivered in glass bottles. Recycling bins had appeared all over town. They appeared to empty themselves when they became full; very efficient. Rosemary didn't know how she had ever lived without the waitresses. So what if she had to eat white bread and frozen peas for a few days! Soon enough, she would be in the cabin, able to order anything she pleased.

Rosemary hadn't taken the time to assemble any luggage after the fight with Nate, so she'd been wearing the same clothes for the last two days. She figured it was a fair bet that she could order a new outfit, maybe even a winter coat for Colorado. The waitress had listened to her request politely, and had paused before delivery:

"Cold weather clothing does not comply with the current climate. Would you like to reconsider your request?"

Remembering immediately the Rolex watch man's reaction, and its consequences, Rosemary reconsidered. On the tray in front of Rosemary appeared a set of green hospital scrubs. She almost said something, but then thought better of it. The moment she laid her hand on the cloth, the tray disappeared.

Not wanting to push her luck with this particular waitress anyway, Rosemary decided that this might be the time to shove off. She tucked the scrubs into the side pocket of the cooler, which was presumably meant to hold dry goods like granola bars. Fortunately, the Pinto had a full tank of gas, and Rosemary wondered briefly how the gas situation worked. Then, with a growing sense of compliance, she decided she would figure it out as she went. The Pinto came to life with an unhealthy roar, and Rosemary pulled away from the corner and west onto Sixth Avenue toward the freeway. She felt free, and a little guilty. Some part of her said that she should turn around and try to get Nate to come with her, or at least tell him she was going. But another voice kept whispering that he probably hadn't even noticed, and that he'd said he wanted her gone, anyway. Why should she say goodbye to that? The two voices kept growling at each other in her head until she turned the car toward the marina and Nate.

In the end, she didn't get out of the car. She stopped at the boatyard gate and squinted through the morning light at *Clementine*, and spotted the cardboard boxes stacked on her deck. This only increased the volume of voice number two, which kept telling Rosemary that Nate had already moved her out. He said he was done with this relationship the other night, and it was obvious that he meant every word. The pit in Rosemary's stomach churned and for the first time since the chicken nuggets, she felt the deep stabs of grief. This was the last time she would see him, the last time she would ever see their home. But it hadn't all been bad. When *Clementine* was still afloat, things really had been great; in fact, they almost had that life. If things hadn't changed, they might be in Juneau Bay fishing for salmon, painting wildlife landscapes, drinking Alaskan beer in dark bars with men who wore furry boots. This was her chance to cut the cord.

While sitting in her Pinto, Rosemary was jarred from her reverie by the *Cursory Angel* conspiracy theorist, the one with an E name who smelled like dirt and always had something in his teeth. He had seen her in the car, and was waving at her from the back of his boat while yelling something over his shoulder toward *Clementine*. Rosemary didn't have to guess what he was saying. Rosemary didn't want to repeat the events of the day before, so she pushed the pedal and sped off toward the freeway.

12

Nate heard Eli yelling, and had ignored him. Eli yelled a lot. He yelled when the barbeque arrived every night, he yelled when he was out of beer, he yelled when it rained. This bout of yelling wasn't anything different. But it wasn't until Eli barreled through the hatch, nearly tripping over the box of paper-towel wrapped LPs that Nate actually heard what he had to say.

"Man! You missed her, man! She was goddamn here! You missed her, she was in some kind of car, man! She was right outside, looking at the boat, all misty like; it was weird. I totally thought she was going to come back in, man, but it looks like the old lady is gone for good. Sorry dude, wish I had yelled louder."

"She was here?" Nate felt an initial wave of relief knowing that she was all right. But just after that wave passed, he felt himself getting angry all over again. She could have let him know, she could have done something to let him know that she wasn't dead or in the hospital. Why was she in a car? Where the hell did she get it? Where had she been staying? Rosemary hated driving. Nate couldn't believe this was the way she was going to leave him. How could she do it without saying anything? Wouldn't she even give it a chance? They had been married thirteen years for Christ's sake! How could she throw thirteen years out the window over a fight and not even say goodbye?

Eli was still standing in the doorway, looking unsure. He never quite knew when to leave.

"Man, you want some barbeque or something, man? That was pretty harsh of her, man. She didn't like come in or anything."

With that, Eli turned and climbed down *Clementine*'s ladder, and headed back to *Cursory Angel*. Nate stepped out into the sun and looked around, his heart felt like it was going to burst out of his chest, and he felt queasy. He knew he had screwed up the other night, had said some really nasty things. But he never guessed Rosemary would just leave. And where was she going? He sank to *Clementine*'s side rail and looked out on the boatyard. *Lana Turner*'s owners were up and doing much the same as Nate. Boxes were stacked on her deck, and they bustled around packing up. He wondered where they were going to go. *Lana Turner* had always known they weren't going to sail again, Nate wondered why they had stayed here for so long. They were an older couple, white haired, and both wore all natural cotton fibers and rubber soled boat shoes. The woman, Nadine? Noreen? Kept the tips of her white hair dyed different shades of blue and purple. Nate and Rosemary had often talked about how they wanted to be like that couple when they were older.

Had what he said been so terrible? Nate knew that it really had been. He meant some of it, but a lot of what he said had just come out; he wanted to shock Rosemary. He was angry. He knew he had told her to go, but the fact that Rosemary had actually gone made Nate nauseous. Why had he said that? He never wanted her to go. He wanted everything to be back to what it was before the Priceplan, before the signmakers, before everything stopped making sense. He wanted to go back thirteen years when Rosemary had first set foot on *Clementine*. He wanted to take that map of Juneau Bay out of the drawer where she had hidden it, and post it on the wall, so she would know he was serious. In retrospect, Nate couldn't answer why he had been so stubborn about leaving Mussel Shoals in the beginning. *Clementine* had come to them ready to sail. She wasn't much good too far out at sea, but she certainly could have made the voyage up the coast, and with a little work, she could be in Juneau right now.

Nate told her that the marriage was a mistake, that he didn't love her anymore. That had been a complete lie. He was angry, but now he couldn't remember why. He wanted her to stop believing the signs and to open her eyes. She simply refused to recognize that the signmakers were chiseling away the very core of who they were. Processed Pepsi and barbeque were just treats to distract everyone from their real purpose. Nate couldn't believe Rosemary had fallen for their trap. But now—fuck it! It didn't matter. Drink all Pepsi and eat all the barbeque you want. What the hell did it matter. Nate rubbed his temples as he began to hear the pounding beats of the *Dear John* theme song. Christ, this was all he needed. Goddamn Judd Hirsch. Judd Hirsch had an opinion about everything, so why shouldn't that bastard show up now. He wasn't even asleep. This hadn't happened since he was eighteen. Usually the key to avoiding any of the voices was just to stay awake.

He heard the voice, soft at first, and then louder as it began to recite in his head. "Well, you really messed this one up, kid. I tried to stop you, but what do I know? No, I'm just older, wiser and the star of my own sitcom. I don't know anything. What advice could I possibly give you? I only won a Tony for "Art." I don't know anything at all about getting along in the world. Pay no attention to me, I'm just an idiot with five Emmy nominations and a Golden Globe. It's not like I didn't have dinner with President Reagan back in the day. No, I'm just a crazy old codger. Of course, I was on Broadway, but, you're right, I'm just crazy."

Nate particularly hated it when Judd Hirsch listed his resume. He wasn't even accurate about it. Nate had looked up the statistics a few times, and he'd never found anything to support Judd Hirsch's claim that he had had dinner with the president. And, the Golden Globe was suspect too, as were the

Emmy nominations.

"Oh, okay, I'm a liar, too. Big, old, liar with a Golden Globe and a picture of President Reagan on the wall. Don't listen to the liar. Go ahead and mess up your own life, you're doing a fine job of it, so far. You think this fire-trap is going to float? Think again, my friend. This heap of crap wouldn't float if you attached water wings. This piece of shit wouldn't float in a kiddie pool, my friend. Your boat is going to sink tonight, and you'll be alone with your LPs. And it's all your fault."

"Shut Up! I don't have to listen to you! I'm not asleep! Shut the fuck up!"

Nate knew that Eli was watching him yell, and Eli would probably think he was yelling at nothing. He couldn't hear Judd Hirsch's incessant, nasal voice, his over-accented syntax. And Eli couldn't smell the sickening combination of liverwurst breath and cheap cologne.

"I don't have to listen to you!" Nate yelled back. "You want to help? Then tell me how to get her back! Tell me where she's going! Tell me how to take back everything I said! If you can't do that, then get the fuck away from me!"

Silence, except for the *Dear John* theme song. Figures, Judd Hirsch had never been much for confrontation. The deli counter had proved that point pretty clearly. The deli counter was the cause of Nate's incarceration in the institution. His mind, driven half crazy by sleep deprivation, had actually made him temporarily insane. That was what the doctor's had told him, anyway. If only he would sleep, and let his brain catch up with his body. Then he could recover. But Nate knew that sleep was the last thing to cure his insanity. Sleep would only plunge him deeper into the thin lines between reality and television.

Nate felt that now, except he wasn't asleep. The voices had found their way out; they were here. He knew he could silence Judd Hirsch with two of the blue pills the doctor prescribed, but something told him that maybe he should just listen this time. He never listened to anyone, not to Rosemary, not to Eli, certainly not to Judd Hirsch or Harry Hamlin, nor to Mare Winningham. He never listened.

He needed to find Rosemary, he needed to leave *Clementine* behind before he had to see her drown. And she most certainly would drown; Judd Hirsch was right about that. Nate had known that fact for a long time. He could ignore the faulty generator and the cracking planks, but the bow was warped and the wood had rotted so much that it threatened to drop his weight every time crossed the deck. No, *Clementine* would sink. So would all the boats in the yard. *Cursory Angel, Lana Turner*, all of them. Priceplan had known what they were doing when they caged them in. They had offered the illusion of the life they had previously known, but the stakes were low. Priceplan knew the boats would never touch water again, and more importantly, they knew that they shouldn't touch water again.

Nate sank off the rail and buried his head his hands. He needed to leave, that much was clear, but he had no idea how, and really no idea where to go. Where was Rosemary going? That was the only option as he saw it. He would follow her, and then they could start over. She would have to take him back when she understood that he realized how wrong he had been. She would have forgotten all the ugly things he said on Tuesday. Rosemary would realize that Nate was going to spend the rest of his life making up for everything he had taken from her. Off the top of his head, he could only figure that she was heading east. Rosemary really didn't know anyone in Mussel Shoals. No, she must be heading back to Colorado, probably to her mother's place in Golden. If that was the case, then Nate knew it was about a fourteen-hour car trip under the best of circumstances. It suddenly occurred to Nate that he had no idea how the rest of the country—the world—was handling the signmakers. Maybe they weren't even in some places. Maybe there were still places where people were free, where things hadn't changed. The thought gave him enough hope to pull himself off the deck of the boat and begin packing again. But this time, he wasn't going to pack all the crap he had been boxing up. This time he was going to pack for a trip. He would have to travel light, he knew that. Since he really had no money left, his only choice was to hitchhike; surely, there were travelers still out there. Food would get tricky, but Nate felt oddly calm about it. He was hungry now, but Nate was sure that he would figure something out.

It was a scary feeling, going without knowing really where or how, but at the same time, Nate felt as though a weight had been lifted from his shoulders. He felt like the Priceplan had floated away, like everything could be fixed; could all be made right.

13

Rosemary was just a few miles south of Mussel Shoals when the engine made its first clunking sound. It reminded her of someone dropping a wrench into a bucket. The Pinto kept running though, so Rosemary tried to ignore it. She would have turned up the radio, but almost frighteningly, she realized that it wasn't picking up any radio stations. It could have been because the antenna was bent, or the radio was faulty, or maybe there just weren't any radio stations left.

Rosemary was beginning to see the same reality Nate had been facing back in Mussel Shoals. She had absolutely no idea what had happened to rest of the world. Rosemary realized that this seemed odd. While the newspapers had long since departed Mussel Shoals, Rosemary had assumed there was still television. She never paid any attention to Nate's reruns and he never turned on the news, so who knew what information was out there? But the newspapers; they still carried news that took place outside Mussel Shoals, didn't they? Rosemary was trying to remember. She thought about the story of Britney Spears being permanently removed, but that had been more than a year ago...had there been any outside news since then? Rosemary was shaken to realize that she didn't think so. How could that not have been alarming to her? To Nate? The papers still came out every day for a time, and they still reported on stop lights being fixed on Fifth Avenue, and the inspirational story about the school kid who had beaten cancer and gone on to win the fifth grade relay. But, in terms of real news, they had dwindled in content and eventually come to a full stop.

Mussel Shoals was never much of a town to demand real news though. The town was nothing more than a glorified retirement community with a thriving service industry. All the cosmos bars and wine nooks on the Walkabout were usually empty, and they changed hands frequently. The restaurants that stayed around were the Black Eyed Pea, Marie Callender's, and Furr's Cafeteria. In fact, Mussel Shoals was the last holdout for Furr's. They had been shut down all over the country, but not here. And on a Sunday afternoon, it was standing room only as seniors milled around with their trays of Salisbury steak and mashed potatoes, their cartons of apple juice and Saran wrap-covered glasses of milk. A lot of Rosemary's students worked weekends at Furr's. They pushed beverage carts and restocked dishes of green Jell-O squares with Cool Whip on top. Even the grand piano still sat next to the gas fireplace. An elderly man played watered down show tunes and classical medleys for four hours every Saturday and Sunday as the clientele ate their chicken fried chicken or baked halibut with macaroni and cheese.

No, Rosemary could see how Mussel Shoals would not notice if the real news suddenly dropped off. Even the few businessmen, in their towers, were demographically wrong—over the age of fifty—and from what Rosemary had observed now and in the past, they were concerned primarily with the number pages, the stocks and business patterns rather than the events from the rest of the world that might or might not affect them. Rosemary remembered when 9/11 had happened. It was on the radio in the morning, the television all day, the newspapers. This, of course, was long before the signmakers. Rosemary and Nate spent the day glued to their thirteen-inch television set, afraid to breathe, afraid to look away. But the rest of Mussel Shoals seemed particularly unaffected. Furr's Cafeteria was still packed, the line at the Post Office was still a mile long, the old men at the grocery store still milled around, sightseeing the groceries more than buying, all acting as if nothing had happened. Even her students seemed oddly unconcerned. School had been cancelled for three days, but on the fourth day back, no one wanted to talk about it. The students shrugged their shoulders, complacent and comfortable in their world.

Rosemary's students were primarily the children of the service workers: the hotel staffs, the restaurant workers, and the retirement center employees. There was quite a large transitory population that came through every year with the orange harvest and the wine country grape picking season. These kids came and attended school for a couple of months, and just as Rosemary was starting to make a dent on their woefully inadequate level of education....the harvest would be over and they would disappear. Rosemary's students and their parents were much more concerned with their own survival than the news from New York, or even Los Angeles. Although it left a cold feeling in her to realize that it was true, Rosemary realized that they hadn't had any outside news in over a year, maybe more—not since Britney Spears.

Rosemary reached Ventura around two in the afternoon. She had been driving fast—really fast—as fast as the Pinto would take her. There were no other cars on the road, and no activity in any of the towns she passed through. It was too quiet, but Rosemary was trying not to think about it. She wished the radio was working so that she could drown out the growing feeling of despair. She missed Nate, she was afraid out here. Why hadn't she gone into the boatyard to say goodbye? Didn't she at least owe him that after thirteen years? The further from Mussel Shoals she got, the more the grief churned into an enormous feeling that she had really fucked this up. More and more, it became like a dream where she dug herself deeper into trouble, but unlike a dream, she couldn't start this over. She had already left. Even if Rosemary tuned around right now, Nate would know that she had left him behind. Regardless of whether she ever came back, she had already left. Rosemary knew how Nate would react. He never would have abandoned her. The more she drove, the less terrible the things he said seemed to matter. The angry words didn't seem real; they weren't the deal breaker she thought they were yesterday. Aside from getting hungry, the gathering heat in the Pinto was suffocating. She decided that she should pull off and eat, and maybe change her clothes.

As she pulled into Ventura, she could see the parking lots and side streets were empty. It was a Thursday, it wasn't a holiday, it was the middle of the afternoon. Maybe she just wasn't seeing it right, maybe you couldn't see from here if the cars were moving on the streets, maybe they were farther away than they looked. Rosemary pulled into a 76 Station, but it didn't appear to be open. She got out and walked to the station's door, and it pushed open easily. The foodstuffs was mostly gone, a few bags of chips and some candy bars littered the floor. An ancient hot dog lay shriveled on the counter.

"Hello? Anyone here?"

Rosemary knew the answer. Of course, no one was here. Judging by the hot dog, no one had been here for quite awhile. She felt a chill down slither down to her core. Mussel Shoals wasn't like this. People still used money and paid bills and filled their cars up with gasoline and cleaned up hot dogs back in Mussel Shoals. So what happened here? A new worry crept into Rosemary's mind—gasoline. By now, the Pinto was about half-empty. Rosemary had taken it for granted that there would be waitresses everywhere, and they could—would—provide. But not only were there no people in Ventura, there were certainly no waitresses. Rosemary realized that she could be stranded if she didn't figure something out. She wanted to go home. She wanted to go back to *Clementine*.

Outside, Rosemary tried the gas pump. Nothing. She knew there was a switch inside that should turn it on, but that was no guarantee there would be any gas in the underground tanks. Still, it seemed worth a try. Rosemary was a little afraid to proceed; she remembered what had happened to the thieves and criminals in Mussel Shoals. She knew this was technically stealing, but there was no way around it. Once inside, Rosemary went behind the counter. Out of curiosity, she checked the drawer, the money was gone as she expected. People had grabbed everything they could from this place and run. But run where? And why? The signmakers weren't generally threatening; at least they weren't back home. They really didn't go after people who weren't doing something wrong. If you weren't a drug dealer, or a drunk driver, or a puppy kicker, they didn't persecute you. In fact, the waitresses had made life much easier for a lot of people. That didn't really explain situations like Britney Spears though. While Rosemary obviously had not known her personally, the pop singer never seemed like a criminal. She had seemed like your typical blonde, slightly oblivious teen. Rosemary's students played her music often; inoffensive fluff about breaking up with boys or falling in love—typical pop song fare.

Maybe Britney Spears had been a bad person, and maybe Rosemary didn't know. Maybe she embezzled money or stole from her fan club. Maybe she was snorting coke in the bathrooms of nightclubs, her perky, friendly face camouflaging a monster. But if that was true, then what happened to Ventura? Surely, all these people hadn't been drunken, drug dealing puppy kickers? She found it hard to believe that everyone had left town; there must have been trouble here. But what kind of trouble? She wasn't sure she wanted to know. Rosemary thought about the cooler full of white bread and peas in the Pinto, and realized that it might have to last her a very long time.

She couldn't think about what was waiting in Colorado. It couldn't be like this. For one thing, Rosemary's mother was there, and she wasn't a Rolex watch hoarding drunk driver. In fact, she'd just received a letter from her mother last week. They were moving downtown, which was out of character for her family. It was a strange letter. It had said they were being moved downtown and her mother had included the new address. It sounded like they didn't have a say in it, and Rosemary didn't understand.

They loved living in the relative isolation of Golden, despite the fact that her mother was still deeply involved in an ancient land war with the neighbors. The roots of the neighbor's pine tree were technically in their yard, but the neighbors steadfastly refused to recognize that the roots were destroying the topsoil. The ongoing dialogue between them went that if the snowstorm on its way to town was as bad as the weather man said it would be, then the tree might lose that bad top branch and Rosemary's mother would be responsible for removing it. And so on. For years. Rosemary's mother hadn't quite tried email yet, and insisted on sticking to letters and the occasional postcard. Actually, email wouldn't have helped Rosemary any more than her mother. Rosemary and Nate never had Internet access on *Clementine*. In fact, the only place Rosemary had ever used the Internet or email was at school. Even then, she only used it when she had to, which hadn't been for some time. Several years ago, the district had insisted that all teachers activate their district email account. Rosemary had a friend walk her through the process of logging on, but had never touched her account again. She knew for a fact that that experience made her 100% more experienced than Nate was; he stubbornly and somewhat randomly refused to have anything to do with it.

Rosemary began shuffling around behind the counter looking for the pump switch. She had no idea what it might look like, only that there must be one. Soon enough, she found a small yellow button directly below the cash register. She pushed it, but nothing happened. The lights on the pumps didn't blink on. She looked around the store, but button evidently served no purpose. Maybe it was some kind of silent alarm, like at the bank. Except, that by the looks of the place—of Ventura—there really wasn't anyone who could respond. She continued to pat the walls and move papers around. Eventually, in a breaker box under the cigarette case, she found a lever that had numbers labeling the sides. This had to be it. Rosemary took both hands and tried to pull the lever down, but it was stuck. She braced herself against the counter and leaning on it with her full weight, pulled as hard as her body would allow. She felt the lever give a little, and she paused. Rosemary's hands were pounding, the skin on her palms red and irritated. Regardless, she positioned herself again and pulled on the lever with her full weight. Finally, the lever gave way and thwunked to its bottom most position. In the process, it threw Rosemary off balance and sent her careening into the back of the counter. She felt a sharp pain in her back, which knocked the wind out of her, and she tumbled to the floor, wheezing. It was a few minutes before Rosemary was able to stand. She limped to the door and saw the pump lights on and ready to go.

Outside, Rosemary pulled the nozzle out of the nearest pump and inserted it into one of the five gas cans she had found inside. She figured that she shouldn't take any chances, if more towns were like this, it might be a long time before she found more stations. Nothing. Nothing came out of the nozzle, the numbers on the pump flashed and went digital, leaving a row of x's. Frustrated, Rosemary threw the pump on the ground, she would at least be able to make it to LA, and there was certainly going to be someone there. Rosemary got into the Pinto and started to pull away when she nearly ran right into a new sign. She knew for a fact that hadn't been there before, and now it had seemingly sprouted right in front of her.

To Whom It May Concern:
Please be reminded that the cause of war,
Formerly known as gasoline, known as fuel,
Known also as oil has been permanently removed
In the interest of containing conflict and
Promoting healthy social and political
Relationships.
Thank you.

The waitress had given her a car but they had removed gas? What the hell? This wasn't the first time the signmakers had made an incongruent decision, but it was the first time that it had affected Rosemary directly. What was she supposed to do? Where did the gas come from that was already in this car? On second thought, Rosemary guessed that the car probably already had gas in it from its previous owner. God knows what happened to its previous owner, but whoever it might have been obviously didn't have the olive Pinto anymore. In a weird way, it kind of made sense. She hadn't told the waitress that she was trying to go to Colorado; in fact, the waitress had refused to distribute any cold weather gear. The cars the waitresses were giving away were probably just meant for local trips, and isolated ones at that. Rosemary felt stupid that she hadn't thought of that possibility. She also felt a stab of panic as she realized that she was too far from home to make it back on the remaining gas in the tank.

She decided to keep on until Los Angeles, maybe find a telephone, call her school, beg someone to find Nate, and then maybe he would forgive her. Maybe he would go to Colorado with her. Now, in the cool California winter dampness, nearly stranded, she felt endlessly alone and foolish. She really hadn't thought out this trip very well. When she awakened this morning, everything seemed so clear, but here in the full light of day, things were anything but clear. Rosemary changed into the green hospital scrubs right there by the gas station. To the waitress's credit, they were remarkably comfortable. It was just weird. Why hospital scrubs? Rosemary opened the cooler to find the frozen peas were beginning to melt. She ate a piece of white bread and a handful of crunchy peas. It didn't fill her up, and the bread stuck to the roof of her mouth, but Rosemary knew that she needed to eat something, and this was certainly preferable to the shriveled hot dog on the counter of the 76 station.

14

Nate winced as he entered the Priceplan. For all of his fruit throwing, all of his picket signs and megaphones, he had never once been inside. Once or twice, he and Eli had played around with the idea of rushing the store to destroy the racks of bulk paper towels and overturn the bin of big blue bouncy balls. Eli wanted to poke holes in all of the meat wrappers and squirt condiments at the employees. Nate thought Eli's idea was taking it a bit too far, so in negotiating the rules of disruption, had never actually executed their plan. The store was largely empty, an old man pushed a broom down the aisle in front of Nate, and a white haired lady wearing a smiley face button stood at the door.

"Good day! Welcome to Priceplan! Is there anything we can help you find?"

Nate was incredulous. Weren't these people aware that this place was going to be underwater or God knows where in about six hours?

"Uh, no. Not really. Hey, haven't you guys seen the sign by the boat-yard? You know what's scheduled to happen around sunset don't you?"

The white haired lady with the red nametag that read "Nell" replied with a nervous laugh:

"Oh pooh! We hope our loyal customers don't put too much stock to those old signs. The Priceplan family has assured us that they have taken care of the situation and it's business as usual! So don't let that stop you from shopping with us today!" Nell adjusted her nametag and smoothed the imaginary wrinkles from her pink striped blouse.

"But, taken care of the situation? I really, I mean, I think you really shouldn't be in here much longer; any of you. It isn't safe. You have to know that."

Nell paused. "I know that those signs can be um, very persuasive, but I know the Priceplan family wouldn't put me or their customers in harm's way. If they say that it's going to be okay, then I believe them, so you'd better believe it, too! So, young man, don't you worry, we'll still be here!"

Nate walked past Nell, and down the first aisle. His skin bristled just being in here. He couldn't see any other customers, and besides Nell and the old man with the broom, it didn't look like there were any other employees.

He wondered why these two stayed. It seemed obvious that the other workers didn't have the same kind of rock hard faith in the Priceplan family that Nell and broom man had.

Nate found the aisle with the trash bags, opened a box, and pulled out three. He shook out the big "Stretch and Heavy" bags and began walking up and down the aisles stuffing them with supplies. Nate knew he was running a risk here, not from Nell and broom man, but from the signmakers. He had heard stories, mostly from Eli, about people being permanently removed for less than petty theft. Nate had seen the permanent removal of several druggies, who used to hang out by the dock. And while stealing food and survival supplies wasn't the same, it was stealing nevertheless. The way Nate saw it, he would either be removed here or die trying to cross the desert. There was no way he was going to ask those goddamn machines or whatever the hell they were for anything. He could take care of himself, and this was the only way he could see to do it right now. Besides, all this stuff was going to be permanently removed shortly, anyway. The sun had already hit its peak and was just about to start the downward journey, which gave Nate six hours, more or less, to clear out of *Clementine*, and bid her goodbye.

Nate took lots of light packaged goods like crackers and such, and he reluctantly filled the second bag with canned goods, black beans, kidney beans, and tuna—but only the dolphin safe kind. In the next aisle, he filled a bag with artesian bottled water. He threw in a couple of can openers, a camping lamp and a few bottles of paraffin oil, a couple of Swiss army knives, and after some consideration, a hunting knife that he strapped to his ankle. He paused at the empty gun counter. Guns had been removed pretty early on, and now the racks stood empty. Before he headed toward the door, Nate found a waterproof jacket and a sleeping bag that rolled nearly flat. He piled the bags into a shopping cart, his heart beating wildly the entire time. Not only was this the first time Nate had ever stolen anything, but he wasn't sure what would happen when he crossed the threshold. He could be permanently removed, after all, since he was definitely violating one of the most basic laws the signmakers laid down in the beginning.

Years ago, when everything was in chaos, before Mussel Shoals had settled into its elderly complacency with the signmakers, back when people were still throwing rocks at the signs and attempting to tear them down, back when the police were still trying to keep the peace, the signmakers had posted "the basic rules" on nearly every stop sign in town. This was before the town had settled back into its time honored routines of eating at Furr's, filling prescriptions, arguing over whether the mayor should have daffodils or four o'clocks planted in the flower boxes that lined the strand walkway. It was before people stopped caring that the signmakers had, almost overnight, replaced everything thing they had ever known about law and order. Back then, people still cried in the streets when they witnessed a permanent removal. They still had memorial services with no bodies to mourn. They met at night at the senior center and talked about rebellion, and what the President was doing about all this.

It hadn't taken long before people stopped going to the meetings, stopped holding the memorial services, stopped turning to the police, started turning to the signs, and stopped wondering about the silent President. They became comfortable. They found that their needs were being met, and that they had no cause to worry about things as they had before. All of a sudden, the seniors who previously had to scrimp and pinch to pay for their prescriptions found that the pharmacy had stopped charging. They found that the mashed potatoes at Furr's were now entirely free of lumps, and you could have white gravy any day of the week, not just on Mondays. The Jell-O on the desert menu was now neighbors with fresh bread pudding, the coffee wasn't too strong, and it never kept them awake, even if you drank it after five p.m. That was all it took to quell the Mussel Shoals rebellion.

Of course, there were other people in Mussel Shoals besides the seniors, but Nate found himself too distracted by his rage at Priceplan to divvy much up for the signmakers, and he figured it was the same with most everyone else. They all had something else that they were protesting or worried about, and the lack of a few drug dealers and thieves was hardly a deterrent. As soon as the permanent removals became less frequent, it was easy to put it to the back of your mind, especially knowing you weren't a target. It became very easy to keep on living your life.

To Whom It May Concern:
In order to live harmoniously
And avoid conflict, we have
Devised these simple guidelines for survival.
Those who choose not to follow these guidelines
Will risk permanent removal if they decide
Not to correct their error:
1. Do not cause harm or heartache to any other living creature.
2. Do not steal, lie, cheat, or swindle any other living creature.
3. Do not slander your neighbor; behave in a kind manner to all living creatures.
4. Do not take more than you need.
5. Do not become slovenly; maintain your purpose.
6. Contribute to your surroundings, and seek to improve all things.
7. Open your heart to each other, and learn to forgive in all matters.
8. Do not perpetuate ugliness.
9. Do not hold onto hatred.
10. Take care of your loved ones, and all those who surround you.

Of course, there were quite a few inconsistencies involved in the signmakers' guidelines. The signmakers must have realized this, and understood the difficulties in quantifying the offenses, since another round of signs appeared a few days later.

To Whom It May Concern:
It has come to our attention that
Based on your popular soap dramas,
Heartache is a necessary element.
Therefore, heartache will no longer be a
Measurable crime.
We ask that you still refrain; however, we will not be monitoring
Your progress.

A necessary element indeed. Nate had certainly been guilty of it, and he wasn't sure it was necessary; it was simply unavoidable. He supposed it was the same with everyone. He mused that it wasn't as though we need heartache as much as we need to know that the depth of feeling still exists. If that chasm is real, then maybe the ability to love and be happy can also be as deep. People weren't dependent on the idea of heartache as much as they were addicted to the idea of capacity.

Nate neared the Priceplan doorway with an odd confidence. While he had never been suicidal, it hardly seemed to matter anymore. Either he was permanently removed for taking all this stuff, or he would die while trying to cross the desert. There really wasn't another way as far as Nate was concerned. He would sooner be removed before he asked one of those goddamn waitresses for a single drip of water. This was really the only way, so no matter what happened, there was no use in worrying about it. As he pushed his cart to the threshold, Nell turned in alarm.

"Oh, no, young man! You'll need to pay for those items! You can't just take what you want here! You need to see one of our customer service brothers or sisters in any of our cash out lines!"

Nate paused and looked back out of curiosity. Someone had turned on all the cash stand lights, but it was very clear that Nell and broom man were the only people in the place. With a sad sense of foreboding, and knowing it would do no good, Nate stopped his cart and took Nell gently by the shoulders. Her frail frame felt like it would collapse under the weight of his fingers, and her energy wilted visibly.

"Please, don't do this," Nate pleaded. "Don't sacrifice yourself to this place. You and the other guy with the broom; you need to get out of here. Look, Priceplan isn't going to be here come about five o'clock, and if you think that those suits who run this place care about you, you're wrong. They've already figured that everyone has left, and they've left all this stuff up for grabs. Get out of here, now. Come with me, I'll walk you home. Forget this place."

Nell looked confused, and then a little angry, and then even though it seemed impossible, she wilted a little more.

"You wouldn't understand. I've been working here for eight years, I can't walk out. They wouldn't let anything happen to us. When the sun comes up tomorrow, and everything is still here, you'll see! You'll see that all those signs were just for show. I suggest to you, young man, that you walk yourself over to the cash out lines and pay for your purchases before I have to call for security."

Nate looked into her dizzy blue eyes, and he knew that Nell wasn't going to leave. She was clinging to some strange faith that her employers would never betray her. And she might be vindicated in just a moment if the signmakers decided that stealing from a sinking store was indeed theft. Nate turned back to his cart and pushed the front wheels over the threshold. Nothing happened. Nate pushed a little more and shoved the entire cart out the door. Nothing. Another shove and Nate and the cart both were standing on the sidewalk. There was no flash of light; nothing except for the sound of the gulls screeching from the light posts and Nell shouting toward the back of Priceplan:

"Security! We have a shoplifter! Security! Benny! Lloyd! You two back there! Security!"

Nate began wheeling his cart down the walkway to the frontage road that led to the boatyard. Nothing happened. Huh! Guess this didn't quite count as stealing. Nate wondered why, after all none of the stuff was his since he hadn't paid for any of it. But Priceplan would be gone in about five hours now, and Nate figured it might already be off the signmakers' radar. This stuff should hold him, at least until he got across the desert and into Utah. After that, he was sure he'd meet up with some more people, a store, a river where he could fish, something. He felt calm, although there was no real reason to be. Nate was looking at what amounted to a two-month hike unless he figured out some other way that didn't involve stealing a car or hitting up a waitress for help. One option would get him permanently removed, and the other would never happen.

Nate pulled his cart up to the entrance to the boatyard. There was a short ladder that dropped down into the yard, but no ramp to wheel the cart down. Even though he was fairly certain no one was going to come by, he couldn't risk leaving his supplies unguarded while he gathered a few more things from *Clementine*. Then, he saw that the light was on in *Cursory Angel*.

"Eli! Eli! Hey, Eli! It's me! Nate! Up here on the street! Eli!" Eli's unshaven face poked out of the boat's rear hutch, a plume of fragrant smoke billowing out behind it.

"Dude! What are you doing man? No—don't tell me, I'll come up; I need the fresh air anyway, man." Eli climbed down the *Cursory Angel*'s ladder, crossed the yard and met Nate on the street.

"I just need you to do me a tiny favor, Eli. Just watch this cart for ten minutes, and then I'm going. I'm going to Colorado to find Rosemary."

Eli looked confused, his unfocused eyes swam over the cart and then widened a bit.

"Man, you went shopping man! Good on ya, bro! Take all the bastards' shit! I might just head on over there myself later on, man! Colorado, huh? Nice. That's going to be one hell of a walk though, dude!"

"Yeah, I know. Look, can you just watch it a minute? I need to grab some stuff from the boat."

Eli stood by the cart staring into the sun, his hand blocking the light as Nate headed back to *Clementine* for the last time. He grabbed a couple of flannel shirts and the small box where he put Rosemary's wedding ring after she had thrown it at him Tuesday night. At the time, he figured she would calm down the next day and then panic because she thought it was gone forever. Nate smiled remembering how Rosemary had freaked out when she thought she had lost her engagement ring the month before they were married. She had taken it off to wash her hands and it had fallen off the shelf that hung over the sink. Nate had heard her scream from the sleeping bunk and thought she had fallen in the shower. He pulled all the plumbing out before she realized that it hadn't made it to the sink, the ring had fallen into the soap dish. It cost them $125 to get some old man retired plumber from town to come out and replace their U-trap and reseal the piping.

So Nate had saved her ring, and had expected to show it to her only after letting her freak out for at least ten minutes while she searched under the cushions, and patted around the edges of the floorboards. It would have been mean, but at the time, Nate figured that was what you got for throwing your ring at someone—even if that person had said something terrible. He would have showed it to Rosemary before too long. Nate would have opened the box and told her that he forgave her. Now, he was just hoping she would forgive him.

15

The Pinto began sputtering and the clunking returned as soon as Rosemary hit the 405 freeway. So far, she hadn't seen much more life in Los Angeles than she had in Ventura. The freeways were empty, and it didn't look like anyone was around at all. The streets that jutted off the freeway seemed abandoned, no one on the sidewalks, no one in the yards of the single-family homes that lined the area. At the north/south interchange, she saw a hand painted sign covering the freeway exit.

"Last Salvation Rancho Cucamonga"

Rosemary figured someone had painted that sign, and that meant that at least one person must be there, and as it didn't appear that anyone was anywhere else, Rosemary took the south exit toward Rancho Cucamonga. If there were people around, then there must be waitresses. At the very least, she could ask to make a telephone call. She would explain her situation, and possibly get a car to take her back to Mussel Shoals. That was certainly better than the only other options she had, which included running out of gas or having the bottom drop out of the Pinto just as she hit the desert.

Rosemary made it another ten miles, no traffic, nothing. She had battled the coldness in her belly since she left Ventura. What had happened to all these people? Was the whole country like this? The whole world? Rosemary remembered right after the signmakers arrived reading a headline in the Chronicle:

"Prime Minister permanently removed! England in Chaos!"

She knew that it hadn't just been Mussel Shoals that was affected by the signmakers, and she knew that not everything they had done was for the better. It wasn't all free food and shelter. She knew that a lot of people, who probably didn't deserve it, had been removed, especially in the early days. The signmakers had become confused about England's political system. In the confusion, they had promoted Queen Elizabeth to high ruler and had permanently removed Parliament. Prince Charles had subsequently been removed when he tried to usurp her rule, and as a result Prince William was next in line. Oddly, the people of England seemed relatively unaffected after the initial chaos. Of course, that was the distant opinion of the Mussel Shoals Chronicle, which wasn't known for its coverage of world politics.

The Prime Minister hadn't been a bad man, nor had Prince Charles, or that guy who ran into her and Nate's old car. They had all been permanently removed. The coldness crept further into Rosemary's belly. She felt queasy with the knowledge that while Los Angeles, and Ventura, and England and God knows where else were being turned upside down. She had been worrying about bills, and money, wondering if Nate still loved her, worrying about babies. It had all been bullshit, and no one had bothered to tell her because the mayor of Mussel Shoals had been too excited about the new tapioca bar that had appeared at the GroceryMart. Why hadn't anyone cared? Why didn't she know until years later what had really happened? As the icy realization spread that something had gone terribly wrong, Rosemary pressed the gas pedal and rode the fumes toward Last Salvation. There was still time to make this right, still time to go back and tell Nate that none of it mattered, that she loved him, and that she should never have left without giving him a chance to make it better. She would fix this, they would go together to Colorado, or wherever they wanted. They would find a way to make the time in front of them count for something.

16

Nate and Eli sat on the sidewalk together next to the shopping cart. The sun hung low over the water, about an hour from setting. As anxious as Nate had been to head out, part of him couldn't leave until he saw what happened to *Clementine*. The other conspiracy theorists from *Cursory Angel* had cleared out about a half hour ago, slapping Eli on the back as they walked up the sidewalk to the bus stop, carrying a couple of back packs, a guitar and a case of Corona. They gave a couple of bottles to Nate and Eli before they left. Now, the two men sat drinking beer and waiting to find out if their homes would either sink or sail away without them. The elderly couple from *Lana Turner* left around three o'clock. Nate and Eli had helped them haul their suitcases, a couple of boxes of dishes and a lamp in the shape of woman's leg up the ladder to the sidewalk. A cabbie had driven up shortly after, and then they were gone. Nate wondered absently where they were going with their leg lamp, hoping it was to their daughter's nice air-conditioned home where they would have the guesthouse all to themselves and could play with their grandchildren every day. Nate knew that probably wasn't true. As long as they had lived here, Nate had never seen any nice daughter or cute grandchildren show up. The couple always kept to themselves, occasionally waving from the bow of *Lana Turner* when they enjoyed their afternoon martinis. No, they were probably headed to one of the dozens of retirement villages that lined Mussel Shoals. At best, they might get their own mini apartment complete with call box in case someone fell down or had a heart attack. At worst, they would move into a single room and eat their meals in a cafeteria that smelled of antiseptic with two hundred other displaced people.

The last two boats were already empty. Perhaps they had been so for days or weeks and Nate just hadn't noticed. Except for Eli, he'd never really been friendly with the neighbors. Nate knew that Rosemary couldn't stand Eli, and quite frankly he didn't get it. Sure, Eli was stoned half the time, and she did have a point that he smelled like dirt more often than not, but Nate never understood why Rosemary cared. Eli was good people, and he was the only one who was willing to sit here on the sidewalk with him and watch the boatyard fill with water.

"Hey ...I was just thinking, man—and dude, it's totally not a problem if you don't want to—but I was thinking, man, if it would be okay with you, and not to totally bum you off your deal, but, man, I was thinking maybe I could come with you. Not all the way, just part way. I have a cousin who lives in Green River, and man, that place is sweet. So, maybe I could just come with you, just till then. Whaddya think, man?"

Nate felt a wave of quiet relief.

"Yeah, I think that would be okay. I'll have to split up with you when I find Rosemary though. You understand, don't ya?"

"No, man, that's totally cool. Like I said, man, Green River is my stop. My cousin has a fishing cabin there and they roll their own, man, it's like a little paradise."

"You might need some stuff though, you got any traveling stuff? It's going to get cold"

Eli decided against his and Nate's better judgment that he was going to risk a run into Priceplan for some last minute supplies. Nate was wary because the sun was dipping low, but Eli assured him that he would be fast

"Snatch and grab, man. Snatch and grab."

True to his word, about thirteen minutes after sprinting down the sidewalk, Nate saw Eli wheeling out a cart full of miscellaneous cans, a sleeping bag, some flannel shirts, and a wool camping blanket.

"Man, you weren't kidding about the blue hair in there, man! I tried to tell her that it wasn't worth it man, but she's one stubborn old chick. Even tried to get that dude with the broom on me. Ha! Like I can't handle a broom man!"

Nate was intrinsically sad thinking about the old lady and the man with the broom. He knew that there was really nothing he could do. He could throw her over his shoulder and haul her out, but the problem wasn't that he would get her out, it was getting Priceplan out of the lady. Nate knew from the look in her faded eyes that it wasn't going to do Nell any good to save her life if her heart was broken. She had found a home, and even though it was packed with discount sneakers and socks with uncomfortable toe seams, she wasn't going to just stand by and watch it sink.

Nate and Eli were splitting the last Corona when the deep orange sun began to melt into the skyline and spread over the water. It sunk lower and lower, and they watched—just until the last blood orange sliver began to sink when a brilliant flash of light blinded both of them for an instant. It was much bigger than the permanent removals both of them had witnessed in the past; this one seemed to pull in and out for a good ten seconds before it finally evaporated. The first thing either of the men heard was the water, the sound of rushing water. In the fading light and with their freshly lasered eyes, Nate saw a five-foot wave of water rush the shore. He instinctually jumped back on the sidewalk, even though he and Eli were well out of harm's way, too high up to be flooded, and the wall wasn't big enough anyway. The first wave crashed through the empty space left by Priceplan, Nell and broom man, and smacked right into the bow of the boats. *Clementine* groaned audibly and rolled further to port. The pressure of the leftward slant without the wall for support forced her bow to splinter away from the rest of the boat. Nate shivered to see her flail. *Cursory Angel* wasn't faring much better. It was a lower boat than *Clementine*, and it had been completely engulfed by the first wave.

When the water pulled back, a thousand trinkets, pans, and scraps of paper were floating in the water. *Last Man on Earth* was ripped from its gravel post and had been pulled back out to sea with the receding wave. The next wall of water, six or seven feet this time, brought it back and slammed it full force into *Clementine*. The bow separated completely and stubbornly stuck in the gravel, the stern half of the houseboat was pushed back, her lumber exploding under the pressure of *Last Man on Earth*. *Lana Turner*, oddly enough, had made a clean break from the gravel, and seemingly unscathed, bobbed out with the yawning action of the wave as if it was heading out to sea. Nate could almost see it's elderly owners, drinking their martinis on her deck as they headed south to Perth or maybe just San Diego.

When the wave pulled back again, it drug *Clementine*'s stern with her, the last vestiges of her hull shattering and then floating to the surface. *Cursory Angel*, finally free from the Priceplan, floated out and had almost looked like it might just follow *Lana Turner*. But instead, it bobbed and then nosedived to the bottom of the new marina. *Nancy's Hideaway* never stood a chance without her partner for support, and it had toppled over. Nate and Eli couldn't see it after the second wave. Still, it was all oddly beautiful watching *Lana Turner* disappear in the quickly fading light. Part of Nate wished it had been *Clementine* who had made it, but he had known for some time her time was up. Nothing can stay too long in captivity and expect to leave unscathed. The men stood. Without a word, they grabbed their shopping carts and began pushing them up the street.

17

Rosemary pulled the blue cooler down the empty I-10 freeway. The Pinto had made its last sputter about two miles earlier and even though the gauge read a teeny bit over empty, the clunk that haunted her since Ventura had finally taken its toll. She had yet to see a single sign of life. But there were a few more signs, all with the same childish lettering: Last Chance for Salvation Rancho Cucamonga.

Working hard to suppress the scream that was slowly building in her throat, Rosemary tried to inventory everything she knew about Rancho Cucamonga. Car lots were the only things that came to mind. There were lots and lots of car dealerships. And soccer fields. A bunch of her students played on soccer teams that were based in Rancho Cucamonga. But that was it. As hard as she tried, Rosemary couldn't think of anything else. The darker the sky became, the more difficult it was to suppress the scream. Despite everything, she wanted Nate. She wanted more than anything to feel his hand in hers, his warm calmness beside her. Even during the last few terrible years, he was able to exude a calm that had always escaped her.

Clementine was surely gone by now, and as the sun finally set, she felt thick tears roll down her face. Rosemary couldn't believe that she had been naïve enough to believe this morning that she'd be celebrating at this moment. She needed a phone to call Kristi, and then she'd find Nate. Rosemary really had no idea where Nate would go now that *Clementine* was gone. Other than the *Cursory Angel* conspiracy theorists, Nate didn't talk to anyone. Of course, she wasn't any better, Kristi was the closest thing she had to a friend, and she was really just a work buddy.

Rosemary had babysat for Kristi a couple of times, all the while fighting the jealousy she felt over her newly delivered baby girl. Kristi had named her Delilah. Delilah? Wasn't Delilah the one who had cut Sampson's hair? Maybe Rosemary was wrong, maybe she had just known Sampson and someone else had cut his hair. She couldn't really remember what the hair had to do with things anyway. But she knew that somewhere deep inside her the name Delilah made her think of a nasty tempered, hair-cutting cheater. And that was unfair to little Delilah. This Delilah was adorable, and so little. She had been delivered when she was just six months old. That was about two years ago. Now she was toddling around. Rosemary wondered if she would make anyone a decent mother. After all, she was having a hard time just taking care of herself.

The cooler felt increasingly heavier, and Rosemary wasn't sure if anything in it was still edible. Her hands were shaking from hunger. The last time she had eaten was the terrible pea sandwich in Valencia. Rosemary knew that she should stop and at least eat some of the newly defrosted peas, but the idea of stopping on the dark, empty freeway made her stomach churn even harder. So she walked forward into the blackness, trying not to look around her. There were no lights, no other cars on the freeway. For a while, she stayed to the side, but she had somehow wandered into the middle of the freeway, daring a car to come flying down the abandoned stretch and hit her. The façades of civilization that lined the freeway were dark, quiet, empty. Rosemary tried to harness her imagination, but her brain was playing snippets from every horror movie she had ever seen. The thick silence around her seemed to absorb all movement, and the crunching of her shoes on the gritty pavement echoed in her ears. Were they dead? Were the buildings and houses and diners she was passing filled with dead bodies, rotting away to nothingness?

Rosemary kept blinking, holding each blink a little longer than the last, hoping each time that when she opened her eyes, things would be different, that all of this would be a dream. Suddenly she heard a crunch from behind, and it was enough to propel Rosemary forward in a full sprint, the long held scream finally tearing loose. She was stopped in her tracks by a lime green RV with Lazy Daze written on the side that somehow appeared out of thin air. The effort of stopping mid sprint made Rosemary reel back, and she lost her balance. She fell backward over the cooler and hit the pavement unceremoniously with an audible thunk.

"Fuck!"

The noise echoed in the stillness. From her landing place on the freeway she looked up to see the source of the crunch. A sign had sprouted behind her. Rubbing the back of her head, Rosemary pushed herself up on an elbow to read it.

To Whom It May Concern:
It has come to our attention that the boats which
Were originally intended to be in water have been
Unavoidably destroyed
We apologize for your inconvenience and
To remedy the situation we would
Like to offer you a new shelter

Just as she finished reading, the words began to swirl and change. Rosemary sat up as they began to settle into a new message.

We further advise you to make your
Way to a resettlement community as soon as possible
Two are conveniently located in this area:
Downtown and Venice Beach
To Add
We apologize for the delay in delivery
We have already delivered the other shelters
And the new occupants are currently
Traveling to new destinations
We apologize for the inconvenience

Her panic subsided; Nate was okay. Rosemary was sure that the sign would have indicated otherwise if he weren't. Years of reading the damn signs had made everyone proficient in deciphering the signmakers' awkward messages. They didn't tend to pull any punches, and if anyone hadn't made it off the boats, Rosemary was sure the sign would have mentioned it. But what did they mean about a new shelter? Traveling?

The signs said everyone else was headed to new destinations. That meant everyone else had been given RV's or something similar, and they were on the move. Where would Nate go? Nate's whole family was in Mussel Shoals, so if he was traveling, then he must be looking for her. He knew that she would run immediately to Denver. Rosemary felt her stomach drop a little. There was no way to stop the wheels now, there was no going back to Mussel Shoals and pretending that she hadn't seen the nearly abandoned city. There certainly was no pretending that everything was the way it used to be. She would have to continue, and hope everything in Denver was still there. Rosemary's mother never indicated otherwise in any of her letters. Of course, there was a lot that Rosemary's mother didn't say in her letters. No, there really was no other option. She needed to find Nate in Denver.

Rosemary pulled herself back to her feet. Resettlement community? What the hell was that? She knew, of course, that Los Angeles had taken a big hit when the signmakers first appeared, but she always assumed that life was continuing much as it was in Mussel Shoals. The panic sparked by the empty freeway finally dissipated, and Rosemary felt the knot in her stomach unwind. In a strange way, it made her feel better to know that the signmakers knew she was here. It did nothing, however, to alleviate the pervasive creepiness that seeped out of the abandoned buildings that surrounded her.

Pulling the cooler behind her, Rosemary made her way to *Lazy Daze*. The driver's side door was unlocked and when she opened it, she saw that the keys were in the ignition. Quickly, Rosemary hauled the cooler to the door that opened to the living quarters and shoved it inside. Safe inside the cab, she locked the door and then walked the small space of the camper and checked all the locks. There was a small bathroom inside, but the water wasn't running. Tank must be empty, she thought. No matter. A narrow bunk hung over an equally narrow padded bench. The two seater dining booth was identical to the table in *Clementine* and was adjacent to a tiny kitchen that consisted of a mini fridge, one propane burner, and a cupboard. In short, it was actually much nicer than *Clementine*, and it wasn't leaning to the left. The signmakers had upgraded her living accommodations. Despite everything, Rosemary let out a snorted laugh, and she was immediately hit with a wave of Nate. All her anger, the fight they'd had, everything seemed so damn unimportant now. She just wanted him here to laugh at the irony of this camper with her. She could almost smell him next to her.

It was way too late to go back; she'd never make it. Plus, chances were that if she had a camper, Nate had one too by now. She had to keep going. She'd find a phone; try to call. Deep inside her, though, Rosemary knew that wasn't going to work. Even if she found a phone, even if she reached Kristi, Nate was starting his own journey. She knew he'd be heading out after her, even after what he'd said and done, she knew it. Upon inspection, *Lazy Daze*'s gas tank was full. Probably enough to make it to Las Vegas, then she'd figure it out. Rosemary started the engine and pulled forward, heading toward Last Salvation on her way to find Nate.

18

Nate and Eli had pushed their carts nearly to the edge of town before they were cut off by a sign they both knew hadn't been there before. It had seemed to sprout out of the darkness as they approached. The words were still swirling as they stopped their carts, curious:

> To Whom It May Concern:
> It has come to our attention that the boats which
> Were originally intended to be in water have been
> Unavoidably destroyed
> We apologize for your inconvenience and
> To remedy the situation we would
> Like to offer you a new shelter

On the street next to the sign suddenly appeared a faded aqua Winnebago that read "Minnie Winnie" on its side. While Nate stared, Eli responded with typical enthusiasm.

"Sweet! You dudes rock! I freakin' love Winnebagos! C'mon, man! Get in! Let's load up our loot and get the hell out of here! This sure beats walking."

Nate just stared; this was a lot bigger than a Pepsi. It was bigger than a Pinto or whatever it was Eli said Rosemary was driving. Nate had sworn he wasn't going to take any help from the signmakers; he wasn't going to ask any of their goddamn waitresses for anything. He had sworn that he was going to do this on his own, and that he didn't need anything. But this—this was really tempting. After all, they had destroyed his boat, and if they hadn't done that, Rosemary would never have left, and he wouldn't be leaving Mussel Shoals. In a way, he hadn't gained anything from the signmakers. In fact, he had to share his new shelter with Eli. Not that he minded really, and in truth he was glad that Eli was with him, even if it was just part way. But still, it wasn't exactly the same thing as asking for anything. After all, they had just given it to him.

Nate wasn't sorry that the signmakers had inadvertently sunk *Clementine*. He wasn't sorry that he had to leave Mussel Shoals. He just wished now that he had realized he needed to leave before, before he said all those terrible things to

Rosemary, before he learned how sick it felt not that she'd left him. He wished beyond hope that he could roll back the time to that moment when Rosemary had run in the door. This time, he would smile with her. They would make plans and pack and figure out a way to get wherever they decided to go. They would have sat together on the sidewalk with Eli, and the three of them would have drunk that last Corona as they watched the boats meet their fates. Rosemary probably would have teared up over it. She cried over strange stuff, sweet stuff, but still strange.

Nate might have turned down the Minnie Winnie had it not been for his image of Rosemary crying over *Clementine*. He also might have kept on walking if it weren't for Eli's excitement. It was infectious. Just then, Eli was jumping up and down in the Minnie Winnie, continually yelling, "Sweet! Sweet! Sweet!"

So, Nate began unloading their loot into the new, rolling shelter. Nate had no idea how they were going to handle gas, neither of them had any money or if this thing would even make it across the desert. But, it was better than pushing their grocery carts all the way to Colorado and Green River, respectively. It was nice inside. Tan, fake leather seat cushions surrounded a kitchen booth table, a mini fridge was even fitted right into the wall next to a teensy microwave oven. Nate never had a microwave, and it intrigued him. In the back were four narrow bunks, enough for a family. The bathroom was cramped, and there wasn't any running water in the miniature sink, but the toilet appeared to be in working order. The cab was cushy and lightly scented like mangoes.

No, the Minnie Winnie was a class act. It was actually an upgrade from *Clementine* and *Cursory Angel*.

"The guys are going to be so bummed that they missed out on this! Can you believe they were going to road trip up to Santa Cruz? They said it's wicked cool up there. I told them, no way, man. I'm not up for more wandering around; it's time to be with family. That's why I'm going to my cousin, man. Hey man, can I take first drive? I always wanted to roll in one of these beauties!"

So, with Eli at the wheel and Nate stretched out on the lower bunk in the back, staring at the ceiling and trying to remember the green apple scent back into being, they rolled out of Mussel Shoals, and closer to Rosemary.

19

The further Rosemary drove from Downtown, and the closer she got to Rancho Cucamonga, the more uneasy she became. The signmakers had told her specifically to go to one of the two areas, and she was heading in the opposite direction. But she needed to get out of town. Surely they couldn't fault her for that? In truth, Venice Beach sounded more appealing than either Downtown or Rancho Cucamonga. Rosemary had been there as a kid; her dad used to drive her to LA every summer. He would take her to Venice Beach and lead her by the hand as he pointed out the local artists with their stands. He would reach into his pocket and pay men with beards and sun hats five dollars to paint a henna butterfly on her shoulder. They would get ice cream from the little stand on the far north end of the beach and walk among the people, ice cream melting all over their hands and dripping on the sidewalk.

Summer was the only time she saw her dad, but even those trips stopped when he got sick. Rosemary was in the fourth grade and had just turned ten years old. She remembered how old she was because they read a poem that year called "Tuesday I was Ten." At the time, she was dismayed because her birthday had been on a Wednesday. The discontinuity bothered her. Rosemary had flown all by herself to Mussel Shoals the week after school had gotten out in June to spend her usual two weeks with Dad. He was living a little north of Mussel Shoals then, outside of Santa Barbara, in the basement of an old house. The basement had a little kitchen, a low-lying living room, and if you crossed through the bathroom, there was an adjacent room that held a giant utility sink and nothing else. But the bedroom was her favorite. A low hanging water pipe ran directly through the space. Her dad had painted it green and to Rosemary, it looked like a dragon. Actually, the water pipes ran all through his apartment, and he painted each a different neon shade. The living room version was pink, the kitchen's bright yellow, and the pipe in the utility sink room was fire engine red.

Rosemary's mother referred to the apartment as a "shithole," a term Rosemary wouldn't understand until a bit later when she started junior high school and the actual "shithole" was just a memory. She would grumble about sending Rosemary to stay in "that shithole of an apartment." Rosemary remembered the talk, but she was put on the plane every summer all the same. Rosemary would learn much later that the divorce between her mother and father had not gone well. Dad had run off with a nursing student at the clinic where he worked, and Mom had promptly packed up Rosemary and boarded an Amtrak for Colorado. Mom would say later that if they had never left Colorado, everything would have been different. Dad stayed in Mussel Shoals and moved into the shithole.

Rosemary's mother married Chuck about a year later, and soon after that came her brother Kyle, and then her sister Lily. Rosemary remembered being thrilled at the prospect of leaving Kyle and Lily behind for a couple of weeks every summer. She would return every time with stories about the ocean, and ice cream, and henna butterflies. Rosemary even remembered her Dad driving her to the beach and having a man in a turban paint a seahorse on her arm, only to race to the airport to get her on the return flight on time. He wanted Rosemary to take the seahorse with her; he wanted a couple more weeks.

"Tuesday I was Ten" and then Rosemary was in Venice again without Kyle and Lily, without Chuck and without her Mom. Dad met her at the airport, but Rosemary could tell something was different. He was shaking and his smile was watery. He cried when he picked her up and hugged her, and Rosemary remembered wiping away his tears, thinking how lucky she was to have a Dad who missed her this much. He held her hand through the airport and then again in the car while they drove to north to Mussel Shoals. The trip took about two hours, and to Rosemary it seemed like an eternity. Instead of their usual chatter, where Dad would ask a question and Rosemary would chatter away for hours, he sat quiet. Under those conditions, Rosemary knew better than to talk. She watched the side of his face as they drove away from Venice Beach, and toward his apartment.

Once there, he was quiet. They watched TV until after eight in the evening when Dad suddenly perked up and asked what she wanted on her pizza. It was going to be okay, she figured, he was just hungry. That was all. Rosemary breathed a sigh of relief. He was all right. She remembered him watching her eat the pepperoni slices, looking sleepy. After he set up Rosemary's cot in the living room, he tucked her in and kissed her on the forehead.

"I'm sorry kiddo, I've just been a little under the weather, that's all. Tomorrow we'll go to the beach. I'm just so glad that you're here, you know I love you, don't you sweetheart?"

Rosemary drifted off to sleep to the rhythmic tick of the water pipe. Long before the sun was supposed to come up, she awakened with a start. The ticking had stopped, and the silence felt heavy. Rosemary climbed off the cot and crossed to the bathroom. She stared in the mirror, trying to figure out what was wrong, because something was wrong. She turned toward the utility sink and saw a faint glow peeking out from under the door to Dad's bedroom. Her stomach flipped, but she didn't know why. Without wanting to, she mustered all the nerve she had in her little body and stepped out onto the cold linoleum.

After she took the five steps to the door, she knocked softly.

"Dad, are you okay in there? Dad? I'm scared. Can I come in?"

Slowly, Rosemary pushed open the door. The glow came from the bedside lamp, and it cast shadows on her dad's face as he lay propped up on his pillows, mouth open, eyes closed, His mouth and eyes were crusted shut with what looked like thick white cobwebs. Rosemary screamed, but nothing came out. A broken water glass lay on the floor next to him and in the puddle swam a few little white pills. On the bed next to his still hand was an empty orange pill bottle. Rosemary felt as though she was bolted to the floor, that she didn't know what any of this meant. What happened? Dried vomit hung on his chin and stained the front of the pajamas. The smell suddenly seemed overpowering, and Rosemary herself vomited on the floor, the pepperoni making another appearance.

Without feeling herself do it, she crossed the floor and crawled up on the end of the bed. She shook her dad's foot, and then his leg. Then she chanted repeatedly, "Dad Dad Dad Dad Dad."

His head lolled to the side and the orange pill bottle fell to the floor with a pling. The noise sent Rosemary off the back of the bed, and once on the floor, she scooted herself back to the door and back into the bathroom. Once inside, pulled herself to her feet.

"He's sick is all," she told herself. "He said he was under the weather, that's all. He took some pills because he's sick, and he needs a doctor."

Finally, Rosemary eased herself out of the bathroom and headed back toward the phone that sat on a little table near her cot. She dialed 911 and listened to the ring. It seemed to echo in her ear. As soon as the operator answered, Rosemary chanted, "He's sick is all. He needs a doctor. He took some pills because he's sick and now he needs a doctor."

Rosemary's last memory of the shithole was the shock of the cold linoleum as she fell backward and bumped her head. She was unconscious and overwhelmed. She never went back. Dad was in the hospital for three months, and then moved to what Mom called "a home for people like him."
There was no more ice cream, no more sea horses and butterflies, no more water pipe dragons.

Rosemary jolted back into the moment. She'd been driving straight, lost in her memory. She never thought about that night; she didn't remember a lot of it. But now, as she fled from the place of her childhood fantasies, it had all come flooding back. She swore she could smell the ocean although she knew that was impossible. Rosemary tried to imagine Nate's hand on her leg, the way he'd rest his fingers on her thigh when they were in the car together, before all the ugliness had started. Soon, she would find a phone. She would find some way to forget everything she was suddenly remembering. Nate would understand. He was probably with that guy with the E name, the one with the beard who always had barbeque breath. He was safe; he had to be safe.

20

"I never stood a chance you know. It was all jinxed from the beginning. First, fucking Angie goes and practically sells me down the river; but then she never liked me anyway. Everyone knows that. Sure, she opened the door when I'd knock, she'd have a drink with all of us, but did she ever connect, did she ever really look me in the eye? No. She never could bring herself to offer me even the smallest courtesy. It was only because of Marlin that she even tolerated me. I should have known how she talk. Hey, you, boy! You listening to me!"

Nate snapped awake. The gray haired man wearing a sweater vest had been talking at him for nearly an hour. He babbled about someone named Angie and the cost of plane tickets. In his dream, Nate wanted to leave, but something about the old sweater-vested man's eyes held him riveted. It wasn't unlike the deli with Judd Hirsch, and in fact, Judd Hirsch was far more affable than this guy, and that didn't say much. Nate shivered involuntarily. He was cold on the narrow cot, and leaned over to grab one of the camping blankets Eli had stolen from Priceplan. How long had he been asleep? Where were they?

"You're at the Big Top, man! No worries. Minnie here was getting a little hot, so I thought she should cool her jets for an hour or so. Man, you must have been having some kind of crazy dream! You've been mumbling about some chick named 'Angie,' and you were pretty pissed for a while there about your key not working. I thought you'd cracked, man!"

"Big Top? Wher..."

"Ah, sorry, man. Just north of LA is where you are, dude. We're just taking a breather. We can probably hit the road in a few. I put some water in her radiator; she'll be cool from now on."

Eli looked thoroughly pleased with himself. Nate realized that the Minnie Winnie was probably the best thing to happen to Eli since *Cursory Angel* had been wedged under the Priceplan. Eli was glowing. Nate was still baffled. He felt as though he had been sleeping for hours even though they were hardly out of Mussel Shoals. Who was Angie?

"Dude, there's one problem though, dude, and I don't want to scare you, man, because I don't know what the deal is. But I tried the gas pump, 'cause even though we're good now, we'll be out by the time we hit Barstow, but there's nothing, man, just nothing. They must be out here, somewhere. Once the Minnie gets cool, I'll try another joint."

Nate sat up and looked out the window. Running out of gas here would be a problem. Aside from the Big Top sign that was lit for viewing from outer space, there was nothing. No mountains, no trees, no people...just dirt and gas pumps, which were evidently not working. For some reason, Nate hadn't even thought of gas when they took off; he was so overwhelmed by the vehicle that it had never occurred to him. Neither he nor Eli had any money; they didn't really even have anything to trade.

Money had always made him crazy. Nate remembered a big fight he and Rosemary had back when they were first married. It was shortly after buying *Clementine*, and they had been seriously broke. So broke that he had come home to find Rosemary sitting on *Clementine*'s floor, the bills in what looked like a solitaire formation. There were different stacks and different levels of bills. She had them placed in late, really late, and going to collections stacks. There was even a subcategory of already gone to collections. Rosemary was in tears, staring at the checkbook, with an already in collections bill in front of her. Nate remembered vaguely that it was from Sears. She was writing out a check for twenty-five dollars, approximately half of what they had in the bank.

Nate saw her hand shaking, and the silent, fat tears sliding down her cheeks. She had turned and looked at him, her eyes distant and a little glazed.

"I need to send them something; we'll still have $20 left this way. We'll just be okay, okay?"

Nate knew better than to disagree with her. Of course they could live on twenty dollars for the next two weeks. What he really wanted to do was take her out and sit her down to a big dinner, get some food in her, put some color back into her pale cheeks, and stop her hands from shaking. Although he knew he shouldn't, he sat down and told her about his morning, more just to get it out of his head, because he knew that she was the only one who wouldn't judge him for it. Nate had filled the car up with gas that morning, at that time gas was up to $5.23 a gallon, for the low-grade. When he had gone to pay, he realized that his credit card wasn't working, and now he knew why. It was in collections. He had given the attendant the only thing of value that he had on him, the portable CD player and noise reduction headphones that Rosemary had given him for Christmas the year before. I'll be back tomorrow, I'll bring money, I swear I'll pay you back. The kid behind the counter had rolled his eyes and agreed to hold the CD player and headphones for a day, and then they were his, a payment for his silence.

Now, of course, Nate knew they were gone. Twenty dollars to buy groceries for two weeks, and there wasn't a penny left to pay for gas. Rosemary burst into tears at the story. But instead of comforting her and asking questions later, Nate took it as a judgment of what he had done. He exploded. He said a couple of pretty base things, that made her cry even harder. He told her that she manipulated him, that she overreacted, and that her negativity was why they were always in this state. He told her that it was her fault, and even though he knew it wasn't, he couldn't stop talking. Rosemary had just taken it. She cried harder, her shoulders shaking, snot rolling out her nose. Nate had become angry that she hadn't told him to shut up, to back off, so he just kept going, his voice going from loud to thunderous. He dared her to tell him to shut up, to slap his face and stop his ugliness; instead, she curled up into a ball clutching the worthless checkbook.

Nate felt terrible immediately. Rosemary shut off, walked around like she was in a daze, lightly acknowledging his presence but only willing to discuss the weather. Nate tried to tell her he was sorry, that he loved her, but she would only look at him blankly, her eyes already far away. It took months for the daze to wear off, although the faraway look persisted. Nate saw it anytime his voice got loud, anytime anything threatened, anytime Nate got frustrated. He didn't even have to be frustrated at her, and the look would come back. And she would be gone. He wondered where she went. He wondered why he couldn't stop pushing her buttons, and he wondered why she didn't tell him to stop when he was so possessed by his anger.

He missed her. He wondered how far along she was in the olive colored Pinto. If traffic had been light, then she must be past Vegas and nearly to Utah by now. Really, Colorado was only twelve hours away, or so, if the conditions were agreeable. But it was winter, and while that didn't matter in California, it would matter very much in Utah and Colorado. She might have stopped for the night. Nate wondered if she had snow tires on the Pinto, and he was suddenly worried as he thought about the mountain passes she was going to hit outside Grand Junction. Up in the Rockies, she would need both snow tires and chains. He worried that she had neither.

"How much gas do we have left?" Nate asked Eli.

"Oh, well, it's kind of tricky, see. On the first tank, we have like half a tank, but there's a reserve tank on this beauty, and that holds thirty-six gallons. I just don't think we should tap that action till we really have to, man. You want to save that backup for the desert, especially in a Minnie."

Nate knew that some time before Eli lived in *Cursory Angel* with the conspiracy theorists, he had lived in some kind of mobile home. Nate forgot the details, but he trusted that Eli knew what he was talking about. Good thing, too. Nate knew next to nothing about RVs, trucks, or cars in general. He stared out the window again.

"Where is everyone? Shouldn't there be truckers or someone here? It's late, but still..."

Eli shrugged. "Yeah, I know what you mean, man, it's creepy. I'm trying not to think about it much. We should just keep rolling and get to Vegas. There's gotta be people in Vegas, man. It's Vegas, after all."

The Minnie was officially cooled down. Eli wanted to sleep, so Nate took the wheel. They discovered the other gas stations were in conditions similar to the one in Big Top; lights burning, but no gas. Relying on that thirty-six gallon reserve tank, Eli convinced Nate to "just keep rolling on to Vegas." Under the best of circumstances, Nate was a terrible driver, and he hadn't actually driven anything in years; not since that guy totaled their car. As he pulled onto the empty freeway, the Minnie swerved uncontrollably at first, and then straightened out. Nate was afraid to go fast, so he drove out of the Big Top at twenty-five miles per hour, steadily increasing to forty. Then, with his heart racing, he let off the gas. Forty miles an hour was fine. Forty would get them there without him losing control of this rolling box and crashing into the sand along the side of the freeway.

21

Lazy Daze shook violently when Rosemary tried to push the gas pedal over fifty miles per hour. That was the first thing she discovered about her new "accommodations." The second thing was that the blower didn't work. She tried to open the vents to get some of the night air in the stale cab, but instead was assaulted with a cottage cheese smell. Her wandering mind struggled to stay awake, and Rosemary found herself replaying every cringe-worthy moment of the past week. It was a game she played fairly often, ever since she was a kid. Usually, it happened when Rosemary went to bed. As her head lay on her pillow and her mind started to disconnect and fall asleep, she would snap awake with the sudden recollection of something—anything—she might have done wrong that day. Sometimes it was as painless as remembering how she'd tripped on the steps at work that morning; sometimes she agonized over whether her conversation with one of the other teachers had really been as awkward as it seemed at the time. Nate always told her that her face gave her away. It was true. Every single thing Rosemary thought or felt showed in her face. Because of that, people often stopped her on the street and encouraged her to smile, to cheer up. Aside from being aggravating, it was also confusing. Most times, Rosemary was simply thinking about her grocery list or some other benign subject that had forced her to scrunch up her face into a frown.

These were the things that kept Rosemary up nights. She played her days over and over, wondering if she had walked around school with a frown all day, if she actually said what she was thinking at that faculty meeting or if it had just been a dream. It all came from the same place as the rest of her anxieties, the same place that occasionally gave her the irrepressible urge to pull on someone's eyebrow as they were talking to her. Nate thought it was funny. Good thing too, since he'd ended up explaining her behavior to more than a few people. Sometimes the urges backed up on her, bubbled to the surface. Now and then, she'd find herself actually tugging on that eyebrow, or hugging a stranger. That was what kept her up at night.

It was funny when she thought about it. Funny in the same way that reality show hosts pull pranks on innocent people, except Rosemary didn't have a camera crew or a stack of $100 checks to hand to her victims as compensation. Rosemary cringed in her seat thinking about the first time she had met Nate's parents. They had been dating about three months when he finally took her to their house. A perfect little house, the white picket fence and all, which was so different from the houseboat he had been living on when they first met. No, his parents had honest to God flowers growing on the sides of the walkway, and the shutters of the house were painted a mint green to accent the forest green paint on the main building. It was like something out of a Nancy Drew book. Rosemary knew right off that she was out of her league there. These people weren't like the ones she had grown up with. They certainly didn't have a couple dozen cats hiding all over the house, they didn't have last week's dishes rotting in the sink, and they didn't use the living room as an extra bedroom. No, these people were way out of her league. Rosemary remembered nervously smoothing her hair and trying to pick the lint off her sweater as they walked down that flower-lined walk. Nate had smiled at her nervousness, kissed her right in front of the immaculate doorway, and told her that she looked beautiful.

It didn't help. Rosemary felt her hand begin to twitch and as she shook hands with his Leave It To Beaver parents, and sat in the immaculate sitting room with a coffee cup in her hands. She felt the twitch climb up her arm and into her shoulder. She tried to get Nate's attention, but he took her attempt as affection and responded only by stroking her fingers lightly. Rosemary knew she needed to get out of there, because the impulse she was beginning to have was so terrible that she just knew Nate would send her right back to her dorm room and never call again. She tried to tell him again, and he looked at her strangely, but he kept on chatting with his parents about school, and how, yes, he had been sleeping pretty well, so on and so on. Rosemary's shoulder twitch traveled into her leg, which set her to tapping her foot, which caused the coffee to slosh perilously in the dainty cup. Nate's Mother grabbed a silver lined napkin from the coffee table and offered it to Rosemary, her eyes focused on the tiny droplets of coffee that were hitting the ivory rug.

But before she could grab the napkin, the white noise rose up in Rosemary's ears and without control, she turned her coffee cup upside down on the ivory rug. Before Nate could stop her or his mother could finish her surprised gasp, Rosemary was up and had his father's cup in her hands, which she also emptied , followed immediately by his mother's cup. Rosemary was crying as she did it, silently begging her hands to stop, but they didn't listen. Nate just watched, an amused smile on his face. She didn't remember much until they got in the car. She knew she had fallen, and luckily there was enough overstuffed furniture in the sitting room to cushion her impact. She also remembered something about Nate's mother wanting to call someone, the image of his mother waving the phone around wildly. Somehow, Nate had known. He walked her outside and placed her in the passenger seat of the car. After he sat down, he started laughing.

"I know I shouldn't laugh," he said, "but I've wanted to do that for years. Who in the hell gets white carpet? It was begging someone to dump something on it!"

Nate took her back to his houseboat, had gently taken her clothes off and pulled his giant flannel robe around her. He laid next to her, softly kissing her neck and rubbing her hands until the shakes had subsided. Afterward, he made her scrambled eggs, even though by that time it was somewhere around two in the morning. They ate together on the deck of the boat, and he imitated his parent's reactions for her. Nate made her laugh so hard that she choked on a bite of egg. They looked at the stars until the sun began to come up. Rosemary wasn't surprised to find that she had tears running down her face as she drove. For all his faults, his anger, his irrationality, Nate was the only one who got her.

Rosemary began to see something in the distance that made her rub her tired eyes. Lights, lots of them, coming from the downtown skyline. They must have been there this afternoon when she had driven this same stretch, she must not have noticed. The skyscrapers were lit up like lighthouses in the otherwise darkened city. What looked like a large flag was hung on the side of the US Bank building; it had no words, just a symbol that Rosemary didn't recognize, a little like a horseshoe, but with a line through it—weird. Venice Beach couldn't be the last chance for salvation; it looked like there were people downtown, too. Rosemary wondered why everyone had been compacted into these two areas, and what plans the signmakers had for the surrounding suburbs. If it was anything like the plans they had had for the Priceplan, Rosemary knew she was better off hitting the gas and speeding on through to open land. Part of her wanted to take the 110 exit and pull into downtown, see who was there, and talk to them about what had happened here. Another part of her knew she probably didn't want the answer anyhow.

She listened to the larger part of herself and hit the gas. *Lazy Daze*'s engine roared a little as they sped on toward Rancho Cucamonga. Rosemary knew she wasn't going to be able to stay awake much longer, and she would need to use *Lazy Daze*'s latrine at some point. Partially due to the tension and stress, Rosemary had been holding it for quite a while. Just realizing how long it had been since she peed last almost made her wet her pants. The need to pee was really the only thing stopping her eyes from drifting shut. Rancho Cucamonga she told herself. Make it to Rancho Cucamonga, find a safe place to park, and then take a rest.

The downtown lights faded behind her and the darkness seemed to stretch on forever. There were no more lights, no more signs of life. It terrified her to think of stopping in the blackness, but the idea of crashing *Lazy Daze* and lying in a pile of metal, without a hope of rescue, was even worse. Rosemary would have to stop, and she would have to make it. Rancho Cucamonga was only about an hour away, less since the road was abandoned. She could hold on. It occurred to her that after she got on the 15, she really didn't know her way across the country. She assumed that if she headed east, she would eventually hit Las Vegas, and from there Utah, but after Utah...what? She would worry about that when she got to Utah, Rosemary decided. Right now, she focused on keeping her eyes open and finding a safe parking spot when she finally reached the biggest car lot in Los Angeles.

22

Nate was starting to fade as he approached Barstow, and Eli was snoring loudly in the back. Every once in awhile, he would snuffle something that sounded like a word; the last one sounded like "Snargle Rock." It reminded Nate of the *Fraggle Rock* show that used to play on HBO, and it figured that Eli would be dreaming about Fraggles. Eli was proving himself a valuable travel companion. He was the one who had cooled the Minnie Winnie's engine back in Bakersfield, and without Eli, Nate would never have known about the reserve tank, which was holding at half a tank now that Nate had found the gauge. Eli had also been much more practical with his Priceplan shopping than Nate had been. Eli had actually remembered camping blankets and extra bottled water. Eli had also been smart enough to grab a little propane stove and a couple of spare tanks. Because of Eli, they could eat hot food.

Eli was also doing something that Nate found fascinating and disturbing at the same time. Twice now, Eli had finished Nate's sentences. Three other times Eli had answered questions that Nate had only been thinking about. Finishing the sentences could be explained away enough to settle Nate's mind, but the questions really kept him wondering. The first time happened as they were leaving the boatyard back in Mussel Shoals. Nate had been silently questioning his plan of attack, wondering how much water they were going to have to drink if they didn't catch a ride across the Sonoran. Eli looked up from his cart and said:

"I'm not sure, man. I read this one thing that said you can drink either a little every day, or a gallon a day, and you'll still die at the same time. If you drink just a little, then you just make the process a little more painful. Sucks, huh?"

Nate had known full well that he hadn't actually asked Eli that question, But Eli didn't seem to think anything of it, so Nate let it lie.

The second incident was right before Eli sacked out on the bunks. Nate had been looking for the reserve gas tank gauge, thinking about how the cab of the Minnie Winnie was beginning to smell a little like bologna when he heard Eli call up from the back:

"Sorry, man! I forgot to tell you. The reserve gauge is, like, under the flap thingy that hides the fuses that, I don't know, make the lights work or some shit. I don't know what the lunch meat smell is; pretty nasty though, if you ask me, man."

The third incident happened about ten minutes ago with Eli snoring and uttering strange sounds. Nate had been thinking about Rosemary's mother in Denver. Since he had seen Barstow's abandonment, he wasn't so sure about Denver. Was it empty? He knew Rosemary wrote her mother letters fairly often, and he often saw the letters from her mom on the kitchen table. So Denver must be all right; otherwise, Rosemary would have mentioned it, right? Nate had been thinking about the first time Rosemary introduced him, and the way Rosemary's mom looked him up and down, before stopping on his face, not his eyes, but just his face.

"You look Jewish. You Jewish?"

The blunt force comment had taken Nate by surprise, and he muttered something like, "Uh, like a quarter, a quarter Jewish; so, um, yeah, I guess, a little."

Rosemary's mother looked at her and smiled. It was an odd smile, a little happy, but also like she had gas. As he drove down the highway toward Vegas, Nate had been wondering what that smile meant. Was she happy he was a little bit Jewish? If so, why? Rosemary wasn't Jewish, she was Irish. Was she unhappy about his being a little bit Jewish? Why? What problems did the Irish and the Jews ever have? Did she wish he was more Jewish? Did she just like being right about where people's families were from, and was that why she was smiling? These questions had been racing through Nate's mind, when he heard a sleep filled voice from the back of the Minnie Winnie:

"Man, she wants to be right, man. Has nothing to do with whether you're actually Jewish. 'Sides, man, that new dude of hers is Jewish."
Sleeping Eli was right. Rosemary's stepfather was Jewish, but he didn't remember ever telling Eli that. Maybe he had, but even then...how did Eli know he was thinking about that? Nate needed to push the thought out of his mind. They would get to Vegas and then he would see a perfectly logical reason why Eli was answering all these questions.

Nate knew his sleepy eyes were playing tricks on him, because Vegas looked really small; bright, but small. Nate was encouraged by the lights. That must mean people were there. Barstow must have been a fluke. Maybe the signmakers gave the Barstow residents Minnie Winnies, too. Nate could imagine that most people would rather live in a 1980s era Minnie Winnie instead of Barstow. Nate wasn't a desert person though. He had grown up in Santa Barbara until he was around ten or so, then his mom and dad moved him down to Mussel Shoals. Mussel Shoals had been devastating to Nate the preteen-ager. He had gone from soda shops, shopping malls, and the beach, to the retirement community where the old farts in the apartment next door banged on the wall every time he closed the closet door too hard. It was as if they were waiting for him to make noise. Nate remembered a nasty bout of bronchitis he had sometime during that period. The old man who smelled like diaper cream had actually come over and threatened to call the manager if they didn't shut up that damn noise.

Nate bought his first boat with his college fund. It was his, and he never slept another night in that damn apartment afterward. A few years later, his parents moved out of the apartment into a house with a yard, which his mother cleaned with characteristic obsession. Nate could still smell the Lysol antibacterial spray she used to cover the house every few hours. Now, it gave him an instant migraine. She was worried about germs; constantly worried about germs. She wouldn't touch the handrails on staircases, and wouldn't use a cart at the grocery store for fear of transferring E-coli to her unprotected fruit. When Nate had been little, she used to instruct him on how to wash his hands properly, and then reward his efforts with a fresh can of Lysol. They would go around the house together, and spray every little corner. She would laugh, and race him to the sunroom, where they could spray down the plastic plants. Nate didn't really like the game, and it gave him a headache even then, but still, it really was the only game she liked to play.

Nate thought about how his mother would react to this RV, to this new way of doing things. She probably ran the waitresses ragged as is, constantly asking for more Lysol spray and antibacterial wipes. She had always smelled like lemons, not the natural ones, but the clean lemon scent most often associated with cleaning products. He couldn't imagine she could be taking this very well, the Minnie Winnie herself was probably a rolling Petri dish. Lord only knows how many germs were on the steering wheel this very minute.

"Hey Momma's boy, you want to watch the damn road?"
Nate jumped and the Minnie swerved as he saw the gray haired man in the sweater vest suddenly appear in the passenger seat next to him. From the back, he heard Eli mumble something about "nacho dip and peanuts," followed by a loud snore.

"Yeah, I'm talking to you, you pathetic, no-talent hack! You probably came to this town because you watched all those Jimmy Stewart movies, didn't you? 'Oh, I look like that guy and anyone can be an actor!' That was you, huh? Well, let me tell you something. You need definition; you need sharp angles. Right now, you're tapioca. I don't work with folk who don't know how to find their own light. And let me tell you friend, you are in the dark."

"Who the hell are you?" Nate looked briefly to his side but sweater vest was gone. Nate had no idea who this one was. In a way, he kind of missed Judd Hirsch; after all, he at least knew who he was. This new guy was mean, too. There was no call for that kind of talk; after all, this was his Minnie Winnie, well, his and Eli's. From the back, Nate heard Eli snore and then:

"I don't know man, beats me. I'm more of a Scorsese fan. I don't know your oldie directors, man, try asking him some questions next time."
Nate was starting to get used to Eli's quirk. He had never believed in any of that psychic stuff, and still wasn't sure he did. But he had seen enough in the last

four years that anything seemed possible, and if the signmakers could make a whole discount store disappear, then why the hell couldn't Eli read his thoughts.

Rosemary had been the big ghost nut. For years, she swore that she had seen a ghost in her bedroom when she was a kid. She told Nate that she woke up in the middle of the night and immediately felt a cold draft. She started to get up out of bed, and in the corner was an elderly woman sitting in the rocking chair, gently moving back and forth. According to her story, Rosemary had frozen, and then the old lady disappeared. Nate had always laughed at that story. His favorite game used to include egging her on to tell the ghost story when they were in public, when she had been drinking, when they were around their friends—and then shoot it down. It always made Rosemary mad, and she would be pouty for a couple of days, but she always took the bait he set. Nate cringed a little, remembering how mean that game really was. He did it to make her realize how silly it sounded, but the more often he played, it became more about him and less about her.

She was probably somewhere in Utah by now. Nate hoped that she was traveling in a nice, cushy SUV with air conditioning and a CD player, not this house on wheels with the sleeping psychic in the back. Once he finally arrived at her mother's house, knocked on the door, and made Rosemary listen to how sorry he was, then he would never make fun of her ghost again. If Eli could read his thoughts, then Rosemary could have her ghost. He had been an ass. Not just to Rosemary, but pretty much everyone, Eli included. Eli just never seemed to care. Nate had always attributed that to the pot, but Eli hadn't touched the stuff since they left the boatyard, and that was a while ago. Maybe he was just really that laidback.

Nate passed a sign "Vegas 120 miles," the lights should be closer, but it had been over a decade since Nate had driven to Vegas, so he thought his memory was wrong, Nate thought it was weird how there were no cars on the road, no trucks, nothing. Surely the signmakers hadn't taken every, single car away, had they? Nate had known back in Mussel Shoals that the car lots disappeared about the time the waitresses began to appear. The issue had never been addressed, but since Nate had still seen people driving around in their cars back home, then there must be a way to get a car and keep it. He hadn't ever asked. Just like everyone else in Mussel Shoals, he had been appeased by the creamy potatoes and white gravy.

23

Rosemary wasn't going to make it. She had to pull *Lazy Daze* over in a pitch-black Ontario, and after again making sure all the doors were locked, duck into the lavatory. Rosemary knew that giving herself a bladder infection would be far worse than stopping for two minutes, but fear had made her keep driving. Too many zombie movies had taught her that the woman traveling alone in the dark was always attacked and killed as soon as she stopped moving. Not that she knew there were zombies here. There probably weren't. In fact, zombies probably didn't even exist. Well, except for the Haiti voodoo zombies, and those weren't really scary; plus, they were in Haiti. Rosemary kept repeating this to herself as she crossed from the lavatory back to the cab. She expected any moment to have a hand fly out of the darkness outside and smack the window, reaching inside the broken glass and hauling her off into the nothingness.

Despite her expectations, Rosemary started *Lazy Daze* and pulled back onto the road without incident. She was hungry, but that would have to wait, as would sleep. Rosemary knew she needed sleep, but the renewed fear of zombies had boosted her adrenaline enough that she was confident she could make a while longer. She'd seen nothing since she passed downtown, no signs, no lights, nothing. If Nate had left when she did, he might be in Las Vegas by now, and she hoped he wasn't alone. He probably wasn't, and if he wasn't, then he probably with that guy with the E name who sang along badly to Bob Dylan on the deck of *Cursory Angel*. Good, although part of her hoped that by the time she and Nate met up in Denver, the *Cursory Angel* conspiracy theorist would have found some family somewhere, or someplace else he wanted to go.

Rosemary was thinking about the last letter her mother sent her. At the time, it hadn't seemed all that strange, but now it gave her little icy stabs in her stomach. It was the first time Rosemary's mother had told her that she and Chuck were finally moving out of the house in Golden and moving to a "little place downtown." Rosemary thought it odd, because she couldn't imagine her mother wanting to sell her house, but then again, she had always loved downtown Denver. Rosemary wondered if her mother had been trying to hide the truth from her. Why would she suddenly decide to move unless she was being forced to move? Why would the signmakers be forcing everyone to the center of the cities? Granted, Venice Beach wasn't the center, but Rosemary could see how it was a gathering place. It didn't make much sense. Maybe she was overreacting. Her mother and Chuck probably just decided to stop paying their outrageous mortgage and buy a smaller place where they wouldn't have to drive so much. That had to be it.

Rosemary's mother wasn't known for being forthcoming. Secretive wasn't quite the word, more like quietly and accurately judgmental. Rosemary hated it when she was growing up, but as an adult, she hadn't been able to prove her wrong. When she flew back to Denver, alone, after her dad's accident, the first thing her mother said to her in the Stapleton airport, was:

"They're going to try to tell you that it was an accident. I think it's important that you know it wasn't. He's weak, but that doesn't mean that you are. I don't want to talk about this again."

And she didn't. When Rosemary asked questions, her mother would change the subject or outright ignore her. Rosemary eventually stopped asking, even when she got a card from her dad, who was in the Santa Barbara hospital. He told her how sorry he was that he had gotten sick. He told her that he felt bad and taken some cold medicine, but had forgotten that he couldn't take his medicine on top of it. It had been an accident, that's all. Just a silly mistake. He was going to be fine; he just needed to spend some time getting better.

The next letter had been from someone named Ingris Helman, M.D. It explained to Rosemary that her father wouldn't be able to write to her for some time, that she might have questions for him, and he would try to answer them as best he could. Her father was just fine and was staying in a place where he could rest for awhile. He had asked Ingris Helman, M.D. to write this letter because he was a little sick, but that soon he would be better. Rosemary never wrote back. She never called the phone number left by Ingris Helman, M.D. Nor did she ask her mother any more questions about the situation. She had been right. They were trying to tell her that it had been an accident, that he didn't mean it, and it was important that Rosemary understand the truth.

Rosemary continued to receive letters from her dad and Ingris Helman, M.D. Sometimes she read them, and other times she left them unopened in the box that held the Hare Krishna books her father had bought her on Venice Beach. No one mentioned her dad again, and Rosemary began to wonder if the whole thing had actually happened. The postmark on the letters was from the "New Coast Psychiatric Institute." Rosemary never asked where it was or what it was. She didn't really want to know. Even Kyle and Lily, usually quick to harass her about anything, didn't touch her letters or her Hare Krishna books. The only difference was that the yearly trips to California were gone, and in their place, her mother sent her to a summer camp in Black Forest, a woodsy area outside Colorado Springs, about an hour from Denver.

Rosemary found that her fear adrenaline was wearing off, and her eyes were getting heavy again. It had to be around two in the morning, and she had gotten up about nine that morning. But with everything that had happened, she wasn't going to be able to travel much further. A few seconds later, she saw a road sign that listed various freeway exits, among them Rancho Cucamonga. Thank God, she thought. In fact, she hoped she wasn't just seeing things, but it looked like there were lights ahead. A little far off, and on the other side of a hill, but lights nonetheless. All of a sudden, she saw a sign on the side of the road that made her screech *Lazy Daze*'s brakes and pull into reverse on the empty freeway to take a look.

To Whom It May Concern:
The following areas are Stage Two developments
and will be permanently removed in one week's time:
Rancho Cucamonga, Ontario, Victorville, and Apple Valley.
Please plan accordingly.

What the hell did Stage Two development mean? Was that why no one was in the suburbs? Rosemary guessed that the people in these areas, maybe all the areas around downtown and Venice, were being warned. The signmakers must be eliminating the extra space. Rosemary wondered why Mussel Shoals hadn't been touched, at least yet. It wasn't exactly a gathering place like Venice Beach, and they weren't living in the business towers as she supposed people must be doing downtown. In fact, people were exceptionally wasteful in Mussel Shoals. You were hard pressed to find recycling bins; people used Styrofoam and paper towels over cloth napkins. The only redeeming factor Mussel Shoals had were the retirement homes.

In trying to think like the signmakers, Rosemary presumed that they might like the fact that a large population of the town lived in giant group homes; maybe that's what saved them. Then again, maybe they were a Stage Two Development and had better get themselves downtown. It was impossible to say. Rosemary wondered about her friend Kristi with her new baby. Why would the signmakers give her a family only to take away her home? It didn't make sense. What had happened to all the other people the signmakers had given babies to? Had they all been shuffled downtown, to the beach? Her head was spinning. How much time had passed since that sign had been left? As far as Rosemary knew, she could be moments away from being permanently removed by mistake.

She hadn't been seeing things. As she grew closer and saw the "Welcome to Rancho Cucamonga" sign, Rosemary saw very clearly that there were indeed lights. People must still be here, at least until the end of the week. But something else was strange, too. While she still didn't see any people, the cars were untouched. Rancho Cucamonga was a notorious car lot, full of auto dealerships and all things that had to do with cars. Everywhere else Rosemary had been, the cars had been removed, with the exception of a handful of dark, empty and apparently abandoned vehicles she spotted on her way into Venice. But here, all the cars remained, and the roads were different in the sense that there didn't seem to be any roads at all. The whole area looked paved over, all the differentiation between the streets had been asphalted; the entire area looked like a giant car lot. Rosemary slowed down and looked. No movement, nothing. Unable to stop herself, she slowed *Lazy Daze* to a crawl. She was afraid to stop, and since she saw the sign, Rosemary certainly wasn't going to sleep here. She would have to get out of Rancho Cucamonga and find a place along the highway.

Out of the corner of her eye, Rosemary saw movement. A figure darted from behind one of the parked cars to another vehicle. She saw feet sticking out from the side of the car, and as she approached, the feet scurried out of her line of sight completely. Heart pounding and hands starting to twitch, she nervously fingered the pill bottle in her scrubs pocket. Rosemary stopped *Lazy Daze* and cranked the window down.

With a shaky voice she called, "Hello? Um, hello? I saw you move behind the car. Look...I'm not trying to scare you...hello? I just want to ask, you, um, something...hello?"

From the opposite side of the car, she saw a set of hands appear followed by a grubby face wearing a purple stocking cap. It took Rosemary a moment to recognize that she was looking at a teenager, a young teenager, maybe thirteen or fourteen. A small voice barely reached her ears

"Yeah, um, sorry, It's just, we don't see a lot of new cars coming through. I guess you kinda scared me, but it's okay. Are you with the coalition?"

Rosemary shook her head. "The coalition? I don't even know what that is. Hey, are you all right over there? Are you with anyone? How long has that sign been on the highway? What does Stage Two mean?"

The teenager stepped around the car, revealing his emoesque tight black pants and skateboard strapped to his back. "You really don't know, huh? The coalition. We're the holdouts. My mom and dad are part of it. I'm just stuck here, I guess. Where'd you come from, anyway? Everyone else who's been through has been trying to get away from Stage Two." He slowly walked toward *Lazy Daze*, unsure, stopped and leaned nervously against the hood of the Honda he had been hiding behind.

Rosemary killed the engine, and opened the door, setting one foot out. It felt good to stretch, and she felt suddenly and oddly calm, even as her hands continued to twitch.

"No, I don't know what it is. I'm from Mussel Shoals, it's right outside of Santa Barbara...we didn't have anything like this there, but I just came through LA. Is Stage Two what's happening there, too?"

The boy shook his head. "Can't say. I only know that sign appeared about three nights ago; that's when the coalition started. They keep saying that the signmakers won't nuke us if there are still people around. I think they're fucking crazy. I plan on driving one of these things out of town before that happens."

Rosemary thought, he must be older than he looks, maybe sixteen-ish. "Where are your parents, are they out here somewhere too?"

96

The boy shrugged. "They're with the others in the car barn, you know that big red thing—used to be a used Toyota lot. Look, if I was you, I wouldn't stop here. They've gotten nuts. They refuse to leave the fucking car barn, and all they do is pray."

Rosemary stepped a little closer. "Can you tell me what Stage Two means? Do your parents ever talk about what it actually is?"

Another shrug. "Look, I don't really know, but dad says that it means, "shape up or ship out," and then he goes off about what the hell, and the nerve, all that crap; kinda makes him crazy. Basically, they did this parking lot thing for a while. Guess they figured that with all the cars, we must like driving. Works for me, but the dudes upstairs weren't so happy. The next sign was some shit about your "statement of purpose," and they told everyone to go downtown; at least that's what Dad said it meant. Now, we have the Stage Two sign, Dad and everyone says that means we're goners because we didn't do what they wanted. I don't know really. I know I'm out of here in one of these beauties come about Friday night. Screw 'em all, man, screw 'em all. They want to die in the car barn, go for it."

Rosemary was stunned,. She had been right, kind of...they were consolidating people in specific places. "Hey, I don't want to scare you, but do any of these cars have any gas? Do you still have gas here?"

The boy laughed out loud. "No way, man. I mean, not in the stations, that's why everything's like all over the place. Just ran out of gas and no one moved them. That was about the time the "go downtown" sign showed up. Which is really retarded when you think about it. I mean, like, how are we supposed to get to downtown LA if we don't have any rides. But, I have a plan."

With this, the boy walked toward Rosemary, and his face lit up with expectation. "Now, you can't tell anyone in the car barn, but you're totally not going to go over there, right? I mean, you really shouldn't. They lost their marbles over there. So, you wanna know my plan?"

Rosemary nodded slowly.

"When we got the warning about the gas, it was like this sign in the middle of everything. I filled up five of those big plastic jugs, you know, the ones that you're supposed to put water in. I did it at night, broke into the station, flipped the pump on, and bam. I'm set. I'm not getting removed man, got a buddy of mine, he's working on the car right now, making sure it'll get us outta here."

"But where will you go?" Rosemary was amazed at his planning; her eleventh grade students back in Mussel Shoals could hardly plan what they were going to eat for lunch, much less have the foresight to devise an escape.

"We're taking off to San Fran. My cousin's up there, and he said Golden Gate Park is kickin' right now. If I have to live with a whole bunch of people, I'm doing it in Golden Gate. Gonna try to get Mom and Dad to go, but I kinda think they won't go for it. Preacher dude like sucked their brains totally out."

With that, the emo teenager gave her a crooked grin that displayed several thousand dollars of orthodontia work. He was about to say something else when a voice rang out from the blackness.

"Jeremy! Jeremy where are you?"
The kid's face went visibly pale.

"Shit. That's my Dad. What the fuck? He hasn't left the car barn in days; didn't think he'd even notice I was out here."

A figure slowly emerged from the darkness, walking quickly toward them. Rosemary jumped back and started to scramble back into the cab. The man started running, before she could slam the door he was in her face, pulling the door open.

"What the hell are you doing out here? Get the hell away from my kid, lady!"

He let the door go as he spun around and grabbed Jeremy's arm. "Jeremy! Get back to your mother, now. Now! It's almost time, son. You can't be out here!"

Rosemary felt her breath constricting. Under normal circumstances, she would have been much less afraid of this guy who was obviously just looking for his kid, but tonight in the abandoned parking that was Rancho Cucamonga, he made the blood freeze in her veins. He didn't look like a monster, he looked like a soccer coach. He was tall and athletic, in his early forties, and wore running shorts and a polo shirt. In the artificial street lamp light, he looked drawn, shadows collected under his eyes. He pulled Jeremy forward as he started toward Rosemary again. Jeremy wrenched his arm free.

"Dad! Leave her alone! She wasn't trying to kidnap me, we were just talking! C'mon, let's go, I'll come back with you, just let her be."
Behind his dad's back, Jeremy gave her a wild look. Rosemary hesitated, trying to pull *Lazy Daze*'s door closed. The soccer coach pulled back and flung it open. Despite herself, Rosemary let out an involuntary shriek and tried to scoot back. A strong arm grabbed her wrist and pulled her out of the cab and onto the ground. Rosemary stopped herself from slamming head first into the pavement with her free hand. The pain hit like a knife and radiated up her arm. Stunned and scared, she rolled back to see Jeremy pulling the soccer coach off her.

"Stop it, Dad! C'mon, let's go! She had nothing to do with anything. She was coming from LA. Just freakin' chill; let her get out of town!"

The soccer coach stopped a moment, considering. "Jeremy, stay out of this. You don't know what kind of people are out there right now. For all you know, she could be one of them. You ever stop to think about that? Where'd she get the gas? None of these cars have run in months, and here comes this one. She's probably one of those goddamn waitresses or whatever they're called."

Recovering from the fall, Rosemary scrambled to her feet, a dull ache in her belly. "I'm not a waitress! I'm on my way to Las Vegas, and then to Denver. Your son was just telling me what the signs meant, that was all."

The soccer coach looked like he was about to respond when another figure came sprinting out of the darkness.

"We've got to get back! There's been another sign, there's no time."

He started to say more, but stopped as he saw Rosemary. In the light, she could see he was older than the soccer coach, his potbelly causing him to pant from the effort of his rush. Rosemary suddenly doubled over with a cramp that pierced her stomach. She struggled for breath; thought she felt a warm wetness between her legs. The horror that she was bleeding overrode the panic that had set in. She fell back into *Lazy Daze*'s side. The cramp began to subside although the wetness was increasing. As she looked up, she saw two men and Jeremy staring at her quizzically. Finally, the soccer coach broke the silence.

"Jesus, you need some help. Are you, I mean do...are you alright?" Rosemary looked down to see a dark stain spreading down the leg of the green scrubs. A cold chill filled her chest. A word played in her head, afraid to be said aloud. Miscarriage. She was a little late for her period, but she hadn't thought it meant anything. After all, it never had before. She tried to respond, but another cramp interrupted her words. Through the pain, she heard Jeremy's voice.

"See what you did Dad! See that! You pulled her out! You made her fall!"

As the cramp began to pass, Rosemary glanced up. The two men were still staring dumbfounded. She took the opportunity to pull herself back into the cab of the RV and slam the door, hitting the lock before they could respond. Her hands were shaking as she tried to turn the key. The engine roared to life as the soccer coach let out a high-pitched scream. Rosemary turned her head to see a sign, newly formed, not a foot from *Lazy Daze*'s door. The soccer coach let out another sound that sounded like a wounded animal; it sent chills up Rosemary's spine. She looked back to the sign and saw the cause of his fear.

It has come to our attention
That Caleb Markson has
Caused grievous harm to another being
Please take it under advisement that you are
Currently in probationary status.
Please revise your statement of purpose.

The soccer coach took off running into the darkness, Jeremy followed. Before the potbellied man could respond or try to stop her, Rosemary hit the gas and pulled out of Rancho Cucamonga, the car barn in the distance, the lights fading behind her.

24

Nate knew something was wrong. For one thing, he had been here before, and he distinctly remembered some outlying casinos and suburbs on the edge of the city. He had driven to Vegas with some college buddies years ago and knew for a fact that there was a casino/restaurant/bar along this highway that looked like an old timey ranch house. It had even had horses in the back, and a makeshift barn. The bar was set up like an old west saloon. Nate remembered it because his buddy had gotten them kicked out, and the owner told them they were never welcome there again. Nate couldn't help grinning a little at the memory. His buddy, whose name he really couldn't remember, had decided that since he wasn't driving, he would start drinking. They had stopped for an early lunch, and instead of eating, the buddy had ordered three whiskey shots. The whiskey shots had turned into tequila shooters and the tequila shooters had quickly turned into an altercation with a guy in a faded gray suit at the end of the saloon. Nate and the other guys had hauled their inebriated friend onto the front porch of the ranch house, only to lose their grip on him and be forced to chase him out back to the horse paddock. Nate remembered laughing uncontrollably—he'd had a couple of shots himself—as his buddy drunkenly scaled the paddock fence and tried unsuccessfully to climb onto an old brown horse by pulling on her mane. The guy who owned the place had hauled him out with one hand and hit the whole traveling party with a lifetime ban from his establishment.

Nate was sure the ban would be lifted now; after all, it had been fourteen, maybe fifteen years. He had been too young to drink at the time, he knew that much, but not too young to have a fake ID that identified him as a thirty-five-year-old man from Santa Fe named Joaquin Odujami. It generally only worked if the bartender or bouncer hadn't read the name, or looked the picture. Nate had to stand in front of a blue sheet, which was supposed to simulate the background of the DMV photos. Problem was, he was too tall for the sheet. It had been hung to accommodate the freshman girls who wanted ID photos taken, and Nate was a good foot taller than any of them. So, he had to crouch down so the white paint wouldn't show above his head. The result was an uncomfortable shot in which Nate looked alternately hunched over, or like he was squinting.

It didn't help either that the fake New Mexico DMV information on the back of the ID was crooked, or that Nate looked pretty far from being someone who would have acquired the name Joaquin Odujami. But it had done the job at the ranch house.

Nate knew the ranch house must be coming up; he vaguely remembered that it was around the fifty-mile marker. But instead of the ranch, or anything for that matter, all Nate saw was flat desert. The Vegas lights were blazing in the distance, but they looked small and compact. The suburbs and surrounding areas were dark. Nate felt nervous; he wondered what Rosemary had found when she had driven through here. Had she stopped? Maybe she was still here...he didn't even let the grain of hope enter his head. While it was a nice thought that she was right now sleeping in a nice Vegas hotel room, and they would "accidentally" run into each other in the lobby of some casino, he knew that wasn't going to be the case.

Rosemary had left this morning, Eli had seen her around eleven, and it was now about one the next morning. If she had driven straight through, it was possible that she had already hit Denver. More likely, she stopped somewhere around Green River or Grand Junction. She wouldn't stop in Vegas, she hated Vegas; it was too crowded and too expensive. Nate tried a couple of times to get her to take a road trip out here back in the early days, before the signmakers. But Rosemary always rolled her eyes and acted like she didn't hear him. She hated the desert, and truthfully, so did Nate. He never wanted to live away from the water.

He heard the bathroom door open and the swoosh of the toilet. Eli sat down next to Nate with a bottle of water in his hand. He offered it to him and he accepted by taking a swig.

"Man, I had the craziest dreams, man. Where are we? How far did the Minnie get us?"

"We're almost to Vegas, twenty-five miles. Although, there's something weird, you've been here before right?"

Eli nodded "Yea, it's been awhile; came out here with the roomies four Christmases ago, lost all our grocery money for the month on a blackjack table; sucked, man."

Nervously, Nate said, "I don't want to sound paranoid, but doesn't it look different to you? Shouldn't we be seeing stuff by now, buildings and shit like that? It's been like fifteen years since I was here, but I remember this place right about here, and now there's nothing. And the lights, I mean, I assume that's the Strip, but it looks really small."

Eli shrugged "Couldn't say man, couldn't say. It's late, I don't remember a damn thing about driving in, man. We rented something like the Minnie here, and one of the roomies drove while the rest of us were enjoying some herb in the back. I don't remember lights; don't remember much man."

The reserve gaslight flicked on; they were down to about three gallons in the tank. The Minnie guzzled the gas and Nate was actually surprised they had made it this far. He figured she was getting about ten miles per gallon. It scared Nate to think about how they were going to fill her up again, if they would even be able to, or how would they afford the gas. Eli didn't look worried about anything. He wandered to the back of the Minnie and was now sitting at the booth eating Vienna sausages out of a can.

"You wanna switch, man? You okay to drive us on in? I don't mind driving, man. Just let me finish here and you can grab a snack."

"Yeah, alright, that's probably a good idea. Hey Eli, I don't know quite how to tell you this, but you know about that thing you do in your sleep, right? You've actually done it when you were awake too, just not as much..."
Nate heard Eli scraping the Vienna sausage sauce from the bottom of the can with some kind of metal utensil—yet another thing Eli had remembered to grab from Priceplan.

"Oh, man, I'm sorry, man. The snoring, right? The roomies used to make me sleep on the deck of the boat sometimes, man, I know it's kinda intense. Shoulda warned ya, man. Sorry 'bout that."

"Not the snoring, I mean, yeah, you snore, but I don't care, I meant the other thing you do, the talking, the other guys must have told you about the talking."
Eli climbed back into the passenger seat; there was a little Vienna sausage juice in his beard.

"Heh, no talking, man, Wouldn't doubt it, but they never told me. What did I say?"

Nate hesitated. "Nothing; never mind. It wasn't bad, just mumbling stuff; no big deal. You want to switch here or in town. I'm fine until we reach the lights."

"That's cool man; whenever. I like the Minnie; sure as hell beats the boatyard. Wonder how your lady's Pinto is holding out, man. Those things are tanks. She's probably halfway across the country by now."

"No, I think she's in Denver, or pretty close by now. Her mom's in Denver; that's the only place she would go."

Eli grew silent staring out toward the lights. His fingers found the Vienna sausage sauce, and he wiped it off his beard and into his mouth. Nate passed a sign marking the exit for the freeway, West Hills, and Business District. He guessed that the lights were coming from the business district and pulled off on the ramp. He was now feeling a light panic, but Eli didn't seem to notice. There had to be something by now. According to the sign, they were cutting through a suburb; they should be surrounded by stores and houses. Instead, it was just the flat desert. The lights loomed ahead, and Nate stepped on the gas, ignoring the fuel light on the dashboard.

25

Rosemary drove out of Rancho Cucamonga keeping an eye on the rearview mirror. She wasn't about to stop anywhere close enough that she might be mistaken for being in the permanently removed zone. She was still shaking from everything that had happened. The cramps had subsided and the bleeding had stopped. Still, Rosemary couldn't shake the fluttery nervousness that had taken their place. She desperately wished she could fast forward time, teleport herself to Denver and Nate. She wondered now if her Dad's cabin was even still standing. If what was happening in Los Angeles was happening in Denver, then it probably wasn't. No matter, they could find a place in downtown Denver. Rosemary had always loved that neighborhood. Sixteenth Street Mall was what the Walkabout wanted to be, but due to the overwhelming number of senior citizens, never would be. The Sixteenth Street mall was a fifteen-block open-air mall lined with shops and restaurants, bars, and coffee counters. Buskers and musicians lined the street, and electric buses ran up and down stopping each block. The city kept Christmas lights on all the trees, even in the summer, so it always looked like there was snow twinkling in the night.

Rosemary brought Nate there for spring break the first year they were dating. It was really only a few months after the coffee incident at his parent's house. Rosemary decided he should go back with her, and he agreed. They took an Amtrak because the plane tickets were outrageous, and her 1980 Dodge Colt would never have made it across the desert. At fifty-nine dollars a ticket, the round trip seemed like a bargain, but what the ticket counter didn't tell you was that the train took three days, and the bargain tickets gave you little more than a cot and a lavatory so small that you couldn't close the door once inside. Rosemary hadn't been ready to take their relationship to the "peeing in front of each other" level, so she had requested an extra bed sheet from the housekeeper and hung it in front of the door. Nate would stand in front of the sheet and poke at it with his finger while she squealed in protest.

The first day had actually been romantic, after the initial shock about their "cabin." Nate was in a good mood; he joked with the waiters in the dining car, sat with Rosemary in the lounge, and drank Heineken until the sunset. They stumbled back to the cabin and fooled around on the lower bunk until they both fell asleep. Rosemary had awakened hours later on the floor, having fallen off in the night, cold and queasy. Nate was sitting straight up, eyes open, having an argument with no one.

"I don't care what you hosted or didn't host. Never got that Emmy for 'Taxi,' did ya? Huh! Had to wait for the sympathy vote almost ten years later, didn't ya! And you have the nerve to come in here and tell me....what's that? I don't think so buddy. I saw Art, talk about phoning it in. That is not your number; get the hell out of line! You came in here with that number, you can't do that, you just can't do that!"

Rosemary had seen him do that before, and she had an idea about what was going on. Of course, she had no idea who Nate might have been talking to, but she had seen this kind of thing before. This was well after the Mary Elizabeth Mastrantonio incident, and Rosemary knew about Nate's diagnosis. She leaned over the cot and lightly touched his shoulder, shaking it slowly.

"Baby, Nate, honey...wake up, baby. You're dreaming again. It isn't real, baby. C'mon, wake up."

Instead of gently coming to, Nate turned to her, and with the glaze of sleep still covering his wide-open eyes, took her wrists and squeezed. Rosemary screamed instinctually, but Nate was still asleep. He squeezed harder and pushed her into the wall, where her head hit a low hanging shelf, and the sudden smack made her bite down on her tongue. Rosemary tasted blood and panicked immediately. She screamed again, and in struggling to free herself from Nate's iron sleep grasp, fell over the small black overnight bag she left on the floor. She fell out of Nate's grasp and landed squarely on her hip. A sharp pain radiated out through her body, and Rosemary was momentarily paralyzed by it. By now, there were voices at the door, knocking, demanding to know if everything was okay in there, warning that they were coming in if no one answered. Rosemary looked over at the bed at Nate, the sleep gaze had snapped out of his eyes and had been replaced with sheer horror. He was frozen, staring at Rosemary sprawled on the floor, her wrists already showing the bruises he had left, a smear of blood on her face from her damaged tongue. Nate fell forward and scrambled toward Rosemary, cupping her head in his hands.

"Oh, God, baby! I did this? Oh, God! Are you okay? Oh God, oh, God."

Tears were streaming down his cheeks and the voices at the door grew more insistent. A key turned in the lock and the bellman burst in, surrounded by half a dozen other faces.

"What happened here? Step away from her, sir. Miss, are you alright?"

Rosemary looked at Nate, who was pressed against the wall, tears in his eyes, and grief on his face. "I'm fine, I had a dream is all, and I fell out of the top bunk. Stupid, really; I sleep walk. I never should have been up there. I'm fine; I just bit my tongue and woke myself up. That's all, really. I'm sorry to wake you up."

It had taken some convincing, and Rosemary had to hide her wrists behind her back so the porter wouldn't catch a glimpse, but finally they all left.

Nate curled up on the floor, head in his hands.

"Oh, God, what did I do? I...sorry doesn't even come close. I would kill myself before I'd hurt you. You have to know that. Oh God, what can I do?"

"You can get me some ice," Rosemary said, "and then you can stop this. You didn't mean to; you were asleep, I shouldn't have tried to wake you up like that. You were having that dream thing again, the celebrity thing, this one was something about an Emmy, and Taxi, and a number."

Nate paled a little and nodded. He left and came back with a bucket of ice as Rosemary rubbed her bruised wrists and tried to ignore the throb in her hip. He sat up with her the rest of the night, replacing the ice and staring at the wall. He refused to tell Rosemary what the dream had been about, but he did tell her about the clinic his parents shipped him to when he was a kid. A juvenile psychiatric hospital disguised as a sleep clinic. Nate had been there for months before his parents took him back home. The more he talked, and the more buckets of ice he brought her, the more Rosemary felt like she belonged to someone, to something. She wasn't just the extra kid any longer, the loner, the oddball; she had a match, a place, and the more she looked around the room, the more she fell back into his arms and into the old comfort of the water pipe dragons.

Rosemary stopped *Lazy Daze* as soon as she crossed a small hilly stretch that almost completely blocked the Rancho Cucamonga lights. Nothing was in sight, just flat desert. After double-checking the door locks and the door to the living quarters, Rosemary realized that she couldn't keep her eyes open any longer. Sleep took precedence over fear, and she walked to the back of *Lazy Daze* and lay down on the bottom bunk. It was still warm enough that she didn't want the blankets, and just as she started imagining Nate's face, she was asleep.

26

Nate drove through the nothingness toward the lights. As he grew closer, he breathed a sigh of relief. The lights of the Strip were really there, and there were people, and he saw waitresses on the corners, just like in Mussel Shoals. The fuel light flashed angrily, and he heard a sputter from the front of the Minnie.

Eli looked up from his daze. "Man, good timing, man. Looks like we got here right on time. Told you the Minnie wouldn't let us down, man! I freakin' love these things, man, they're like karma mobiles."

Nate pulled off the road next to a roach hotel with a faded sign that read "Stage Three Development Community. Welcome" Across the street, the Strip was introduced by the Luxor and it's huge pyramid entrance. The sight of it was overwhelming. The black glass seemed to stretch into the sky. The spotlight that usually rotated around the peak was dark, but in the city light, the figure seemed to merge with the night sky. The parking lot of the Luxor didn't have any cars, certainly no Minnie Winnies, but there were dozens of single and double rider Vespa scooters. Most of them were plugged into what looked like large power strip stations. People wandered the parking lot, moving down the sidewalk, talking, and laughing as if the rest of their city hadn't been removed. Most were carrying plastic buckets, presumably full of coins or poker chips. Nate turned around to Eli, but he was gone. A second later, Nate found him on the sidewalk next to the Minnie doing a strange little dance and shaking his arms. Nate climbed out cautiously and leaned over to stretch his stiff legs.

"Man, I just got a little cooped up, ya know what I mean, man! Just gotta dance it out, man! C'mon, man! Dance it out with me!"

Despite himself, Nate laughed. He couldn't get over how none of this seemed to faze Eli at all; he really seemed thrilled by everything. Eli apparently wasn't wondering what Stage Three meant, he wasn't wondering how they were going to afford more gas, if there was even any gas in this town. It looked to Nate like the signmakers had maybe gotten rid of all the other vehicles that needed gas. Nate had a sudden vision of himself and Eli, straddling each other on a two-seater electric Vespa all the way to Colorado. But despite all of this, Eli was dancing away on the sidewalk. He gave Eli an obligatory shake of his arms and leaned over to stretch his legs again.

"C'mon, man! Let's go find out how to get the Minnie rolling again, man! Time's a wastin'. Your lady is probably all holed up in Colorado by now. I sure as hell don't want to drive the desert in the daytime, the Minnie can't take that kind of pressure, man...she's an old lady."

With that, Eli was bouncing down the street. Nate locked the Minnie Winnie's doors and checked the door handle to the sleeping area to make sure it was bolted, not that anyone could steal anymore; the signmakers looked down on theft, petty or otherwise. Still, it was habit. Nate caught up with Eli and they proceeded down the Strip. They crossed the empty street and cut across the Luxor parking lot, and knots of people smiled at them as they walked toward the entrance.

Nate wanted to stop and ask them about the gas, but Eli seemed to be on a mission. As they passed, Nate snuck a look into the plastic buckets that everyone seemed to be carrying—no coins, only chips. Nate suddenly wondered if there were any coins here...after all, if you were going to eliminate the suburbs, gasoline, and unsuspecting Priceplans, wouldn't you go after money next? Made sense to Nate, especially since money certainly caused more problems and sadness than gas and Priceplan ever had. Nate remembered a theory Rosemary told him one night as they had been drinking beer on the deck of *Cursory Angel*, back before Priceplan, before everything changed. She had turned to him out of the blue and said:

"I think we like being unhappy. Really. I think we work very hard for it. You take all the things that we claim make us unhappy away, money, property, health problems, whatever, and people still look for something new to hate. It's like that song; you know that Joni Mitchell song about paradise. We say we like nature and being free, but really, we only want to cage it up and look at it."

Nate hadn't responded, and Rosemary had grown silent. At the time, he just thought she was being apocalyptic again; she got that way when she had anything to drink. Now he wasn't so sure that she hadn't been wrong. These people looked totally happy surrounded by the plastic palm trees and neon pyramids. They looked content to be carrying around their buckets of plastic money. For all of the illusion, Nate had to wonder what they were working on to make themselves unhappy, and how the signmakers were going to try to fix it.

Nate and Eli entered the Luxor through the double doors that were cut into the side of the pyramid. A doorman in a red uniform with shiny brass buttons opened the door for them with a wide smile.

"Welcome to Las Vegas! We welcome you to the Luxor! Have you just arrived?"

Nate nodded his head while Eli seemed fixated on the shiny buttons.

'Well then an especially big welcome! Please see our front desk for information; the agent will have a whole packet to get you oriented to the new Las Vegas!"

The new Las Vegas? Eli seemed unfazed as usual, as his eyes became slightly glassy with the overpowering sight of thousands of people milling around, some at the slot machines, which as Nate suspected, were now only accepting poker chips, and some lounged near the bar, drinking out of glasses rimmed with exotic flowers and ornamental monkeys. The Egyptian arches loomed in front of them, and Nate became dizzy just looking up at the rows and rows of stacked rooms. Palm trees sprang from planters and reached for the point that was only a dot in the ceiling. The front desk area to his right was filled with lush looking sofas and greenery. A line led out of the restaurant and Nate was hit with the smell of hot food, reminding his stomach that the last meal he'd eaten consisted of yesterday's stale saltines. He suddenly felt lightheaded, and just as he tried to grab for Eli's shoulder, he saw only blackness.

When Nate opened his eyes, he felt cold leather beneath him, and saw about a dozen faces staring at him in worry. He coughed as his nose got a whiff of Eli's Vienna sausage breath. Eli was directly over him.

"Whoa, man! Welcome back, man! You okay? You fell like a log, man. I never saw anything quite like that one! Hey everybody, I think he's okay. Thanks for the cushions and all!"

A pretty Asian woman, somewhere in her early forties, maybe, appeared directly over Nate's face. She touched his neck with her slender, cold fingers, feeling for a pulse. She stopped on his ceratoid artery and looked at her watch. The fingers felt good, the cold cushions felt good, but everything else felt numb. Nate could still smell the food, and it made his stomach turn a little. The woman looked up from her watch.

"I think you'll be alright. Your heart rate is up a little, and you're a bit pale, but it doesn't look like you hit your head too hard. I'm sorry, my name's Caroline. I'm a doctor. You passed out. Do you know where you are, sir?"

"The doorman said this is the new Las Vegas. We just got here."

"I think you're fine," she said, smiling. "When was the last time you ate? Low blood sugar will knock you out faster than anything."

"It's been awhile. I had saltines this morning, but we have food in our car, my friend and I were only coming in to see about gas and the information packet the doorman talked about. We don't really have any money or poker chips or anything. Maybe if my friend could grab the packet we could just go back to our..."

Caroline smiled gently, as she pushed the long black hair away from her face. "You don't need money or chips to eat here. The signmakers take good care of us. I'm sure you saw the sign on your way in. We're Stage Three. Nearly everything is self-contained here. You don't need to worry. We'll get you a plate; don't move. Is there anything you don't eat? We have a buffet table so you can have anything you like."

Nate reeled back, and the energy it took to speak exhausted him even more. His voice came out little more than a whisper. "I don't want any of their goddamn signmaker food. I don't want...." He tried to continue but felt his voice fading out. Nate saw Caroline exchange a worried glance with Eli.

"Okay," she said, carefully. "That's fine. I'll just go get you some other food, not from the signmakers. Would that be okay? Is there anything you don't eat?"

Nate felt relieved; they hadn't been completely taken over.

"Meat, I don't eat meat. Do you have orange juice? I feel shaky."

"Sure, just sit tight and don't move, I'll be right back."

Caroline's pretty face was replaced with Eli's slightly worried one. "Dude, you sure scared the hell out of me, but man, people are nice here, man. The desk lady gave me this book, said we needed it. She also said that if we wanted a couple of rooms to just say the word, man, that's some niceness, see, man. The karma mobile didn't disappoint."

Nate sat up. His head rushed to his eyeballs and he thought for a second that he would pass out again. His hands were shaking so badly that he couldn't hold them still. He had been lying on one of the sofas that led to the front desk. On the sofa across from him sat a little old lady, her white hair puffed out like a poodle. She was counting her chips and humming the Jeopardy theme song. She seemed oblivious to Nate or Eli.

Eli began reading from the cover of the dark bound book. It had a picture of the Strip lights on the front and the inside pages looked like the hand-made paper sold in stationery stores.

"Welcome to the New Las Vegas! Whether you are relocating, or just passing through to another Stage Three community, we hope you will enjoy our beautiful city! In conjunction with the signmakers, the Las Vegas hospitality board has created this booklet to guide you to the new way of living here in 'New Vegas.' If you have any questions, please do not hesitate to ask any of the friendly wait staff, which you will find in many convenient locations throughout the city.

"Let's start with 'Getting Acquainted.' Whether you are making the move to New Vegas or just joining us for the night, you'll want to take advantage of our legendary Vegas showroom hotels and nutritious buffets. The signmakers have removed the need for money of any kind, so don't you worry about the finances! Just jump in line and remember, take only what you need! Our friendly front desk staff in any of our fine New Vegas establishments will be able to arrange temporary or permanent housing for you and your family."

Caroline returned with a red plastic tray that held a plate of what looked like pasta with a creamy sauce, broccoli, and garlic bread. Next to the heaping plate, stood a tall glass of orange juice and another of ice water. Eli's jaw dropped an inch.

"Man, do you mind if I hit the buffet line? That looks good! You got BBQ over there?"

Caroline gave him a warning look as she placed the tray on the low end table next to the couch. "Feel free to go to the buffet; just remember to take only what you need."

Eli ran toward the buffet. Nate gingerly reached for the orange juice but his shaking hands sloshed the glass. Caroline took the orange juice out of his hands and held it to his lips.

"I suspect you might be hypoglycemic. Have you ever been diagnosed?"

Nate shook his head as she held the glass to his lips.

"Here, just drink this first, we need to get you a little stabilized, and then you need to dig in. Hope you like pasta."

Nate gulped the entire glass and the smeary effect of the bright casino lights began to fade a little. His hands stopped shaking, and he reached for the hot plate and the fork next to it. The pasta was wonderful, the sauce a minty Alfredo with mushrooms and artichoke hearts. The broccoli was steamed just enough to be soft without turning mushy, the bread a perfect blend of garlic and butter. Nate knew he should pause and make conversation with Caroline, ask her questions, find out about the gas, but he couldn't stop. She waited patiently as he wolfed down the noodles. It wasn't until the pasta, broccoli, and most of the garlic bread was gone that he came up for breath. Nate hadn't eaten like this in a long time, not since he and Rosemary were confined to her teacher's income. He'd become accustomed to all meals having something to do with rice, tuna and saltines. This was a feast.

"I'm sorry, I'm so rude. I'm Nate, that's Eli." In his food-induced blindness, Nate hadn't even realized that Eli was back, gnawing happily on a barbequed turkey leg.

Caroline accepted the hand Nate offered. "It's my pleasure. You're getting some color back. Do you feel better?"

Nate nodded through a mouthful of bread and then covered his mouth. "Thank you, this is great. I had no idea Vegas would be like this, now. Sorry I passed out on your floor...I didn't realize how hungry I was until we stopped."

Caroline took the empty plate from Nate and placed it back on the red tray.

"You really shouldn't worry about it. That's why I'm here after all. We have travelers from all different experiences show up at our door. Since we're at the end of the Strip, fainting happens more often than you might think. It's overwhelming; a lot of people think we've turned into monsters, or robots or some other crazy thing. They don't expect to see what they see."

Nate took a long drink of lemon-tinged water from the glass Caroline offered him. "Yea, about that...Eli was reading the book, but what is this?" Caroline smiled. "The book really will answer all your questions. It's hard to explain the transformation without sounding callous, just please take us up on our offer of a couple of rooms for the night—or we have a suite with two double beds. Whatever your plans, you should rest, you won't do anyone any good if you make yourself sick, or fall asleep at the wheel tonight. After a blood sugar attack like the one you've just had, you're likely to feel markedly tired; you shouldn't push it. Give us a night. Who knows? You might want to stay."

Caroline was right about the drowsiness. The extreme hunger had been replaced with a sudden and violent urge to close his eyes. "No, I can't, my wife,

Rosemary, she's in Denver, I have to get to her, I screwed up and she left, and our boat sank, and this guy in a sweater vest thinks I'm tapioca." Nate knew he was babbling, fighting the urge to curl back up on the pleather sofa.

"Well, stay the night and start fresh with some rest. It's nearly four in the morning; after all, if you've been traveling all day, you need the break."

Caroline motioned to the girl behind the front desk, who came around the counter to bring Caroline two keys. Simultaneously, a bellhop with more shiny buttons and a young man with an apron appeared to alternately remove the food trays and show Nate and Eli to their room. Nate could barely walk, and Eli supported him with his arm around his waist.

"Man, I think you're in some kind of noodle coma, man. Doctor lady is right, man. We'll sleep and get you better, and then we'll take off tomorrow. Don't worry, man, your lady will still be there, and Minnie will still be waiting. This is sweet, man. Never stayed in Vegas in style before."

The bellhop took them up fifteen flights in the elevator to room #1563. The opened door revealed a two-bedroom suite, with a living room, mini bar and fireplace separating the two spaces. There was a patio door across the room that presumably opened up to a balcony. Nate patted Eli on the shoulder and shuffled off to the bedroom to the right. He barely pulled the sheets down and peeled off his t-shirt and pants before crashing down to the bed, asleep before he hit the pillow.

27

The winter sun started baking *Lazy Daze* a little after eight in the morning, and soon, Rosemary woke up drenched in sweat, gasping for breath. She had shut every possible entryway when she locked up last night and therefore cut off all possible supplies of fresh air. Rosemary's throat felt raw, and she was dizzy. She suddenly realized that she had no water, save what must have melted off the peas last night. As she opened the lid, she reeled back from the stink of the melted peas. A couple of inches of water sloshed around in the bottom of the cooler, which had soaked the bread, and the peas were bloated and overripe. Rosemary groaned, considering her options. She either drank the pea water or held out until she reached Las Vegas. The stink washed over her in a wave, and Rosemary felt her stomach begin to heave. Slamming the lid down, she lurched forward to the RV door, barely making it outside into the warm winter desert air before she dry heaved. She'd wait until Las Vegas—it was only three or four hours away. Opening the cooler and drinking its rank water was not an option.

The next sensation that hit her was an intense need to pee. She barely made it into the lavatory and with the door wide open, tried to relieve herself. The burning sensation crept up through her bladder and into her gut. Nothing came out, and the sensation increased with the effort. Rosemary knew what this was, and she started crying from frustration and pain. She had intermittent bladder infections as a kid and as she got older, they grew to be purely situational. If she wasn't drinking enough water, taking enough bathroom breaks at school, or taking care of herself in general, this was the first sign. She shouldn't be surprised; she hadn't been doing anything to make sure it didn't happen.

Fuck! Fuck! Fuck! Rosemary smacked the side of the lavatory with her open palm and the effort made *Lazy Daze* shake a little. What other fucking thing could happen? She buried her head in her hands. What next? What to do? She should have gone to the car barn with Jeremy, the soccer coach and pot belly, and let them sacrifice her to the car lot gods or whatever crazy thing they had planned. At least then she would know that she had been of some use. As it was, Rosemary was likely to die in a goddamn, motherfucking, 1980s RV with a mountain scene painted on the side. Fuck! Rosemary caught a look at herself in the teeny mirror over the lav sink. Her face was red, eyes puffy and bloodshot.

Her dark blonde hair was black with sweat and plastered to her head. The front of the green scrubs was soaked with sweat and dried blood. Rosemary didn't need a mirror to smell herself, smell *Lazy Daze* in general. It smelled like sweat; like frustration.

Trying her best to ignore the mixed messages that her bladder was sending her, Rosemary stood up and leaned against the lav sink as a wave of pain and lightheadedness washed over her. She turned on the faucet. As she expected, there was nothing. Why would there be? Rosemary knew that the only way there would be water in the faucet was if someone had filled the tank next to the sewage. And, on top of it, the only way the faucet would have enough pressure to pump the water was if she had had the opportunity to plug in the generator, if it still worked. All those ifs, and here she was, leaned over a dry sink, trying to ignore the consequences of poor planning. Thanks a lot you motherfuckers. Thanks a lot for the new goddamn home you bastards. Yeah, this is goddamn great; a motherfucking RV! An RV with no gas, no power; goddamn nothing.

Rosemary held the wall and used it to swing herself out of the lavatory and into the dining booth. She needed to drive; she needed to get to Las Vegas. Either she would die here or she would die there, but she just wasn't ready to assume that Vegas had been removed. Rosemary told herself that it was worth the chance. Trying to ignore her suddenly rumbling stomach, Rosemary looked down at the stained hospital scrubs. She'd left her clothes in the Pinto, which was stuck on I-10. There was no way to cover up the stain. Fuck.

Las Vegas was about four hours away; surely she could make it until then. If there was anything left, maybe she could raid a pharmacy or even a grocery store and get some cranberry juice for her bladder, and a new pair of pants. What had she been thinking? That this would be easy—just a drive to Denver and that was it? Oh, yeah, she'd just jump over to Colorado, and with no problem at all get one of those waitresses, none of which she'd seen since Mussel Shoals, to hook her up with everything she needed. She'd move into Dad's cabin, and as soon as she was unpacked, the signmakers would deliver a baby. And then, only if she wanted him back, Nate could join her, all contrite and apologetic, and together they would be the perfect family. Nate's eyes would never again spiral downward until they were nearly black. He would never tell her in that deadly focused voice that it was a mistake, that their marriage was a mistake, that she was a mistake. He would never again accuse her of being too accommodating, of not being able to stand up for herself, of being weak. He would never watch her cry and walk out the door.

All of that would stop; instead, she would have the Nate who returned once his eyes were green again, the one who honestly didn't seem to remember why she was upset. The Nate who wanted to help her, hold her. She would have the Nate who woke up terrified night after night in fear of accidentally hurting her during one of his dreams. She would also have the Nate who made her eggs at two in the morning, wrapped her in his flannel robe; the same one who had almost been lost during a stint at the psychiatric hospital as a little kid.

She would take that guy back, and they would raise their perfect baby in a cabin in the woods, and never again even have to think about the desert, or boatyards, or anything but the future.

With renewed strength, Rosemary closed the door and latched it before she crossed to the cab and gave the drum in the passenger seat a light tap. She started the engine, rolled down the window, and trying to ignore the stifling air, pulled out on the highway. The road stretched toward nothing. The sign in LA had been wrong; the last chance for salvation lay ahead, somewhere on the other side of the desert.

28

The crisp white sheets smelled like chocolate, just like rich, dark chocolate that was fresh out of the wrapper. Nate rolled onto his side and buried his head into the chocolate pillow. He had no idea where he was, what time it was, or how to find out, but what he did know was that this was the most comfortable bed he had ever slept in. It seemed to wrap around him and hug. They call it memory foam, Nate thought lazily, as he breathed in deeply. He cracked his eyes open and saw the digital alarm clock on the bedside table: 9:23. It was later than Nate had slept in years. For a moment, he thought about what it would be like to stay here forever. He could send Rosemary a letter, maybe someone had a phone, convince her to come back to wherever he was. Why would she protest? This was perfect.

He was snapped out of his reverie by Eli's voice from the next room. He was singing "Hotel California," and underneath that, Nate could hear the television. He groaned as he remembered where he was, and how he had come to be in this perfect bed. They had to get going; he couldn't stay here. He couldn't just send for Rosemary and pretend as though nothing had happened. Memory foam or not, he had to get up. Nate felt a sting of embarrassment at having passed out in the lobby the night before. He remembered the doctor, Caroline? He remembered her saying that it happened sometimes, that he hadn't been the first, but still.

Nate stumbled to the door wearing only his boxer shorts, his clothes strewn haphazardly on the floor. He honestly didn't remember shedding them. Eli was lying back on a periwinkle sofa, the guidebook from the night before in his hands. The television was indeed on and playing some sitcom.

"Good morning, man! I only beat you by 'bout an hour. I wasn't as crashed out as you were. I should have driven before you got all zingy on me, man. Hey look at this, man, this is a trip. The TV, they're only playing "Will and Grace" reruns; crazy."

Nate had never seen "Will and Grace," so Eli's amazement had little effect on him. Nate sat down on the sofa and rubbed his eyes.

"Sorry about last night, Eli, thanks for getting me up here. Guess I should have eaten something while we were driving. Sometimes I get a little crazy when I don't eat for awhile..."

"No worries, man, no worries. Hey, this book is wild, man. You gotta take a look. They call it 'New Vegas' now, and it's like all electric and shit; all the booze is gone. Those umbrella drinks everyone was carrying around last night... you remember the ones?"

Nate nodded.

"Yea, well, it's all fruit juice and soda man, no more booze, or smoking, actually I think that's good, I freakin' hate cigarette smoke man, gets in my hair. You should hit the shower, dude, you're smelling a little ripe. You'll like it, man, it has that massagy head and the soap smells like oranges."

Nate stopped rubbing his eyes and looked up. Eli was actually very well groomed. His hair was shiny and combed away from his face, he had trimmed his shaggy beard, he was even wearing new clothes, a black t-shirt and a pair of fatigue print shorts; new flip flops, too. Seeing his gaze, Eli laughed.

"Yeah, man, they left clothes up here last night or this morning or some-time. I took these, but if you wanna swap, lemme know, man. Lemme know."

Nate shook his head, stood up and stretched. The morning light was filtering into the room through gauzy curtains, and it accented what Nate only vaguely remembered about the room, the small balcony beyond the curtains, the sitting area, and the two bedrooms on either side. On the wall were hung pictures of Egyptian gods in neon colors, and arty photos of Vegas. Nate turned and slowly moved into the bathroom. There was indeed a clean pair of jeans, boxer shorts, a t-shirt, and flip-flops waiting for him on the shelf. On the counter sat a hospitality kit that included a razor, shaving cream, toothbrush, tooth-paste, shampoo and soap. Eli was right; it smelled like oranges.

More than anything in that moment, Nate wanted to stand under the showerhead, then pull on the clean clothes. But a dawning realization was slowly hitting him. He charged into the other room and startled Eli, who dropped the guidebook on his chest.

"Who brought the clothes?" Nate demanded.
Eli shook his head. "No idea, man. They just showed up. Dude, chill! It was probably that doctor chick or the bellman. It is a freakin' hotel after all, man.... So freakin' paranoid."

Nate considered Eli's words. It was possible, after all, it was indeed a hotel and had always been a hotel. On the other hand, he had never stayed in a hotel where they brought you free clothes. But maybe Eli was right. Maybe the doctor from last night had dropped them off. He'd already given in to the sign-makers by accepting the Minnie Winnie, was it that big a deal to take a change of clothes and a shower?

Swallowing his reservations, Nate went back into the bathroom and turned on the water. Eli was also right about the massaging shower head, Nate could have stayed in there all day. But as his senses returned, he remembered fully why he was there. They had to get going.

Nate emerged in his new clothes, looking considerably more cleaned up than he had in weeks. *Clementine* had had a shower of course, but in order to take a hot shower, one had to mess with the generator, plug the power cord into the outlet provided by the Priceplan, and then be happy with the five minutes of hot water the effort provided. As a result, Nate was constantly disheveled, unshaven, messy and wrinkled. Today was the first time in a long time that he looked like the guy who used to work at the Chronicle, the guy Rosemary had married.

"C'mon, you ready? We've got to figure out what to do with the Minnie Winnie, do they say anything about gas stations in that book?"

"Well, man, you want the good news or the bad news first, no don't answer...you want the good news. Those crazy ass oil wars that we've been killing each other over, know the ones?"

Nate nodded impatiently.

"Well, man that's all done, man, all the oil is gone; the signmakers totally got rid of all the oil, the gas, all of it. I mean, not like the oil in the ground man, but now it's totally off limits to us. Permanent removal if you even try to go after it. That's why all the scooters out there are electric, man."

Nate shook his head. No gas? Really? Why did the signmakers give them a gas vehicle to drive? Where did the gas come from that was in the reserve tank? How did they create enough electricity to run all this?
Eli looked up from the book.

"Don't know, man. Can't say. Haven't gotten to the part where they talk about where the electricity comes from; maybe it's like that Penn and Teller magic shit. Can't really say. But I don't think the signmakers were trying to screw us, man. Really. I think they just get confused sometimes, like maybe we were just supposed to live in the Minnie, and not try to drive her. Don't really know, though."

"Hey, Eli, remember last night when we were driving? Remember I told you how you do this one thing, and then I never told you what it was?"

Eli nodded.

"Yeah, man, and it wasn't the snoring. I remember."

"Well, you just did it again. You answer questions I never ask out loud. You do it in your sleep sometimes, too. You're usually right, too, for what it's worth."

Eli looked a little stunned, and then he grinned. "Huh, well, you probably say more than you think you do, man. Most people do. Hey, wanna get some grub downstairs before we try to get the Minnie going? I think that front desk chick can help us out."

Nate folded his dirty clothes on the bed, and smoothed the sheets before they headed out the door and down to the lobby. The Luxor's lobby was as busy as it had been last night. It was the same scene. People with plastic cups full of poker chips cheerfully wandered here and there. The scene was unreal; a huge Middle Eastern cityscape filled one triangular edge of the casino. Nate could see lights in what must have been offices before everything changed. He supposed now that some lucky families were living in the façade overlooking the fake desert.

Nate paused at the sight of the buffet line. It was neatly organized around a maze of indoor palm trees and sand motifs. He smelled eggs and toast, and again felt slightly dizzy. Eli charged forward, looking back only when we realized Nate wasn't following him.

"Dude, c'mon, man. You don't know when we'll eat again. We gotta get rollin', man, and if you flip out on me again, that's gonna freakin' suck."
Nate backed away.

No. I can't. I'm going to the front desk. I'll ask them where they have the other food, the food they brought me last night. I just can't eat this."

Eli shrugged, turned and walked toward the line. Nate headed back to the front desk. Surely, they would help him out. That doctor last night...Caroline? She'd brought him food that wasn't "created" by the signmakers. They had to have more somewhere. Behind the long desk, a bored woman was reading a magazine. As soon as she saw Nate approaching, she snapped to attention. As he got closer, Nate realized she was little more than a teenager. She smiled as he reached the desk, her round face looking slightly maniacal.

"Hello there, sir. How can I help you?"

Nate stumbled over his words, realizing how odd he sounded. "Um, last night there was a doctor down here...."

The girl cut him off. "Yes, sir, Dr. Sakanai was on duty."

Nate took a breath. "Yeah, that's her; she said her name was Caroline."

The front desk girl looked slightly annoyed. "I'm sure she's right, sir, I wouldn't know. Do you need to reach her? Dr. Sakanai is off duty, but we have a staff physician on call to assist you."

Nate caught the impatience that leaked into the girl's voice. "No, that's not it. It's...I know this sounds weird, but she brought me food last night that wasn't from the signmakers, that was real food, I guess I was hoping someone could help me out with that. I can't, I mean I don't have any cash though to pay for it, and I...."

The front desk girl was looking at him confusedly.

"Sir? I'm not sure what Dr. Sakanai told you but there isn't any other food. The buffet line behind you is provided by the signmakers, as are all the buffets in all the casinos on the Strip. I'm not sure what you mean by 'real' food."

Nate felt a growing nausea in his stomach. He should have known, he was too out of it last night to think it might have been a trick. The front desk girl began again.

"The food is cooked by our staff if that's what you're worried about. It's only the ingredients that are provided, that will all change when we enter Stage Four. Have you received a handbook yet?"
She started to reach under the desk, but Nate shook his head, stopping her.

"Yeah, no, I mean, I goddamn have one already...I just...fuckin' signmakers."

The front desk girl's face froze momentarily, then she stepped back, looking nervous. "Sir, I need you to refrain from using that language. Cursing at me could be interpreted as a threat, and if you had read your handbook you would know how the signmakers react to abusive behavior."

Nate felt his temper starting to rise, so he stepped away, slowly backing off into the lobby. The round faced front desk girl watched him retreat, her face in a fixed frown. Nate repeated to himself that it wasn't her fault. She was probably eighteen at most; she would have been a kid when the signmakers first showed up. She didn't know any better.

He felt some despair as her words finally sunk in. Caroline, Dr. Sakanai, whatever, had lied to him last night. The clothes he was wearing were probably from the signmakers. Nate suddenly felt itchy, his skin crawling with the realization. The voice behind him made him jump.

"Hey, man, didya find some grub? You should try the eggs over there, man. They have little bits of spinach and bacon, but the buffet chick told me that it was some kind of soy bacon. Right up your alley, huh?"

Nate spun on his heels, facing a surprised Eli.

"We've got to go. Now! This place is infested, can't you see that? There isn't anything here that the signmakers haven't made! Even the hotel room. I shouldn't have been so stupid last night. We need to go."

Eli shook his head. "Man, you've gotta chill. You're gonna have like an embolism, or cardiac or some other medical thing if you keep this up. We need to figure out how to go first. Have you talked to the desk girl?"
Eli looked behind Nate at the round faced front desk girl. She was eyeing him warily.

"Alright, man, judging by how she's checking you out, I'm gonna take that as a yes. Let me try, then we can go. Just stay put and don't go postal on me."

Nate paced slowly watching as Eli approached the desk. The front desk girl gave him the same maniacal grin, and Nate watched as she tried to offer him a second guidebook.

Eli suddenly took off in the direction of the bar, carrying the guidebook. "Bartenders, man, they know everything. Besides, man, I always think clearer with a little mango juice in me. C'mon man."

The clock over the front desk read 10:45, Rosemary would be sitting at her mother's table, maybe drinking coffee; maybe she would be taking a walk in the woods around her folks' house. Nate wished he could ask her how she had gotten out of Vegas.

29

The burning sensation in Rosemary's bladder had been replaced with an urgent and overwhelming need to pee. Rosemary was trying to ignore it, because she knew what would happen if she once again stopped *Lazy Daze*, went to the lavatory, and just sat there. Nothing, except she would have to fight the pain to get back to her seat. Her lower back was starting to throb. She was thirsty but the thought of drinking the rank water in the bottom of the cooler made her want to dry heave. The good news was that she had finally passed a sign marking Las Vegas as 150 miles away. That was a little over two hours without any traffic. She still needed someone to be there, she needed water, something to relieve the bladder infection that was growing steadily worse. She needed to know that there were other towns besides Mussel Shoals and downtown LA that were still functioning. She should have gone to Venice Beach, Rosemary thought as *Lazy Daze* rolled along. She could have figured out how to tell Nate where she was. Rosemary had no idea how she would have done that, but in her present state, it seemed she was much better off there than she was out here.

Rosemary mused about her romance novel, the only one she'd written that had ever been published. It seemed like that happened in another lifetime. Had she really been successful, even for a year or so? What had happened to her? How did she fall into the trap of scraping ends together on a trapped houseboat? The first time Rosemary had seen the acceptance note from the agent, she thought to herself that this was it; she was set. She had been so freakin' young. Nate never discussed it, almost as if he didn't recognize her as a writer at all. He seemed interested in it when they first met, but over time, he just never brought it up again. It was a big deal to have a book published, a really big deal, and even though it was only the one, and it never really made any lasting money for her, it was a real thing. Statistically, you were more likely to be struck by lightning than to get published; damn him for not letting her feel like it was important.

Another voice piped up from the back of her head. "You don't need for him to 'let' you do anything. If you feel unimportant, it's not his fault." Great! That's fine advice from someone who never had to feel like the biggest thing she ever accomplished meant nothing to someone else. What psychology book did you pull that crap out of? The voice responded, "You taught him that it wasn't a big deal. You can't blame him for how you are." Oh, how I am? I'm the only reason that Nate never ended up in jail or in the welfare line. Every time he came up with some even stupider idea to harass the suits, I was the one who talked him out of it. I'm the one who can wake him out of those fucked up dreams or whatever he has; I'm the one. There's nothing wrong with me. Nothing. It's him; he yells, he blacks out, he drug me down into the mire with him. I don't know who I am if I'm not taking care of his ass. The voice was silent. Finally, the only noise was the hum of *Lazy Daze*'s wheels and the roar of the wind in the window.

She wondered about her mother's letters. If other places were like Los Angeles and Rancho Cucamonga, then how was mail getting delivered? In Mussel Shoals, there had still been a post office. Who was driving or flying the mail back and forth from city to city? What happened if someone wrote a letter to an area that was Stage Two? Rosemary was suddenly hit with the realization that she hadn't seen a plane in the air in quite some time. Mussel Shoals didn't have an airport, and Santa Barbara only had a small one. You had to drive to Los Angeles for any major flights. Mussel Shoals wasn't even on any flight patterns, so she hadn't noticed when planes stopped passing overhead. Out here though, she should have seen something by now, but she hadn't. What happened to the planes? It was probably the gasoline. She knew planes took some kind of fancy something else, but it was probably all gone. So, how were the letters being delivered? And where did the electricity come from to light the downtown, the boardwalk, hell, even the car lots.... Who was manning the power stations? If the signmakers were banning gasoline, why weren't they banning the other fossil fuels, like coal? Rosemary's head hurt.

She couldn't decide if she was suddenly cranky with Nate because she felt terrible, or if feeling terrible and being cranky at Nate were two entirely unrelated things. Cranky wasn't really the word for it anyway. She realized somewhere on the way to Vegas that if she caught up with Nate, if they lived together in the cabin in the woods with their baby, or dog or whatever little fantasy she had planned out...if she did that, then she was saying it was all okay. It was fine for him to have said those words. It was okay for him to treat her the way he did sometimes. The grief in her stomach was back, and it was gnawing at her in tandem with the burning infection. Could she really expect that just because the scenery was going to be different, Nate would change completely? After all, she had been blaming all his problems on the Priceplan for a long time, years in fact. Over and over, Rosemary would repeat to herself that he would find another job as soon as the Priceplan was gone. He would be happier, as soon as the Priceplan was gone. He would let go of the anger that had eventually consumed him, as soon as the Priceplan was gone. She wasn't so sure now. But Nate had been angry before the Priceplan, he'd blacked out sometimes, and he sure as hell had said terrible things to her before Priceplan appeared. Priceplan was just an easy target; that was the only difference.

He never laid a hand on her, not since that night in the Amtrak when he had been sleeping. Rosemary had actually never been hit by anyone in her whole life. She sometimes wondered what it would actually feel like. While Nate had never hit her, he came close. So close in fact, that Rosemary had been afraid. She left *Clementine* and walked up and down the street popping her anxiety pills. She never confronted Nate and he never brought it up, so she figured he'd forgotten or didn't care. Rosemary knew when she was going to shut down, it was very much like the sensation when her social anxiety set in, but instead of inappropriate actions, it was a total lack of action. Everything became numb. Sounds became fuzzy, and her hands began to feel like they were encased in giant marshmallows. In a strange way, it was pleasant. She could see lips moving, and she knew something bad was happening, but with the volume turned off, she could pretend that almost anything was coming out. Rosemary remembered one particularly nasty argument with Nate. At one point, after trying desperately to shut everything down, Rosemary ceased hearing the string of insults he was spewing and instead heard him singing "Caro Mio Bien," a lovely opera song she had had to memorize in junior high school.

The fight had started small. Rosemary brought home an ad from her school. They needed a file clerk to help during the last three weeks of the semester. It was a temporary position, and part-time during the day. Basically, they needed someone to come in and help the front office staff do things like clean out the student records and box up the graduating seniors' exam scores. Rosemary and Nate had just finished another month during which they ate rice and canned tuna for eight out of every nine meals. Rosemary thought it was an innocent enough offer, God knows Nate was qualified enough, and it would only take up a few hours each day—and it paid ten dollars an hour.

He crumpled up the ad and threw it in the sink. Then, he skulked away wordlessly to *Clementine*'s cab and leaned against the wheel. She could see him breathing harder and harder, and that was when the marshmallow hands had begun. Rosemary knew she should just go on deck, get out, but the marshmallow spread to her legs and she was suddenly comfortably numb. Nate burst into the living quarters, face red, his eyes darkened to near black.

"Don't you goddamn tell me how to get a goddamn job! I'm the one protecting this family while you could care less. I'm the one trying to change things while you're up there supporting the goddamn signmakers. I'm the one; don't you forget that."

More insults followed, but suddenly his ugliness turned to, "Caro mio bien, trace ciero mien, na tol mia lieche, ahaha so pendure!" The words floated out of his mouth in a beautiful soprano voice. Rosemary stared in amazement, her eyes not locking on Nate's, but instead following the words as they manifested themselves and floated around the kitchen. Beautiful. Nate stopped abruptly and stomped out onto the deck, pounding the cabinet door as he went.

Rosemary didn't know why he was mad. Maybe she had been condescending to him when she discussed the ad after their tuna and rice leftovers.

She hadn't meant to imply that he couldn't get a job, but maybe she had sounded too confrontational; she didn't know. She never asked about it again. She told her principal that Nate wouldn't be able to come in; he had another offer. It was a lie. When Nate would speak to her about anything, she would smile vaguely and respond with something about the weather. The weather was the only thing that didn't seem to piss him off. Now, here in *Lazy Daze* as she raced across the country to find him, Rosemary wished she had thrown that job ad right back at him, told him to fuck off and get a goddamn job. She should have told him how unfair it was that she not only had to make all their money, but that she had to take all his shit. She wished she had told him that he was being selfish and mean. She wished she had told him that there were things she could do, that she had options, that she didn't have to be with him. She was worth something. But she hadn't. Now, no amount of yelling at the desert would fix it. A sign flashed: Las Vegas 95 miles. Rosemary pushed on, not sure of what she wanted to find.

30

Eli's mango juice was in a margarita glass rimmed with bright colored sugar crystals and a glassy blue monkey that clung to an orange slice. The bartender was a surly old guy who bore an uncanny resemblance to Mick Jagger. His nametag read 'Sal'. He regarded Nate suspiciously.

"Nothin' for you huh? Well, aren't you the fancy one?"

Nate tried to ignore him. He needed to let Eli ask the question, otherwise they'd never get out of here.

Sal turned away from him and back to Eli. "Goddamn juice bar's what I'm runnin' now. You young men should have been here back in '93. You woulda seen something then, none of this Disneyland buffet line, poker chips that don't count for a damn thing crap. Then you have the goddamn welcome wagon over there, all their booklets and try this and try that. When I ran this bar, you had to be first rate to be in the Luxor. The owner, Jerry, he's spinning in his grave to see all this, I'll tell you that!"

Eli asked what Nate was thinking. "What happened to the owner, man, was he removed?"

Sal squinted at him. "No, goddamn it, no. Heart attack. About two months after all this shit started happening. Not that Jerry coulda done anything about it; he got the same goddamn deal as the rest of us."

Nate's turn. "What deal was that, where does everyone live here?"

Another squint. "You ask too many questions. You should ask 'em one at a time. I want to answer you, but I don't know which one you want first. Which is it? What the deal is, or where is everyone?"

Nate swallowed."The deal, tell us about the deal."

"Eh, the deal. Okay, you listening? All these signs start popping up all over the goddamn place, talking about statement of purpose or some shit, then people just start disappearing. I'm sure you saw it wherever the hell you came from, too, the light and then—blamo! Gone. That went on for a real long time, until the Stage Two crap started. Stage Two was like this. They take all those fuckers in the suburbs, then they cram 'em all in here; well not just here, but all over the Strip. We actually lucked out, believe it or not, Circus Circus is like a goddamn romper room. We just got all the chicks with double chins and the men who wouldn't know a designer suit if it hit 'em in their ass. All the integrity's gone. Goddamn Disneyland, that's what this place is."

Nate was afraid to ask, but carefully he ventured on. "What happened to the areas around the Strip? Is that what Stage Two is?"

Sal slammed the plastic pitcher of mango juice down on the counter. "You and your goddamn multiple questions. You ever listen? I'm in the middle of telling you what the deal is, and you're all yak yak yak. You gonna listen this time? I got other customers ya know."

In truth, Sal didn't have anyone else at his end of the juice bar, so his threat was idle. Still, Nate and Eli both nodded their heads simultaneously.

"Okay, the deal is this. This is Stage Three. That means the burbs are sianara; they got removed last month some time. Don't know about other places. All they ever play on the goddamn TV is some fucked up sitcom and re-runs of the Patriots/Raiders game. Seen that goddamn game probably 200 times already. You know who won? Huh?"

Nate shook his head, his mouth slightly open.

"The goddamn Patriots! It was a goddamn crime. The ref called foul in the last ten minutes and fucked a whole lotta good people out of a lot of money, goddamn bastards. Anyway, the deal. The deal was this. We keep our jobs, we serve our 'statement of purpose' as they put it, and we get a room, any of the buffet lines in town, any time you want 'em, and every so often, a new set of duds shows up in the bathroom. No more money, no more cars, no more bar. Goddamn jamba juice now, not a bar."

Nate started to ask, but Eli cut him off, and then glanced at Nate apologetically.

"We have a gas vehicle outside. Is there any way to get her running again?"

Sal laughed. "Not with gas, but I'll tell you something you gotta keep a little secret. You fellas go to that old McDonalds down the way, not the first one you run into...you'll see—it's one oh, like a second-story balcony thing. You gotta take an escalator to get to it. You don't want that one, you want the one all the way down the Strip, by the Sahara and Riviera. It's a little bit of a haul; if you want, you can take the monorail down there. There's a station down in Harrah's, but I think you'll want to bring your car, take my word for it. You'll have to push your bus or whatever the hell you got out there, some kind of goddamn mini-wagon thing is what some of the people are sayin', but take my word for it, fuckin' amazing."

With that, Sal turned to the couple who had sat down next to Nate and Eli.

"Whaddya think?" Nate asked. "It seems like the best lead we have so far...wonder how far the McDonalds is. Can't be too far; they used to be all over the place out here."

Eli nodded. "Sure, man, can't hurt. We're either stranded or we hit one of those waitresses up for a scooter."

"I'm not asking the waitresses for anything. I don't care what you do, but if it comes to that, I'm out. Forget about it, I know, I know, I ate the free food last night. But that doctor lied about it! I wouldn't have taken these clothes either. We've just gotta get out of here!"

Eli looked a little confused. "Okay, man, whatever, man, don't get all blood pressury on me, dude. I'm not real hot on driving a scooter through Utah either. Just breathe deep, man. Let's go see the McD's."

They walked out the front door of the Luxor and into the wintry sun. As they crossed the parking lot and headed toward the Minnie Winnie, which was still parked on the side of the road, Eli shook his head.

"You just gotta tell me one thing, man, and don't get all steamed. But dude, you were okay with the new clothes and the room and all that jazz when you thought it was just regular people giving you shit for free, right? So why the hell does it make a difference if it's the signmakers?"

Nate was taken aback. Rosemary had never asked him straight out about his issue, he'd never had to defend it. "Eli, Jesus. First off, I wasn't 'okay' with it, I... don't know! That's different! Don't you see that? We're not supposed to be under the thumb of some goddamn thing that's gonna take me out for saying 'fuck' to the front desk girl!"

Eli kept walking across the parking lot. "Whatever, man, whatever. But I still don't get it. You missed out on some seriously kick-ass mango in there; that's all I'll say about it."

The Minnie Winnie was an oven. The sun's heat was filtered by the winter haze, but it had heated up the Minnie Winnie nevertheless, and the heat rolled out in waves when Nate opened the door.

"We should at least try the gas, right? Maybe she'll get us another mile."

Eli shrugged. "Couldn't say, man. She sounded like she meant it last night when she stopped, but go for it."

Eli was right. The key turned and the dash lights flashed, but the engine gave no sign of life. Without discussion, Nate went to the driver's side, Eli to the passenger's side, and with the doors open, and Nate one hand clumsily on the steering wheel, they began to push. Luckily, Vegas is flat. Still, the effort made the muscles in Nate's arm scream in protest, and the heat threatened to knock him under the slow moving tires. Eli wasn't faring much better; he was grunting and his face was red as a beet. They pushed on down the street, both men keeping searching for the McDonalds. It occurred to Nate that the bartender might have been full of shit, and that he was playing games with them. But on the chance that there was some gas stashed there, it was worth the effort. Eli slipped out of his flip-flop and fell backward, but he popped back up a moment later.

"No worries, man, no worries. Just a little fall, man."

They had been pushing for what seemed like forever, when they were passed by a group of twenty something young men with buckets of poker chips.

The guy in the front called over to Eli:

"Hey, you guys need a hand? Where'ya going, anyway? You should get a scooter—way easier!"

Eli yelled back. "Yeah, a hand, man! We're just going to McD's. Can ya give us a little shove?"

The guys crowded around the back of the Minnie Winnie and started pushing. All of a sudden, the speed picked up dramatically. Eli yelled through the cab at Nate.

"You jump in and steer, otherwise we're going to crash her!"

Eli was right; the force of the new help was threatening to push the Minnie Winnie right off the road. Nate jumped in and steered her back onto a straight line. He heard one of the young guys yell up at Eli:

"McDonalds is just up here a little. Telling you, man, the buffet lines are way better. Don't even think this one is open anymore, not since we started going Stage Four."

The McDonalds loomed in front of them. As they closed the distance quickly, they all stopped pushing and the Minnie Winnie coasted up the front drive. The parking lot was empty as expected, except for a couple of scooters plugged into a power station. Eli waved at the guys as they continued their way down the sidewalk.

"Tell you what, man, I don't know what that bartender man was all excited about here. Doesn't look like anything's going on."

Nate noticed a small sign hanging on the door. On closer inspection he read:

To Whom It May Concern:
This establishment is presently a Stage Four
Research and Development Station.
For more information and samples, please see the
Rear entrance.

"Does this fall into your no waitresses thing, man, or are you coming with me to check it out?"

Nate glared at Eli and followed him wordlessly to the back of the building. The employee entrance was open, and inside were stacks of barrels labeled "food waste." A small bell hung by the door and Eli rung it immediately.

"Just a minute. Hold on. Almost there!"

A man with buzzed black hair, standing barely five-two, came bursting out of the front area and stopped when he saw Nate and Eli. "Oh, okay, you're here, I... huh? Who are you again? Are you here for the solar study or the soy bean growth results?"

Nate stepped forward. "Sorry, we're not really here for either, um, I'm Nate, this is Eli. We're just trying to get out of town. We have an RV, it takes gas, but the bartender said you might have some?"

The little man rubbed his head. "Huh, gasoline? You know that's all gone now, all gone, that was Stage Three, we're on Stage Four. You're late, too late for that…huh."

The man turned and started to return to the front of the restaurant. Eli followed him and yelled a little too loudly.

"Wait, man, hold on. What did the bartender mean, man? He said you had something amazing here, and he thought it would get the Minnie running at least through Utah or so. Do you know what he was talking about?'

The little man stopped, and turned. "Huh, well, it's being tested, I mean, it's been around for awhile, so I don't know about amazing, but, okay, it definitely works so far. See these barrels?"

Nate and Eli nodded in unison.

"Inside these barrels is all the food waste; the oil, the grease the artery-clogging crap that people used to eat here. When we turned it into the research station, we cleaned up all the foodstuff and we were left with this. We thought it was trash, but…do you have a minute? Let me show you, well, read this, huh. Well look here, it might ruin your car. I don't know that it won't, but then again it might not. It shouldn't, it should run like a charm. This was around before all this, before the signmakers or any of this all came. It was here, we just didn't want it, but here it is. I put this crap, this grease, this foodstuff into your car. Well, it's not quite that easy, but that's the basics for the layman, I mean, kind of. And there have been some modifications of course, but in a way it kinda runs like gasoline…see what I mean?"

Eli nodded his head as a smile spread across his face. "Yeah, man, I get it, man. Biodiesel, dude. Don't you see what this means, man? We don't need gas, man, we just live off the grease."

The little man looked excited. "Yeah, well, kind of, but not really. We've had to tweak it a bit, no fuel to use as an additive after all. We're testing it now with the mail trucks, so far, so good, kind of, well, not all the time, but it's getting better. What did you say you were here for again?"

In an impatient burst, Nate pushed himself past Eli and stepped right in front of the little man. "Listen, we need to get to Denver. The signmakers…." The mention of their name made Nate cringe but he forced the words out. "The signmakers gave us an RV, but it takes gas, just unleaded gas. We can't use diesel anything, not biodiesel, not any kind of diesel.

Nate turned and began to walk out the door. He was sick of Stage this and Stage that, he was sick of Eli's total non-reaction to everything that happened, he was sick of his enthusiasm, like this was just some grand adventure. Eli and this little man didn't know what was at stake. If Eli didn't get to Green River, then big deal, he'd probably just eat BBQ buffet and play with Mr. Science here all day. But if Nate didn't get to Denver, and soon, he was horribly afraid that he'd never see Rosemary again, that she'd find a way to disappear.

31

Twenty-five miles to Las Vegas, and Rosemary was becoming alarmed. She saw buildings in the distance, but there should be more, there should be suburbs by now, there should be some little truck stop or something out this far. She wondered if Vegas had been subject to the same treatment as Rancho Cucamonga. The bladder infection had spread all around her lower body, and the dull ache in her bladder had turned into a jackhammer pain in her kidneys. *Lazy Daze* was unbearably hot, no air conditioning, and the breeze the window let in was hotter than it was inside. The scrubs were soaked with sweat, sticking to her skin. Occasionally, she reached up to push her matted hair out of her eyes. Despite everything, she was vaguely hungry, but the pain in her back, combined with the heat, made even the thought unbearable as well as impossible.

She thought Nate must be in Utah by now, at the very least, and figured he'd probably beat her to Denver by a day or so. She wished there was a way to contact her mother, let her know he might be showing up. Just then she remembered that she'd never told Nate that her mother had moved downtown. Oops. He would automatically head to the house in Golden where they spent Christmas a few years ago, and find a new family in it—or nothing at all. Rosemary knew it was likely that Golden had been permanently removed, that her mother had bent the truth about "selling" the house. Chances are she was informed and moved downtown to a place provided by the signmakers. Rosemary wondered if she was living in Brook's Tower...she had some friends who lived there when she was a senior in high school and had become infatuated with it. At forty-two floors, it was the tallest apartment complex in the city. Rosemary had briefly been involved with a guy who lived on the thirty-ninth floor and from his balcony, people looked like ants; in the distance you could see the mountains. Vin was the flute player in a band called Canned Toast, even though no one really played much of anything in Canned Toast. It was mostly a vehicle for the lead singer to deliver his spoken word, which usually had to do with the injustices of the transit system. Vin and the other five members would doodle around on their instruments in the background, not playing any particular melody. The result was a confused mishmash of noises.

At the time, it hadn't much mattered to her. Rosemary would drive from Golden to downtown every weekend to go to the Mercury Café and listen to them, fighting her anxiety ticks. She'd sit in the front row, usually accompanied by a girlfriend, and stare dreamy eyed at Vin and his flute. It didn't matter that Vin ignored her before, during and after the show, Rosemary simply considered that his artistic temperament. He'd only acknowledge her after the instruments were put away and the stage was being broken down. Then he'd sit at her table, her girlfriend long gone, and bury his head in his hands and dry heave. Rosemary would wait for Vin to raise his head and let him rant about the music, and how the bastard management at the Mercury wanted to limit their contract, they wanted music, and they wanted to move Canned Toast to Poetry Slam night. Week after week, Rosemary followed this same routine until finally, the Mercury followed through with its threat. That night, the Canned Toast front man, a scrawny blonde guy named Clay, threw one of the band's new speakers into the bar area, narrowly missing the manager who had just delivered the bad news. Vin tried to throw the other speaker until a crush of Mercury patrons grabbed him and pitched him kicking and screaming down to the floor.

After that, Rosemary went to Vin's Brook's Tower apartment, where Canned Toast played to no one. After they were done, she would sit by while Vin and Clay slammed tequila shots and smoked weed. Rosemary would stand out on that balcony and wonder what it was like to live there, to be an adult, to worry about your dishes, and be able to decorate your bathroom any way you wanted. She also wondered what it would be like to have the freedom to stay over at Vin's anytime she wanted. At the time, Rosemary was a virgin. The farthest she had ever gone was making out with Mike Cunningham after a football game at her high school. When she met Vin, who was twenty-two and built like a young Keith Richards, she knew he was no Mike Cunningham; this was a man. Never mind that he didn't seem to know she was around very often and had a serious moody streak, never mind that Clay was always around so Rosemary hadn't even gotten close to her virginity shedding plan. Once they made out and he had grabbed her breast, but then Clay knocked on the door and Vin went back to pretending she wasn't there.

After becoming wildly frustrated, Rosemary decided one night that she had to take action. Instead of knocking on the door, Rosemary waited in the hallway for Clay. She was going to tell him what was what. She'd worked out the speech in her head and was going to tell him she needed some time alone with her boyfriend whether he liked it or not. Rosemary practiced it in front of the mirror at home and judged that she had come across as tough but fair, assertive but not bitchy. It was perfect.

Clay showed up about nine that evening after Rosemary had been waiting for nearly fifteen minutes. To her, those minutes felt like hours. She was in the middle of running the speech in her head when he showed up. She looked good that night and she knew it. She also knew that Clay was checking out her black velvet t-shirt that showed off her cleavage, the tight black skirt, the stars and stripes tights and combat boots that showed off her figure perfectly. She put the outfit together especially for this night, and once she got rid of Clay, she was going to make her move. She would not be the last among her friends to have sex; after all, she was already sixteen, and all but two of her friends had already lost it..

She stepped in front of the door to block Clay, her hands starting to shake. He stopped and looked at her curiously, an amused smile on his face.

"You...a...you going inside or just hanging out here all night?" Rosemary took a deep breath and tried to launch into her speech, at the same time the shaking in her hands took over and she found herself fighting the urge to stick her finger up Clay's nose. The effort of trying to combat the sudden urge, made her forget the beginning of the speech, and so she started in the middle, right where she had been when Clay had arrived.

"It's not so much to ask, I need some time with Vin, too, and tonight you need to give us some time as a couple to do the things that couples do, I like you, but he's my boyfriend and you're here every night. I think you should be more considerate of our relationship."

Clay started laughing. He looked her up and down with a slight twinge of disgust in his eyes. "Boyfriend? You actually think he's your boyfriend? You're just a goddamn groupie. You're nothing to us. We let you hang out because we're not like those fucked up bands that don't ever see their fans. You think he's your boyfriend because you go here every night? That's a good one."

Clay started laughing, and Rosemary felt something unhinge in her gut. The string of self-control that had been holding her together unraveled. Her hand had gone flying toward Clay's nose but he saw it coming and naturally assumed it was meant to be a punch. He tried to move but wasn't quite fast enough, and the finger she'd aimed at his nose went directly into his eye.

Clay yelped with pain, grabbed at his face and yelled, "Goddamn bitch! What the fuck!"

Rosemary ran down the hallway and hadn't looked back, not even when she heard Vin's door open. She never saw him again, never called, and he never called her. Rosemary knew that Clay was right. She had been a groupie. She finally succeeded in shedding her virginity the next fall with none other than Mike Cunningham. He was on the varsity football team by then and while he was decently polite about the whole affair, it lasted about seven minutes, about the same amount of time it had taken Rosemary to poke Clay's eye. It wasn't the stuff of Rosemary's romance stories, and it certainly hadn't been what she was expecting, but it was over, and most importantly, she wasn't the last one.

Sitting behind the wheel, Rosemary wiped a bead of sweat from her forehead. According to the signs, she should be deep in the Vegas suburbs by now. She wasn't surprised, really, just curious. There were buildings ahead, probably the Strip; made sense really, what else did you need? From the distance, Rosemary was nearly blinded by the light reflecting off the rooftops of the buildings. She shielded her eyes and wished madly that she had thought ahead enough to ask for some sunglasses from the waitress before she left Mussel Shoals. Strange, she wondered what was making them do that, it looked like panels of some sort. Maybe they had always been there, Rosemary didn't know. She had never been to Vegas before, and just like Mike Cunningham, it was proving to be rather anticlimactic.

She approached a sign directing her to the business exit. Rosemary pulled *Lazy Daze* across the empty freeway and onto the ramp. Good thing the freeway was empty; normally, she was a wreck about driving, especially if she had to get on a freeway. *Lazy Daze* was burning gas fast, and she had tapped into the reserve tank about thirty miles back. It was still moderately full, but Rosemary knew it wouldn't get her much past Vegas. Her plan was to either find gasoline here, which was unlikely and would depend on some kid like the one she met in Rancho Cucamonga who had a private stash he or she was willing to share with her, or trade *Lazy Daze* in on something else. If the Strip was still here, then maybe there were waitresses. If there were waitresses, then she could get another family car, siphon the gas out of *Lazy Daze*, hold it for a reserve fill up on her way to Utah, then worry about the next step there. *Lazy Daze* burned too much gas; it wasn't practical and it was a hot box. Maybe the waitresses could fix her up with something that had air conditioning.

As she approached the Strip, the first thing Rosemary saw was an unlit sign hanging over a slum hotel that read "Stage Three Development Community. Welcome." So she had been right. This was what was going to happen to all the Los Angeles suburbs, and what had probably already happened to Denver. This was what Stage Three looked like. She had to admit, it was impressive. There were people going in and out of the casino across the street, and little brightly colored Vespa scooters vroomed up and down the street. People in pairs and groups walked the sidewalks, some carrying plastic buckets, presumably full of coins. Rosemary was so relieved at the sight that she started crying. She didn't even realize it until she felt the tears coursing down her cheeks. There were waitresses here for sure, and she would just trade this thing in and get back on the road—right after she found something to ease the throbbing pain in her kidneys and bladder, stocked up on water, and maybe had a bite to eat. After that, she'd be on her way. She would be only be a day behind Nate, and maybe, somehow, he would figure it all out, look for her mother downtown. Maybe Rosemary wouldn't be too late.

She passed the slum hotel and slowed down to a crawl. The people on the sidewalk looked curiously at *Lazy Daze*, and Rosemary knew they stood out; she in her blood-stained green hospital scrubs piloting her giant RV. She figured she looked like she was from another planet here in Stage Three Las Vegas. But never having been here before, Rosemary had no idea where to stop. The minute she spotted a waitress standing on the corner, she screeched *Lazy Daze* to a halt. The waitress was giving a new pair of shoes to a young woman, and the things looked like orange flip-flops from the street. Maybe that meant they gave away other kinds of clothes here, not just hospital scrubs.

Rosemary pulled *Lazy Daze* over to the side and got out, her lower back and bladder screaming with pain. The effort of swinging down from the cab nearly made her pee her pants and collapse to the ground. She felt the insulating air overpower her senses, and it nearly knocked her back. Sweat poured down her face, and she reached for the door handle but missed. Rosemary lunged forward grabbing at nothing. A group of blonde girls came running from across the street, dodging the Vespas. Through her dizziness, Rosemary wondered why they could get into the casinos. They didn't even look eighteen.

"Miss? Miss? Are you okay? You don't look so good, miss. Do you need help?"

Rosemary stumbled into the street and was nearly hit by a passing purple Vespa.

"I'mmm jussst fine, I jus neet a carrr, and, then I'll beee goininggg."

Rosemary listened in horror to the way her voice slurred, but she couldn't stop it; in fact, even the effort of saying the words aloud was exhausting. She wanted to curl up in the street right. An overpowering sense of dizziness was settling down around her making her legs feel like Jell-O. A wave of nausea overpowered her viciously and she suddenly dry heaved, spitting up a drizzle of saliva but nothing else. The girls surrounded her and grabbed her by the arms. She tried to protest, but her weakness prevented it.

"Maybeeee a sitttt down."

Rosemary smelled citrus shampoo from all sides and heard a frighteningly loud voice in her ear

"Okay, we need to get her up to the hospital floor. C'mon lady, we'll get you in there. You must have been on the road awhile. Don't worry, just hold on and try to walk."

Rosemary's rubber legs barely held any weight, and she felt the marshmallow take over her extremities. The girls seemed to carry her, weightless, from the street into the Mirage. The swirling images, blinding lights, and cacophony of sounds accosted her simultaneously causing her nausea to return with a vengeance. A wave of cool air hit her in the face and gave her a sudden, bone deep chill. She felt the sweat freeze to her body and started shivering violently. The citrus voice in her ear said,

"Jesus! She's having a convulsion!"

From the other ear she heard,

"She's burning up! Hey! Can someone get the doctor?"

The last thing Rosemary saw was a swash of black hair and dark brown eyes, a hand on her forehead, and a voice saying something about the elevators. She closed her eyes and gave into the blackness.

32

"Transesterification. That's the process. It's really just a big word for how we convert this food oil, or vegetable oil, or even leftover gasoline if we had any, into a diesel fuel compound."

The little man's face was bright red with excitement; he actually looked like he might explode from the intensity of his explanation.

"There's another method of course, and we're refining it right now so it's more accessible, but you can burn just straight vegetable oil if you make the proper modifications to your car. You'll need two tanks, one to boil the oil, and to filter and convert the energy. You'd be fine with either in Vegas, but where did you say you were headed?"

Nate was near his fill of this talk. It was almost noon, and he was anxious to do something, see the vehicle that could save him and Eli, or just be done with it all and start finding another solution. His voice was notably agitated. "We're headed to Colorado, and I've already told you, the engine isn't diesel. We can't use your fuel in it, anyway. Do you have anything that works like unleaded gas?"

The little man was already moving through the swinging doors that had once led into the kitchen of the McDonalds. He glanced behind and motioned with his hand. "C'mon, I can't explain it well; it's better that you see, c'mon."

Nate and Eli followed him through the doors to see that the kitchen and lobby of the restaurant was filled with lab tables, stills and test tubes full of colorful liquids. A small racetrack with teeny car shells circled the lobby area. The cars looked like the remote control toys kids played with, but these had been stripped and replaced with tanks of green gloop. The other area was lined with what looked like greenhouse panels. There were two other men in lab coats standing in the corner of the lobby, carefully wiring a solar panel to a car battery.

"I want to show you this, just so excited, we never get visitors, it's so rare. The Vegas people don't come in here much anymore, not since we fitted the casinos for energy. They all have the scooters, so they don't care about the long-transit options. It's all very exciting. We're so close. We'll be Stage Four next month at this rate."

Eli's face was twitching with a suppressed grin. "Stage Four, man, you keep saying that. But what else could they do here, man. It seems totally like peaceful and nice."

The little man smiled. "Yes, but you have to ask why it's all so nice, and why we have the energy, don't you? You could guess, go ahead...it's so exciting. It was last month's conversion, it's really very perfect."
He paused, as if Nate and Eli were going to guess, and then looked a bit let down when they didn't. "Well, I'll tell you anyway; you'd never have guessed it. We converted the power plant to solar energy. They had to keep the power plant until the last minute, you can't remove that until you have a better idea, and we did—we do—we had a great idea. If you were a bird, you'd see all the casinos were fitted with a full set of cooperative solar panels and energy cells. They're all connected, like a stand of aspen trees. We linked them to every building on the Strip. We're able to store enough power in the day to keep all the lights on at night. They were a little spotty for a couple of nights, don't get me wrong, but we fixed the battery cells and converters. But now, oh it's just so beautiful. That's Stage Four, we, well, lots of us, we're the only ones here right now, but the engineers are working on the advancements to turn this whole town green You must have come in from the west, yes?"

Nate and Eli nodded, a little dumbfounded.

"You didn't see the greenhouses. We currently have the country's largest greenhouse complex, which is devoted entirely to soy, other greens too, of course, but mostly soybeans, and on top of that, we use non-acidic farming practices. That's being taken care of by the agriculture group, but it's really very exciting. You know the argument right?"

Nate and Eli shook their heads; Nate's mind was spinning.

"Soy crops, they can grow anywhere, but you have to put additives into the ground, acidic compounds and the like. They leak into the water table and pollute the water supply. Big deal down in Brazil. You really haven't read up on it? Huh. Anyhow, the agriculturists are developing an organic additive to replicate the same acidic process without harming the water table. That way, the land can be reused, the crops rotated, which could be done anyway, but with the organic farming practices, you don't have to worry about damaging the land. Well, where was I going with this...oh yes, soybeans. They're amazing. You can use them in our biodiesel compounds. As of the next full moon, well, that's how I figure it, about a month or so, all the meat products will be removed from Vegas and replaced with a self-substantiating soybean product replacement. We don't deal with the food so much, that's being worked at over at In-N-Out Burger."

Nate shook his head. "But, why, I mean, I'm a vegetarian anyway, but it seems like the signmakers don't care about that stuff. What does it have to do with the energy and the cars?"

The little man was digging madly through a stack of papers. "Oh, they care about the land waste mostly. Huge amount of resources go into keeping livestock. The signmakers gave us this memo, it's somewhere, I don't know, but it said something about borrowed land and animal waste. But food isn't really our deal here. We're working on the energy. The solar works beautifully for the casinos, but we have a definite transportation problem. I don't know, but if I had to guess, the signmakers didn't expect people to be moving about so much; guess they must have thought we stayed in one place more than we do. That's why you have the car you have."

Nate interrupted little man. "Yeah, what's the deal, with that? I mean, we were given this thing only to discover that gas is no longer around? How did the gas that's already in it, get there?"

Little man rubbed his thin fingers along his head. "They removed all the cars, but they come back sometimes. If they were full when they were removed, then they're full when they return. If I had to guess, I'd say they didn't see that it would be a problem. They're not psychic, you know. That thing you have out there, they probably thought you'd move it off the street and live in it. Didn't think you'd haul it across the country before you settled in together."

This time it was Eli who interrupted. "No, man, we're not living together. I'm getting off in Green River."

He glared at Nate a little, Nate knew he was being a little bit of an ass, and Eli was all pissed off about the waitress thing, but damn, he'd never acted like this in all the years Nate had known him. Nate rolled the words around in his head, something wasn't right here.

"Wait a minute; this place can't be totally green, not without some kind of signmaker voodoo. I mean, those casinos must have a ton of trash every night, and the water to wash the dishes, that doesn't sound very Stage Four to me."

The little man was now pulling them to the racetrack. "The trash isn't the problem, that's being stored, it's going toward a fuel development project. The water for the dishes is all refiltered, like a fountain, but that's not my department, either; they work on the water and natural gas issues over at the Taco Bell. Here, this is what is going to get you across the desert."

The little man stopped in front of the track. He pulled down a UV lamp and held it over the car covered in solar panels. After a couple of minutes, he flipped a switch, and the car took off around the track. It circled and circled, nearly running down the two engineers with their battery.

"I've wanted to test this for some time, but no one has left Vegas for awhile. People get here and just tend to stay. It's really pretty simple. The solar energy runs the car and simultaneously charges the battery. That way you can travel some at night. Right now you need a full day's charge to get four hours in the dark, but it's getting better. The one I have in mind is a hybrid; you'll love it. I made it myself. It's a biodiesel convert. We put in a Mercedes five-cylinder D1 engine with a catalytic converter to assist with climate conversions; used to be for reducing diesel emissions, but you don't need to worry about that anymore. The point is, only use the biofuel when you need it, and the sun will take you all the way in."

Nate shook his head. "But, we don't have anything to buy this from you, we, you wouldn't just give us this thing, we can't!"

The little man pointed out the window. "It wouldn't be free; it'd be a trade, an experiment. We don't get a lot of raw vehicles; that Minnie Winnie out there would stay with us. I have a lot of ideas just looking at her. You'd need to report back to us, and we'd send someone out to collect the vehicle of course. You'd be test drivers only. We have a similar car that would be sent out when we heard from you, you'd need to stay with the car until we get there to pick it up. You'd be our guinea pigs. We don't know how it works. We've been wanting to take her out, so you could do us a big service—if you're willing to take the risk."

Eli was twirling his hair nervously. "The risk?"

"Well, naturally, the risk. We don't know quite how the backup power system will hold up, and the biofuel tends not to convert properly in cold weather, so it's particularly good that you're going to Colorado. We've been dying to put together some cold weather trials, but you hardly get that here. It's possible that you'll only get a few hours of energy out of her each day, then the biofuel freezes and you're stuck. But, that's hardly likely, I mean, maybe a little likely, but the point is that you get to test her out, and get to where you're going. We have a sister station in Greeley; they've already started their Stage Four operations out of the old slaughterhouse. You drop her off there, and they test the results. It's brilliant."

Nate was incredulous that this little man would just "give" them a car, science experiment or not. "I don't get it. What's to stop us from driving to say, Laramie, and never turning your fancy car in at all. What if we're thieves, axe murderers, bad drivers?"

The little man laughed. "Well, if you were thieves, you would probably have been permanently removed by now. We had a lot of that in the early days around here, you'd better believe. And as far as running off with the car, same thing would happen, I expect. The signmakers are probably aware of the deal we're making right now, and if you end up in Laramie, well, too bad for you, I suppose. And if the two of you can drive that huge thing, then you can' t be all that bad at driving. The test car runs just like a car, stick shift, it's actually a Honda frame, 1988, good year for Hondas."

Nate and Eli shook hands with the little man. Nate didn't care how he got across the desert and the mountains, as long as he wasn't too late. If the Honda with a Mercedes heart would take them, he would have to take the risk.

33

Blackness. Rosemary tried to open her eyes, but they felt weighted. Around her, she heard beeping, voices, the clanging of metal; she couldn't make out any one sound long enough to tell what it was. She felt neither hot nor cold; she felt totally numb, like waking up after the appendectomy surgery she had when she was a teenager—except she wasn't waking up. The voices were calm, so she stopped trying to open her eyes, instead surrendering herself to the blackness.

She heard her father's voice through the black.

"I'm sorry kiddo, I've just been a little under the weather, that's all. Tomorrow we'll go to the beach. I'm just so glad that you're here, you know I love you, don't you sweetheart?"

Somewhere beyond, she heard the tick of the water pipe, and on the edge of her numbness, a cold breeze. Rosemary tried to reach out, but her arm was made of lead. She fell back into the voice, into the tick of the water pipe.

Rosemary's dad had come to see her when she was in the hospital. She was eighteen, not ready or able to face how sick she actually was. He had been out of the institution for a couple of years by then, living in a halfway house. He sent letters; Rosemary read them sometimes. Her mother had called him for the first time in a decade when Rosemary went into the hospital. She had been in her senior Spanish class when she doubled over in agonizing pain. Two hours later at the Denver Health Hospital, she was told her appendix had ruptured and she was rushed into surgery. Rosemary remembered feeling confused more than anything; she hadn't felt much other than a stomachache, and she thought it was cramps.

The most confusing thing for Rosemary at the time was her mother's reaction. She had actually said goodbye to her as the nurses pushed her gurney down the hallway. In a rush of panic, Rosemary realized that her mother expected her to die. She had called her father so he could come and say goodbye as well. When Rosemary had woken up in the recovery room, for a minute she thought that she actually might be dead. This was heaven, or hell—or wherever people went when their parts stopped working. The only clue that she was still alive was that everything hurt, and turning her head nauseated her.

Rosemary was wheeled back to her room by a silent nurse whose only statement to her was, "It's only your appendix; don't overreact." Dad had been sitting in a plastic chair in her hospital room; a magazine lay in his lap, unread. He stared across the room blankly. Rosemary made a sound that was supposed to be a hello, but it came out as a grunt. Dad had lurched forward as if she had scared him. A smile spread across his face.

"Hello, sweetheart. I've been here with you all night, well, your mother and Chuck were here for a long time, too. Your mother's down in the chapel. Your brother and sister are somewhere around here. You want me to find them?"

Rosemary shook her head slowly, the motion sending a new wave of nausea through her body. She tried to speak, and instead started crying. He looked old; his thick, dark hair had receded back to his ears, and was streaked with silver. Deep rivets lined his face; his eyes were aged. He moved carefully, too aware of his actions, a subtle discomfort permeated everything about him from his stiff manner to the overly ironed button-up shirt he was wearing, which was tucked perfectly into a pair of pants that fell short on his ankles. He perched on his chair instead of sitting in it, and it was obvious that he was out of place here, not sure about how to talk to Rosemary. He moved to the bedside and held her hand; his was damp and awkward.

"I'll just get your brother and sister; I know they're here somewhere."

With that he left. About half an hour later, Lilly and Kyle came in, sat by the bed and told Rosemary everything that she was missing at school, what Mom had flipped out about yesterday, how it was so totally unfair that Lily couldn't go to the dance because Mom said she could and now she was a total liar. They talked and talked. Rosemary heard about half of what they said. Instead, she was thinking about the people that used to live above Dad in the shithole. They made peanut butter balls; basically, peanut butter rolled in oatmeal and baked. Rosemary didn't know why the memory had come back to her; she hated them. They stuck to her teeth, and the neighbors always used chunky peanut butter, which made Rosemary choke. Still, she ate them when they were offered. Dad never came back. He didn't come back when she graduated two months later. She was left with the tick of the water pipe and the memory of peanut butter on the back of her teeth.

"Miss? Miss can you hear me? If you can hear me, try to open your eyes."

The voice was gentle but persistent. Rosemary felt the numbness wearing off, which was replaced with a violent chill. She cracked her eyes, blinded by the bright white light above her.

"Okay, there we go; she's coming around a little. Good girl. Miss, you're in Hospital Sector Five, in the Mirage Hotel and Casino. Don't be alarmed, you're going to be just fine. You came in here with quite a fever; 104 degrees to be exact, and a nasty kidney infection. We've been cooling you down for quite awhile. You're in an ice bath now, so don't be alarmed."

Rosemary was suddenly acutely aware that her scrubs were gone and she was in some kind of shallow bathtub, ice packs covering her body, over which was some kind of blanket with a blue glow. An IV line ran from her arm to a metal stand. The chill made her body rock, and a throbbing pain shook in her head.

"Whoa, whoa there. Calm down, sweetheart. We need to get your body temperature down. Don't try to talk much now, don't worry. In a few minutes, we're going to move you to a nice room, and you'll get to sleep for a while. We'll take care of you here, don't you worry. Can you tell me your name sweetheart?"

Rosemary opened her parched mouth and managed a raspy, "Rosemary McLeod, I..."

"Shhhhh, it's okay, don't exert yourself. You should still be unconscious; it's a miracle you're awake now. You came in alone, one of the gals ran down and looked in your car and got your things. Don't you worry. Do you need us to tell someone that you're here, sweetheart?"

With great effort, Rosemary managed, "Dennnverr."

"Okay, I think that's enough for now, your temperature is going back up a bit. If you're going to Denver, you're going to have to wait for a little bit, we have to get you well. Just lay back and breathe deep for me."

With that, Rosemary fell back into the hot, cold blackness.

The next light Rosemary saw was a pinpoint; bright; moving. She felt her eyelid being tugged open, the dryness making it stick. Voices surrounded her, Rosemary felt hot, and even the thought of moving made her lightheaded. She was out of the tub and in a bed. Out of the corner of her eye she could see the metal handrails that adorned every hospital bed. She tried to move her hand to the rail, but the effort was like trying to run through water. She managed no more than a quiver. It was enough for the voices to notice.

"Rosemary, kiddo, can you hear me? I'm Dr. Niogi. The nurse told you before, but you are in the hospital here at the Mirage Casino. Don't try to talk; you have an oxygen mask on to help you breathe. Just try nodding."

Rosemary cracked her eyes open a bit and saw a youngish East Indian man, the one with the dark hair and eyes that she faintly remembered from the lobby. His face was very serious and he spoke with a slight accent. He had his hand on her wrist, timing her pulse. Rosemary didn't feel his touch at all. He placed her hand back on the white sheet and wrote down a number. He noticed her alarm.

"You're on a lot of medicine right now, and you don't have all the sensations you should have. Don't worry about that. When the medicine wears off a little, they'll return. Do you feel strong enough to talk a little? At least listen to me talk?"

Rosemary nodded; her head felt like it was filled with an ocean tide.

Dr. Niogi pulled over a rolling stool and wheeled up to the bedside. "You came in with a severe kidney and bladder infection, and a high fever. You also were dehydrated; your electrolyte balance was low. Basically, you're falling apart."

Dr. Niogi smiled; it looked out of place on his too serious face. "We ran some blood tests. I suspect you had a miscarriage. Did you know you were pregnant?"

Rosemary shook her head violently, tears forming in the corners of her eyes. That meant the bleeding, the fall in Rancho Cucamonga.

Dr. Niogi, somehow reading her mind, placed his hand on hers. "Calm down kiddo, please calm down. When you came in, we saw evidence of bleeding. We still need to run some tests to be sure, but if it was a miscarriage, then you were very early on in the pregnancy. It's very common. It doesn't mean you won't ever be able to have children, it doesn't mean that at all."

Rosemary pulled the oxygen mask off with great effort. "I fell. I was bleeding; it hurt a lot."

Dr. Niogi replaced her mask. "That may or may not have anything to do with it. Typically, first trimester miscarriages happen because something wasn't developing properly. Usually it has nothing to do with what the mother is doing, or not doing for that matter. Please try to stay calm. I know this is hard; you came in with a very high fever and a kidney infection. You're on antibiotics to treat the infection and your fever is dropping, but you're still very sick. We'd like to keep you for a couple of days until you're back on your feet."

Rosemary tried to swat at the mask, her hand choosing not to obey her command. Dr. Niogi reached over and lifted it away from her mouth.

"No! I can't stay here! I...have to get to Denver, my husband is there, or on his way there anyway. My mother..." Rosemary realized for the first time that she didn't even have her mother's new address with her; she only remembered the cross streets. She suddenly felt dizzy. Dr. Niogi replaced the oxygen mask. Exhausted, Rosemary felt her eyes fluttering.

"Kiddo, don't worry. We need to get you healthy first, and we still need to confirm that it was indeed a miscarriage. You need rest now, we'll figure out all of this together. Later." His voice was hypnotic. "You're going to be okay, we'll take good care of you here. I'll send someone in with some ice chips; I think you're ready for that."

True to his word, a short girl with a blonde ponytail came in with a cup of ice. She pulled the mask away and gently slipped them between Rosemary's cracked lips. The coldness felt wonderful against her raw throat. She felt her eyes beginning to drop. The nurse replaced the mask and silently closed the door behind her. Rosemary drifted off, the remains of the fever carrying her into another dream.

34

The Honda looked like something out of those Area 51 documentaries. It was low to the ground, and the frame of the old car was still visible. But solar panels had been attached to every possible surface. On closer inspection, there were thousands of little wires that ran from the panels to a collection of car batteries, which were housed in the trunk. In turn, a network of cables that ran over the exposed trunk and under the car to the hood, connected to the newly transplanted Mercedes five-cylinder D1 engine. There were lots of new looking attachments to the engine, but Nate didn't have the foggiest idea what they were. He hoped the little man wouldn't require them to know too much about this thing. Nate had a feeling it would take days just to explain the cable connections.

"The fuel tank is where it always is, but you have to lift off the panel like this before you can fill it up—if you need to. I'm actually, um, hoping that you never need to use the fuel and that the solar will take you all the way through Utah. It should, we've run the numbers and they've said as much. Let me show you how to refuel."

Nate tried to pay attention, but found himself distracted and impatient as the little man showed Eli the five extra plastic gas cans full of biodiesel that were stored in the back seat of the Honda. They took up the majority of the space, and Nate was wondering where they were going to put their stuff, the food, the sleeping bags.

Eli turned from the little man and with a hint of impatience in his voice said, "Man, you gotta chill, man, it's one thing after another with you, man. We'll put the stuff, like, on the floor, or we'll, like, shed some of our stuff man. I'm sure science dude here could do something with all that Priceplan crap, right, man?"

The little man looked confused and slowly nodded. Eli turned away from Nate and back to the little man's description of how and when to fuel the car.

"You don't want to fill her up until you really need the power. The biodiesel doesn't hold up well in cold temperatures—tends to freeze in the gas tank, so leave it in storage as long as possible. It has to do with the compound. See, we don't have any actual fuel to add to the mixture so we have to depend on the food oils, but they coagulate when the temperature drops. We're pretty close to fixing that, but for now, you'll just have to watch it. The car batteries will automatically charge throughout the day; you should have a charge now since they've been out in the sun all morning. Here's a map that will lead you to Greeley, I'm sure they'll make sure you get to Denver or wherever from there. Don't stop unless you have to, daylight hours are precious. Let's get you packed up."

They were all standing behind the McDonalds. The other two scientists had become very excited once they'd seen the Minnie Winnie through the window. The five men had pushed her up the little embankment and into the parking lot behind the former restaurant. Eli was already headed over to the Minnie Winnie with the plastic crate the little man had given him. Nate followed, a little stunned that this was all really happening. Inside the Minnie Winnie, he and Eli loaded up the canned food, can opener and a box of saltine crackers. Nate grabbed the sleeping bags and both his and Eli's jackets, and as an afterthought he pulled the camping blanket from the bunk. There was a lot left behind, clothes, the camping stove, and the propane tanks. The little man nearly squealed when he saw them.

"Oh this is just wonderful, that's so useful, just so useful; you have no idea."

As it was, the small load barely fit into the back seat, crammed around the fuel tanks and crowded on the floor. The crate wouldn't make it into the door, so Eli just dumped the food on the floor, on top of the camping blanket. Nate's stomach was growling, and he guessed Eli's was too, but it was already nearly two o'clock and the sun wouldn't be in the sky much longer, if they didn't leave now, they would have to wait another night. Eli turned to him.

"It's up to you, man, but I say we go. I'm going to ask the waitress over there for like a doggie bag or something man, some take out man, I'd ask if you wanted anything man, but I know how wiggy you get."

Nate glared at Eli, who promptly turned and jogged over to the waitress who was about ten feet from the McDonalds. Nate saw the silver tray appear with a large brown bag. Eli took the bag and started jogging back, yelling:

"C'mon man. I got something for you, man. Even if you don't want it, man, you'll need it. I don't want you to like pass out on me again, man. Here, you eat; I'll drive the first shift."

Eli thrust the heavy bag that smelled of barbeque into Nate's hands, and then went to the driver's side of the Honda. He shook hands with the little man

"Don't worry, man, we'll make it. Do they have, like, phones or something, man? How will they tell you we got there okay?"

The little man shook Eli's hand vigorously. He was flanked by the other two scientists. "They'll send word; we have an active mail run going from here to there. You might pass one of our biofuel mail trucks on the way. They're just wonderful; our first green vehicle."

Eli looked confused. "Dude, I thought you said the biofuel didn't hold up...isn't that what we're testing? But, I don't get it. You already have the mail trucks..."

The little man's eyebrow twitched with annoyance. "Well, yes, yes, that's true; the mail trucks use our biofuel now. You're not testing the biofuel, well, you are in a way....here's the thing. You have a new compound of fuel for the car, we're testing an anti-freeze agent derived from the soy beans. But, the main thing is the solar panels. The mail trucks need improvement. Now they can't stop on their route without risking coagulation. We need to perfect the solar panels. That's what you're testing; mostly, that is. But if you use the fuel, we need to know how it holds up, see? The mail trucks break down; not all the time, but enough."

The thought occurred to Nate that he should take advantage of this and send a letter to Rosemary. He was pretty sure he could remember the address, maybe. In Golden. But, he was stopped with the realization that the mail truck would get there as quickly as he would, so there wouldn't be much point. Instead, he waved at the little man and the beaming scientists, and climbed into the passenger side of the Honda. The seats were a rusty brown; they looked polished, like they had never been sat in. Eli sat down behind him. The engine started up and the scientists on the sidewalk gave a little round of applause. As they rolled down the street, men and women with their plastic buckets waved at them. Eli picked up speed and they sped out of Las Vegas and into the desert.

35

In her sleep, Rosemary could hear the tick-hum of the monitor beside her hospital bed. She felt the sheets, stiff and overly clean. The air smelled like ammonia and sickness. It struck her as funny that with all the changes, the permanent removals, the consolidating cities, the electric scooters, that the sign-makers hadn't been able to fix this, make the hospital smell like cherry wood, or strawberry cookies. In her dream, Rosemary was sitting on the chair next to her own hospital bed. She could see herself; she saw her mouth twitch as she considered the idea of cookie-scented hospitals. Outside in the hall, nurses and doctors wearing scrubs, just like she used to have, scurried here and there carrying clipboards. Rosemary moved from her chair and stood over herself.

Her nose was crooked. It had been since her first year of college. She was playing mud soccer on the field outside her dorm with the girls on her floor. She slid for the ball, and her nose collided with Gina Westbank's knee. Gina had been overly apologetic, but everyone convinced Rosemary that it couldn't be broken; no way it was broken. Rosemary's roommate even told her that if it was really broken, it would be bleeding. The other girls crowded around her and said that she would definitely know if it was broken, that it would really hurt. They didn't respond when Rosemary told them that it really did hurt. The girls then told her that she would know if it was broken because it would move. They seemed to ignore the fact that although it was bitterly painful to test it, the nose was definitely moving. The result was Rosemary's crooked nose that now had a slight bump.

In her dream, Rosemary reached down and touched the nose, straightening it gently back into position. And instead of springing back, it stayed. Rosemary then ran her finger down the bridge, smoothing the bump into a thin, smooth surface. There, back to the way it should be. Rosemary then opened her mouth with her right hand. With the left, she reached in and slowly moved the crooked bottom front teeth back into order. She ran a fingertip across the chipped upper top tooth and replaced its tiny missing part. Then, as a finishing touch, she drifted a finger across the whole row; removing all the plaque and making them shine. Perfect.

She felt the dream fading, started feeling the hot/cold, the scratch on her dry throat. She was snapped back into her body against her will. Sweat lined her brow, and Rosemary could hear the monitor's tick-hum. Her arm itched where the needle stuck into her arm, the one that connected her to the IV a few feet away. She realized with horror that she had wet the bed, Rosemary tried to sit up but the effort exhausted her. Her heavy arm reached for the red call button mounted on the side guardrails. She barely made it before her head fell back onto the pillow. She heard the door click and the blond ponytail was back, clipboard in hand, checking the monitors. She leaned over Rosemary with a stern face.

"Yes? You called us. Can I help you with something? Are you feeling uncomfortable?"

The blond ponytail pulled the oxygen mask away from Rosemary's face long enough for her to say, "The bed, I, it's the bed, I'm sorry, I didn't..."

Blond ponytail pulled back the bed sheet, and frowned. "Don't worry; we'll get you cleaned up. It's alright."

It was hardly a reassurance, but Rosemary couldn't manage to respond. Her eyes were heavy with pressure and sleep. As she passed out, she was being rolled to one side by strong hands while blond ponytail pulled the sheets from under her. Like a child, Rosemary thought, as she gave into the heaviness and let her mind float far from the hospital bed.

After the surgery, Rosemary hadn't heard from Dad until Christmas. He sent a package to Rosemary's Mom's house. Inside was a box of chocolate, and a wrapped present for Mom. Mom had left the gift unopened until well after Christmas, and even after New Year's. Rosemary had been home from college, and on the night before she was going to go back, they sat down to open the box.

"I'll bet he sent your present to your dorm honey, he probably didn't think it would take so long to get there, and he wanted you to get it before you came home. It's waiting for you in your dorm room, I'll bet you."

They didn't talk about how strange it was that he had sent Mom a present in the first place. With the exception of Rosemary's surgery, they hadn't even spoken in years, much less exchanged presents. As they sat together in front of the little wrapped box with the gift-wrapping kiosk bow, it seemed even stranger to leave it unopened. It was a snow globe. A tiny dancing snowman holding a sign that read "Plow Me" inside. When you wound the knob on the bottom of the globe, the little snowman would spin and the sign would wave back and forth. Rosemary and Mom stared at each other for a couple of minutes, both afraid of their reactions. Finally, they burst out laughing. Mom reached for the globe and shook it up, showering the obscene little snowman in plastic snow. They drank coffee and laughed about what must be waiting for Rosemary back in her dorm room.

When Rosemary arrived the next day, there was no package, or card; nothing. She sat on her bed, a bit stunned. She hadn't received a present from her Dad in years, and she certainly hadn't given him one, but in that moment of

146

realizing that he had deliberately cut her out, it stung. She sat down and wrote him a letter that night. Rosemary never sent it; instead, she folded it neatly and placed it in her journal. A couple of months later she took it out and read it again. That was after he sent her his letter. Dad's letter was much worse than the lack of a snow globe. The letter was unexpected, and mean, and sad. It told Rosemary that he wouldn't be managing in a half way house much longer, that he would disappear into the institution, a "place for people like him."

The letter was addressed to Rosemary, but the content was not. It outlined step by step how she had destroyed the marriage. Point one was that Rosemary had never been there for Dad when his father, her grandfather had died. Rosemary had to read it twice. She had only met Grandpa Pete once, and then as a toddler. All she remembered of Grandpa Pete was his shoes, hard leather shoes at her eye level. The rest traded about various points of contention ranging from not appreciating his efforts to fix up the house, to not going to Aunt Dee's funeral. Rosemary was suddenly glad that she hadn't sent the letter she had written after Christmas. She read both and then tucked them away in her journal. Sure enough, the next week, Mom called to tell her that Dad had to go back into the institution for a little while. He had stopped taking his medication and had relapsed.

"Guess that explains the snow man, doesn't it honey?"

Rosemary was lifted back into consciousness briefly as the hands laid her flat onto dry sheets. She felt a thin blanket being pulled over her legs. All of a sudden, she wondered what day it was, and what had happened to *Lazy Daze*. The idea of having to find gas for *Lazy Daze* overwhelmed her mind. It had to happen and it wouldn't happen. Rosemary's hand floated back up to her face and she felt her nose. It was back to being crooked, without checking she guessed that her teeth were also back in place.

She placed a hand on her empty belly. For a few weeks, they had been a family, and she hadn't even known it. Would Nate have agreed to leave if he had known? She felt spent and weighted. Rosemary felt a pace, rhythmic like a drum welling up inside. Maybe irrationally, she wanted Nate more than ever right now. She closed her eyes, trying to feel his arms around her.

36

The greenhouses really were impressive. The little man at the Mc-Donalds hadn't lied. As soon as Nate and Eli pulled out of the city, they started seeing the greenhouses. Nate was actually surprised that he hadn't seen them from the Strip, long, low rows covered with moisture-trapping muslin. They stretched for miles into the desert. Little electric farming carts were plugged in by the road. Inside the houses, Nate saw people walking the rows, spraying and planting. He figured that this must be where the bulk of the people worked. It would make sense that the Vegas residents would mostly work night shifts, since the heat at high noon was unbearable; Nate figured that accounted for the huge number of people who seemed to be milling about during the daytime. As they pulled past the greenhouses, they saw what looked like the beginnings of a wind-mill forest. A few turbines were standing, and men and women were hauling the parts of the rest around a big field. Nate saw the sparks of a welding machine and caught a glimpse of one of the biofuel trucks the little man had talked about pulling another turbine to its feet. Eli nearly drove off the road.

"Sweet, man. Man, I freakin' love those things. They look like something out of the Wizard of Oz; freakin' love 'em."

Nate still had the bag of waitress-produced food on his lap. His stom-ach was doing flip-flops but he refused to touch the food. Fuck them. He could take care of himself. He had found food, he had things he could eat, he didn't need a goddamn waitress just handing him something that he could get himself. He he'd figured out the car, hadn't he? Nate hadn't needed to ask one of those things for some goddamn scooter, had he? No, people were still making cars; people were still making it work. They didn't need the signmakers.

He wondered how Rosemary had fared with the gas situation. She might've ended up in something like this as far as Nate knew. She would have been running low on gas around Vegas. The little man hadn't said anything about a woman coming through town looking for a car, but maybe little man wasn't the only one making these in Vegas. Maybe Rosemary had a diesel car and just had to pick up a few tanks of fuel. Nate liked that idea; she probably had been given a diesel RV and just had to get the biodiesel to make it run. Any-how, she was in Colorado by now. He wished to God he could remember the address. He knew how to get there, it was off I25 to Sixth Street, follow it all the way out, and it was the curvy road by the courthouse in Golden. A straight shot. Rosemary's folks lived in a modest looking ranch house; green paint, long driveway. He could find it.

"Dude, I got you some tofurky, man. I don't know much about that veggie stuff you eat, tofurky was all I could think of. It's in there, man. I also got some fries for both of us. Can you hand me the box, man?"
Nate glared at Eli.

"Man, you've got to calm down, man. It's not like we had a choice, man, we had to hit the road. Little dude back there told us as much; you gotta take off when the batteries are fully charged, like when they've had some time in the sun. If we'd have waited man, we wouldn't a had any backup power for nighttime. Didn't you hear anything he said man?"

In truth, Nate hadn't heard the little man say that, he had been too busy worrying about when they were going to leave, and where their stuff was going to go in the backseat. Without saying anything, he reached into the bag and shuffled around the cardboard containers. He lifted one out that had "Fried Potatoes" printed on it. He handed it to Eli who one handedly opened the top, placed it in his lap and began shoveling fries into his mouth. Nate couldn't watch.

"Disposable containers pollute don't they? Seems like your waitress friends are confused about the whole 'going green' thing."

Eli looked briefly at Nate and through a mouthful of potatoes, laughed, spitting potatoes pieces on Nate's shirt and arm. "Dude, your really didn't hear anything little dude said did you? He told us to keep all the trash, take it to Greeley, that goes for everything man, all the paper or whatever man that we use from here to there, toilet paper and everything. It's gross, man, but they turn it into compost, man, recycling man. Dude, you should really listen."

Eli went back to his potatoes. Nate didn't respond. Instead, he put the food bag on the floor, leaned his head back, and closed his eyes. Sleep came easily. He felt himself losing consciousness and drifting off to the rhythmic lurching of the car.

Heavy lidded and fully aware that he was dreaming, he turned his head to the driver's side of the car. He wasn't in the Honda; instead, he was in the old Toyota that he and Rosemary used to own. The one with the cracked dashboard, that always smelled of water rot. In the passenger seat was the gray haired man in the sweater vest. He was driving fast, a mean little smile on his face. Nate looked in the backseat. Rosemary was asleep in the back, stretched out. She shifted and curled up in the fetal position, her wrist curved in at her face the way she always slept. She was wearing some kind of hospital clothes, like the surgeons wore. Her eyes were moving beneath the closed lids, darting back and forth. Nate reached back for her and had just touched her soft hair when sweater vest reached over and smacked his hand.

"Get the hell away from her! Can't you see she's sleeping! You can't touch a woman when she's sleeping; they get pissed off at you. Don't you know anything? If you want to make it in this business, you better get one thing straight. You stay away from women. I'll tell you where women got me, I'll tell you that. They got me Europe, that's what. They got me some B-lister buying out my mansion and telling his friends it was mine, that's what women got me. Goddamn Angie. Goddamn it. Don't trust a woman to tell the truth boy, you hearing me?"

Nate stared at sweater vest, his mouth open a little. He almost missed Judd Hirsch; at least he knew who he was. Judd Hirsch could be nasty but this guy gave him the willies.

"She told me at the door that she was going to bed, she told me to have a good time and make sure the door was latched when I left. She goddamn knew we were screwing, she knew it. Then later on, it was, 'Oh, no, I had no idea.' Well, boy...fuck her. And that little tart, you need to know something before you go to this audition boy, you need to know who you can and cannot trust in this town, and who will land you in a villa in fucking Poland. You have any idea how cold Poland gets boy?"

Nate looked back at Rosemary. She had tried to stretch out on the seat and one leg was falling off, threatening to drag her onto the floor of the car. Nate reached back again to push her leg back. Sweater vest slapped him across the face, the car swerved and as sweater vest grabbed the wheel, Nate saw oncoming lights in the windshield.

"Dude, wake up man!"

Nate opened his eyes; his face was covered in sweat. Eli had one hand on the wheel, and the other was across Nate's chest.

"Man, calm down, you nearly jumped out the car, man! Who's Angie? You were all yelling about her, saying she could go to hell. I always thought you were an atheist man, I didn't think atheists had a hell."

Nate leaned back, wiped his head. He reached into the back and grabbed one of the water bottles. He took a gulp and put the lid back on. This might be my atheist hell, he thought, science without any reason or explanation. No choice but to accept whatever someone else thinks has to happen to you. This might just be it.

"Man, that's pretty pessimistic don't you think? Besides, there's lots of reasons for the Honda, man, it's all science, how can you possibly complain about that, man? This is like atheist heaven, you know, if you guys had a heaven."

Nate turned his head. "You did it again. "

Eli shook his head. "Like I said before, man, if you want me to stop doing whatever it is that freaks you out man, quit thinking so loud."

37

"You can guide the wand yourself, and I'll just tell you when it's in the correct position. You'll want to guide it all the way back until it reaches the cervix."

Rosemary looked at the internal ultrasound wand with horror. The long, thin wand, dripping with ultrasound gel looked decidedly uninviting She looked up at Dr. Niogi who smiled reassuringly, while blond ponytail nurse behind him looked impatient.

"Rosemary, it's alright. This is really the only way we can tell if you're still pregnant. If you prefer, we can compare hormone levels, but that would mean that you will need to stay a bit longer. We would need to take a blood sample now and compare it with another in one next week."
As though reading her mind, he continued.

"A pregnancy test is going to be inaccurate right now. Even if you did have a recent miscarriage, your hormone levels are going to be high enough to show a positive result."
The thought of staying another week in Las Vegas while Nate was in Denver was enough motivation for Rosemary to close her eyes and take the wand.

"Alright, Rosemary, we're almost there. Good girl, there, right there."
Dr. Niogi paused a moment. "Alright, Rosemary, you can remove the wand. I'm so sorry; it is as I suspected. There is no heartbeat. I'm very sorry."

With the wand extracted and Dr. Niogi and his grim-faced nurse gone, Rosemary allowed the tears she'd been holding back to start flooding her eyes. She shook with silent sobs. For what, she asked herself, for something I didn't even know was there? For someone I have no way to care for? She wrapped her arms around herself and curled into a ball, letting her sobs rock her to sleep.

38

By the time they reached St. George, the Honda was making a thwump noise, and doing a strange little jump. It was still light outside, so Nate knew it couldn't be a power issue, and besides, the batteries were supposed to take them for quite awhile after the sun went down. Plus, there was always the trusty crap gas with which that little man had filled the backseat. Nate knew all of that, but every time the Honda did that little jump or he heard the thwump, he shivered, predicting that it was going to die at any time.

"Goddamit, man! Will you cut it out, dude? That 'cranka-cranka' noise is nothing. This isn't just some car, man! You can't just be all like 'oh God, the car is broken' when you didn't even bother to listen to the instructions."

This was the first time Nate had ever heard Eli raise his voice. Even when he had been annoyed back in Vegas, back in the casino, he hadn't spoken above his normal tone. This time, however, he actually sounded mad.

"And, yeah, I am actually mad, man! I'm pissed off that you were so 'oh God look at me' about this in the first place, and then all you do when we're actually going where you want to go, is piss and moan, man! Piss and moan! You want to know why your lady left you? You want to know?"

Nate couldn't speak. He was so stunned that any anger he might have felt was, at least for the moment, displaced by the new Eli.

"She goddamn left, man, because you haven't stopped bitching for years! I've lived next to you for thirteen goddamn years, man, and for way too many of them I've heard you fighting. Jesus man, everyone heard you fight. You fucking piss and moan about your terrible life and don't even realize what you had, man. You had a boat, and a lady, so what you didn't have any goddamn water. We didn't even have a bow! You had a goddamn bow, man. We were like six feet under dude. You were just leaning. That's fucking nothing, man! Nothing! Do you know how goddamn unsanitary the roommates were? You have any idea? You think I went up to the sidewalk everyday with you because I actually thought that the goddamn Priceplan would actually go away because you threw some soggy peaches at the suits, man? No! I went up there because the roomies had farting contests that started at ten in the morning and lasted pretty much all day. Disgusting, man! Throwing fruit may be low class, man, but it sure smells a lot better."

Nate started to open his mouth but was cut off.

"And yeah, man, I know I did it again, man. You don't have to point that out every goddamn time it happens. I've always done it. You think I haven't known what you were going to say before? Only difference before is that it wasn't anything interesting enough to comment on, man."

Nate shook his head. He wanted to respond, but was still too shocked. Instead, he managed a weak, "Okay."

Nate reached over and took the empty French fry box off Eli's lap and put it back into the bag. "You want your barbeque chicken sandwich?"

Eli nodded, his face red. Nate pulled out the little box, opened the lid, and placed it on Eli's lap. Then he dug around in the bag and to his surprise, found a little stack of cloth napkins, tiny little squares. Nate pulled one out and laid it on Eli's leg next to the sandwich. Without speaking, Eli grabbed the sandwich one handed and began to shovel it in, dripping BBQ sauce all over his hand. Nate closed the bag and turned toward the window.

He wanted to be angry. How dare Eli talk to him like that! After all, wasn't it because of him that Eli was even on this trip? Eli wouldn't even be here if Nate hadn't decided to go. He'd be following the farting roommates to Santa Cruz.

"Dude, it never occurred to you, man, that I might have a Minnie of my own if you weren't with me? The signmakers must've thought we were a couple, man, that's why we got one, not two. That Minnie as much mine as yours, man, so lay off. You're on my trip, too, man, and if it wasn't for me, you'd be stuck in Vegas right now, man, so shut your trap."

Nate felt small. The anger he wanted to feel was washed away with a sudden case of oh, shit, he's right. He hardly recognized the new Eli, his face set and red, smeared with BBQ sauce. Nate knew he was right, he had had it easy, relatively speaking. Rosemary had to drive all by herself, and no doubt she had to figure out this biofuel thing all by herself, too. Nate guessed that she had a pretty hard time back in Vegas. She had left with only her small bottle of medication, and surely that had worn off by now—although, the hospitals the signmakers would make would surely be wonderful. Nate imagined that you could ask a waitress for anything, and the doctors had found a way to cure you within minutes, just like the Honda, here. Surely, medicine had caught up.

Las Vegas was not Rosemary's kind of town. The crowds would have her popping pills and still wanting to pull on people's sideburns. She might even do that weird dance she did when she mixed the pills with a drink. Nate could count on one hand how many times that had happened, but it didn't stop him from bringing it up to Rosemary every once in awhile. In truth, it was possibly the funniest thing he had ever seen, but to Rosemary, Nate knew that it was just another in a long line of public embarrassments. The debut night for the dance had been at his frat's Cinco de Mayo kegger. Nate wasn't a big frat member; he was only allowed to hang out there because he had a bunch of buddies who were members. They took Nate in because the guy who had his room previously had knocked up his girl while he was home at Christmas.

Nate took Rosemary to the party even though he had already seen her anxiety behavior in full swing. She assured him that she was all right; she wouldn't repeat the performance that she had given at his parent's house a few weeks prior. She had these relaxants, they took away the ticks, she promised. They had only been there about an hour when Nate lost sight of Rosemary in the crowd. He checked the bathrooms, the kitchen where everyone was smoking weed, and finally found her on the dance floor. She was doing the Linus dance from Charlie Brown Christmas. Arms straight down, head down and chin on her chest; she resembled a stiff clogger. Her legs, however, were flying this way and that. The indiscriminate flailing of her legs only seemed to accentuate the stiffness of her upper body. Her face was pinched into a ball, and she looked like she wanted to stop, but that someone was forcing her to dance. It reminded Nate of that really bad Lambada movie that came out in the 1980s or the early 1990s. The lead Lambada girl had to dance for the evil slumlord or else he would cut off payments to her family's kidnapper or something like that. That was the kind of determination Nate had seen in Rosemary as she danced. He stepped in and took her by the arm. She had looked up at him with large, scared eyes.

"I danced."

Nate nodded and led her off the dance floor to the back deck of the frat house. In the fresh air, Rosemary managed with shaky hands to find the pills in her purse and take two dry mouthed.

"I'll be better in a minute. I got nervous, and I couldn't see you. I heard the music; I danced. I didn't mean to embarrass you."
Nate smiled, holding back the laughter. "You were fine. Besides, those assholes are so drunk in there they won't even remember this party tomorrow."

Rosemary nodded, and together they had walked back to *Clementine*'s predecessor, Unmentionable Causes. Nate spent the night drinking homemade mai tais on the deck of the boat with Rosemary and listening to her recant all the stories that involved her dancing the Linus dance in public. By the end, she was laughing so hard tears were pouring out her eyes. Nate was drunk on mai tais and couldn't stop staring at the way her neck poured into her shoulders and the glimpse of bra strap that snuck out every time she leaned forward.

Eli looked calm now; his face was less red, and he even voluntarily handed back the food container and tiny napkin to Nate. He still didn't say anything, except to roll his eyes when Nate recalled Rosemary's bra strap.

39

The ice chips were back, and Rosemary nearly choked as one slid all the way down her throat. Blond ponytail pulled her hand back and looked alarmed. When she was sure Rosemary was still breathing, she relaxed and with a gloved hand, took another and slipped it between Rosemary's lips. Rosemary looked up at her face. Her eyes and expression was blank. She barely even seemed to breathe. So far, Rosemary had hardly even heard her speak. She followed the doctors around and wrote in that clipboard, and from what Rosemary could tell, she spent the rest of the time fetching ice chips. Rosemary's head felt a little clearer, her stomach felt empty, her throat raw, but the medicine fog had lifted almost completely. Rosemary reached up and took the cup of ice chips from blond ponytail.

"When can I leave?"

Blond Ponytail looked annoyed. "As soon as Dr. Niogi discharges you. You're much better, but we need to get you on an oral antibiotic, and Dr. Niogi is switching your anxiety medicine."

Rosemary looked confused. Blond ponytail continued.

"We found the bottle in your pocket. You can still take the medication but you need a variety that is safe in the event that you become pregnant again."

Rosemary interrupted her. "But, I wasn't trying to get pregnant in the first pla...."

Blond Ponytail talked over her, her voice annoyed and distracted. "We recommend, of course, that you not take any medication that isn't absolutely necessary during your pregnancy. You are still being treated for dehydration, but we'll bring you a meal before too long."

Blond Ponytail talked like a robot; every word perfect and careful. She talked like one of the waitresses. Rosemary mused that she might be a waitress for all she knew. It made sense that if they had waitresses that filled needs, then they would have waitresses for medical needs, too. The only sign that blond ponytail was indeed flesh and blood was the uncomfortable look in her eyes, and the fact that on closer inspection, one eye was blue and the other grey. Blond ponytail would be quite pretty if she didn't look so grim.

"The doctor will be in to check on you soon. Do you need to use the restroom?"

Rosemary realized that she did, and very badly, too. She nodded. Blond ponytail rolled her blanket back and took Rosemary under her shoulders, pulling her around and to her feet. Rosemary's legs felt like Jell-O, but they held. Blond ponytail maintained her grip on Rosemary with one hand and pulled the IV tray with the other as they slowly walked across the small room.

"Dr. Niogi does not believe in the overuse of catheters. He believes they may further aggravate severe urinary tract infections such as you have. I apologize for this inconvenience."
Once in the bathroom door, blond ponytail planted Rosemary on the toilet seat and promptly turned and walked out, closing the door behind her. Rosemary could see her shoes under the door. Blond ponytail waited for the flush and then entered, and they repeated the slow waddle back to bed. Rosemary was exhausted with the effort.

Breathing heavily, she managed, "What's your name? What should I call you?"

Blond ponytail again looked annoyed. "Morgan, my name is Morgan. I am the only nurse for these wards during the day. At night you will have a male RN named Will; you have not met him yet. I leave at seven in the evening, about an hour from now. After that, it will be Will's job to take care of you."

Rosemary processed the information slowly, letting it wash over her more than inform her. She didn't remember much. "Thank you Morgan, for the ice, and the bathroom."

Morgan looked uncomfortable and blinked too quickly. "You are welcome. I will return later. Dr. Niogi will be in by and by to see how you are doing. Would you care for me to turn on the television?"

Television? Rosemary hadn't owned one or watched anything in years. Since the signmakers, and especially since she had begun her journey, Rosemary had assumed that there was no more television, just like the phone lines and the Internet had been permanently removed.

"Sure, I mean, there's still TV?"

"Yes, Las Vegas is programmed to "Will and Grace.""

Rosemary had no idea what "Will and Grace" was, but it would be nice to break up the time. Morgan turned and reached over her head to the television controls. The show flipped on and without a word, Morgan left. Rosemary was fascinated. No commercials; just one episode after another. She didn't know who was who, but it didn't matter, everyone seemed to be living in one fancy apartment. Rosemary felt herself drifting off to sleep to the lullaby of the laugh track.

40

For the most part, St. George had been permanently removed. Nate wondered where the signmakers had moved everybody, since the only other comparable city was Provo, which was way up north next to Salt Lake proper. Nate was pretty sure that Salt Lake City was still around, although probably much like Vegas, consolidated. But, St. George now consisted of a long line of greenhouses, that looked like a forest of solar panels and what used to be a row of barns. The barns had been outfitted with the solar panels and were flanked by the turbines Nate and Eli had seen the Vegans erecting. As he stared at them from the Honda window, way off in the distance, he saw some movement near the bars, some scooters, and even a tractor up against the barn wall. It made sense, Nate thought. It made sense that if you can have a biofuel car, then a tractor can't be all that hard to figure out. This must be some kind of farming project. The fields beyond the barns were green and lush, rows of perfect fruit trees. The greenhouses were no doubt growing the same soybean crops the little guy in Vegas had spoken about. The sun was dipping rapidly, but the car kept going. The thwump noise had even stopped, although it was replaced by a disconcerting clang from the back end.

Eli hadn't spoken to him for about an hour. His face had relaxed, however, which gave Nate hope that he would cool off before long. Nate knew he was being an asshole, he generally knew every time he was an asshole, he just couldn't stop. He had been so focused on getting out of Vegas that it never occurred to him that Eli might've wanted to scrap Green River and stay there. Nate had never quite seen Eli so happy as when he was lying on that hotel furniture, or piling his plate on the buffet lines—even though the barbeque was about to become soy. He must have one hell of a cousin in Green River, Nate thought. Nate didn't allow the thought that kept badgering him at the edge of his mind that Green River might not be there anymore, that at best it might have been changed into a research station. Eli's cousin and the homegrown weed very likely were moved to a bigger city, or removed altogether.

"Man, cut it out man. I know that could've happened, man, I just gotta see for myself. Always meant to move there, man, couldn't believe I stayed on *Cursory Angel* for so long with the roomies, man. Always meant to move back to

157

Green River, dude. Freakin' sweet there."

Eli's voice didn't sound angry anymore, it just sounded spent. He turned to Nate. "Man, you mind switching for awhile? I'll catch a nap and then we'll trade again, man."

Nate just nodded. Eli slowed the car on the empty highway and with the engine still running—they were afraid to turn it off—ran around and swapped seats. Almost immediately, Eli nodded off and began his strange sleep muttering.

Nate was trying to remember the last time he had used a telephone. He desperately wanted to call Rosemary's mother, and even though he knew Rosemary might not answer, she would at least know that he was trying, that he was on his way. He wondered what she had seen on her way out. Surely she had taken this same route, the trip through Arizona and New Mexico was longer and harder to get to from Los Angeles, and Nate wanted to think that she had ended up driving her biofueled RV all the way to Denver without any problem at all.

He wondered if she had her medication, or if she had found enough food. She wouldn't be stubborn like him and would probably have gotten take out from the waitresses just like Eli. Rosemary was probably just fine, by this time cleaning up the dinner dishes with her mother while Chuck and Lily watched television. Nate wondered suddenly if "Will and Grace" was the only program the signmakers had spared. He had never seen it before this morning, but even from that, it didn't seem like the kind of thing Rosemary's perpetually cranky stepfather would ever watch. Chuck was more of a baseball guy. Nate didn't figure that the phones were even working anymore. It was hard to say, he hadn't seen any in Las Vegas, and even the phones in the hotel room had been removed.

Nate saw lights coming at him in the distance. The sunlight was rapidly fading, and in the oncoming darkness, he picked out two headlights. Probably the mail trucks the little man had talked about. As the lights came closer, his suspicion was confirmed. A giant, ugly, and well-used truck barreled by him, it's owner honking and waving. It made Nate feel normal again, connected. It helped to know that there were other people out there going on with their lives, things running as usual.

"Good and settled aren't you?"

Nate jumped and the Honda swerved, causing Eli to mutter something about green beans.

Sweater Vest was in the rear view mirror, sitting in the tiny space between the fuel cans and the door. He looked crowded and angry. "I've been sitting here for God knows how long listening to your sniveling crap. You want to know what your problem is? Do you?"

Nate shook his head staring into the rear view mirror.

"Goddamit boy, you are catering to a woman. You want to know what catering to a woman gets you? Do you? It gets you a goddamn man's haircut and a headache one day before shooting. That's what it gets you. And for what?

So those goddamn models can all shave off their hair now and call it classic? Is that it? Is it? She did it for that goddamn soap opera. You know that; everyone knows that. And if the producer had been a man, a real man, then he would have said 'Fuck You.' That's right boy, Fuck You! I'd have my bombshell. Instead, I had a prepubescent boy. Goddamn women."

Sweater Vest turned to the window and back again, looked like he was going to speak and then clammed up. He just sat there in the back staring at Nate. Nate managed a whisper:

"Who are you?"

Sweater Vest lunged at Nate and he felt a cold wind hit the back of his head. "Goddamit, boy! I was in Poland, not the Congo for Christ's sake. I'm still on the A-list; you know I am. I used to be welcome anywhere I went and now I have to put up with some nobody, no chin, no angles, no nothing apprentice asking who I am? This is not a good way to get a call-back."

Nate snapped back to attention and as he did, he realized the sun was completely down; the absence of any light on the road or any traffic had plunged them into pitch darkness. Nate was barreling through the blackness, lights off, his foot pressed all the way to the floor. The engine was roaring, and the thwump noise was back, and it had spawned a clank from somewhere underneath the car. Instantly, Nate slammed on the brakes, his heart pounding and his hands numb. The Honda lurched forward and began to spin out. Nate spun the wheel trying to keep up with the motion. The Honda finally slid to a halt after throwing Nate and Eli into each other. As it finished its final rotation, Nate sat back, breathless at what almost happened. He was afraid to look, He could have been driving through the desert for all he knew. Eli was still fast asleep, although now he was now listing the ingredients for animal crackers. Nate turned on the lights, and to his relief he was still on the roadway. He must have been out for at least half an hour of blind driving. It seemed like Sweater Vest's visits were always brief, but Nate always lost time.

He turned his numb hands and legs back to the Honda, whose thwump was now more pronounced but whose clang had stopped. Nate was terrified at what he might have done. Eli slept on, oblivious to the fact that Nate had nearly killed him, in fact oblivious to everything but his shopping list. Gathering himself, Nate continued into the night, not looking back, working hard to control his shaking hands.

41

"I'm sorry, kiddo, I've just been a little under the weather, that's all. To-morrow we'll go to the beach. I'm just so glad that you're here, you know I love you, don't you sweetheart?"

Rosemary heard the voice through the darkness. She wanted to open her eyes, but sleep provided a delicious weighted feeling that kept them closed and allowed the voice to float closer and closer. After the letter, Dad had been sent to a different institution, this time back in Colorado. The doctors never explained why they moved him, but Rosemary had received a typed note from the institution in Glenwood Springs that acknowledged her as his next of kin and thus the person ho had power of attorney over her father's estate while he was hospitalized. When she called the hospital, she was informed that her dad had written a living will some time back that named her as his sole beneficiary and gave her power of attorney should he ever be hospitalized again. Rosemary's first reaction was a snort. Power over what estate? The shithole back in Santa Barbara? The trunk full of belongings that he had kept at the halfway house prior to his most recent breakdown?

It wasn't until almost a month later that Rosemary was contacted by a lawyer who had an F name who smelled vaguely of cat urine. Cat man showed up at her dorm in Santa Barbara, and while he talked about the legal documents he had come to deliver, Rosemary couldn't stop staring at his yellow teeth; she was completely preoccupied with the black something wedged between the two front ones. It wasn't until she heard "cabin" that she tore her attention away and started asking questions. Essentially, cat man explained, the terms of her father's hospital care were well outlined; she didn't need to worry there. However, she was now the executor of a small fishing cabin on the Colorado River. It was unlikely, cat man said with a lisp, that her father would ever be able to live there on his own again, so it was a fairly safe bet that she could do with it what she wanted.

She felt empty as she walked cat man to his car and watched him drive away. She felt like her dad had already died, and she had just been given the proof. The ice cream on the boardwalk and the water pipe dragons were almost gone from her memory. She had to stretch to taste the ice cream and the water pipe dragon grew still more elaborate as her mind worked to recreate the memory. She had come back to Santa Barbara for college because part of her wanted that life back, wanted him back. She had never gotten up the nerve to call, and now it was too late. He was locked up in the mountains, and a million miles away. Unlikely to live there again was what cat man said, and what he meant was that it was unlikely her dad would ever get out of the institution. Rosemary couldn't even force the tears; her heart felt like stone.

"Rosemary? Can you open your eyes for me, kiddo? Rosemary, we need to do a little checkup and then you can go back to sleep."

Rosemary cracked her eyes and saw Dr. Niogi's serious face near hers. She wondered why he was calling her kiddo; she was probably older than he was, since he looked to be in his late twenties. She felt a cold disk on her chest and opened her eyes all the way to see the stethoscope over her heart and then her lungs.

"Breathe in as much as you can and then let it go."
The effort made her chest hurt and her head begin to swim again. Blond ponytail was gone and next to Dr. Niogi was a tall man, in his early forties, with frizzy dark hair.

"Okay, this sounds a little better. Rosemary, this is Will, he will be with you the rest of the evening. We're going to lean you forward so I can get another listen, alright kiddo?"

All right or not, they took her by the shoulders and leaned her forward, which was the most movement she had accomplished since Morgan had hauled her to the bathroom earlier.

Rosemary felt the cold disk and then Dr. Niogi and Will lowered her back on the pillows. A light fog descended, and Rosemary watched, half amused as Dr. Niogi spoke rapidly to Will, who in turn pulled a large needle from a medical supply drawer. Numbly, Rosemary watched as he drew a small amount of blood from her forearm. Dr. Niogi pulled up the rolling stool.

"So, I imagine you are still feeling quite tired. Do not be alarmed, we need you to rest and recoup right now, you are going to be fine. As Morgan told you earlier, your fever is down and you're dehydration has been treated. Those two things alone will make you feel much better. I want to make very sure your infection is cleared up before you are discharged. Infections of any kind can be very dangerous. We'll need to keep you here for another day at least, but we'll be able to send you home very soon."

Rosemary's head was swimming, she didn't have another day, she needed to go, but the Jell-O in her arms told her that there was no way she was leaving tonight.

"I don't live here, I'm going to Denver, my husband is there, he doesn't know where I am...I need to call him."

Dr. Niogi looked a little surprised. "Rosemary, you are aware of the telephones, are you not?"
Rosemary shook her head.

161

"The telephones were permanently removed during Stage Two; we are now entering Stage Four. It's been quite some time since we had need of telephones. We do, however, have the capacity to send a letter in our mail truck. I provided some paper and a pen if you would like to write a letter. We can send it out tonight."

Rosemary was confused. "You have trucks? You have gasoline? The signs told me it was removed."

Dr. Niogi again looked a little surprised. "No, kiddo, it's a biodiesel truck. We have many engineers and scientists working on our Stage Four conversions. The mail trucks are very recent, very modern. In fact, I will have Will bring you a Las Vegas guidebook. It answers many of your questions. In the meantime, did you want to send a message?"

Rosemary shook her head.   "Can't remember the address; they were moved downtown. I know the intersection, and that's it."

"That may be enough; our mail runners are very proficient."

Rosemary gave in, although she had a million more questions. She took the notepad from Dr. Niogi and began to write, only to find she had no idea what to say.

Dear Nate,
I hope you get this. If you do, please don't leave. Please wait for me. Something's happened. I need to tell you in person. Please wait for me. Please. I'm on my way. I love you, more than ever.
Rosemary

She folded the note and handed it to Dr. Niogi. She started crying when she realized again that Nate didn't even know where her mother lived. He would drive to the spot in Golden just to find a green field. He would turn around, or keep going; he would be gone. She would never see him again, and she didn't know how to stop it.

"Rosemary, is there more? Tell me the intersection and the city and I'll get this ready to send for you."

Rosemary turned her head away. "19th and Sherman, Denver, his name is Nate McLeod. Not that it matters."

She heard Dr. Niogi's footsteps as he left the room. Rosemary stared at the white wall until she began to count the individual dots of light. Her stomach was knotted with grief, and although numb, the rest of her body vibrated in sympathy.

42

The raindrops started as a fine mist and escalated to healthy thwumps on the windshield. Soon enough, the thwumps became artillery fire and were soon accompanied by some of the most spectacular lightning that Nate had ever seen. Nate was about seventy-five miles out of St. George, the low-lying mountains in the distance reflected off the lightning and then were lost to the blackness. The rain proved to be so powerful that the windshield wipers were useless. The lightning rolled out of the sky and sprawled across the mountains, stretching its fingers as far as it could go. As soon as the boom of the thunder hit another ball would roll, eventually splitting and reaching for the Honda. Eli had finally woken up, and although unaware of the near accident Nate and Sweater Vest had caused, he was struck silent by the fireworks show outside the car. It looked far away, but the thunder made them both feel that it was right on top of them.

Unfortunately, for Nate and Eli, the scientists who had engineered the Honda had neglected to perform some basic maintenance procedures such as replacing the shredded windshield wipers and repairing the defroster. The windshield begun fogging up from the base and quickly spread up to the ceiling of the small car. The defroster blasted, but nothing happened. Eli reached over and switched the gauge to air conditioner as Nate tried to drive and wipe the windshield with his sleeve. Nate didn't even ask, although it made little sense to him. Eli turned his head briefly as he rolled down his window and then started rubbing the windshield with his hand.

"Man, you really never did that? The air conditioner and the defroster are directly linked, man, the air dries out the car and gets rid of the steam, man."

Nate didn't respond, had slowed way down and crept along the dark road as he too rolled down his window. The rain immediately began pouring in, soaking his left shoulder and arm. The lightning rolled again and the thunder answered with a thud that made the car shake. It was followed closely by a deafening crack and sparks flying from a tree about 500 yards away. Flames shot up and were subdued almost immediately. The shock made Nate swerve, and the car nearly ran off the road into the shrubs on the side of highway 15.

"Holy shit, man! Holy shit! That tree, man! Did you see that tree?"

Nate was rubbing the windshield with his sleeve again, as the rain increased in intensity and hardened into icy balls that flew through the open window, one pegging Nate in his left eye.

"Ow. Shit! Ow!"

Nate began to crank up the window, but the steam increased and he stopped. Instead, he slowed to just under fifteen miles per hour and prepared to pull off the road. Nate heard Eli gasp.

"Man, you can't stop, man! You gotta keep moving, man. Just go slow— we're gonna get hit like that tree if you stop the car, dude! Just keep going!"

Nate realized Eli was right. A sitting target was much easier to hit than a moving one. Besides, with all the wiring and scores of metal straps that were holding the Honda's solar panels in place, they were a lightning rod. Nate sped up a bit, as the steam seemed, for the moment anyway, to be stabilized. The hail was joined by sheets of rain that washed the Honda from all angles, and the wind had made it impossible to tell which way the storm was blowing. It seemed to be coming at them from all directions.

"Man, I hope the solar panels are tough, man. This hail, man, crazy. Oh shit! Did you see that?"

Nate turned his head quickly to see more sparks flying from a tree way off in the distance. Like the tree before, this fire flared and then was beaten down. But then, in response to Eli's concern, they both heard the sound of glass shattering.

"Okay, it's alright, we'll be okay." Nate repeated the affirmation to himself quietly, and grew in volume. Eli picked up on the chant.

"Okay, it's alright, man, we'll be okay."

As the rain pounded, Eli turned his head and stared at the lightning crashing over the distant hills. Nate glanced in the rearview mirror. Sweater Vest had returned to his cramped spot, a dark grimace, somewhere outside of a smile smeared his face.

"No...." A sick weight filled Nate. "No! You get the hell out of my car! I will not black out during this you bastard, I'll kill all of us this time, get out god-damit!"

Sweater Vest turned up the corners of his lips and showed the edges of his teeth, his eyes seemed to darken with the effort. "You'll do what I tell you, you damn sniveling, worthless pile of shit. You think I'm going to invite you back on set after what you've pulled out here? Imagine, ordering an artist, the creator—a visionary—off the set. In my day, you would be thrown out on your ear. Good thing management likes you boy; otherwise, you'd be sweeping the executive floor with all of the other losers."

Nate looked straight-ahead and then to Eli.

"Eli! Can you hear me, Eli! Wake me up, Eli!"

Eli couldn't hear Nate's voice, and continued to stare out the window at the rolling light. Nate felt an icy cold stab in his gut. Right now he could be barreling across open land. Nate, Eli and their wonder Honda would all crash into a tree.

No one would be by to save them, and they would die of their injuries, alone and forgotten, by the side of Highway 15. Nate pressed his foot all the way down on the brake, and braced himself for the pressure of the dead stop. The Honda flipped around the road and stopped, facing the wrong way. Eli still didn't notice, and instead set about rubbing the windshield with his shirtsleeve. Nate reached out and grabbed Eli's shoulder. The touch felt real, but he couldn't feel the texture of the cotton t-shirt Eli was wearing courtesy of Las Vegas hospitality.

The Honda lurched forward and sputtered, but the brake pedal flopped uselessly on the floor of the car. The speed increased on its own, and Nate struggled to drive and wipe the windshield. Suddenly, the steam seemed to increase tenfold, and the entire windshield was clouded. Nate tried desperately to keep the car in a straight line, as the speedometer crept spun from fifty to sixty-five, seventy-five, and then eighty-five. The engine began its thwump noise again, and the dash shook violently. Eli still seemed oblivious; he stared out the window, eyes wide as he watched the lightning send sparks from another tree far on the hillside.

"No integrity, that's your problem, boy. You all have no integrity. I should have won a thousand times over for the sheer integrity of my work, but you think those bastards noticed? You think they cared? No. They want car chases, tits and ass, sidekicks. You'd make a great sidekick, boy, you know that? Know what a sidekick does? Nothing. Nothing but die and support the main character, that's where you're useful. You'd get that part in a heartbeat. You have no integrity; you can't ever be the hero, can you? You'd have to stand for something, wouldn't you boy?"

Sweater Vest's voice was deadly calm; the words were steady, pounding like a train. Nate tried to scream but the volume was gone, and his voice came out as a flood of hot breath that fogged up the windshield even worse. Sweater Vest continued, the words becoming incomprehensible, the car swerving and sputtering, barreling through the wave of rain and hail. Nate's hands felt glued to the steering wheel, and the sick weight in his stomach was steadily rising up through his chest, his throat and finally appeared, as the bitter taste of bile filled Nate's mouth. He spat it out, covering the steering wheel and the dashboard. Dizziness overcame him and even his terror couldn't stop his head from falling forward. All of a sudden, he felt a hard slap across his face, and a voice in his ear.

"Wake the fuck up, man! Jesus Christ! Nate! Wake Up! Jesus! Give me the wheel!"

Nate's eyes snapped open as he saw Eli pushing him into the window and grabbing the wheel. Through his fog, he saw Eli pull up sharply on the emergency brake. Immediately, the Honda lurched forward and began to swerve. Nate felt Eli grab his leg and push down on the brake pedal. The car lurched forward and both men slammed into the windshield. They finally stopped with a loud whump from the engine, and the piercing sound of screeching metal.

The pain in Nate's head was so intense that tears filled his eyes. It radiated down his neck shoulders quickly, and he felt a sticky warmth rolling down his face. Through slitted eyes, he saw Eli lean back in the passenger seat. His right temple had an ugly gash and blood was pulsating out of the cut. He looked stunned.

"Nate, man—what the hell, man? You had one of those, I don't know, dude, blood sugar fits or some shit, man. You were out, man. Dude, you all right? You awake?"

Nate managed a slight nod and then leaned back.

"Man, you started yelling at somebody to get out of the car and then you just pushed down the pedal, man, and wouldn't stop. Thought you were going to kill us man. You might've killed the car."

Nate started to speak and found his voice rough and sore. "Eli, I, I...didn't mean to—Eli, I'm sorry. Are you okay?"

Eli had taken off his flannel shirt and was pressing on the wound cut with the sleeve. "Yeah, man, just hit my head. Jesus, man, what happened?"

Eli offered Nate the other arm of the shirt, Nate leaned over a bit and began wiping the blood from his forehead. "How fast were we going? What happened?"

Eli tore off the flannel sleeve and began wrapping it around it head to cover the wound. "Dude, you didn't get going all that fast; don't think this thing even goes all that fast. Guess you topped out at, like, I don't know, fifty miles an hour. I got you slowed down quite a bit before we crash-landed, man. Look, I don't know what happened, you freaked out man."

Nate felt his head and painfully found the cause of the bleeding, a wide cut right above his hairline. He pressed down with the shirtsleeve. "I've got to tell you something, Eli, it's part of the reason I think Rosemary took off. I...it hasn't been this bad in years, must be the stress, I don't know. But it's different this time. You'd better drive from here on out."

The two men sat in the car in the middle of highway 15, in the midst of the never-ending electrical storm. The panic in their stomachs was beginning to settle, as Nate started from the beginning. He told Eli about Judd Hirsch, Harry Hamlin, Mary Elizabeth Mastrantonio, the institution, Rosemary; Nate told Eli everything. Eli sat silent, eyes wide. As Nate got to Sweater Vest, Eli rubbed his eyes.

"Man, I know that guy though, man. Let me think it out for awhile, dude, but I know who that guy is."

Nate swapped places with Eli, the rain outside washed the clotting blood off his face. He stood there in the road for a minute, letting the cold soak his skin, watching the timid sun rise and daring the lightning to strike again.

43

The morning light streamed in through the blinds and awakened Rosemary. For a moment, she felt a sedated panic until she remembered the night before and found her bearings. She felt like she had been here for days; in fact, it had only been one day. Her head felt clearer, the pressure in her chest was lighter, and the overwhelming nausea wasn't present—at least for the moment. Someone during the night had removed the oxygen mask and replaced it with small tubes that ran around her ears and into her nose. Will. That was the name of the night nurse. Will must have done it. She looked to the bed stand and saw the guidebook Dr. Niogi promised her last night. As she reached for the book, she realized how desperately she needed to pee. To her surprise, there was a red call button clipped to the bed rail. She pressed it down twice.

A moment later, Will stepped through the door. He looked different to her than he had last night. Then, he looked huge; now, Rosemary realized that he was actually of fairly average height, and his hair was pulled back into a shrimpy ponytail. Rosemary hadn't noticed before, but his features seemed too big for his face; out of place.

"Good morning, Rosemary! You must be feeling a little better today. Do you remember me? I'm Will. I'll be with you here for a couple more hours until Morgan comes back on. I bet you probably need some help getting across to the bathroom, am I right?"

Rosemary nodded; suddenly tense. Will was already moving the IV cart to the side of the bed and pulling down the rail.

"After that, we'll see if you feel like eating something, I think that will make you feel a thousand times better."

Just like Morgan had done numerous times the day before, Will scooped Rosemary under her arms and effortlessly landed her on her feet. Despite her wobbly legs and the pounding in her head that accompanied each step, they made it to and from the little bathroom without her passing out. Will then left the room wearing a wide grin on his mismatched face. He returned with a tray of Jell-O and some sort of clear broth.

"I know, it's a weird breakfast, but I want to start you out slow. In a couple of hours, if we can keep this down, we'll get you something more substantial."

Rosemary took a sip of the broth. Her stomach cramped and then relaxed, reminding her that she hadn't really eaten since she left Mussel Shoals. She gobbled down the Jell-O and soup, the effort exhausting her. Will looked up from the chart he was filling out at the end of the bed, and grinned again.

"Nice job. Give it a little while, and we'll get you round two. Dr. Niogi wants to release you later on today, this afternoon I think. But before then, we want to get your strength back up. Your kidney infection has been flushed out for the most part. He'll probably send you with some oral antibiotics; good thing you got here when you did. You'll need to rest for few days, though. We'll arrange a room for you with the front desk."

Rosemary shook her head.   "No, I can't, I have to keep going, I can't stay here."

Will scrunched his face, reset the clipboard on the end of the bed. "Well, you'll have to convince the doc on that one. I'm just telling you what he's going to say. You need the rest though; otherwise, you'll kick that infection back up again. You're in no shape to drive." The concern was evident in his voice. "Besides, that big ol' RV you were driving is flat out of gas and will not be going any further. They had to push it off the road. We can figure out how to get you where you need to go, but you really should take it easy for a few days."

"I can't, my husband, I have to get to Denver, he thinks I'm there, I don't know how to tell him I'm here, the doctor sent a letter last night, but it's not going to make it in time. If he leaves Denver, I'll have no way to find him. I don't know where he'd go." Rosemary felt hot tears in her eyes and the lump in her throat that threatened to burst forward with a sob.

Will looked sympathetic. "Look, Rosemary, I can tell you this much. Denver is fine. My sister works in a clinic in Capitol Hill, and she's sent letters. She's fine, it's Stage Four, the baby stages of course, but they're getting there. Chances are your husband will end up downtown and the waitresses will help him find a new pad. It's pretty cool, really. I assume you came from LA? You were mumbling in your sleep about it."

Rosemary nodded.

"LA is just now going to Stage Three; you haven't seen anything yet," Will continued. "Stage Four means self-sufficiency, no wasted space. When you are a little stronger later on this morning, we'll take you outside. You'll see. All that space that used to be offices, empty rooms for meetings, hotel rooms for tourists, all of that has been converted. The signmakers changed it all. Look at the guidebook, the greenhouses, they're, wow, just look at the book. It'll answer a lot of questions. My point is, Denver is even better than Vegas. Our greenhouses, the soy fields outside of town, they're all new. Denver's had them in place for a while now. Everyone's been moved downtown; that happened when they converted to Stage Three. But you'll just have to see. They'll help your husband, I'm telling you. They did that here, the waitresses had addresses, everything. They'll probably set him up with a place and you can get back together with him when you get there."

Rosemary choked back the irrational tears. "He won't talk to the wait-resses; he'd never do that. I know him. I'm afraid he'll get there and turn around, or keep going somewhere. By the time I get to Denver, he'll be gone. It's all my fault."

Rosemary couldn't stop the tears anymore. "I left. Don't you get it?" Her voice was shaking. "I left. He knew I'd go back to Denver, but I ended up here instead. Now he's in front of me. He's probably there by now and all he's going to find is an empty field where my mom's house used to be. He'll never ask for help from the waitresses. He'll just turn around and disappear."

Will sat down on the rolling stool, scooted up to the bedside, and hand-ed Rosemary a tissue. "You can't do anything by worrying about it. Besides, you could have died yesterday if you hadn't made it in here. You couldn't help it; it wasn't your fault. Now if you want to get out of here by five this evening, you'll need to get some strength back. That means rest. Take a nap. We'll bring you more food soon. We'll help you figure out a way to Denver; I have some ideas. Till then, no use worrying about things you can't change. If you sent a letter, it'll get there fast. Maybe it'll get to him, but you don't know. Look over the guide-book; it'll orientate you some."

With that, Will squeezed her hand and walked out of the room. Rose-mary closed her eyes and immediately crashed asleep.

44

Miraculously, the Honda was still running. The thwump sound was significantly louder and the brakes sounded like metal on metal, but it was still running. Eli had been driving all night. The solar batteries had given out before they had reached I-70, but Eli had stopped and showed Nate how to fuel the car with the biodiesel. It had actually worked. Although, Nate noticed the consistency of the fuel was drastically different than it had been in Las Vegas. In Vegas, it had been all liquid, now it had clotted—coagulated—probably from the food grease that was its key ingredient. Still, it had gotten them to daybreak. Now with Eli at the wheel, Nate slept in the front seat, his head wrapped with the sleeve of the flannel shirt.

He was dreaming of Rosemary. In his dream, she was in a tub full of ice. Her face was red and she was crying. The room was stark white and there was a blond girl next to the tub, staring numbly at her. Nate screamed her name, but his voice caught in his throat, he tried to run to the tub but suddenly his legs were incredibly heavy. His eyes kept closing and he would fall asleep on his feet, leaning against the wall. In the dream, he was awakened by the sound of her crying. Nate jolted awake, the movement sending a sharp pain down his neck and spine. Since the storm, Nate had been growing increasingly sore, his neck throbbed, and the cut on his head felt like fire. Eli didn't look much better. There were circles under his eyes and the sleeve that wrapped his head was dark with blood. Nate felt guilty, and wondered silently why Eli hadn't just thrown him out of the car and kept going. He would have been justified in doing so, especially after Nate had explained about his disorder. He knew he must have sounded crazy.

"Dude, you're not nuts," Eli said. "I know nuts. I'm not gonna leave you by the side of the road, man. But I'm especially not gonna let you drive. If nothing else, the Honda needs to get to Greeley. This thing is a science advancement, man, we're like the astronauts, man. If we don't make it because you flip out and drive us into a tree, then little man's gotta start all over again, man. That'd be tragic, dude."

Nate got a sudden case of shivers.

"Man, don't get creeped out, man. I don't hear all of it, just the really

170

loud parts."

Without responding, verbally at least, Nate leaned back against the window and stared at the desert going by. They must be nearly through the San Rafael by now, Nate really had no idea how long they had been driving at this point. The Colorado border couldn't be too far away, and neither was Green River. Nate didn't have to say it; Eli heard him and sighed audibly. Nate turned back to the window. He wondered what the dream had been about. He liked to think that he would know if Rosemary was in trouble, although he couldn't imagine what kind of trouble she could be having in Denver. He didn't allow himself to honor the nagging insecurity at the base of his mind that kept whispering that she might not have made it at all, that she might have crashed into a ditch, or worse.

It suddenly occurred to him that he had left Mussel Shoals without saying goodbye to his parents. Not that they would notice, much. He really only stopped by every few weeks anymore, even though they lived in south Santa Barbara, not too far away; their idea of retirement heaven. He would have to call, if he could, if there were still telephones. Or write from Denver. Send it on one of those big, ugly mail trucks back across the desert. He would have to explain what had happened.

His parents didn't particularly care for Rosemary. Not that it mattered much. Ever since their first meeting, his mother had been overly polite about her, turning the conversation to another topic whenever it came up. The closest to approval that Nate ever saw was the onslaught of baby gifts that they received at the wedding. When Nate finally told them that they didn't want children, his mother had stopped mentioning Rosemary almost completely. Nate's father, however, never mentioned Rosemary at all. But, hell, he never really mentioned Nate, either. After he gave them the McLeod family seal at the wedding, Nate's father seemed content to pretend that Nate was still off at college and not a grown man with a houseboat of his own, and a wife. Nate didn't care much to tell the truth. He felt numb toward them most of the time. He learned how to tune them out while he was still a kid, not care, not depend on either of them for anything. Now he saw them simply out of habit.

Nate's head ached from the accident. The pain radiated out from his temples and his neck was bitterly sore as well. He knew that Eli had to be feeling the same, but he hadn't mentioned it. Eli hadn't even really talked about it at all. Even after Nate's explanation, he'd just taken the wheel and kept on going. It was strange, he should have been pissed. Nate quickly tried to turn off the thought before Eli picked up on it and responded. That weird ability really scared Nate; made him feel exposed. Even though Eli said that he didn't hear everything, he heard enough. Nate was about 99 percent sure Eli had listened to his conversations with Sweater Vest back when they were in the Minnie Winnie. How could he be so damn calm about it?

"He's calm because he's onto you, kid."

Nate was actually relieved to see Judd Hirsch squeezed into the space that had been previously occupied by Sweater Vest. Judd Hirsch he knew; he could make him go away. Judd Hirsch leaned forward so his mouth was directly next to Nate's ear.

"He's calm because he thinks you're crazy. You don't get angry at crazy people, it just makes them crazier. He plans on taking you to the next big city, dropping you off at the local loony bin and driving on into Greeley without you. No Rosemary, no Denver, nothing. Rosemary will just assume you disappeared. You didn't want her, after all. You meant what you said, kid. It's easy to be calm when you have nothing to lose except the dead weight in the passenger seat. You think he wants to be stuck with you around his neck like some kind of damn albatross? You're bad luck, kid. You destroy things; you break them."

Nate faced forward and shut his eyes. "Shut the fuck up. Get out of this car and take your goddamn friend with you."

Judd Hirsch laughed under his breath. "Oh, listen kid, he's no friend of mine; yours either. You'd do well to watch the company you keep."

And just like that, Judd Hirsch vanished. No theme song, no name-dropping, no awards show bravado. Nate looked at Eli in the driver's seat, staring ahead, humming "Stairway to Heaven," and tapping his fingers like miniature drums on the steering wheel.

Nate heard in his ear: "You're bad luck, kid. You destroy things." There couldn't be any more mental hospitals or asylums out there, not with the sign-makers. They had to have come up with something different, something better than the arm restraints and the needles full of sedatives. Surely, they had a better way to fix a kid's insomnia and night terrors than to pump him so full of sleeping pills that he was trapped in his mind for days and weeks at a time. Eli wouldn't try to drop him at that kind of place, anyway. Just in case, Nate decided that he should maybe drive the next shift.

45

Rosemary had graduated to miso soup and soda crackers by the time Dr. Niogi made his first round. Will had been replaced sometime during this period by stiff faced Morgan. Rosemary missed him. She wondered if he had been serious about helping her find a way to Denver. He was probably just trying to calm her down. It didn't matter though; she wouldn't be going anywhere unless she could convince Dr. Niogi that she was much, much better.

"Let's see," the doctor said, leaning over her as he read the chart. "Your fever has officially broken and is now almost normal, just a little high. Your kidney infection, as we discussed before, will need a little ongoing treatment, but the discomfort should have passed by now."

For the most part, it had. She still felt a slight ache in her lower back, but she was damned if she was going to mention it to the doctor.

Dr. Niogi paused and hung the clipboard back on her bed. He rubbed his face, the words obviously hard to say.

"Once you get to Denver, you need to arrange to see an OB. I'll give you a couple of names. You need to tell the signmakers as soon as you arrive, they'll arrange for living accommodations and work."

He sighed and continued. "Truth be told, I don't want to release you yet. You haven't even been here twenty-four hours. You need to rest or else the kidney infection that we've suppressed will come back much worse than it was this time. You're eating, which is good, but you're still weak and ill prepared to be traveling. But we have to move you, since we're not equipped to house patients for longer than a couple of days. We have a floor here at the Mirage just for hospital patients. I want you to stay there for at least a few days, then I can check up on you."

He paused, and drank in Rosemary's panicked face. "But something tells me that no matter how much I want you to stay, you're not going to do so. I'll let you go as soon as you get a full meal. We have these antibiotics for you, take one every day until the entire bottle is gone. Don't stop taking them just because you feel better; you need the full cycle. We also took the liberty of filling the anxiety medication that was in your pocket. I switched the prescription, so in the event that you are pregnant again in the future, you do not need to worry about taking your medication. I'll be back a bit later, so try to get some rest."

Dr. Niogi hesitantly placed two pill bottles on the nightstand. As he turned to leave, he bumped into Morgan, who was just coming into the room. She jumped to the side and her face reddened. Rosemary couldn't tell if it was anger or pleasure. She quickly composed herself and crossed to the bedside. After she removed the miso soup bowl and placed it in a plastic tub on the floor, she paused and looked at Rosemary.

"I shouldn't even perpetuate this, and it's none of my business, but Will wanted me to tell you that he'll be back before you leave. He said not to worry, and that he's figured out something."

Morgan paused. "I hope you realize that he could lose his position here if he gives you special treatment—lose his position or worse. It' not advised to favor one patient over another," She said. "You're not the only person to end up here like this, you know. Everyone is on their way somewhere. No one thought Las Vegas would even be standing, and no one is prepared to travel. You're not so special that Will should have to move out to erecting wind turbines just because you can't figure out whatever you need to figure out on your own."

Rosemary was speechless. Her face was burning and she was at the same time indignant and embarrassed. Her arms were heavy with responsibility and guilt. At the same time, she wanted to slap Morgan across her unhappy, pale face. She wanted to shake her by the shoulders and scream, "How the hell do you know what I can do?" But she didn't. Instead, Rosemary stuttered a little but said nothing. She hadn't asked Will for anything; he had volunteered. But Morgan was right; it wouldn't make much of a difference to the signmakers. They saw what they saw regardless of the intentions.

Morgan gave Rosemary's efforts a disdainful look. "You really have no idea how things operate here. You kept crying in your sleep about gasoline, you really think you can just pull into the filling station and get a tank of gas still? I don't know why you left home, and quite frankly, I don't want to know. I just want you to understand that not everyone here is buying your act."

With that, Morgan turned on her heels and left the room.

Rosemary was stunned. What act? She wished Will was back, or even Dr. Niogi, so she could ask them about Morgan. She'd worked with Morgans before, and so the intellectual part of Rosemary kept telling her that Morgans would always be unhappy, always miserable, always have a stick up their ass. Rosemary had been a Morgan in certain regards, too. She understood what it was like to look at the world with a cloud of discontent hazing your vision.

None of these thoughts helped, though. Rosemary was shaking; she desperately wanted one of the little red pills from the newly filled prescription jar. She restrained herself, though. She didn't know how long she had to make them last, and she wasn't going to put herself in the position of running out like she did on the trip. So instead, Rosemary lay back and fought the urge to rip the IV out of her arm and race out of the casino hospital wearing just her backless gown.

About forty minutes later, Morgan reappeared with a tray, which held more soup and half a cheese sandwich. She silently plopped the tray down on the side table and glared Rosemary down as she left the room.

For her part, Rosemary fought the nearly irrepressible urge to yank on Morgan's blond ponytail and jab the soup spoon right between her eyes. Rosemary almost laughed as she imagined Morgan having to go on her rounds with a soupspoon impression on her forehead. Morgan took Rosemary's amusement as a challenge and glared even harder.

The routine between them continued throughout the day, and at around noon, while Rosemary was eating a boiled egg on wheat toast, Morgan stopped and stared. The urge to pull the ponytail was still there, but the soupspoon urge had changed as the utensils had been taken away. Now, Rosemary was looking at the half an orange on her tray, wondering what it would look like smeared all over Morgan's face.

"The doctor will be back in at about one o'clock. Hopefully, he will release you then."

Rosemary, with her hands shaking madly, couldn't resist. "What do you care? Why don't you back off?"

Morgan's stiff face morphed with the hint of a nasty little grin.

"Because I know what kind of person you are. You've depended on someone else your whole life. Now you're here, and you cry and whine about how terrible things are, but you don't do a damn thing to change them. I listened to you when you were delirious, crying about your husband, your mommy, why this and why that. Some of us have had to take care of ourselves, and it infuriates me when someone like you gets themselves in trouble and then bitches and moans about how terrible their life is. That is why I care, because you are an affront."

Rosemary's hands were vibrating the bed. She began to speak, but her mind went blank. Before she could stop herself, she lunged over the side of the bed, yanking out the IV. She was too fast for Morgan to react, and she grabbed the blond ponytail. With an immense feeling of satisfaction, she pulled Morgan's head back so far that ponytail nurse lost her balance and fell backward onto the floor. Rosemary landed on top of her and with her free hand, began rubbing the orange, which she had grabbed from her egg plate, all over Morgan's pinched face. She smashed it into Morgan's nose and forced it into the corners of her mouth. Rosemary felt high, she could feel the marshmallow sensation wash over her limbs and for an instant, she felt her herself rise above her body.

Suddenly, she was pulled back to reality as Morgan got her senses back and threw Rosemary off and into the bed frame. In her weakened state, Rosemary easily flew back and felt her head hit the bed rail. Morgan struggled to her feet, scraping bits of orange off her face. She looked disheveled, disrupted. Rosemary knew that what she had done would probably mean the end of her time here in Vegas, but she really had trouble regretting it. The satisfaction that came out of seeing Morgan's perfect little sweater and white collar stained with orange juice greatly outweighed the consequences.

Morgan began to speak and it came out as a sputter. She stormed out the door.

Rosemary's euphoria quickly faded and was replaced with an icy horror as a sign grew up from the floor. It started as a crack in the hospital linoleum and Rosemary shrunk back as the post rose steadily skyward the top blossoming into a stop sign shape. The letters appeared fuzzy for a split second and then clarified.

It has come to our attention that
Rosemary McLeod
Has committed a violent act against another citizen
Please consider this a warning to
Cease your behavior.
Thank you.

Fuck, fuck fuck, fuck, fuck! What had she done? Rosemary hadn't even thought about the signmakers. A warning? Fuck. Dr. Niogi came bursting in. He jumped back at the sign, his face flustered.

"What happened in here? Morgan said you attacked her? We need to get you back in bed; you shouldn't be up yet quite yet."

He came around the bedside and eased Rosemary back onto the pillows. Then he rolled the stool over to the bedside and sat down. As they both watched, the sign folded in on itself and shrunk back into the floor.

"Okay, you need to tell me what happened. I can imagine that this has something to do with that anxiety medication that you're on, and I imagine that you have been off of it for at least two days, which isn't good, especially with the stress."

Rosemary was shocked that he wasn't kicking her out the door.

"I, I'm really sorry—I couldn't, I get these urges sometimes. I couldn't stop myself. And she just kept talking and insulting me. I got so mad. I tried not to take the pills, I need them for later. I don't know, I'm really sorry, I should probably go. I have a warning! The signmakers...."

Dr. Niogi shook his head.

"You don't need to go anywhere; a warning is just that, a warning. I know it's a bit jarring, but try not to let it rattle you. While we don't have a big staff, we do have other nurses that will take care of you while you're here. For now, I think you need to take one of your pills."

In one graceful movement, he reached across the hospital bed, and took one little red pill from the bottle. For a moment, Rosemary could smell the cleanliness of his shirt, and tie. She swallowed the pill obediently and lay back.

"Good. Look, don't worry about Morgan; she'll be fine. It's perfectly understandable that you might have a little breakdown, you've been off your medication, and this is a very stressful time for you. And quite frankly, there have been times when I was tempted to rub an orange in Morgan's face myself."

Rosemary laughed despite herself.

"You need to understand though, the transition here in Las Vegas hasn't been an easy one. It's smooth now, but Morgan had some ugliness that she dealt with and she's been a bit edgy since. I shouldn't say more, it's not my place. But don't take her personally. Are we alright?"

Rosemary nodded. Dr. Niogi checked the puncture wound that was left from Rosemary pulling out the IV and determined that it was probably time to remove it anyway. He left her alone.

Rosemary's hands were still shaking badly, and she fought back the urge to vomit. Why had the doctor been so damn calm about the sign? Why had the doctor told her so much about Morgan? In most places, people would simply have let the issue lie—if they hadn't asked her to leave first.

This hospital was different, and Rosemary couldn't tell if it was because of the signmakers, or the combination of people that had ended up there. Maybe there were new rules about hospitals, maybe doctors didn't have to keep their distance, stay aloof and professional anymore. Maybe the signmakers had issued a decree that stated it was suddenly all right to act as you felt, for good and bad. Maybe not. Rosemary looked at the clock and saw that it was about one; she had only a few hours to convince Dr. Niogi—and herself—that she was all right.

46

About twenty miles outside of Green River, Nate and Eli saw the hand painted sign.

Turn Right for Resistance

Nate hadn't commented, and Eli pretended like he didn't see it. Neither of them had any idea what it could mean, but even without discussing it, they were happy to pretend that the next right turn didn't exist. Eli rubbed his eyes.

"Man, I gotta take a break, man, just for a minute, man, gotta, you know, man. Need a restroom break. I got a bad feeling. I should be seeing something out here by now, man. There used to be houses and cabins out here, and now there's nothing. I got a bad feeling. There wasn't anything in Green River that the signmakers would want to save."

Nate didn't respond. He didn't remember ever driving through Green River, and honestly had no idea whether the signmakers would save it. Judd Hirsch had given him a headache. It had started in the back of his head and now had rotated to the front, a stabbing pinpoint of pain in his right temple. The light seemed unnaturally bright and his peripheral vision was now blocked by a kind of black cloud. Nate had to turn his head completely to look at Eli. He looked tired; there were bags under his eyes.

"Tired of you"

Judd Hirsch's voice rang in his ears, making his temple throb. He had been hearing the "*Dear John*" theme song play over and over in his right ear for about an hour. He had avoided looking at Eli because every time he did, all Nate could hear was that voice whispering, listening; he saw Eli's true intent now. Judd Hirsch was right; Eli was looking to dump him somewhere. He was glad Green River was gone; he'd have to keep driving, give Nate time to figure out how to get the car back. Nate still had a part of his brain that kept repeating that he had no business driving, not after what happened last night. The migraine drowned it out for the most part.

"Look at you. Goddamn waste of my time. Show up late, get there late, why don't you just roll over and let the other nobodies take your place, you pathetic piece of shit?"

Nate whipped his head around making the blinding pain in his temple ricochet around his head and send a thousand stabbing pinpricks into his eyes. His vision blurred and then cleared to reveal Sweater Vest sitting in the back seat of the Honda.

"You're already late. You know how many directors are going to hold your spot in line? One. I am the only friend you have, you worthless background performer. You've played the background your entire life and now you're letting this little piece of shit take your audition. You're letting him tell you when and where and how you'll run your life. You know damn well what's going to happen when you get to a city. You know, and yet you still keep on sitting in your own life like a goddamn passenger. You make me sick, you worthless embarrassment to the union. In my day, your SAG card would be burned in the street and we'd dance on the ashes. You got that, boy? You got that?"

Nate closed his eyes and shook his head violently, trying to erase the voice. The pain wrapped around his head and engulfed his vision. Nate saw only darkness with speckled starts of light when he looked up. He felt hands on his shoulders from a distance, as if he was somewhere in space, and the hands were barely touching the surface.

"Wake the fuck up you worthless piece of method crap! You need to be in 'character?' I'll tell you about your character! You've so far played the role of the self-serving doormat. You let everyone walk all over you, you kowtow to women, to your agent, to the law, and now to your goddamn chauffer. Still want to talk Stanislavski, you maggot? Go ahead, go ahead and tell me your motivations. I'll tell you about motivations—my motivation is to stand on that goddamn stage and tell those motherfuckers to go screw themselves. That's my motivation! And if you make me lose that opportunity just because you can't get your pathetic ass to the audition, then I promise you, you will pay. You'll pay all the royalties I stand to lose in an international release. You'll pay for every inch of film we wasted on your talentless ass, you'll pay for craft services. You'll never work in this town again, you hear me! Now get your ass in gear and drive!"

Nate's vision snapped back into focus and over him, he saw Eli, his face red and sweating, a small cut oozing blood on his cheek. Nate felt the weight of the asphalt on the back of his head. Suddenly, the pain in his temples vibrated and filled his vision. For a moment, a wash of white light blinded him. Then the darkness came, and through his pain, Nate let it drag him into sweet unconsciousness.

47

Dr. Niogi finally released Rosemary at four o'clock, when the sun was already hanging low in the Vegas sky. He had given her a business card to show at the front desk so she could get a room for as long as she wanted. He also supplied her with a pair of gray sweat pants, a matching t-shirt, and a purple hoodie, which Rosemary tied around her waist. She did not intend to go to the front desk, but also had no idea where *Lazy Daze* had been taken, or even how to get gas to make it run. She wandered into the elevator and pressed the lobby floor. Rosemary was still weak, but the throbbing in her kidneys had subsided. In her pocket, she carried the two pill bottles. She almost laughed at how unprepared she was to cross the remainder of the desert—to say nothing of the Rockies.

The lobby was packed with people carrying plastic buckets of chips. Rosemary had left the guidebook upstairs, but she had read enough to know that the poker chips had been the new currency during the first transition. Now, even though they were unnecessary, the habit was dying hard. Rosemary was amazed at what she hadn't seen during her inauspicious arrival. Giant palm trees framed a lush garden path which, according to the signs, led to dolphins and tigers. Rosemary stared, her mouth open. She wondered if the signmakers had left the dolphins and tigers or if they had been transplanted back to their natural homes.

The lobby was a collage of bright signs, greenery, and cushy carpet. The rooms and the buffet lines fed everyone and anyone in town, and the waitresses were on hand to supply electric scooters. Rosemary had considered the scooter, but she knew it wouldn't get her very far. After her ordeal, she definitely didn't want to risk a dead engine in the middle of the desert. She would die for sure this time. She had also read about the greenhouses and the soybean crops. Rosemary wondered what Nate's reaction to all this had been. Even he couldn't claim that this was wrong. It was beautiful in a strange way. The entire city was on its way to being self-sufficient.

Rosemary also learned that each casino had its own hospital floor, each specializing in different things. The Mirage focused on infections and viruses, Circus Circus held the pediatric ward. The Luxor had a chronic illness ward on its top floor. According to the book, medicine was being advanced rapidly.

Now that money had been removed, medications were now freely dispersed and research was made possible by the signmakers free from lobbyists and expensive funding. Rosemary learned that the antibiotics that had been dripping through the IV into her system for the last 24 hours were a new breed, a new advancement. They acted much like traditional antibodies, but worked with a quickening agent, a metabolic stimulant that caused the effects to be felt much quicker, therefore reducing the risk of long-term damage due to chronic infections and fever. This was all in the appendix of the guidebook, along with the new cancer and AIDS treatments that were being developed in anticipation of the Stage Four status.

The setting sun blinded Rosemary and reminded her that she had been indoors for the last twenty-four hours. She stumbled a little coming out the door and was caught by a tall man. She started back before she realized it was Will, dressed in his scrubs, apparently about to start his shift.

"Careful there, good thing I found you. I was hoping they would hold you until five or so when I came on shift, but this is lucky. How are you feeling?"

Rosemary held up her hand to block the sun.   "Better; a little weak, but better."

Will moved around her so his body blocked the sunlight and she could stare directly at him. He grinned. "The doc called me to come in early, told me about your little run-in with Morgan. Heh, can't say as I wouldn't have done the same thing."

Rosemary couldn't help but ask. "I had a warning, a sign, right there in the room! I don't even know why I did it. She was just so goddamn bitchy."

Will snorted a laugh as he led Rosemary to a bench by the Mirage entrance and sat her down. "Morgan's on warning; not from the doc, from the signmakers. She, too, had a sign spring up right in her room last month saying that she was not fulfilling her purpose. She used to work in the soy fields, think she liked it better, as you guessed she's not really much of a people person. Trouble is, she has a nursing license, she came here about three weeks ago in a panic. She's, um, tense. It has nothing to do with you, she scared off two patients last week. Can't help but think the signmakers are not too happy with that. Don't worry about her. I have news."

Rosemary leaned forward as Will smoothed back his frizzy hair.

"I got a buddy who drives the mail trucks, he's leaving tonight for Denver, around seven o'clock. He's not supposed to take passengers, but the signmakers don't seem to care; only the engineers really give a hoot. Something about liability, the trucks are experimental, you see, all biodiesel, and they're afraid they'll freeze up in the mountains. Anyway, I asked if he could take you into the city and he said sure. All you have to do is be there before seven so you don't get left behind. Here's the address. His name's Kevin, and he usually brings his dog; hope you're not allergic."

Will handed her a note card with an address on it.

"It's about two buildings down, below the McDonalds, you'll see, it looks like a little shopping plaza thing, just go in the front and ask for Kevin, I told him to expect you. If I were you, I would get something to eat first, though, he doesn't like to stop, the trucks do their best traveling in a straight shot."

Rosemary stared at the card and shook her head almost imperceptibly.

"This is—wow—thank you, Will. Thank you so much. Are you sure he won't get in trouble? I don't want him to be removed or fired or whatever else."

Will shook his head. "He does it all the time, the other drivers do too, they just don't advertise, it if you know what I mean. He took a couple to Salt Lake last week. They were traveling through from LA, just like you."

For the first time in awhile, Rosemary began to feel hopeful.

"Do I need to pay him? What with?"

Will again shook his head. "No, didn't you read the handbook? Money doesn't matter here. He does it because I think he likes the company. It's a lonely job. Don't get freaked out, he's not all 'hey baby' or anything. You'll see; he's harmless, a little chatty, but harmless. Look, I need to get in before I'm late. Can't believe my luck, you could have been anywhere by now! Feel free to stop back up if you have any questions, just, you know, keep it on the down low, know what I mean? Help yourself to the buffet line in there, this is one of the first veggie convert hotels. If you want meat you can still get it on the west end of the Strip."

With that, Will flashed another grin, stood up and sauntered inside.

Rosemary stared at the card in her hand. It seemed way too easy, but it was her only shot. The clock on the casino in front of her read 4:40; she had a little time before she needed to catch the truck. Rosemary took Will's advice and headed inside for the buffet, her head clear for the first time in days.

48

A pinpoint of light flashed over Nate's field of vision. He heard movement on all sides of him, slow and careful. Instead of the spongy asphalt, there was something soft under his head. As he focused on the source of the softness, he was overcome with the piercing pain that he had felt before Sweater Vest had shown up in the Honda. Now the pain was more evenly distributed, his entire head pulsed. As if in sympathy, an aching pain in his chest vibrated in tune. He moaned softly as the light moved across his closed eyes. He heard the shuffled movement cease; excited voices became clearer and clearer.

"I think he's coming around...Eli! C'mere! Your buddy's waking up. Hey, can you hear me? Hello?"

Nate cracked his eyes a little and saw a thin faced man with a scraggly beard that appeared to have been grown more for lack of shaving equipment than for personal preference. Nate found himself looking at the uneven patches of reddish bristles that jutted from the man's face. He realized with a jolt that he had been taken somewhere; he was inside some kind of structure. He struggled to sit up, only to feel several sets of hands gently holding him back. Eli came running into his limited line of sight; he had a bandage above his eye and the beginnings of bruises on the opposite cheek.

"Whoa, dude! Calm down, man! Chill! You're okay, you just got knocked out. You're fine, man; well, mostly fine."

Nate felt his panic subside as Eli hunched over him, staring down.

"Whaaa....where am I....are we?

Eli grinned. "You're lucky you're injured, man, or else I'd hafta kick your ass. You remember your freak-out? Stupid question man, I bet you don't remember a thing. I was getting ready to pull off to the side for a pee break and you flipped the hell out. You grabbed the steering wheel, and basically nose-dove us into a tree. Lucky for you I wasn't going all that fast, and I've gotten really good at dealing with your crazy ass."

Eli grinned again. The scraggly bearded man was standing next to him wearing the same kind of crooked grin. Nate's confusion overcame his pain for a brief moment.

"Dude, this is my cousin! Rennie, meet Nate. Sweet, huh? It's a small

183

freakin' world after all, huh? Rennie and the others scraped you off the street and took you down here. They patched me up, too."

Nate closed his eyes and reopened them, hoping that when he did, this would all go away and he'd be in Denver. It didn't work. Eli and Rennie were joined by a smallish girl, probably seventeen at the oldest. Her clothes hung loosely on her, and she looked nervous. Nate glanced around and noticed the dirty concrete walls and the absence of lights, except for several oil lamps that sat on long tables. Nate didn't see any windows and the air smelled stale.

"What is this place?" Nate managed to whisper, the effort making his rib cage throb.

Eli gestured behind him. Nate saw several more people standing nearby, their physical details obscured mysteriously in the long shadows.

"It's the resistance, man. Right up your alley. Thought you'd be thrilled. More specifically, we're in some kind of old bomb shelter, right?"

Eli looked to his lookalike cousin for confirmation. Rennie started to answer, but was cut off by a voice that rose out from the dark corner.

"It's not just 'some old bomb shelter,' it's the last holdout of human- ity. This is a genuine lead lined fallout shelter. It has its own ventilation and a generator to run the fan and electrical. Only about half a dozen of these puppies made in the entire country that are up to snuff."

The thin girl next to Rennie moved quickly to the corner taking with her an oil lamp. As the shadows lifted, Nate saw a ragged man in his early forties. He was lying on a table that appeared to have some kind of mattress fragments spread out for comfort. His right leg was covered in a thin blanket. His cheeks looked hollow, and Nate could see even from a distance that his eyes were not only sunken, they also had taken on a yellowish tint.

"I'm Paul, this is Sarah, my daughter. You've met Rennie. There are about ten more of us, though they're hiding in the corners, evidently."

With that, more bodies moved forward, some with slightly embarrassed smiles. Nate laid his head back, overcome with the pain that was beginning to turn back into a pinpoint focus. He closed his eyes as Paul continued.

"Lucky we found you, you'd be sitting ducks out there otherwise. This is the last place they'd be able to find you. They can't see through these walls."

Nate felt the words melting around him. He heard rustling at his side and felt a cool wetness on his forehead. He drifted off as *Dear John* began to well up slowly from the corner of his mind.

49

Rosemary was still full from pasta and Greek salad when she set out in search of the mail truck. The building was easy enough to find, just where Will said it would be across from the McDonalds. She couldn't help but wonder why the fast food restaurant still existed. According to the guidebook, Las Vegas was going vegan very soon. The last meat-based buffet items were slated to be removed by the end of the month. The yellow arches now looked ominous and out of place, and there were no vehicles in the parking lot; just a couple of scooters. Upon opening the door, Rosemary was almost tackled by a giant Great Dane with mint blue eyes. His shiny coat was black and white like a Dalmatian, and he stood over six feet tall on his back legs. His weight pushed Rosemary back into the wall, and he stood there for a minute grinning down at her before he jumped down and clumsily ran down a hallway.

"Um, hello? I was told to ask for Kevin, is he here? Will sent me, from the Mirage...hello?"

Rosemary heard a door slam at the end of hallway and the Great Dane came bounding happily back followed by a round little man with a prominent bald spot. His face was speckled red and despite the lines around his eyes that told her the man was at least in his late sixties, there was a fire in his pinched eyes that defied his age.

"Rosemary? Are you she?"
Rosemary nodded. Kevin threw up his hands delightedly.

"Wonderful! Just in time, we're just about to roll. No one's here, so your timing is impeccable. I'm Kevin, this is Mr. Reynolds. I named him after Burt. Hope you don't mind dogs, he's my traveling partner. Aside from a little snoring, he's very agreeable. Did you eat? We don't get much of a chance to stop, the fuel tends to clog otherwise. There's a bathroom on your right if you want a last pit stop. Just meet me through that last door when you're ready."

Without waiting for an answer to any of his questions, Kevin and Mr. Reynolds trotted back down the hallway and through the last door. Rosemary found the little bathroom and for a minute stared at herself in the tiny mirror. It had been a very long time since she had actually looked at herself. Her pale skin looked blue around her dark eyes, and her dark blond hair hung in clumps.

She looked thin, tired, and ready for a long rest. Rosemary pulled her hair back and gathered it with a rubber band she had picked up in her hospital room. She splashed a little water on her face, nervously fingering the pill bottles in her pocket. The idea of spending the next ten hours in a truck with Kevin and his small horse of a dog was terrifying, and her hands had already started a mild level shake. She popped one of the red pills, and tucked the bottle back in her pocket. After one last look, she headed down the hall toward the truck.

The mail truck proved to be much more comfortable than she had expected. There was a small sleeper chamber behind the front seats, big enough for a tiny cot and Mr. Reynolds's blanket, on which he stretched out, a green stuffed alligator in his giant mouth. Rosemary had never really been a dog person, but she had to admit that Mr. Reynolds was charming. Kevin also proved to be charming, and as Will had cautioned, rather talkative.

"Alright, here we go!"

He started the engine with a roar, and pulled out onto the Vegas streets.

"Will said you've been pretty sick, tried to drive straight through in an RV. Bet those scientists were thrilled to pieces to get their hands on that thing. Gas cars are few and far between, nowadays. They need them to run tests on. Keep your eyes open for the soy fields as we leave, it's something else, I'll tell ya. Never would've imagined that, I'm just glad that I got this gig. Most everyone else works shifts in the fields, or on the turbines. That's our solar backup plan. Here they come, lookie there; quite a sight."

Rosemary saw the greenhouses stretching farther into the desert than she could see in the darkness. People wearing smocks and aprons walked the rows with spray cans, buckets, or pushing wheelbarrows. No one seemed connected; they were all intent on their individual purpose.

"I think it looks wonderful, so peaceful."

Kevin chuckled. "Well, to each his own. I'd go crazy out there hauling beans. I need company, that's why I love passengers. Used to drive a Greyhound; lots of company there, course. Mr. Reynolds had to stay behind. He's going on ten years old, that's old for Danes. You have a dog? Wonderful creatures, dogs. You know, Danes were originally herding dogs, they hail from..."

Kevin's voice droned on becoming a comforting backdrop, and from the back, Rosemary heard Mr. Reynolds' muffled snoring. She found her eyelids closing but fought to keep them open. The last thing she needed was to offend Kevin and find herself in the middle of a bean patch without a ride. She lost the battle as Kevin began to explain how Cesar Augustus had used Great Danes in ancient Roman military negotiations. Her eyelids closed and she fell immediately into a dream about the cabin that had grown so far from her mind.

In the dream, the cabin was untouched, Nate was waiting on the deck, his green eyes warm. He was waiting for her; he had kept the cabin from being removed. As Rosemary approached the deck, he turned and smiled, warm and familiar. She rested her head against his shoulder, listening to his heartbeat, Nate's arms moved around her stroking her hair. Kevin's words became the rapid babble of the river, the syllables inconstant and murmuring. Rosemary took Nate's hand and guided to her belly, which had swelled, while his other hand entwined in her hair. Through the dream fog, Rosemary felt a pang of reality and tried to chase it away. The deep hurt grew anyway in her belly, spreading outward, creating static in place of the river's murmur. She groaned and shifted in her sleep, trying to regain what she had lost.

50

"I don't know, man, maybe it's the lead in the walls, maybe it's just that we're underground. Whatever it is, it seems to be off the signmakers' radar."

As usual, Nate hadn't asked the question. Sarah was standing nearby, folding scraps of gauze together to make a bandage. Nate breathed in the stale air as he looked around the stark walls of the last holdout of humanity, as the injured man in the corner had put it. Lead walls didn't seem to make much sense, but Eli was right; whatever it was, the signmakers definitely didn't know these people were here. They never would have let them get this sickly. Nate erased the thought. If it weren't for the signmakers, these people wouldn't even have to be down here. Trying to steady his voice, he turned to Eli.

"Why aren't you pissed off?" he asked, as Eli helped Sarah change the bandage on his head.

"Oh, I was, man. Yeah, damn right I was. Lucky thing you were unconscious during most of my being pissed off. Before I got too peeved, Rennie came running out of the woods like some kind of wolverine! Shit! Scared the crap right out of me. I didn't even realize it was him until we were down here. Haven't seen him in, like, oh Jesus, ten years? Freakin' lucky, huh, man?"

Lucky was not exactly what Nate was thinking as he glanced around the concrete bomb shelter. He'd been awake long enough to realize that he had a gash on his head and more than likely had broken a rib in the crash. Other than that, the pounding from inside was only growing stronger, regardless of the extracurricular injuries he'd suffered. He fought off the voices, but the music beat like a drum. He struggled to concentrate on what Eli was saying. Behind the music, he kept hearing a chant:

"Tired of you, Tired of you, Gonna find a way to dump you, Gonna take the car. Gonna find a way to dump you."

The rhythmic beating of the words made Nate feel as though he might puke. His head felt airy, disconnected. He stared at the room around him through the growing din in his head. It was a dismal scene. In addition to Paul, Sarah and Rennie, ten men and women sat slumped around the room. They were thin and ragged looking. In fact, it seemed as though they'd been here for years. Paul was on the table in a corner, and it was obvious enough even from the short time Nate had been there that something was wrong with his leg. He had also become aware of a pungent smell, the smell of something rotting that made his stomach roll and contract. Sarah, who hadn't yet spoken, ran back and forth between Nate and her father. Nate had seen her lift the blanket covering his right leg and apply wet towels. As she scuttled away with Nate's spent bandage, Eli leaned in and whispered in Nate's ear. His voice was barely audible through the near deafening roar in his own head.

"From what Rennie's told me, man, Paul jacked up his leg a week or so ago. It got infected but he won't go back up, and he won't let any of the others get any medicine from the signmakers. They've been hiding out down here for a few months since Green River was removed. It's a bad scene, man, bad scene."

Eli shut up as Sarah moved quickly past them to her father. The two men watched her lift the blanket gingerly, releasing more of the rotting smell that had been plaguing Nate since he'd been down here.

Nate leaned as close as possible to Eli, whispering quietly. "They're starving...."

Eli looked around cautiously as he whispered back. "Yeah, sound familiar? Mr. I-won't-eat-at-the-buffet-cause-I-don't-know-where-it-came-from."

Nate bristled and glared at Eli, even though he knew his bearded traveling companion was right. Nate looked around at the thin figures lining the dark walls and shivered. The *Dear John* theme song pulsed in his head, as Paul groaned and gently pushed Sarah's hands away from his leg. But he also felt a sudden surge of anger. Goddamn signmakers! This was all their fault. He flashed to Rosemary's face after she'd seen the sign about the boatyard. She had been so happy, so goddamn happy, she'd shut up if she saw this place.

Immediately, he felt a wall on his anger. A voice moved through his crowded head. Nate was only slightly relieved to hear Judd Hirsch.

"Well kid, I tried to warn you. This is exactly where you shouldn't be, you never listen. But why should you listen to me? After all, who am I? I don't know anything. I certainly don't know how to maintain an active career for over three decades, do I? No. Just ignore me. I don't know anything about anybody. So, when I say that you're one step away from being buried alive in this cave, I wouldn't know anything about that, would I? He got you down here, he took you through Green River, he knew these whack jobs were down here. He wants to leave you here. He's acting now, look at his eyes. You can tell he's not feeling it."

Nate squeezed his eyes shut, trying not to look at Eli. He wasn't trapped, no one was holding him hostage. He just needed to stay calm, needed to get to Denver before Rosemary left. He tried to concentrate on her face. Despite his efforts, another voice took up where Judd Hirsch left off.

"You fucking baby! I put my name on the line for you, you little pansy. Now, you're letting this nothing tell you that this is all your fault. You know why he wants to keep you here, don't you? He's probably going for the same part, and judging by you curled here in the fetal position, he's going to get it. You've got to get up, you've got to stop this. You need to make him shut up. You're going to die down here, and no one will ever know what happened to you. You'll choke to death on dirt and no one will care. Your woman will move on; forget about you. No one will know who you are, and it's all his fault."

Nate rubbed at his face, trying to erase Sweater Vest's words. He felt Eli's hands trying to hold his back. Through the fog, he heard Eli's voice as if from a distance.

"Jesus, man! Knock it off! You're rubbing your bandage off, man! Chill!"

Nate lacked the strength to fight Eli. He was shaky and weak. He saw Eli settle back against the wall, looking at him cautiously. Sweater Vest continued, his voice steady and dark.

"You need to take him out if you're going to get out of here. It's your only chance. The others won't stop you. It's him. He's the reason you're stuck. He's the reason you're going to miss your chance. If you don't do it, you'll fade away. They won't even know your name in a year, much less ten, and it's all his fault. He took your woman away, he told her to go. It's his fault. He's killing you."

Nate closed his eyes. The pungent smell of rot faded as Sarah replaced the blanket over Paul's leg. Nate heard some of the others shuffling around. Eli's voice sounded distant, distorted.

"Rennie, man, I've gotta get him oughtta here, he's gonna flip out on you guys like he's been flipping out on me for the last two days. He needs, Jesus, I don't know, something."

Eli's voice was overridden by Sweater Vest's calm and deadly delivery.

"He thinks you're crazy. Do you hear that boy? He thinks you're crazy. You're all you have boy, you're all you have."

Nate twisted away from the sound, struggling to shut up the noise inside his head.

"Shut up! Goddammit, shut up!"

Nate didn't realize he'd said it out loud until he cracked his eyes to see Eli standing overhead. Rennie stood next to him, and a few of the shadowy figures were on the perimeter. Eli turned to Rennie.

"See what I mean?" He turned back to Nate. "Listen, man, I've gotta go back up...." Rennie looked immediately alarmed and started to interrupt. Eli held up a hand to stop him and continued. "No, really, man, I'm going back up. I'm gonna see what I can do with the car. Very least I can grab some of the supplies from the back and bring them down here."

Paul's voice rang out from the corner.

"Rennie! You told him? None of that signmaker shit is going to touch our door!"

Eli turned his head, openly annoyed.

"Jesus, man, calm down. We have other stuff, too. Not much but, I don't know, some fruit cups or something. We took them with us from Mussel Shoals."

The activity caused the noise in Nate's head to subside momentarily, and he tried to concentrate on Eli's words. Judd Hirsch and Sweater Vest were wrong. Eli wasn't going to leave him; he didn't think he was crazy. Rosemary would wait for him. He'd get out of this place and find her.

51

Rosemary woke up close to the I-70 junction in Utah. She was cold, her eyes heavy. She turned her face and started to find Mr. Reynolds at eye level, staring her down with a dog grin.

"Oh, I'm sorry I fell asleep, where are we?"

Kevin scratched Mr. Reynolds' head and eased him back onto his blanket with one hand.

"No worries there, Will said you'd been pretty sick. Hell, sleeping's all that one does every trip." He motioned back to the Great Dane with a friendly smile.

"You feeling better? Best way to travel I think, all asleep. You miss all the time. We're about midway through Utah, not quite halfway there. Amazing how fast this trip goes when there's no traffic. We'll need to stop around the Grand Junction area, I have a drop-off to make, and we could all use a restroom break by then, I imagine. Mr. Reynolds' is a champ at this trip, but that's the maximum for him to hold it, huh boy?"

Mr. Reynolds whined and slapped his tail against the side of the truck.

Rosemary reached behind her and scratched his ear. "What time is it?"

Kevin shrugged his shoulders. "I'm guessing around one in the morning; never keep a watch with me. Damn things aren't worth a darn if ya ask me. Since the atomic clock was dismantled, it doesn't mean a darn thing really. You knew about that didn't you?"

Rosemary sat up and shook her head. Kevin continued.

"Most folks think it was just an accident really, you know the one I'm talking about, doncha? Boulder? Not too far from where you're going. Yeah, whole damn thing disappeared about two months ago. Way I see it, it doesn't make any sense that the signmakers would remove it; after all, it's not bad. You can see why they removed all the guns and drugs—even the gas—but the cesium atom? I mean, I think it was some damn kids got in there and screwed it all up. Doesn't affect much as far as I can see. We follow the sun and the moon, there was time before that big ole clock, and there's time after. Bet it sent all those scientist types in a tailspin. Surprised you didn't hear about that one, the engineers in Vegas were sure in a tizzy."

Kevin chuckled at the memory.

Rosemary phrased her question cautiously. "We, my husband and I, were from Mussel Shoals, near Santa Barbara. You know it?"

Kevin shook his head. "Can't say as I do, but I don't do runs west of Vegas."

Rosemary proceeded, stuttering a little. "Are, are all the towns you see like Vegas? I mean, Mussel Shoals was just like normal, I didn't know any of this was going on. The signmakers sure, but people still had cars, they went to work, there was money, it wasn't really that different."

Kevin pulled a handful of doggie biscuits out of a paper bag on his side of the truck and offered them to Mr. Reynolds who eagerly began crunching.

"Well, I'll tell ya. I don't know any more than anybody else, except that I see a lot of places you wouldn't see otherwise. I can tell you this much: if things there weren't all falling to hell, if there were a lot of group-type homes, like hospitals, or nursing homes, that kind of thing, then you might not have had a lot of changes. Now, the cars, the gas, the money, I bet that's changed. It's better this way though, take my word for it. There's been a lot of changes in the last month. I bet if you went back to Mussel Shoals was it? I bet if you went back there right now, you'd find a whole heap of new signs all over the place, and all those cars'd be gone. That's how it happened back in Vegas, anyway. They moved everyone downtown, and then one day all the cars were removed. Sure were a lot of angry people, but they got over it. People are only angry if they think someone's paying attention; like kids ya know?"

Rosemary's head was spinning. "But why this last month? Why didn't I know anything was happening? What happened to the news? Television?"

Kevin shook his head. "Can't really say, except looks to me like the stuff that's going on, the soy bean fields back in Vegas, the turbines, even the vegetarian food—which is taking some getting used to let me tell ya—took a whole lot of time to get done. I think it's all happening now just because it wasn't ready before. Don't know about the television, the news. I take it you weren't much of a TV watcher before?"

Rosemary shook her head.

"Nate, my husband was, but I never really cared much about it."

Kevin smoothed is thinning hair back. "Good. I think that's good. Stuff'l rot your brain right out. I used to love watching the ball games and some of those reality shows where you'd get a bunch of people living together, you know? Guess you might not, but one day, it all cut out. No explanation. The sign came round a day or so later, said that communication would now be done through letter correspondence. That gets you to me."

Rosemary was incredulous.

"Why, though? It doesn't make any sense. They had television back at the hospital."

Kevin laughed.

"Oh, those reruns? Yeah, they started piping those in about a month ago; guess they figured we needed some kind of entertainment. I think I've seen every episode of that show now. They'll catch on after awhile, maybe change it to MASH; love that one. I don't know a lot of the why's, but I can guess. You wanna hear a good guess?"

Rosemary nodded.

"Alright, here she goes. I think they cut out the television and the radio, Internet, all that jazz in the beginning because of how riled up folks got. You got to keep people under control if you want to change anything, too easy to organize all those angry people together if they can communicate with one another through phones, and emails, and television. I think they cut it out so we wouldn't have a full-scale war on our hands. Maybe I'm crazy, and granted I think the signmakers are a real blessing, but I think nothing would've changed if we'd had our say in it. We're stubborn like that, ya know? Folks say they want something different, something better but when it comes down to it, we sure as hell don't want any help getting it. My little girl, when she was about four or five, used to run around telling everyone 'I'll do it myself!' She meant it, too. Dropped a whole tray of food in a restaurant one time, everyone looked at me like I was the monster who made her carry it. What they didn't know was that if I hadn't let her try she'd have pitched a fit bigger than all that spilled food. I think most folks are like my little girl. We'd rather make a big mess and say we did it ourselves before we let anyone step in and carry our tray."

Kevin fell silent. Rosemary felt oddly calm; she liked this man. She could see him with his little girl, maybe a pretty wife.

"How old is your little girl now?"

Kevin perked up with the change of subject.."Oh, she's nearly thirty now; 'bout your age, I'd say. She's in Decatur, works with the water recycling people. Smart one she is, heap of a lot smarter than her old man. If it wasn't for my truck license, I'd be in the bean fields. You have kids?"

Rosemary hesitated and realized that she was actually comfortable, more comfortable talking to this man than she had been talking to Nate in years.

"No, not yet anyway. I, I actually had a miscarriage, that's why I was in the hospital in Vegas." Rosemary realized that this was the first time she'd actually spoken the words, the lump in her throat climbed higher choking her. 'I ... my husband, he's been out of work for a long time. I don't know what I was thinking; we didn't even have anything for a baby...." Rosemary swallowed the sob that rose with the words. " I need everything to change, I need to find him."

Kevin reached over and squeezed her hand.

"That's a real shame, but I'll bet you're right, I bet things will change for you. You'll love what the signmakers have done with Denver. You find your husband, you let them set you up in one of those big buildings downtown; they'll assign you work, don't you worry. He won't be out of a job there. Even if it doesn't work out the old-fashioned way, I bet you can adopt a baby. They take care of it for you now, you know? My daughter has a little boy, she requested him and a few days later, there he was. Beautiful little guy, too. No more forms, no more waits. You'll see. Used to be you had to be a damn millionaire to adopt; now, they look at what's in your heart, and they take care of the rest. I have a feeling you'll be just fine."

Rosemary eased back as Kevin told her all about his daughter, Ella, and her little boy. The love in his voice overshadowed her worries, and she allowed herself to relax for the first time in days.

52

Nate woke with a start to the sound of Eli spilling a bag of canned food on the floor. There wasn't nearly as much as Nate remembered taking from the Priceplan. Through his fog, he remembered that they'd left quite a bit behind in Las Vegas. The men and women were excitedly sorting through the contents of the small shopping bag that Eli had pulled from the back seat of the Honda. Nate didn't even remember his leaving. In truth, he had been in and out of sleep for the last few hours, fighting off Judd Hirsch and Sweater Vest. They had quieted down, but the voices had been replaced with a high pitched light that seemed to bore into Nate's pupils. He closed his eyes, but he still felt the pressure, the whine of the electricity. He felt like he was going to vomit, and the sight of the food made him realize that he hadn't eaten for over a day now. Eli grabbed a can of pre-made tuna salad and came trotting over, looking pleased with himself.

"Here, man, signmaker-free food. I don't want to take much away from these guys, they ran out of supplies, what, two days ago?"

Eli looked to Rennie for confirmation; he nodded back. Paul spoke from the corner, his voice hoarse.

"We raided stores before Green River was permanently removed; we've taken care of our people. We're just waiting for backup to arrive from Salt Lake."

He leaned his head back, his eyes closed. Eli glanced at Rennie before answering.

"Yeah, man, you're welcome, too...it was no problem man...I can see everyone down here's just great. Good job, man!"

Paul started awake, leaned forward, wincing in pain.

"Fuck you! Who are you, anyway? What? You bring us a few cans of food and you think you can judge us? We're fighting this thing; what are you do-ing?"

Sarah came flying past, giving Eli a warning look as he started to retort. Nate watched as she helped her father lie back down, briefly checking his leg. The smell was stronger now, overwhelming. Through his pinhole vision, Nate saw the wound for just a moment before the girl covered it back up. There was a large cut, the flesh around it purple and black. Yellow puss leaked from the edges, staining the blanket. Nate was suddenly glad for his lack of clear sight; nevertheless, he gagged and fought the urge to dry heave. He pushed the can of tuna salad away from him. Eli persisted.

"C'mon man, you have to eat something, you can't pass out on me, and I need you to get back up there."

He leaned in closer.

"Nate, dude, you don't want to stay here, man. We're outta here, soon as I can get the Honda to start. Hell, maybe we should just take off even if it doesn't. Someone's gotta find us on the road."

The pinpoint light glared brighter than Nate could stand. He groaned with the icy pain that accompanied it. He heard the movement around him and it made him dizzy. He could still hear Eli's voice whispering in his ear; something about the car, something about the solar panels. Fuck, he couldn't concentrate on the words. The light shut them out. He began to hear a sharp sound growing in strength and proximity. It sounded like a stick or a pole being smacked against a wall. Thump, thump, thump.

Nate tried to visualize Rosemary's face, her hands; he tried to remember her smell. Thump, thump thump. Eli's voice stopped. He became aware that Eli had moved away from his ear and out of his immediate space. Nate clawed at his ears, trying to block the noise. Thump, thump...it grew louder and louder.

"He thinks you're crazy, he's trying to get rid of you, he thinks you're crazy, he's trying to get rid of you. He'll dump you somewhere, he'll leave you here, he thinks he holds the cards. He thinks you're crazy."

Sweater Vest's voice was little more than a whisper, but somehow it overpowered the steadily growing sound of the stick hitting the wall. Behind his eyelids, Nate saw Sweater Vest sitting in a director's chair, a hand carved walking stick in his hand. The details were elaborate, ornate; they curved into a hollow carving of an orb at the top.

"You're losing it. You gave me Gandolph's staff, you crazy fuck. What in the hell would I have to do with Gandolph's staff? You're turning out to be a huge disappointment; I can't see why they recommended you, fought for you. You're a hack! You give me every little thing you ever saw on TV. I'm surprised I don't have a pet monkey and homemade pink prom dress. You wasted your life watching that television crap day after day. You want to be a TV actor boy? Is that what you're made of? Pathetic."

Nate watched in stunned silence as Sweater Vest slammed the staff into the floor, chipping the concrete with each blow. A slow smile spread on his face, his teeth yellow and ragged. Nate scrambled backward, slamming his head into the wall. From outside his head, he heard scrambled movement, felt hands pulling him down. He fought against the pressure, trying to twist away from them.

He suddenly snapped awake; Sweater Vest was gone, but the chant had only increased in strength.

"He thinks you're crazy, he's going to leave you here, he thinks you're crazy..."

Nate felt arms grabbing him around his waist, felt his body moving toward the door. Through the bright pinholes, he saw a long hallway, saw the faces of the starving resistance fading away. He slumped against a wall while a heavy metal door was thrown open. Arms reached down and pulled him up. Nate felt the rush of icy air and the frozen ground beneath him. His head and eyes cleared for just a moment, and he saw Eli, panting, leaning against a tree. Nate sat up a little, groaning with the effort. Eli stumbled forward, closing the metal door as he approached Nate.

"Dude, that's it, man. We're out. I was about to flip out, too, but I'm just not as good at it as you, man. Dude, you awake?"

Nate managed a nod, the pinpoint of light was fading, Eli's voice became a little clearer.

"Can you walk, man? C'mon, let's get to the road. We'll get the car going together. Maybe there's someone who'll pick us up, remember science dude said there were mail trucks...."

Nate pulled himself up with considerable effort. The tomblike air of the bomb shelter vanished. Eli started to take his arm, but Nate waved him away.

"I...I'm alright, I think I'll be alright."

53

By the time Rosemary, Kevin and Mr. Reynolds had reached Grand Junction, it was near three in the morning, or so the clock on the postal building indicated. The trip had flown by. Kevin had told Rosemary all about his daughter and her little boy, and his wife, who died from diabetes about five years ago. He told her all about their wedding, their first apartment in Decatur, Ella's birth, her crazy high school boyfriends. By the time the mail truck pulled into the garage, Rosemary felt like she had known Kevin for years.

As soon as the door opened, Mr. Reynolds perked up and climbed from the back, over Rosemary and out the door. He made a beeline for the grassy median behind the garage. Kevin laughed.

"Told ya! Grand Junction's as far as he can make it. We'll be here for a little bit, there's a washroom down the hall, and there should be a waitress out front if you're hungry or need anything. Don't wander too far, I'll find ya, when we're ready."

Rosemary found the little bathroom and when she was ready, she headed out the front door to find the waitress Kevin had mentioned. She was hungry again, and she wasn't about to let this opportunity go by. From experience, Rosemary knew that Grand Junction was about six hours from Denver. It'd probably take even more time since it was beginning to spit snow. Rosemary pulled the purple sweatshirt from around her waist and pulled it over her head, enjoying the crisp night air. She was worried about something they had seen on the road, outside of what used to be Green River. There had been a car by the side of the road. She had interrupted Kevin and drawn his attention to it, but he told her that stopping was not an option. Evidently, there were still people living in the area, and a mail truck had actually been robbed a little over a month ago. Kevin wouldn't stop, but promised to tell the Grand Junction people as soon as they arrived. They would go back and make sure the owner of the car wasn't hurt.

Somehow, Rosemary had a feeling about the car, a panicky feeling that she couldn't understand. There was no reason for it, except that the car looked so out of place all by itself. It was hard to tell in the dark, but it looked like it was all set up with some kind of panel system. Kevin had told her about the solar cars the engineers were working on back in Vegas. Don't worry, he said. He explained that they do test runs on all their cars between Vegas and Greeley, and that they would know what to do to fix it. He'd sounded so sure, but Rosemary had trouble shaking the image from her mind. She imagined *Lazy Daze* by the side of the road outside of Rancho Cucamonga, how she should have accepted help from anyone she could find. She felt much better, but still shaky. Rosemary reached into her pocket and dry swallowed one of the antibiotics. She fingered the other bottle and then put it back in her pocket. She didn't need it. For the first time since high school, she didn't need it.

In addition to telling her all about his family, Kevin had also told her more about Denver. Evidently, it had been consolidated to the downtown area, a little of Capitol Hill and that was it. Denver was working on a wind power initiative, and had already begun the soybean fields courtesy of the research and development station in Greeley. Kevin knew exactly where 19th and Sherman was, he would take her there, don't you worry. She didn't have the heart to tell him that finding her mother was the least of her worries right now.

Rosemary spotted the waitress about a block down. With a nervous look on her face, she started out. She didn't want Kevin to leave without her, but he had said it would be awhile. The streets were dark; the mail station seemed to be the only thing out here. Rosemary wondered where they had housed everybody since there weren't any skyscrapers, or business towers. The waitress more than happy to deliver an egg sandwich, French fries and bottled water. As Rosemary headed back, she saw Kevin on the sidewalk, looking from side to side.

"Kevin! I'm over here!"

He squinted into the darkness and waved.

"There ya are! Guess that waitress moved on me; used to be right out here. Hold on just a second and let me get a bite and we'll be on our way."

Rosemary shivered in the cold, her senses heightened by the early hour. Mr. Reynolds came bounding from the back of the mail center and plastered himself against the glass as he saw Kevin hustling back up the sidewalk. Kevin carried a little bag like Rosemary had, and a plastic bowl with what looked like dog food.

"Alrighty there, gotta give Mr. Reynolds a little dinner break. Lucky for you and me, he's fast."

They headed inside, and Rosemary stretched her legs on a plastic waiting chair. Kevin set about filling a second bowl with water as Mr. Reynolds wolfed down his dinner.

"Hey, can I ask you....where is everybody here? Where did they house everyone?"

Kevin pointed at the street and to the right.

"Mesa State, they moved everyone onto the campus. They left a few buildings but not many. Left this one for mail. There's no one here now. We drop it off and they come to sort it in the morning. I left a note about that car we saw, don't you worry. They'll send someone back to make sure it's not stranded. It'll be all right. I know that spooked ya a little. It is strange, I'll give you that. Don't see many folks out on the road anymore. But I'll bet ya it's one of those super solar hybrid science machines the engineers in Vegas are always working on. They don't have it right yet; have a hell of a time finding people to test drive 'em. Seems like they never quite make it past those wind turbines back there in Vegas. Fact, this is the farthest out I've ever seen one. Anyhow, I think Mr. Reynolds is all done, best get him back in the cab before he falls asleep here on the floor."

It was true, Mr. Reynolds was laying beside his empty bowls, eyes drooping.

"Yep, once you miss your opportunity with this one, you're done. He'd sooner sleep here in the lobby than climb back up into the truck."

As the truck pulled out and back onto the road, Rosemary looked around for lights. The campus was brightly lit, but that was all. It was lonely here, and she wondered if Nate had felt the same way when he came through; if he'd come through. She nudged the thought out of her head. She nibbled on a French fry as she tried to imagine him with her Mom and Chuck, and Lilly nearby. Maybe he would be laughing about all this, and they'd all be telling "goofy Rosemary" stories. In truth, she hated that tradition. In it, her mother and sister would tell anyone who cared to listen all the embarrassing things Rosemary had ever done. Included on the list was the time she had run into the sliding glass door, breaking her little toe. They never talked about the toe, but they did revel in mentioning what her face looked like when Rosemary realized there was a door in the way.

It drove her as crazy now as it did when she was thirteen. Lilly had always been Mom's ally; they were more similar than Rosemary and her Mom. They even looked alike; same round face, same curvy hips and big boobs, even the hair. They both had long, curly black hair that Rosemary ran her fingers through as little girl, wishing it were hers, while her mother sunbathed on the porch. No, Rosemary looked like her father, angular face, hazel eyes, even his caramel colored hair. When she was growing up and had gone anywhere with her mom and Chuck, people usually assumed she was Lilly's friend; no one believed they were related.

"Ya alright over there? Lookin' sad, you're not worrying about Denver again, are ya? Let me tell you why you shouldn't be worrying so much."

Rosemary turned her head toward Kevin and daydreamed about the things he told her; rooftop gardens and soybean fields surrounding the city. It was a beautiful vision; Rosemary just hoped it wasn't too late.

54

The sun started to peek out from around the horizon around half past five. Although Nate knew it would be another hour before it was in the sky, and longer still before it was high enough to charge the solar panels, it came as a big relief. He was curled up in the front seat, a blanket wrapped tightly around him. Eli was much the same on the driver's side.

The cold air held the chanting voices to a dull static, and Nate almost felt normal, although deep in the pit of his stomach he knew he'd crossed a line by allowing the voices to go places he'd always been able to defend before. Eli had fallen asleep despite the freezing temperatures. Nate watched him breathe in and out. He had no idea whether Eli had been able to fix the car when he'd come to get the food. He had been afraid to ask. Nate felt weak; his spirit felt drained. Eli had always followed him, Nate had called the shots; now, he was little more than an infant. He also knew that Eli was barely holding back his anger. The part of Nate's brain that had defrosted despite the cold, night air sighed and accepted Eli's frustration. Of course he was pissed; he'd been cleaning up after Nate for two days. Now, they were stuck by the side of the road with two options in front of them: a basement full of starved shadows or a broken car on an abandoned highway.

At one point, a truck had rumbled past. It never slowed, and the lights disappeared into the night as fast as they had arrived. Eli had jumped out; waved uselessly at the darkness. Nate hadn't reacted. He had already known the driver wouldn't stop. What's more, he knew the truck shouldn't stop. He didn't need Sweater Vest or Judd Hirsch to tell him that, he felt it. The truck rolling on in the night felt like inevitability, it felt like a weight dropping and settling at the bottom of a lake. Eli had climbed back into the driver's seat, and without a word fallen asleep.

To take his mind off his frozen toes, Nate tried to remind himself of all the things he loved about Rosemary—as a safeguard against his darker thoughts. He tried to remember how she first looked when he saw her in that class in Santa Barbara. He almost smiled thinking about her reaction whenever anything scared her. Nate remembered the time he had burst into the houseboat unexpectedly when Rosemary was cooking over the propane stove. At the time, she was stirring a big boiling pot of something. First, she had frozen, obviously trying to figure out what the noise was and what to do. Then, she had turned and with closed eyes hurled the big spoon at the doorway, hitting Nate precisely in the middle of his forehead. She then opened her eyes, recognized what she'd done, and screamed. The entire series of events had taken less than five seconds, but it had taken her more than half an hour to calm down. Initially, Nate tried to be sympathetic, but couldn't stop laughing. The idea that in her adrenaline-controlled state she could fend off an attacker with a ladle struck him as hilarious.

He also loved the way she developed a deep wrinkle over her right eye when she was trying to concentrate on something. Her entire face would squint up, and this big rivet would form. It became deeper and more pronounced if she was trying to follow one of Nate's explanations. The depth of the rivet had become Nate's indicator of whether his idea was just a little crazy, or totally nuts. Rosemary was entirely unconscious of it, too. He had brought it up once, and she looked at him, rivet in place, and shook her head. Nate considered it his secret, something he knew about Rosemary that even she didn't know.

All these little memories helped, but they made his stomach ache with anxiety. He had no evidence that she had even gone to Denver. He had been thinking about the cabin she had talked about when her Dad passed. Nate had never seen it; Rosemary remembered it only vaguely. It had been passed on to her, along with a mountain of hospital bills and credit card debt. Most of that had been forgiven or paid off with the insurance money, but not all. Nate had pleaded with Rosemary to sell the cabin. They could pay off her Dad's Master-Card, the last remaining hospital bills, upgrade the generator on *Clementine*; but she had refused. Stubborn. She might go to the cabin. Nate wondered if it was still there. If it had met the same fate as all the cabins in Green River, then it likely had been removed some time ago. Nate assumed that Denver and the surrounding area had been consolidated Vegas style. He really had no idea how to find her once they hit the city, if she was indeed there. He sighed, the cramps in his stomach increasing with each new worry.

"They didn't think it would be a hit, you know. Horror never makes the Oscars; never gets any recognition. I showed them, I pulled their heads out of their asses, is what I did. You have potential, boy. You could make it big, boy. You remind me of Adrian. He didn't listen to the Hollywood motherfuckers who ran me out of town. He followed his heart. Next thing you know, he's kissing Halle Berry. I know talent; you need to let go of all this crap, boy. You need to keep your eye on the prize. You'll be the reason I get to move out of motherfucking Poland. You want to know how cold Poland gets in the winter? It'll freeze your balls off."

Sweater Vest's voice whispered in Nate's ear. He closed his eyes and tried to block it out, tried to chant something that would drown it out. The only thing he could remember was the pledge of allegiance.

"I pledge allegiance to the flag...and the republic for which it stands..."

The voice continued; unaffected.

"You need to drop the dead weight. Potential isn't enough, you need wings. You'll never get far enough to make anyone remember if you keep babysitting and letting the piranhas nip at your flesh. You're stuck; it's their fault. You keep catering to him, you let him insult you, you let him walk all over you; you're letting him get in your way. For what? What is he doing that you couldn't do? And faster? You'd be there by now if it hadn't been for his crying." Nate squinted his eyes shut.

"of the United States of America and the republic for which..."

The voice became louder, more intense. "You're letting that little whore jerk you around too. You've let her lead you around by the balls for years now. She's made a laughingstock out of you. She fucked other men in your bed, she laughed in your face, she loathes the sight of you. She left you because you weren't useful to her anymore; you were too old, too crazy, too weak. She's laughing right now in the arms of her lover. She left you for him, you know. She left you for him. She left you for him."

Nate was shaking side to side and kept repeating the words.

"the republic of the United States of America for which it stands, one nation..."

Unrelenting, Sweater Vest continued. "He has a great big cock, she does things with him that you know nothing about. All that shyness, all that fake sweetness; it's an act, a game, and you fell for it. Without her, you could be great. You could be somebody. Right now, you're a little boy following his mommy around. Pathetic. You need to break the tie. You need to take your power back. You need to stand up and be a man."

The voice suddenly cut out and was replaced by Judd Hirsch.

"Kid, he's telling you the truth, you need to stop this bullshit and do something about it, I've been trying to tell you for years, maybe you'll listen to Roman. He's a fucking genius you know. We worked on a project years ago; never made it to print because of the goddamn accountants. It would have brought me back, made them notice. Don't make my mistake kid, don't let your chance go by. You could be famous, you could be a star."

Judd Hirsch's ramblings actually took the edge off those of Sweater Vest. Roman's ramblings? Nate began to breathe deep as he continued to repeat:

"The United States republic one nation, under God, forever and ever..."

The voices melded into one, and faded. Nate realized that every muscle in this body was tensed. As he opened his eyes, he felt an intense pain in the side of his head and saw Eli's face hovering over his. He realized that Eli was straddling him, pinning his arms back.

"Man! Freakin' Christ, man! You alright? You awake? Your head, man. Your freakin' head, man!"

Eli fell back into his seat and Nate reached up to the pressure point on the side of his head. His hand was sticky with warm blood. As he turned to the window he saw it was shattered, the sealant holding the spider web pattern dangerously in place,

"Man, you kept muttering the pledge of allegiance, like from school man, and banging your head, I tried to stop you but you were like a freakin' rock. Least you didn't try to jump me again. But damn, you all right?"
Nate shook his head, the pain swimming from side to side.

"I...no...I, we need to go...can we go? I need to get there, they're getting worse. I need to see her, show them they're wrong. They're wrong, I know they're wrong."

Eli collapsed back against the seat. "Look, the Honda isn't going to start until the sun charges her up or the gas unfreezes. Either way, man, that's not going to happen for a while. The sun just came up, man; I can't make nature happen faster just because you're freaking out again. You're just going to have to let it go, dude."

Eli reached into the back and handed Nate what looked like a clean mechanics rag. Nate pressed it against the side of his head, the fresh pain making his shudder.

"Eli, I have to ask you this, it's important. You saw Rosemary in a car back in Mussel Shoals, didn't you?"
Eli nodded his head, confused.

"I, it's, I mean, was she alone? Was there anyone else in the car, like a guy?"

Eli's face was incredulous. "No, man. She was alone. Is that what all this craziness is about? You think she ran off with some dude? You really are nuts. Did you forget that I was there for part of that argument? I heard how you were talking to her, man, I would have left your crazy ass, too. I don't know her as well as you, man, but I would bet my life that she isn't off with some other dude. You have a good lady, the fact that you haven't run her off before now is a miracle."

Nate leaned back. "A simple 'no' would have done."

Eli's face was turning red. "No, it wouldn't, man. You think I didn't hear what you were thinking earlier? All that nasty shit you were thinking about her? Scared the shit out of me. You need to let all that anger go, man. It's not on her; it's all about you. Rosemary did what she had to do, and now you have to suck it up and try to get her back. If you go at her all angry and accusing her, she's going to kick your pathetic ass back to Mussel Shoals, and good on her if she does. Keep with those thoughts you had earlier. The ones about her wrinkles and her face when she got spooked. That's what you need to concentrate on, man, not your fucking paranoia about some other dude that doesn't exist."

Nate turned away. He knew Eli was right, but the darkness that had gathered at the back of his thoughts wouldn't release its grip. As he dabbed the blood off his face, he tried to replay more pleasant memories.

55

As the mail truck approached the Glenwood Springs area, the sun began to rise over the mountains. Big, white flakes drifted lazily down and blew past the windshield. It was cold in the cab; Mr. Reynolds had folded himself under his blanket and was snoring soundly. Kevin slowed as they approached a sign.

> To Whom It May Concern
> The road system in and around Glenwood Springs
> Has been deemed wasteful
> Please be advised that the remaining
> Route is considerably narrower.
> Proceed with caution

"Huh," snorted Kevin. "Didn't count on that. I knew it was coming, they've warned us about it for a few weeks now, but I'll be interested to see what they came up with."

Rosemary remembered vaguely the elaborate highway system in and out of Glenwood Springs; it had cut into the canyon and had multiple levels. She thought she remembered her mom telling her about the landslides in the area, but Rosemary had been here only a few times. After her father had been sent to the institution, she tried to visit, but she got only as far as the canyon highway the first time before she turned back.

The second time she made it to town and up to the institution, but her father had been "feeling sick" that day, so he was unavailable. The first time she saw him while he was in the hospital was nearly a year later. She had flown to Denver and driven her mother's minivan the four hours to Glenwood. It was about twelve years ago, she was newly married to Nate at the time, and brought with her a mini album from their wedding. Her dad had been invited, but of course, wasn't well enough to leave the hospital. Rosemary sent him the invitation hoping they would give him a day pass, or that he would respond, but he hadn't; not even with a card. She never told anyone of her disappointment, never told them she even invited her Dad. Rosemary knew her mother would think it was crazy and knew what her response would be:

"Why in the world would he be able to come to your wedding? He's in a loony bin; he's not at summer camp."

Intellectually, Rosemary knew that she was exactly right and her father probably couldn't have come, even if he wanted to. Emotionally, she wanted him to try.

He looked thin when she saw him finally, and very much older. The gray in his hair was no longer in streaks. In fact, for the most part, his head was shaved. Rosemary remembered wondering if he had wanted it done or the doctors forced it on him. He smiled quietly. It was the first time since Rosemary's operation that they had seen each other. She went in with a list of questions she wanted to ask, among them the wedding and her hospital stay. She wanted to know why he hadn't said goodbye, why he disappeared. She wanted to know what he thought about, if he thought about her. However, when Rosemary saw him, wearing ill-fitting jeans and a yellow t-shirt, the questions disappeared. He looked fragile, breakable. Mentally, she tucked her list away and smiled back.

He asked her about Nate, he wanted to know about living on a house-boat. He wanted to hear about her job, her friends. Whatever started out awkward became soft. By the time Rosemary left, her heart was light. The choking sob that she had swallowed on the way to Glenwood finally dissipated. She never told her mother about the visit. As far as Mom knew, Rosemary had taken the car for the day to visit friends down in Colorado Springs. Rosemary wasn't sure why she didn't want her to know, it just seemed as though something too fragile to mention would be broken by talking about it.

About six months later, the attorney who had contacted Rosemary before called to say that her father had been moved to a halfway house in Lakewood, nearly four hours away. Rosemary occasionally received postcards from her dad with pictures of downtown Denver. It was almost as if he had forgotten that she grew up there. Eventually, they slowed to one or two postcards a year. Rosemary wrote back and included photographs of Nate and *Clementine*. Once, she even sent a very small shell she'd found on the beach. It was enough—enough to remind her that he really did exist.

Kevin snatched her from her reverie with a loud "Whoa," and Rosemary swiveled her head across the windshield to see what had alerted her new friend. In place of the canyon highway was a two-lane dirt road that seemed to follow the path of the lower highway tier. Everything else had been removed and fresh, young trees had been planted where the dirt had been disturbed. The river was high with runoff, and chunks of ice stuck to the sides and occasionally broke off before they hurtled downstream.

"Didn't think they'd do that. Well, you ready for an adventure?" Kevin grinned and put the truck in gear, crawling forward.

"We're so wide, is it…will we even fit?"

Kevin laughed.

"We'll see soon enough. The signmakers know about our trucks, so I figure they wouldn't try to run us off the road quite yet. Lucky for us, or unlucky I guess, this side is not nearly bad as leaving Glenwood."

Rosemary automatically grabbed for a seatbelt only to find that there were none present.

"Is Glenwood Springs still here? It's so small; it doesn't seem like much to save."

Kevin was squinting through the snow, slowly navigating the road. "Oh, yeah, they moved everyone in from the surrounding area. No more cabins or lodges. All those hotels here gave everyone plenty of room. They run water purification research out here. The signs say they're trying to figure a way to irrigate crops without adding chemicals. Quite a task if you ask me. Do you have any idea how many chemicals used to be in drinking water? Baffles the mind; our livers must be made of steel. I'll tell you..."

Kevin began another tangent as he inched along. Rosemary contentedly eased back and watched the snow fall into the river as Kevin's voice rose and fell with his story.

56

By now, the sun was rising steadily, but the Honda still wouldn't start. Nate knew it was too soon, so did Eli, but still every time the engine ground and died, he felt himself slip a little more. He tried to follow Eli's advice, which was that every time a nasty thought started to get its claws into Nate's head, he should try to replace it with something. But Nate was having trouble combating the latest one. Every once in awhile, Eli would look at him and shake his head to indicate that he was listening to the ugliness, and even that became increasingly annoying to Nate. Who told him I needed babysitting? Why was he so concerned all of a sudden? It seemed to Nate that during this trip and throughout the years he'd known Eli, he didn't know a damn thing about his family, his love life, if he was straight, gay, anything. Nate had no idea.

"Man, don't turn this on me. You don't know because you don't ask. Simple as that. You want to know?"

Nate stared at Eli blankly, still spooked by Eli's psychic radar.

"I'll make it short, man, so you can go back to your gloom and doom. I'm straight; I just don't see many ladies. None ever came around the marina. Believe it or not, I was actually engaged once, a long time ago; before you moved into the neighborhood. My folks live in Pismo. Dad ran a hardware store and my mom's a paralegal. That enough for you? Satisfied? I have a sister, married a rich guy, moved to Boise, popped out three kids. She sends me inspirational audiocassettes about how I should go to college, become a stockbroker, and move to Wall Street. You imagine me on the Street, man? Crazy. Doesn't matter, man. You still need to concentrate on whatever the fuck it is you're working out man."

Nate's head was throbbing from the incident with the car window. The bleeding had slowed, but a thin trickle still oozed from behind his ear. Nate wondered how much blood you could lose before it became a problem. Between that and the gash on his forehead from the previous accident, Nate had lost plenty. Eli tried the engine again; it didn't even stir this time.

"Okay, man. I'm going to put the biofuel out in the sun. Maybe that'll thaw it out some. Just stay here. You should've eaten when you had the chance. All those cans are long gone now, man."

With that, Eli opened the driver's side door and climbed out. He cracked the rear door enough to pull out the congealed cans of biofuel. To Nate, the stuff looked like the grease pan his mother kept underneath the sink when he was growing up. Whenever you threw out grease, you scraped it into the grease can, and the result was a can full of lardy fat speckled with bits of bacon and burn smudge. That grease can made Nate become vegetarian when he went to college. The smell of the solidified bacon drippings and their transformation into the milky white paste overwhelmed Nate whenever he looked at a hamburger or slice of bacon.

The memory wasn't pleasant, but it was a distraction. Suddenly, Nate began to smell a musky cologne and automatically began shaking his head.

"No no no no no no no no."

His chant was answered with the full-force return of the voices.

"He thinks you're crazy; he's going to leave you here. He thinks you're crazy. Drop the dead weight. He thinks you're crazy."

From the edge of his vision, the bright light returned, this time moving from the outside in. Nate shook his head and tried to push it away. Judd Hirsh was sitting in the driver's seat, staring at him coldly. From the back of the car, Nate heard Sweater Vest's voice rise like a siren.

"Drop the dead weight, boy! You want someone to feel sorry for you? You need someone to babysit you? He'll leave you here, he'll leave you to the wolves, boy. You'll starve with the rest of the groundlings and your chance will be gone forever."

Nate's mind turned nonsensically to a game Rosemary's mom had sent them last Christmas. A coin trapped in a metal sphere. The trick was to remove the coin. Nate had spent days spinning it, dropping it, and shaking it only for it to fall apart in his hands, releasing the coin. So simple. All along it had been so simple.

Nate watched Eli shake the gas cans as the musky smell grew stronger, overpowering. He heard the chant; ranting, unrelenting.

"He thinks you're crazy. He thinks you're crazy."

Eli tromped around outside on the snow-powdered Earth, shaking out his legs. The musk was stinging his senses and Nate sneezed loudly. Eli didn't notice, just kept on doing his shake-walk. Nate became dizzy from the scent, and he opened the door to feel the crispness of the air, but the scent lingered and turned sour. Suddenly, Nate began to feel a pounding in his head. Every step Eli took reverberated in his skull.

"No no no no no no no no no no no no..."

The chant didn't help; in fact, Nate heard a chuckle that caused him to turn and discover Judd Hirsch sitting stone faced beside him. As he slowly faced forward again, he was blinded by the sun and felt a hand cover his mouth.

"I see how it is now. You need someone to tell you what you already know, what you've already seen with your own eyes? I see it now. I thought you were more...more powerful than that. But if you want to spend your life having someone else convince you of what you already know, then so be it. I'll hire another face, another set of lights for my movie. They'll forget you, you'll fade away."

Nate tried to scream but the hand held tight.

"You know what you saw. You don't need this coward, this eunuch out here to tell you what you saw. She pulled out of your little shithole, driving a Benz, accompanied by a younger, richer, more exciting version of you. She's with him right now. She's naked in his bed, laughing at you, feeling sorry for you. She knows you know where she is, and with whom. Women are snakes, and you're the rat, boy."

Nate thrashed back and forth, the pounding increasing with each step outside. Nate tried to reach the windshield. Eli would finally see and he'd wake him up, tell him it wasn't a Benz, there wasn't someone else.

"She's got you half down her throat; you're fighting the dying light, boy. If you had any balls, you'd claw your way back out and strike her down, her and her new boyfriend. I doubt you'll do that though, any more time here and you'll be in her belly. You need to get out of here. He won't let you. He's holding you back from your fate. He's holding up filming of my greatest work, and I hate wasted film, Nate. Time is money, Nate. It's his fault you're stuck; it's his fault she got away. It's all his fault. You're going to piss away the chance of a lifetime because you are too much of a pussy to stand up for yourself."

Nate was clawing at his face, trying to remove the hand, and this had finally drawn Eli's attention. Somewhere on the periphery of Nate's senses, he felt Eli's hands, heard his voice. They were like phantoms, insubstantial.

"Look kid, you need to listen to the boss, here. You need to grow up, kid. Stop blaming everyone else and do something. Show that little bitch what happens when you're disloyal. You have to do this; it's my career on the line, your career, your entire purpose. You were meant to be big, kid. If you piss and moan it all away, then you better believe I'll personally come after you."

Eli's voice and hands broke through only vaguely. Nate was trying to pull the sweaty hand off his face but the grip was like iron. It was holding his head straight so that Nate couldn't turn to see Sweater Vest or Judd Hirsch.

"I don't know why I've put up with you as long as I have, boy. You sit here in love, or so you think, and the joke's on you, boy. The joke's on you! She isn't thinking about you, she's worrying about what matching panty set to wear to bed tonight. She's a whore, boy! A whore!"

Nate felt his body hit hard ground, but the iron grip on his mouth persisted. He was rolling, and from a distance, Nate felt a sharp stabbing in his back.

"He's killing you! This is what dying feels like, boy. You're letting him kill you; you're weak, you're inconsistent, you're all wrong for this role." Roman's voice was suddenly replaced by that of Judd Hirsch.

"It's true kid, you need to raise your fists. If you don't, you'll die here in God knows where, alone. You have to make it there, you need to take care of your business; you need to fulfill your purpose."

In the background, Nate began to hear a chorus of voices; he picked out Mare Winningham, Mary Elizabeth Mastrantonio, and Harry Hamlin. All were chanting and shouting, all at the same time. The volume increased to a din, and the vibration caused a hairline crack to stretch across Nate's head. He felt it split. All of the voices and worries and suspicions he held had breathed life into their beings. Nate at once felt overwhelmingly lightheaded and relieved. His fear was gone, his mind made clear. The struggle that affected his physical body seemed nothing more than an interesting diversion. He saw Rosemary in Denver, clear as day, in her silk pajamas, drinking coffee at a glass table. Next to her a man nibbled on toast, moved his pencil across the crossword. She looked happy, content. Nate reached out and tried to flip their coffee cups, cram the toast down his skinny lawyer or doctor throat. He imagined tearing that glass tabletop out from under them, raising it overhead, holding it just long enough to see their frightened faces, listen to them plead, and then let it swing quickly down, silencing the apologies, the laughter at Nate's expense.

Eli scrambled to his feet, wrenching his way out of Nate's hands. As though he were watching a movie, Nate saw himself stagger after him. He watched from a plush, red velvet movie theatre seat as Eli made it to the bomb shelter entryway and tried to pull the metal door open. He heard screaming, a girl, then Eli joined the chorus, the noise broken and scratched from disuse. In another moment, Eli would be inside, the metal door slammed shut. Nate shivered with anticipation, his arms and legs perfectly numb.

This was the way Nate would miss his purpose, this was what happened to the weak. The voices melded and lowered. Nate was amazed to hear Roman's voice flow out of his mouth, and he saw as if it were a movie all the moments, all the scenes, things, knowledge he didn't have. He saw Mia Farrow in her pixie boy haircut, he saw Adrian Brody huddled in a bombed out building clinging to an officer's coat. He saw Angelica Huston's young face peeking in the doorway, he felt the cold sweat on his chest, the urgency, the secrecy. He tasted the champagne as it washed down a couple of Quaaludes, he saw a nest of brown hair.

Nate's hands reached forward, pulling Eli back, leaving the metal door gaping open. Words without meaning sputtered from Eli's mouth. Nate watched the giant screen as he threw Eli down the concrete stairs, scattering the shadows that hovered around the edges. Nate watched, numb, as he pulled Eli's head back and slammed it forward into the lead-lined wall. The sickening crunch made Nate cringe in his seat but he didn't look away. Nate looked at his hands and arms covered in blood. From a distance, he felt his fist wrap around something solid, Roman's carved staff was dripping with blood. From his red velvet seat, he swung and swung until the yelling stopped, until the rain shower of blood stopped spattering his face, until it was quiet, until he clawed his way out of the snake's throat.

57

Kevin had been right. The highway out of Glenwood Springs had been rougher than the way in. The snow had compounded itself and began to stick to the ground, concealing the edges of the road. It was the first time during the trip that she'd seen Kevin's forehead knitted with a concentration capable of stopping his stream of chatter.

Rosemary sat back quietly, watching the edge of the road, sensing his tension. Any other time, this would have spooked her, and she reached automatically for her pill bottle when Kevin became quiet. She didn't do well when people around her were upset; she folded in, took it personally. But this time, she left the bottle of pills alone. Things were different. Rosemary was able to distinguish Kevin's tension about the weather from resentment toward her. She wanted to tell him her epiphany, but on top of breaking his concentration, the explanation required a lot of back-story that she wasn't sure Kevin wanted to hear. Without looking away from the road, Kevin seemed to pick up on her excitement.

"I think the signmakers are going to catch on to what a bad idea these little roads are pretty quick, but not before someone goes off the edge."

Rosemary had been thinking about her father's cabin, the one she had originally taken off to find. It seemed so silly now, especially since she had seen what was left of Glenwood; a row of hotels that housed scientists and their families, all of whom had something to do with the water treatment plant nearby.

Oddly enough, the hot springs were spared, and there were lots of people out in the pools as the snow fell around them. Rosemary knew the cabin had been removed; it only made sense. It invaded upon nature; it wasn't necessary. Out of her deep comfort, Rosemary ventured a comment to Kevin.

"You know, my father used to own a cabin here. Left it to me when he passed. That's where I was headed originally; good thing I changed course isn't it."

Kevin smiled through his concentration. "That so? Yeah, it's probably gone now, unfortunately. Must've meant a lot to ya and your dad. Did he pass away recently?"

Rosemary felt something unhinge in her, but instead of her usual reaction, she instead felt a deep heat through her solar plexus that spread out through her entire body, covering her in a deep calm.

"No. No, it's been a little while. Is this, talking bothering you? Do you need to concentrate?"

Kevin laughed easily. "Lord no. I've been jawing your ear off the whole trip; it's good to hear your voice."

Rosemary's fingers felt tingly, but instead of the marshmallow sensation, she just felt still, focused.

"It's been about ten years; we weren't close, although it was better with him the last few years. He was sick, schizophrenic, in and out of hospitals. In the years before he passed, he'd been pretty much out on his own. Spent some time in a halfway house here in Glenwood and met a woman. That's when he moved to that cabin. He'd bought it a long time ago; never thought he'd live in it again. Mixie, that was her name. Ever heard that name? I didn't even know it existed. Little pale thing, scared to death. Wouldn't eat in front of anyone, I met them up there one year, only time I ever saw the place. She stayed inside the whole time; ate in her room. My dad talked about her like she hung the moon. Talked and talked about how beautiful Mixie was, how talented. She painted pretty well, too. She'd been in the institution back in Glenwood for clinical depression. Is the institution still there?"

Kevin shook his head.

"Not sure if it is," he said. "I bet at least part of it's been transformed into regular housing or all-purpose hospital care."

Rosemary continued, the words flowing out smoothly, calmly. She felt her belly release a little with every sentence.

"It looked like a lodge. Had big pine columns; a real log cabin look, but it was big. The lobby looked like any ski lodge you'd ever see out here. Only way you would ever know it was a hospital was by the IV carts in the corners and the monitors everywhere. Nice place, really. Better than where I've been living for the last thirteen years. I should have gone crazy, I would have been better off."

Kevin chuckled.

The marshmallow feeling permeated Rosemary's throat, but instead of bringing anxiety, it was like slipping into a hot bath.

"After my dad left the institution and was in the cabin, we'd exchange letters every so often. It was a beautiful place. Perfect. River nearby, a deck built around a big tree. Raccoons used to climb out on the deck at night. Dad had a whole book of photos of them; used to send me one every once in awhile. We were all right there toward the end. He was gentle; loved animals. You know he taught me how to talk to squirrels when I was a little girl? You make a clicking sound behind your tongue. They come running; you better have something for them, though. Otherwise, you'll have some unhappy squirrels on your hands."

Rosemary demonstrated the tongue click while Kevin continued to chuckle. The road was widening a bit and his forehead was unfurling. Rosemary

214

continued to talk, quite unable to stop herself.

"I had just talked to him the day before it happened. He called me, and of course, he never usually called. He told me he had some things he wanted me to read; he sounded strange."

Kevin ventured a question.

"Strange how? Sick?"

Rosemary shook her head.

"No...not really. It, it just scared me. I called my mom in Denver, still don't know why; she'd never come up here. Not for any reason." Rosemary paused, considering her words. "But something about what I told her made her promise she'd make sure. That scared me more. I didn't sleep at all that night; stayed up until sunrise. I knew the phone was going to ring before it did. I made Nate answer it."

Rosemary felt her voice getting smaller. Kevin glanced over at her, concern washing his face.

"It was this little lawyer guy, damned if I remember his name. He'd contacted me in college when Dad went into the hospital here, and now he had called and I didn't want to talk to him. I thought maybe Dad had just been put back in the hospital, but Nate's face; God, it was blank when he handed the phone to me. He only does that when it's bad, when he's trying to not tell me how bad it is."

Rosemary's voice slowed to a whisper, each word heavy.

"They found him in the river. His pockets were weighted down with rocks, but most of them must have fallen out because he floated back up. They..."

Rosemary's voice broke a little, but she was compelled to finish it; to let it out.

"The lawyer called it an accident—a fucking accident. Who stuffs his pockets with rocks and wanders into a river, by accident? They did it 'cause Mixie's Catholic, and they wanted a whole hoopla at the funeral. Wouldn't do it if it was a suicide. I don't know what difference the words make. He still did what he did, except one lands him in hell and one is up to God's standards."

Rosemary rolled the word "suicide" around in her mouth. She could count how many times she'd ever said it. She had no idea why she was letting all this spill out just now. Lost in her compulsion, she continued.

"Not that Mixie should have said anything at all; she went back to the hospital. It was up to me, and Nate—he was there through the whole thing. He carried a lot of it. He greeted people, he was social, he made phone calls and arrangements; he made me eat. Dad was buried in a ridiculous gold colored coffin with crucifixes all over it. When they splattered the holy water, no one knew what to do. Mixie was the only Catholic there, and she was so medicated; she could have been at Disneyland for all she cared."

Kevin shook his head.

"Wow, that's a...wow. For what it's worth, though, I don't think anyone can decide what sends you to heaven or hell," he said gently. "I think that's up to you, and it sounds like your Dad loved you and his wife, and that's what counts. Not all that other stuff."

Rosemary shifted in her seat, she felt lighter; free.

"I've never told anyone that. I mean, I've never said it out loud. Nate was there, but I've never really even talked about it with him. Thank you."

Kevin put his right hand on her shoulder briefly and then returned it to the wheel. "You don't need to thank me, honey. I knew you were an old soul when I saw you; now I know why."

As the truck finally pulled out of Glenwood Canyon and onto open highway, Kevin breathed a sigh of relief. For the first time, Rosemary looked at the road that stretched ahead with hope rather than fear. She finally understood that she could handle whatever lay in front of her.

58

Nate stood staring at the metal door that led to the bomb shelter, a long, greasy red stain ran the length of it. Confused, Nate looked at his arms and hands to find that they were stained the same grotesque color. A bloody tree branch lay on the ground a few yards away, its placement both deliberate and random. He heard the frantic voices below and tried to make sense of them, but it was no use. Unsure what he would find, he stooped down and pulled the door open. Sarah screamed immediately and her voice brought back a flood of sensations. Nate remembered lifting the door, kicking Eli's broken body down the narrow flight of stairs. For a moment, Nate remembered being afraid of Sarah's high pitched scream. He felt panic as outraged voices rose at him from the shadows of the cave. He heard sobbing and for a moment wanted to join in, but only for a moment. Suddenly, the feeling was gone, replaced by Roman's voice and Roman's actions. Expressionless, Nate slammed the door shut, silencing the voices below.

Nate tried to make sense of the thoughts in his head. They were swirling, rambling. The only thing he was sure of was Rosemary. He needed to get to Denver, he needed to find her in her fancy new room. He needed to show her that he knew. Nate had been pacing near the metal door for some time, and the sun was high enough in the sky now, but the idea that the Honda might run again seemed far away. Nate needed to make sense of the sign that had appeared several yards away.

To Whom It May Concern:
Nathan McLeod has committed
Grievous harm to another citizen
The nature of the incident is unclear to us
And as a result is under investigation
Please review your statement of purpose
This is a warning that
Your behavior from this point on
Will affect our ultimate decision

Nate tried to tear his way through his scattered thoughts. His face ached, and was tender to the touch, the throbbing in his head had dulled and the voices were low. The images, however, were not. Nate had trouble focusing his eyes. He had one thing he clung to, the one thing he knew was true. Rosemary was in Denver, he needed to find her, he needed to show her that he knew. He needed to show them all that he wasn't a patsy, wasn't a fool.

Nate walked back along the path, brushing the blood stained snow away with his bare feet. He didn't feel the cold, didn't feel anything except the power that was coming back. The incident was erased. Whomever had done it was now free. Nate walked back to the Honda with a grin on his face. He heard Roman's voice in his throat; he opened his mouth and let it out.

"Finally, boy. You've finally arrived. Took miles of film to get it out of you, and now you're ready. Keep walking, boy, they're coming for you soon. You'll meet them on the road. You'll teach that little bitch to treat you like a fool."

Nate began walking, past the sign with its meaningless words, leaving the last ties to his old life behind.

59

An hour or so later, as Rosemary, Kevin and Mr. Reynolds approached the Highway 24 turnoff, Rosemary was laughing as Kevin related the story of his wedding. Mr. Reynolds was awake and panting in Rosemary's ear, and she was slowly feeding him dog biscuits, which he happily accepted.

"....and then, when we finally got to her vows, the damndest thing happened. Motorcycles! Motorcycles, if you can believe it. A whole gang of 'em pulled through. She just kept right on talking; couldn't hear a damn thing she said. Everyone was leaning forward. I stepped closer, but still nothing; nothing except motorcycles."

Rosemary was laughing so hard she could hardly ask her question. "Why didn't she stop and wait?"

Kevin scratched Mr. Reynolds' head. "Don't know! Asked her that later and she said she was going to cry. Motorcycles were the only thing that saved the wedding! Problem is I had no idea what she'd vowed! Neither did anyone else, for that matter! Years after, she'd turn to me when I was giving her a hard time and she'd say, 'Look here, buster, I never vowed to put up with your garbage. You don't even know what I vowed!' And she was right! She could have vowed to give me a hard time and make my life miserable...I still agreed!"

Rosemary gasped for breath and rubbed Mr. Reynolds behind his ear. "But she didn't do that. You were happy."

Kevin was still smiling from the memory. "Oh yeah, we had our moments, let me tell you. She was a firecracker, didn't let anything go, didn't let me get away with anything. What I wouldn't do to have one last good fight with her. Her nose would twitch when she knew she was wrong, you see, then I'd know I could win. Eventually, she'd give in, and we'd end up laughing."

The snow had thinned out a bit, but Rosemary knew the higher up they went, the worse it was going to get. It would only be an hour or two before they reached Denver, and Rosemary was giddy with excitement that would have been fear an hour ago. She popped another antibiotic without even fingering the other pill bottle.

Kevin saw her and asked, "How're you feeling? You seem pretty good, 'specially considering how sick Will said you were. He told me about Morgan. Boy, that little one's a character, heard you taught her a real lesson though.

Hope you don't mind me saying!"

Kevin chuckled quietly. Rosemary's initial wave of embarrassment washed over her, and she found herself giggling, too.

"Yeah, I guess so. Sure didn't mean to; hope she's alright."

Kevin tapped the steering wheel lightly.

"Oh, I'm sure she'll recover. I know her from her brother. He was a buddy of Will's back in the old days. Big time gambler; lost his shirt every other week. Seemed like Will was constantly bailing him out of one crisis or another. Don't know what happened to him, know he wasn't too happy about getting sent out to the bean fields, although if I were him, I would've been happy that I didn't have to live that kind of life anymore. Not like the bean fields are hard duty after all. All the people they got there in Vegas? I tell you, shifts are pretty short, get to be around all that greenness all day; sounds a heap better than getting run out by bookies. No, after Morgan got her warning and moved over to the hospital, her bother... can't remember his name... Theo, Teo, something like that. Anyway, he wasn't around anymore. Maybe he moved on, maybe he was removed, can't say. Hit Morgan pretty hard though, that's why she's such a little snit to everyone. Not nice to say, but damned if it idnt' true. So no, you don't need to worry. Whatever it is you did, I'm sure there's a line of people behind you that want to do the same."

Rosemary cleared her throat and took a drink of water from a plastic bottle. "I feel much better. Better than I have in years. I think it might all work out. Can't imagine what I would've done if I hadn't met you two."

Kevin grinned and patted her shoulder. "Oh, it's me who's grateful, haven't had such good company in years! Say, did I tell about the reception yet? It was something else, big chocolate cake, three layers high with a white lace trim and...."

The welcome cadence of Kevin's voice moved along with the disappearing highway as they pulled the final stretch into the city.

60

Nate was just a hundred yards away from the Honda when he saw a large truck heading towards him. He felt Roman's voice deep inside him and let it out.

"There it is. They're looking for you boy. Stop them before they reach the car; they'll find your 'incident.' They'll try to stop you if they know."

Nate waved his arms back and forth over his head and felt the air as it tried to escape him. He grinned at the power he owned. He'd been reborn; he was now worthy of his role. The truck slowed to a stop, and a man and woman got out. The man was in his late thirties, thinning brown hair, wind burned face. The woman seemed to be younger, dark skin, thick hair. Nate stopped himself from leering. He needed to stay focused.

"Hey, you alright there!" The man yelled. "That your car down the way?" He yelled again, indicated the Honda down the road.
Nate waved back.

"Yep, good thing you found me. Damn near froze to death last night. Solar panels don't work for shit, pardon my French!"
The man smiled and crossed the empty highway.

"No pardons needed. After a night in the cold, you can cuss all you want! I'm Ben, this is Gabby. We had a note on our desk this morning saying there was a car abandoned somewhere near Green River. Guess you were the one, huh? We need to take you in; you look pretty banged up. C'mon, we'll get you back to Grand Junction and get you taken care of."

Nate had nearly forgotten about the tenderness on his face, the blood on the side of his head and his bare feet, which still felt no cold. If it hadn't been for the slight look of horror on Ben's lined face, he would have forgotten completely. He reached up and touched the gashes on his cheeks, felt the dried blood in his hair.

"Yeah, crash landed because of the snow. Car's down completely. Where'd you say you were from?"

By this time, Gabby and Ben and were ushering Nate into the big truck, they squeezed him into the long bench in the cab, and Gabby immediately pulled out a first aid kit and began to wipe the blood away from his face. Ben set to pulling a blanket from the back and wrapping Nate's cut and frozen feet in it.

221

"Your feet should be frozen through and through. It's a miracle they aren't completely frostbitten. As it is, they just look a little road worn."

Gabby interrupted him. Nate was enjoying the closeness of her hands, her face leaning into his. She noticed his eyes following her and pulled back. "We need to get you into the clinic back in Grand Junction. We should have brought more medical supplies with, but the note didn't say anything about people, just a car. Is there anybody else back there? Are you alone?"

Nate looked her directly in the eyes. Clearly uncomfortable, she averted her gaze. Amused, he replied, "All by myself. Leave the car behind. Those scientists said they'd come get it if anything broke. Is there a way to send word?"

"Of course," Ben responded. "We'll send a letter as soon as we hit town."

Ben put the truck in gear and began the five-point turn to get it faced the other way. "You a scientist out there?"

Nate leaned back, Gabby scooting as far away as she could. "Nope, test driver. Just trying to find my way to Denver. Think anyone can help me with that in Grand Junction?"

Ben nodded. "We'll figure something out for you. We have mail trucks heading out that way all the time. You can probably hitch a ride with one of the drivers. Pretty standard practice. There's also a transport truck heads to Denver; brings fertilizer for the soybean fields. That might be your best bet."

Nate stared ahead and smiled to himself. He'd be there soon; he'd show her that he knew.

61

To Whom It May Concern:
The Following Community Is Presently
A Stage Three Community.
Stage Four Preparations Are in Place.
Please Be Prepared.

"Told ya! Told ya they were making some changes, huh?"

Kevin's voice was excited as the mail truck passed the sign. Rosemary was relieved to see the outline of buildings in the distance. It looked like the skyline, although it was lonely to see without any of the surrounding buildings.

"Yep. See what I told ya? It's all about downtown now, little bit of Capitol Hill, but mostly just downtown. Pretty much moved everybody into the office buildings; capital building, too. Deliver a lot of mail there, I'll tell ya."

Rosemary was amazed to see the fields of soybeans and the greenhouses that stretched in all directions around the city. They seemed to fold into the plains that used to lead to the airport, and blend in with the mountains to the south.

"How far do they go? The crops?"

Kevin stretched his hands on the steering wheel. "Oh, they go clear down to Colorado Springs. That's still there, mostly because of NORAD. Rumor has it they tried some big military action somethingajig down there in the beginning, but I don't see how it would happen. We got a letter you see, photocopy of what some whackadoodle claimed was correspondence between Washington, DC and Los Angeles. I don't buy it for a minute. I think somebody got real creative and decided to write a bedtime story."

Rosemary was intrigued. "What did it say?"

Kevin glanced over. "Oh, the letter? Oh that. Well, I never saw all of it, it circulated around all the casinos for quite a while. Since there isn't really a 'mayor' anymore back in Vegas, there wasn't any specific person for it to go to. Just floated around. I heard about it from a little redhead named Jana who works the front desk over at Circus Circus. Nice little gal, she organizes the staff, cleans room sometimes, you know..."

Rosemary was too curious to be patient. "Kevin, the letter, I'm dying to know. What did it say?"

Kevin laughed softly. "Sorry, caught a tangent there. The letter, let's see. It talked about some 'plan' the government had to take care of the signmakers. Said the president had been put on emergency status, gave control of the city to Villaragosa—LA, that is. Vegas was never supposed to see it."

Rosemary shook her head.   "But how? How did it get out?"

Kevin's face scrunched up a bit and then released. "Not sure there. Jana said it came with a note attached, not typed, but written. Said that they'd stolen the letter and they were sending it all over the country. Said everyone needed to see it. I still maintain that it's like that atomic clock disappearing. People with too much time on their hands, and nothing to do with it. I tell you what, and mark my words, they'll find the bunch of jokers who sent that out. That is, if the signmakers don't first."

Rosemary was still intrigued by the idea of the secret letter. It was just the kind of thing Nate would go crazy over. She wished he could hear this.

"Did it talk about the 'plan?' How could they possibly expect to fight the signmakers?"

Kevin tapped the steering wheel in an invisible beat.

"That's the part I think is wackadoodle. The other stuff I'd buy for a dollar—president going into hiding? Hell, we hardly saw him in the first place. Hiding wouldn't be much different. But the plan was the crazy part if you ask me. I only know what Jana told me; she read it, not me. She said they had pinpointed the signmakers in Australia, bombed the bejesus out of it, evidently."

Rosemary's jaw hung open. "What? Australia? That is crazy! Even if it was right, the signs are still here; they were wrong. They can't just go and bomb places can they? I mean, wouldn't Australia bomb back? Wouldn't we have heard about this somehow? You know, besides the conspiracy letter?"

Kevin laughed. "You're preaching to the choir, here, Rosemary. I hear ya on all that and more. What I want to know is why they think the Aussies could or would have the resources to step up and make all this happen. They don't—didn't—even have the atomic bomb. Hell, most places out there in the desert—outback, they call it—don't even have running water! You know how they treat the natives there? The aborigines? It's like looking at our American Indian policies a hundred and fifty years ago, or less, sadly. You know the government down there used to claim that it was the legal guardian of any aborigine baby? They even used to..."

Kevin caught his own tangent and took a deep breath.

"All's I'm saying is, if anyone around here could do all this, I don't think it's Australia. And you're right, whatever we did down there to mess them up, well, it certainly didn't affect the signmakers much, did it?"

Rosemary shook her head. Even though what Kevin said made sense, that it was not only improbable but impossible that the government would have made such a horrible decision, it sent chills down her spine. Rosemary had been so absorbed in the conversation that she hadn't noticed Kevin pulling into a long complex. It looked like a series of storage units. It was the Highland area, just north of the bridge and I-25. Rosemary was amazed at what she saw. Across the bridge, she could see the entire downtown area, virtually untouched. She couldn't see many of the streets, but she spotted the Vespa scooters zipping around through the snowy streets. Kevin pulled all the way into a garage where a large man in a jumpsuit was directing them, he held up his hand to signal a stop. Kevin turned the key and killed the engine.

"Well, here we are. That's Claude there in the black; good guy, real good guy. Now don't run off, I need to help them get this offloaded, but you need some directions to say the least. Washroom's toward the front; meet me up there in a few."

Rosemary nodded. Her legs were numb. Mr. Reynolds was jumping around excitedly in the back making a snuffling woof sound. When the door opened and Kevin exited, he bounded out, and just like in Grand Junction, headed straight out the garage door to the grassy field behind the mail center. Rosemary swung herself down and on pins and needles inched her way down the hall. Her legs finally regained some feeling by the time she reached the washroom Kevin had told her about. She nearly ran into a crowd of young men all wearing the black coveralls, they looked appreciatively at her and despite herself, Rosemary blushed a little. It'd been awhile, and she had some sense of how she must look right now, after a hospital stay and nearly 15 hours on the road.

The mirror confirmed her fears. Her face was pale and thin. At least the blue circles around her eyes were gone. Her hair was still pulled back tightly, and it was a good thing, since it was greasy after days of neglect. Rosemary suddenly remembered an article she had read years ago, when she was in college, about a woman who had stopped washing her hair altogether. The woman claimed that your hair created its own natural oils and it cleaned itself. She'd looked pretty decent in the picture, considering she hadn't really bathed in fifty years. Looking at her own hair, Rosemary wondered how her hair could look so bad after a couple of days.

Rosemary couldn't get the letter out of her head, looking at herself in the mirror, she mouthed the word: "Australia?"
It didn't make any sense. Probably what Kevin said; some kind of joke, like those people who sent chain letters. Bunch of kids got together and made a bet they could scare a whole bunch of people.

Rosemary wandered to the front of the building and looked out through the glass. She saw the rooftop gardens from here, just as Kevin had described. They were beautiful. Running along the sides of each of the tall skyscrapers were long solar panels. They blocked the windows in some places, but Rosemary supposed that as they shifted upward to catch the sun, it would be like the blinds opening. Back from the garage, Kevin and Claude, interrupted Rosemary's reverie.

"Alrighty. We're set back there for a bit, anyhow. Brought Claude up here to introduce ya, but also because he says he actually saw that letter. The one that showed up here had a different note. Thought you might like to hear another conspiracy theory."

Kevin winked and motioned to Claude, who was rolling his eyes.

"Great, you know I come up here to meet the nice lady, and he introduces me as a crazy man. Just great. I'm Claude, very nice to meet you. Did you find the loo alright?"

Rosemary was mesmorized by his slight accent. "The what? I'm sorry?"

Claude motioned over his shoulder. "The toilet; er... the bathroom?"

Rosemary shook his hand. She was pleased to feel the calm inside her. At this point she would normally be feeling jittery and nervous. But today, in this place, she felt like she could take on the world.

"So, yes, the letter," he said. "I only saw a little bit, and the rest is all us guys sitting around sorting mail and chewing the fat, I believe, as you say."

Rosemary nodded. "I'm just curious. It's the first I've ever heard of this," she said. "I came from a tiny town back in California, Mussel Shoals?"

Claude shook his head slightly. "Hmm... sounds nice, never been to California. Well, ours came with a note; a long one, too. Handwritten, not like the letter, which was typed but had been copied, and not on a copier, either. Looked like those purple ink roll machines they used to have. Anyway, our handwritten note said Australia was only a diversion, and that the government had another target. It said they sent missiles out to who knows where at the same time. Australia was meant to distract the signmakers. I wouldn't give it much credence though. There's another guy in the back who heard that we bombed Holland. Who would bomb Holland? I'm sure if you ask around enough, you'll hear a half dozen more targets too. I'm with Kevin on this one, kids playing games, causing worry for reason. Anyway, see, that's all I know. And it's not anything at all, really. Just more garbage for the pile. It was nice to meet you, Rosemary. I hope we see you around here soon. If you need work here, request us. We could use some prettier faces than those jokers back there."

Rosemary smiled and again shook his giant hand. Kevin started to head out the door.

"You coming? You said 19th and Sherman, right?"

Rosemary nodded.

"Well, way I see it, I can either give you terrible directions that'll get you lost, or I can take you out there. I'd welcome the break, really. Gets me out of sorting. Mr. Reynolds is eating his lunch in the back; he'll never know I'm gone. C'mon."

Kevin trooped down the street to a bike stand where three Vespa scooters were parked. Each was plugged into the building with a thick black cable, and all had large baskets attached. Kevin unplugged one, climbed on, and patted the back.

"I'm know, it's not real ladylike, but unfortunately there aren't any waitresses out here to get you your own, and we need the rest for delivery. But if you'd like, we can get ya one on the other side of the bridge."

Rosemary climbed on behind Kevin strapping on the helmet he handed her. "No. It's okay. I don't know how to drive one anyway. Are you sure this is alright? I mean, I took your time anyway out here..."

Kevin turned around. "Nonsense, I can't just leave you out here can I? Anyway, your folks live right close. Just hold on; we'll be there in a few minutes."

Rosemary grabbed Kevin's shoulders just as he took off, riding expertly through the matted snow. The cold air in her face felt good; clean, like a new start.

62

The fertilizer truck was bumpy and loud, but Nate barely noticed from his place behind the cab. The front seat was occupied by a young man who had been traveling from Salt Lake and wanted to work with the wind turbines in Denver. Nate had tuned him out miles ago as he babbled about how Salt Lake was only Stage Three and didn't have the turbines yet, but that Denver was already Stage Four and how exciting it was. Tim or Todd, something, Nate didn't care. The driver was silent too. Hadn't even shook his hand, not that Nate cared. The only communication he'd heard from the driver was a grunt when he showed up at the pastures where they were loading the fertilizer.

Ben and Gabby had been true to their word, they had taken Nate all the way into Grand Junction where they tried to check him into some kind of clinic that they called the hospital. Nate had agreed to a shower to wash the blood off his mangled face, and then he had walked out, past the stunned doctors, and past Ben, who just watched and shook his head. Nate had taken a set of scrubs from the closet and a pair of slip-on shoes; no one stopped him. The signmakers were evidently still deliberating his fate; good thing, too. He didn't need much time; just enough to get to Denver and Rosemary. After that, he'd be content to do whatever they asked of him. He still had no idea what happened to Eli, but he didn't much care anymore. He heard a chanting in the back of his head whenever his thought wandered in that direction.

"cover it up cover it up cover it up cover it up..."

Now he was here, nearly at Glenwood Springs. The roads had narrowed and the driver waved his hand at Tim/Todd to shut him up. Good. Nate was sick of hearing about his sister in Denver and how "cool" the soybean fields were, and had they read that crazy letter that had been going around? The letter rang a bell with Nate, but he didn't listen long enough to hear anything that Tim/Todd was saying. In fact, Nate was fantasizing about what he would like to do to Tim/Todd to make him shut the hell up. From his undignified floor seat in the truck cab, Nate had to look up to see the back of Tim/Todd's head; he could easily grab his skinny neck and twist, ever so quickly. He nearly laughed thinking about how easy it would be. The only thing stopping him was the signmakers. He needed a little more time; another "incident" and the signmakers would be much less likely to consider the first one an accident.

This was where Rosemary's little cabin was, somewhere around here. She had probably come through here with her lover; they had probably gone looking for the little cabin with its river view and its big oak framed bed. Nate liked to imagine how her face looked when she discovered the big, blank spot where it had been. Did she cry? She liked to cry, she liked to manipulate him into feeling sorry for her. No more. He wasn't falling for her bullshit anymore. Roman's voice rose up and he had to swallow it back down his throat so it only reverberated in Nate's ears.

"Told you, boy, you're almost there; you'll be there by sundown, just in time to catch them falling asleep in each other's arms. Then you'll be ready. It'll be masterpiece, boy, it will be my finest work. We're all counting on you, boy. Just a little while longer and you'll be there."

The driver breathed a sigh of relief as they pulled into town. He turned off in front of a hotel and looked around to face Nate and Tim/Todd.

"Need to refuel. Don't go anywhere. Be right back."
Tim/Todd turned around and faced Nate. "Hey, say I never got your name!" Nate stared at Tim/Todd for a full minute, not breaking his gaze, until Tim/Todd broke his line of vision and looked down nervously.

"You never asked."
Nate enjoyed Tim/Todd's obvious awkwardness, and even more his timid reply.

"Oh...sorry..."
Nate dismissed the boy, and returned to his thoughts of Denver and Rosemary. Roman would help him find her; they would lead the way. Nate was only the messenger.

63

The four-story brick building at 19th and Sherman was almost dwarfed by the skyscrapers that framed it. The city was magnificent. Rosemary and Kevin had driven over the bridge and through Lodo with its brick lofts, now occupied by those who were once homeless—or close to it. The street looked bare as they passed the Red Cross Shelter, and there was no one sleeping in the snow. It hadn't really been on their way, but Kevin made the detour to show Rosemary the changes. When they paused, he explained that the Red Cross Shelter was the new hospital, and the homeless—its previous residents—had been moved out into the lofts and office buildings. Doctors had been provided, medications distributed for the mentally and emotionally disturbed. The same had happened in Vegas, Kevin said. The difference was extraordinary. People once trapped in their own minds were now functional, and those who still struggled were given light assignments in the hospital where they could be monitored. Rosemary couldn't help but think of her dad. Where would he have fit in all this. Whatever happened to Mixie?

The downtown area was changed, too. The 16th Street Mall, similar to the Walkabout in Mussel Shoals, had remained an open-air mall, but the stores were dramatically different than before. Instead of high priced boutiques and clothing stores, the façades now advertised job training spaces—where people could get ready to assemble the turbines that were part of the Stage Four status—and small clinics and schools. From the storefront windows, Rosemary saw children seated in rows with books. Buffet style dining places now occupied the spaces that once housed fancy steak houses and martini bars, and their menu items consisted of organically grown vegetarian food. As Kevin explained, that had "led to some unhappy folks for awhile."

Rosemary could just imagine. People out here liked to think that be-cause they lived in Colorado, they were genuine cowboys and deserved to eat buffalo and deer whenever they liked. Vegetarian food must've gone over like a lead balloon. But, now that it was the only option, Rosemary didn't see a shortage of people in line. Little electric scooters lined the streets, and the solar panels that covered the skyscrapers were overwhelming.

When those wind turbines are up, "'specially out there by where DIA used to be," Kevin had said, "these'll just be used as daytime backup. That's the plan, anyway."

Kevin slowly passed The Brown Palace, the historical hotel with its ornate carvings and moldings, a city block big and standing as a giant triangle in the middle of the city. Rumor had it the building was haunted, but they said that about the building on 19th and Sherman for that matter, just as Kevin explained.

"Just a story for bedtime again, but that's the rumor. I thought you were kidding when you first told me the address. Only reason I know the place is that one of our sorters lived in that building before he moved on to Kansas City. Said he saw all sorts of weird things. Ask your family about it, tell me what they say. I love a good ghost story."

As they pulled up to the brick building, Rosemary was filled with nervous excitement. She had no idea whether Nate would be here or not, or even if her mom was still here. But, for the first time in her life, she knew she would be able to handle whatever it was that she found. Kevin turned off the engine at the front door.

"You want me to come up with ya? Happy to, if you want."
Rosemary shook her head. "No, I'll be alright, I think. Whatever happens, I'll be alright."

Rosemary dismounted and unfastened her helmet, then she leaned in and gave Kevin a long hug.

"Oh, I have no doubt of that darlin', remember, you need me for any reason, just walk on down there. You saw all those waitresses; ask for a scooter. They're easy to drive, you'll see. There's even a shop down there that gives lessons I think. You remember the way back to the mail warehouse?"
Rosemary nodded.

"Even if I'm back in Vegas, Claude'll be there. He's housed here. He'll take care of whatever you need."

Rosemary nodded. Kevin grinned and waved as he pulled out onto the snowy street.

64

Past Glenwood Springs Tim/Todd was still quiet. Nate was enjoying the guy's discomfort tremendously since their earlier exchange. The driver even seemed on edge. He'd turned around as they exited the Glenwood Canyon and spoke to Nate.

"You okay back there? Not too bumpy is it?"
Nate had savored the long pause before his answer. "It's charming. Best truck ride I've ever had."

Since that, no one had spoken. The trucker had gone back to his silent concentration and the boy had begun fingering a long string of beads that he had taken from his pocket. Nate leaned back in the quiet and listened to Roman's plans.

"International cast, groundbreaking, real, and edgy. It's going to show humanity for what it is, in your face, without apology. No reasons, no excuses. It's going to show everyone what it's like when everyone shits on you and you're left with nothing. It's going to show everyone what a winter in Poland feels like. That's right. I'll be welcomed back with open arms. I'll be famous."

Nate could see the film reel on the back of his eyelids. It showed him entering the posh bedroom, black silk spread thrown to the floor, black silk sheets wrapped around their bodies. Rosemary's little frame, her breasts barely covered, would start back, clutching the darkness around her. Her man, blonde, tall, would stand and charge, demanding an explanation. Exposed in his nudity, he wouldn't see Nate's reach; he would barely have a protest out of his throat before Nate twisted it, threw him aside, and moved forward.

The film became grainy. Nate strained to see, but the reel went empty. Roman wasn't done yet, it was up to him. Only he could finish the movie.

65

The names were handwritten on the buzzers below. Rosemary was relieved to see "Parks" written in her mother's scrawly hand on the last buzzer. Rosemary rang twice before she heard a voice from above her.

"Hello? Anyone down there?"

It was Lilly! Rosemary nearly wept with relief. She backed up from under the awning and waved up. "Lilly! It's me!"

Lilly's young face lit up. "Rosie! Rosie! Mom! Rosie's here! Hold on, I'll let you in!"

Lilly disappeared and Rosemary's mother's face took her place; she looked incredulous.

"Rosie! Baby! What are you doing here! Oh, what a wonderful surprise! Lilly's on her way down! Sweetie, you didn't write. How in the world?"

The door burst open and Lilly collided with Rosemary, nearly knocking her off her feet. Rosemary hugged her back so hard she thought her arms would break. She was home. When Lilly finally stepped back, Rosemary saw that she wasn't a kid anymore, not by a long shot. Her long black hair streamed down her back and hung in effortless ringlets. Her face had lost its baby fat and her hips, once on the plump side, looked smooth and curvy. Rosemary at once forgot all her childhood jealousy, all the tension, and hugged her again.

"God, you're beautiful!"

Lilly snorted sarcastically and grabbed Rosemary's hands, leading her hard wood stairs.

"Vegetarian buffet. It's killin' me, but I did lose like half my ass. Mom's gonna freak! We never thought we'd see you again! How in the world did you get here?"

They paused before opening the fourth floor door.

"It's been, um, interesting. Hey, before we go in—this is going to sound strange—but, is Nate here?"

Rosemary knew the answer even before Lilly shook her head confusedly. Rosemary took a deep breath and breathed out her expectations before her mother tackled her with another hug.

233

66

By the time the soybean fields had begun to appear in the distance, Nate started to hear the soundtrack to Roman's masterpiece. It had begun to matter less and less why he was going to find Rosemary and whether he did. He still harbored a little worry that he didn't exactly know where she was. Could be any one of the tall skyscrapers that dotted the horizon line. He had asked Roman where to go, but the voices had been silent. No matter; he would find her somehow. The soundtrack played on in his head, discordant notes seemed to argue with each other; Stravinsky-esque, but far more brutal. It was like nails on a chalkboard, no words just jangling, mismatched melodies.

Tim/Todd had resumed his nervous chatter. This time, he was going on about some letter that was all over Salt Lake now, some copy of a letter that had landed about a month ago. People kept making copies, sending them around, getting everyone all riled up. Tim/Todd sounded very adamant about its importance. Nate was just watching the shape of his mouth as he talked, the bits of spittle that flew from his lips every so often.

"It's really bad. The letter says the president has gone on emergency status and some code has been put in place. I don't remember what; it didn't make any sense. But he's not in charge until the plan is completed; too dangerous is what the letter said. That's why we haven't heard from him, why we haven't heard from anybody. Don't you think that's weird? That we haven't heard from anybody?"

The truck driver grunted in reply, while Nate heard a C# chord clanging in his ear.

"Dubai's gone. All gone. We bombed the shit out of it. But that's not the worst part. According to what the letter said, the worst part is that we were wrong—on purpose. We were trying to distract the signmakers. Not only did the guys who dropped the bomb do it because they were commanded to, hear that? Under oath to serve their commanding officers they pushed the button, they got removed, sure that happened, but also, I mean, Dubai! Dubai's gone! All so we could send other bombs to some other crazy place when they weren't looking."

Tim/Todd seemed to be searching is memory; his forehead was all scrunched up in concentration.

The truck driver looked as if he had finally had enough.

"Son, I've been listening to your crazytown talk for nearly six hours now. Now you want us to believe that our government bombed Dubai just to distract the signmakers from the fact that we actually wanted to bomb what...Jupiter or some horse shit? That letter you claim was so real? I saw one too, probably sent out by the same jokers, 'cept this one was in Boise a few months back. That one said we bombed Moscow, buddy of mine told a while back that he'd read we'd bombed Japan. Bullshit. All of it bullshit. Besides, they removed the damn guns lord knows how long ago. You want me to buy that they'd remove the guns and leave the bombs behind? I drive this route once a week, and it's not like I mind the chatter, but c'mon, give us a break. None of this makes a damn bit of sense. And I went to college, I'll have you know."

Tim/Todd's face seemed to brighten from the response. A spray of spittle accompanied his words.

"No! It makes sense! I can't believe you guys haven't seen the letter! It's everywhere now! Before I left, I got a letter from my buddy in Baltimore; they'd seen it. Someone got hold of some kind of top-secret letter, made copies and sent them everywhere! It makes sense, I'm just not explaining it very well. We bombed Dubai so the signmakers would be so preoccupied with finding those bad guys that they wouldn't notice that we sent off like five other nukes, but toward this other place...where did it say...Iran maybe?. Now the shit's gonna hit the fan. The guns—I've thought about it; I have—and you know, they didn't get all the guns all at once. It took awhile. There was still talk in Salt Lake about people who'd gone underground, hidden out. They still had guns. I figure the signmakers didn't find them all; not right away, anyhow. Figures it'd be the same with bombs and all that other stuff; maybe they didn't know it was there until it was too late."

He gestured back to Nate, who stared blankly at him. The truck driver's face was getting red now.

"Now I can hear a lot of bullshit, and a lot of big stories, lord knows I've seen enough over the last few years to make me believe anything, but that's just ridiculous. Everyone knows that the whole government got their incompetent asses removed when this showdown began. Anyone who thinks that we've had the time or the means to be going after some God-forsaken desert somewhere; well, they're just crazy!"

Tim/Todd backed down at the sight of the trucker's red face. He seemed to sink back into his seat. From Nate's low perch, he heard the low rumble of a G minor scale, played repeatedly up and down the octaves.

67

Rosemary's family was on their second pot of coffee and Rosemary had already been force-fed two grilled cheese sandwiches, kosher pickles, and half a peanut brittle loaf before three in the afternoon, all courtesy of the waitress at the front of the building. Her mother talked non-stop about all the changes, the new apartment, the scooters, and the vegetarian food. That was the worst, she said. What did they have against a good steak? At least they let us keep the coffee pot, thank God for that.

Chuck sat quietly back but occasionally would refill her coffee cup, and pat her on the hand. Lilly was still beside herself. She was training to work on the wind turbines. There was a training center in the 16th Street Mall, and she was going out to the fields next week to begin work. Mom and Chuck worked with the daycare downtown. Rosemary had almost laughed out loud when they had told her that. It wasn't a far stretch to imagine her mother, but grumpy old Chuck?

Rosemary could see the logic behind it. Neither one of them were healthy enough to be out in the fields or on the turbines. They weren't educated to be scientists, or doctors. But they were valuable. Together, they had raised three kids. It wasn't a far stretch to see the signmakers assigning them to what they did best.

She recounted the entire trip in between mother's anguished facial expressions when she described the hospital, and before she dared ask about Nate. Everyone looked at her blankly.

"Have we seen him? Not for years! Not since your dad passed. I cried for hours after you two left, thinking of you living in that crooked little boat. Why would he be here? We had a letter arrive yesterday for him, didn't open it though."

Rosemary was surprised at her reaction. She knew that she should be devastated to find out that her worst fears were true that he'd gone on to somewhere else. But, instead she felt a calm. Lilly interrupted her mother's Nate rant.

"We've got to take you down to the assignment office tomorrow. They're real strict about people coming into the city and not working right away.

You'll be alright tonight, but much after that you'll get a warning to get to work. I go to training at three in the morning every day; goes till one in the afternoon." Rosemary choked on her coffee when she heard Lilly say three a.m.

Lilly laughed. "Yeah, you heard me right, three a.m. You get used to it; the signmakers aren't real smart about some stuff, sleep schedules being one thing. Anyway, I'll take you tomorrow. They'll probably give you an apartment, since you're married and all; it'll be good. It's crowded here."

Rosemary could see that it was crowded. The hardwood apartment had two bedrooms and one tiny bath. The living room was about the size of *Clementine*'s cabin. Rosemary could easily see that she would need to find her own place. That would be better anyway. Then, when Nate showed up, she would have everything ready.

Chuck appeared with yet another pot of coffee as Rosemary's mother launched into what she did at the daycare. Rosemary felt safe as she basked in the warmth of the small apartment.

68

The fertilizer truck rolled into a small barn outside Denver at around six in the evening. The sun was already down and the stars were just beginning to peak. Nate had been humming his soundtrack intentionally for the last ten miles, daring one of the two men to tell him to shut up. Not surprisingly, they hadn't said a word. The trucker pulled into the dirt drive and turned around, addressing Tim/Todd and Nate.

"Alright, here's as far as I go. If you head on down the highway there, you'll hit the city right soon. If you want a ride, you'll need to wait until morning till one of these guys heads out. You can bunk in the barn if you're interested."

Tim/Todd bolted from the truck; Nate slowly crawled over the seats, stretching his legs before touching ground. He saw the trucker pull Tim/Todd aside point over to where a bunch of men stood huddled around a campfire. Nate laughed out loud. He was probably telling him how to get away from the scary man. Nate started follow Tim/Todd but was blocked by the trucker's hand across his chest.

"Son, I think you best hit the road. You probably got family waitin' on you in the city. You'd best get walking. Are we understood?"
Nate swallowed Roman's voice which told him to tear this man apart. He instead offered his hand and an insincere smile.

"Sure do. Appreciate the ride."

The trucker looked at his hand and walked away. Nate grinned. He enjoyed his new power over people. The trucker was nothing, and neither was the sniveling little weakling who'd been babbling for the last six hours. It was certainly not worth getting removed over, just to lose a little of the tension that was due somewhere else. The highway was dark; the city still appeared to be about ten miles out of town. Nate was surrounded by soybean crops and fruit trees wrapped in plastic, new buds not yet showing. There was no moon to light the way and the electric lights at the barn were limited to one overhead lamp inside the barn where a crowd of men was already unloading the fertilizer. Nate turned and walked toward the highway. Didn't matter anyway. She'd still be there, he'd be in the city by midnight, and he'd start looking.

Alone on the highway, Nate could allow Roman's voice to rise and fall with the wind. Snow was blowing around him but he didn't feel it, not even through the thin scrubs material. It was like he'd been reborn, given powers no one else had. Roman's inspiration came pouring out through his mouth and into the night.

"It's a love story, a dystopic love story. Everything's a dystopic love story if you think about it. It all starts with happiness and flowers, and then you have to face the reality of the situation. People screw you over, people turn cold; they stop caring. This will show them what happens; this will make them decide where they stand. It'll have them on their feet at Cannes. I'm welcome at Cannes, you know. They love me at Cannes. It's the bloody Oscars where I'm unwanted. If only that little bitch hadn't testified, if only she hadn't lied." Roman was calmed down and faded out by Judd Hirsch.

"It's about time, kid. I finally felt secure enough to have the costume mistress hem my pants and order that new shirt. I'm an odd size you know; have to special order everything. Very tall, I'm actually very tall."

The voices swirled and mixed, creating the distant soundtrack. Nate opened his mouth to sing the noise as he walked toward the light.

69

That night as Rosemary lay on the couch wrapped in a fuzzy blanket, her stomach full and her mind clear. She thought about Nate. He could be on his way still, she supposed. If he wasn't here, she really had no idea where he'd go. She was almost sure he wouldn't have stuck around Mussel Shoals. Besides, from what Lilly told her, the signmakers had released a new list of towns that were being consolidated in preparation to move them into Stage Two. Mussel Shoals was on it, and all the people were going to be moved into downtown Santa Barbara. It gave her chills, but also answered a lot of questions that had been nagging for days. Of course, she hadn't noticed a huge change in life in Mussel Shoals; it was still Stage One when she was there.

According to Lilly, Stage One was the "getting to know you" phase. That was where the signmakers tried to calm the residents and meet their needs. Stage Two was the consolidation, elimination of wasteful spaces and replanting of the land that was left behind after removal. Stage Three was as she had seen in Las Vegas, the first big step to self-sufficiency. This was when the solar panels were implemented and the signmakers weaned the community off fossil fuels. Stage Four was the breakaway stage. That was why Denver and Vegas were trying madly to get the wind turbines up on time. Stage Four meant the end of the backup. The citizens would be responsible for their own resources.

Lilly explained that she had learned in class that Las Vegas had actually lost its power plant a bit early during Stage Three. The signmakers had put too much dependency on the solar panels. As a result, there were too many blackouts, too many power outages. To correct it, a sign had been put up last week outlining the new phase guidelines. Rosemary couldn't help but feel the excitement in the air. For all the complaining her mother did about the small apartment, they looked happy.

Chuck no longer sat for days at a time watching the television; now, he taught preschool kids to play soccer with foam balls. Lilly wasn't preoccupied with her nails and beauty school. She was going to be out in the fields, working on the turbines. She understood the science behind them, too. Rosemary had never heard her explain anything even vaguely scientific. And, from her mother's accounts, her brother, Kyle, and his wife were happily working on the water treatment system up in Missoula. Rosemary had crinkled her nose at hearing Missoula and made her mom laugh.

"I know, quite a departure isn't it?" They'd moved up there not too long after the signmakers arrived, thought he could hide out there in the Montana mountains. Her mother went on to explain that Missoula was the only town left in Montana. Turns out you really could fit all the people in the state into one small town.

They'd all made it all right. Rosemary wondered about Nate; was he stuck out in the cold somewhere? Had he gone somewhere else with the *Cursory Angel* conspiracy theorist, E name with the foul breath? Maybe the two of them had taken off for San Francisco or found themselves a new boat somehow and sailed on.

Anything was possible. Rosemary found herself missing the warmth of his body against hers, the way his hand would always cup her breast as they slept, even if he was in a dead sleep. He'd find her; he had to. She'd go with Lilly, get her assignment, and get set up in an apartment or room or whatever they gave her. She'd be ready when he finally arrived; he'd see that she'd changed.

70

Shortly before midnight, Nate reached the city limits. His legs should have been numb with the effort of the seemingly endless hike, but they felt strong. Nate looked around at the whipping snow. He should be cold, but the wetness didn't seem to affect him anymore. He grinned and looked up at the sky. She was here; he could sense her, out there somewhere. Roman's voice rose and fell, ordering the gaffers and best boy around, pulling the script supervisor from whatever task she had gotten involved in, making her look at the text line for line. He yelled at the sound technicians to raise the boom out of his shot. It was going to be perfect.

Nate could hear the others in the background too. They were all getting ready. Harry Hamlin was adjusting his Clash of the Titans robe, Mare Winningham was brushing fine strands of brown hair out of her face. Judd Hirsch stomped back and forth, practicing his lines over and over. Nate couldn't quite hear him, but saw the movement on the back of his eyelids. Soon they would start rolling, soon.

71

Two in the morning came early. Lilly was overly apologetic about waking Rosemary up, but she didn't mind. Everyone in the house went to bed so early that two a.m. didn't seem oppressively early; they felt active, refreshed. Mom was already brewing a pot of coffee, and Chuck was in the shower. Everyone went to work early, Lilly explained. That way they could conserve the energy at night when people would normally be burning lights late.

About two thirty, Rosemary and Lilly headed down the street. All around them, people were streaming out of their doors, heading to the 16th Street Mall. Everyone seemed in good spirits, greeting each other, hugging. Rosemary had never seen anything like it. To her, Denver had always seemed a standoffish city. People were hesitant to greet you, or return a smile. It had, in a big way, bred and encouraged Rosemary's social anxiety. When she went to college, the shock of having people act open and forward scared her to death. Rosemary hadn't taken any of the anxiety medicine since Vegas. She wasn't even shaky, although she felt like she should be. She was embarking on a new life here; she was starting over. She was going to get settled and wait for Nate, have everything ready for his arrival.

Rosemary dreamed of him last night. They were together in one of the rooftop gardens that dotted downtown. He looked beaten up, his face had cuts and gashes. He walked toward her, slowly at first, but faster and faster. Rosemary heard strange music, discordant melodies, chords that didn't belong. He ran full tilt toward her, his green eyes blank. Rosemary had called out, but he didn't respond. She held her ground until it was obvious he meant to barrel her over. At the last minute, she pulled aside, and Nate flew off the edge of the building, plummeting to the street below. Rosemary had felt the sick worry for a moment after she woke up, but it dissolved as she told herself it was only a dream, just her worries about him. He was all right; he was on his way.

Lilly parted from Rosemary at what used to be The Brown Palace gift shop. It was a little alcove in the doorway of the grand hotel. Rosemary saw that the signmakers had maintained the elaborate lobby, the tea area, and even the elaborate brass carvings. Lilly explained that it was all housing now; the suites had been allocated to families, the smaller rooms to individuals and couples.

243

The staff, previously unseen as they moved through the series of basement level passageways, now walked proudly around the hotel. Some worked on the buffet, others were stationed at the front desk. The rest, Lilly explained, had been assigned elsewhere. Before Lilly took off down the street, Rosemary caught her arm.

"Hey, I promised somebody I'd ask. My friend, the one who dropped me off yesterday, said that your building was haunted. I promised him I'd find out if anything ever happened to you all while you've been there."

Lilly smiled. "Well, don't ask Mom or Dad unless you want twelve hours of stories. All I've ever seen is pretty minor stuff. I think it's just the wind or something, but the cabinets have a tendency to open themselves, and the water turns on sometimes. It's probably just the pipes, but ask Mom. She definitely has other theories. See you later! Good Luck!"

With that, Lilly bounced down the street, while Rosemary walked into the ex-gift shop and got in line behind a young woman wearing medical scrubs. She turned around and smiled at Rosemary.

"Hey! What a change, huh? I used to work here in the hotel years ago. Never thought they'd let anyone in for under a grand a night! I'm Gloria; just came in from Salt Lake. Where're you from?"

Rosemary shook her outstretched hand. "Rosemary. I'm from California—Mussel Shoals—don't suppose you've ever heard of it?"

Gloria shook her head and went on to chat about how she was hoping to get another job in the hotel, with the food service. She went to culinary school, she explained, was excited to work on the buffet lines. They chatted for about five minutes before Gloria was in front of the brunette waitress behind the check stand. She listened patiently while Gloria explained her skill set. Rosemary began to get nervous. She didn't really have any other skills besides teaching. She wasn't very hot at science, and she certainly couldn't cook or be of much use in a hospital. The waitress presented Gloria with a receipt. Gloria squealed with delight and turned to grin at Rosemary.

"Got it! This is perfect! Hope to see you around!"

Rosemary stepped up to the counter, and the waitress addressed her in a very businesslike tone.

"Welcome to Denver. Please tell me about your skill set."

Rosemary stammered a little. The waitress cut her off.

"Please speak clearly so we can best understand."

Rosemary began again. "I used to be a teacher. I taught history, to high school students. I also like plants, but I don't have any experience with them."

The waitress seemed to be computing her response. "I understand. Do you require housing?"

"Yes, please."

Another pause before the waitress responded. "Is a roommate acceptable or are you traveling with family?"

"My husband is not here yet, but he is on his way to Denver." Rosemary hoped she wasn't lying.

"It is normally our policy not to hold housing for residents who have not yet arrived. We can assign you couples housing for now, but if he has not arrived by the end of the week, we will need to move you in with a roommate. Is this acceptable?"

"Yes, I understand."

The waitress paused and handed Rosemary a receipt that came from under the counter. Instead of numbers and amounts, it showed her job assignment and housing printed on it.

Job Placement:
Educator
Please report to Glenarm and 16th Street as soon as possible
Housing Assignment:
Brown Palace Room #617
Please see front desk for key and additional information

Rosemary walked away stunned. She was going to live at the Brown Palace? She didn't know how that was possible. When she was a teenager, she had walked by the historic hotel all the time, marveling at the carvings, the brass and gold plated moldings. She was actually amazed that it was still here, but then again, it did offer quite a bit of housing. She headed to the front desk to show them her receipt.

72

The sun was coming up as Nate found the bridge that crossed the empty I-25. He grimaced and blocked the sun so he could have a better look at the skyscrapers, their solar panels glinting in the fresh morning light. Behind him was a mail center, and it appeared as though no trucks had arrived this morning. Roman was right. He had told Nate to take the fertilizer transport, that the mail truck would be too slow, that he would delay shooting. For the last stretch of this walk, Nate had been listening to Mary Elizabeth Mastrantonio do vocal warm-ups. She would start out with a low rumble and on one tone raise her voice up to a cat screech. It was driving Nate crazy. He hoped she would lose her voice and be replaced by a mute. He never cared for her, not since she walked onto the set of the Abyss wearing those ridiculous white nylons with her business suit.

Roman was discussing lighting options. Nate was interested in hearing the details, but Mary Elizabeth drowned him out with her siren squeals. The excitement on the set was unbearable. Harry Hamlin had already taken his place, even though Roman warned him that it might be hours before the shooting. Mare Winningham was meditating in her trailer in preparation for her performance. Nate walked on. He was early; he knew that. Roman didn't want to shoot until nightfall, until twilight. It didn't bother Nate, he could wait; he still needed to find the set after all. Roman had kept mum about it so far. Made sense really, this way the paparazzi wouldn't flood the area.

Nate opened his mouth as he crossed the bridge into the city and began to sing softly.

"Out in the West Texas town of El Paso, I fell in love with a Mexican girl..."

A Vespa scooted past him, the driver slowing to pass a strange look as Nate ignored him and sang on.

"Night-time would find me in Rosa's cantina, music would play and Felina would whirl"

He grinned to himself as the scooter passed on into the city. Nate slowed his walk, he had time; he needed the set to be perfect before his entrance.

73

Rosemary loved the little school immediately. She had been there for several hours already and instead of the normal anxiety associated with teaching, she found it exciting. After checking into her room at the Brown Palace, which she found to be a smallish room with dark antique furniture, a queen sized bed and a view of 17th street, she headed down Glenarm. The school obviously used to be a shop of some kind, maybe a Gap; it was spacious and had a storage area in the back. The classes were geared toward fourteen to eighteen year olds—high school students. When she entered, she was greeted by a woman, Tessa, who wore long flowing robes and scarf around her head, and who spoke with a Jamaican lilt to her voice. After checking her receipt, she led Rosemary around by the hand, showing her the area.

Tessa explained that the students arrived at 6:30 and were released at 1:30, giving them time to attend job training classes at the various offices on the mall. Some were learning how to build the turbines, while others were learning about medicine or agriculture. It was left to the student to pick a focus. The purpose of the high school was to advance their reading, and strengthen their math and science skills. Tessa clapped when Rosemary told her that she'd taught history.

"Oh, we haven't had a history teacher come through yet, very important! Good, good!"

Rosemary discovered that there were pod schools all over Denver, and each catered to a small group of students who were essentially in the same field. The Glenarm School taught students who were attending the agriculture training. There was another secondary school upstairs in what used to be a fancy bowling alley, and it catered to the medical students. The space itself was set up like a conference area. Tessa explained that the students all learned together, the older ones helping the younger, much like a one-room schoolhouse from the old times. The teachers took turns with their lessons, helping each other out throughout the day. In this way, each student received a lot of personal attention, and someone was always there to help. Tessa explained that the supplies were kept in the back, but that the waitresses stationed quietly at the front of the space, provided things like textbooks, novels, and other consumable and recyclable supplies.

"You let them know, they get it for you. It's a miracle, no more forms or funding, or budgets; we can actually do our jobs. Amazing, huh?"

That first day, Rosemary observed the classes and hung out on the side, occasionally helping one of the kids with a problem. The students were nice and they looked content, certainly a far cry from the unruly, bored students she taught back at her old school in Mussel Shoals. Tessa hugged her as they left the building that first afternoon at two. Rosemary began walking back to her room, excited to begin her life.

74

Nate wandered the Metro State Campus aimlessly. People bustled back and forth, some stopping to stare at his face, which he imagined must look even more gruesome than it had last night. He could feel the scabs that had begun to form over the cuts and gashes, and the itchiness of the wounds told him that an infection was brewing. He didn't care; soon, it wouldn't matter. Besides, this was how Roman wanted it. He needed to be in character now; he needed to be see the reactions of the people around him. One older lady had actually stopped and gently reached her hand out, waving it around his wounds.

"Honey, we have a clinic in the campus area here. Can we take you over and have them fix this up? You must've had a rough trip out here."
He had just stared her down and held the smirk on his face until she backed away, her eyes avoiding his.

"Well, do as you like then..."
Nate had to swallow his laughter. From what he could see on the campus, it had been converted to housing, and it shared space with what appeared to be a massive elementary school environment. At the time, a crowd of little kids was running on the track field, led by a thirty-ish teacher, who ran backward in front of them. Whatever he was yelling kept making the kids giggle. As he passed Nate, he paused in his yelling for a moment, and looked at him with a perplexed expression.

Good, Nate thought. Good.

Roman was almost ready, just a few more hours. Judd Hirsch was in place in his newly tailored suit. He looked good; he was right, he was tall. Nate walked around the campus, killing time until Roman called places.

By 4:30, Rosemary was enjoying her sautéed tofu and bean sprouts in the lobby of the Brown. Her family had come down to see her room and they were eating together, laughing. She'd seen Gloria behind the line, observing the new procedures. She waved at Rosemary, and a hugely excited smile spread across her face. Rosemary's mother was busy cutting her eggplant carefully into small bites.

"Well, we usually go to the buffet in what used to be the movie theatre.

249

They left the movie seats in place, so they're very comfortable. But this is quite nice. We'll come here now and all eat together."

Rosemary was amazed to see Chuck contentedly eating his veggie burger with barbeque sauce. There had been a time when he steadfastly refused even to try veggie food.

Her mom was thrilled to hear that she had been housed so close to them.

"Just down the street!"

She was right. The front entrance of the Brown at 19th and Sherman was only a few blocks away. Sitting here in the lobby, Rosemary couldn't believe that she had tolerated any other way of living. As the sun began to set, Rosemary hugged her Mom, Chuck and Lilly. They set off up the little hill to their apartment, and Rosemary headed upstairs. She needed to get to sleep since her first full, new day would begin soon.

As the sunset finally yielded to twilight, Nate got off his park bench and began to walk toward the Brown Palace. He really had no idea what it was or where it was, but Roman had been whispering the name in his ear. He simply allowed the voice guide him.

"Brown Palace, boy. I can tell you now. That's where we're shooting tonight. Couldn't tell you earlier, boy, but that's where she is. You'll find her there. She's with him right now, laughing at you. You'll make it stop. You'll show them all that you're no fool, you're no one to be trifled with. Go after her. Keep walking, boy. We're all waiting on you now."

In the background, Nate heard Harry Hamlin clinking his shield, apparently with the sword he carried in the other hand. It was very exciting, especially not knowing which roles the others were playing. Roman wanted it this way; raw, unrehearsed, very exciting. Nate could almost see Rosemary's face, just like in the reel he'd seen earlier. She had the black satin sheets around her, and there was a look of horror and utter in her eyes. This would make him famous; it would get Roman home. It would save everybody. More than that, it was what Nate was born to do. He walked steadily toward 16th Street, toward the electric bus that ran up and down. He needed to head south, now, and he needed to hurry.

Rosemary was drowsy by 6 p.m. She had been studying the guidebook in her room, and its theme was similar to the one she'd glanced through in Vegas, especially the part where it outlined the area's upcoming projects. According to the book, residents were limited to three full showers a week to conserve water. Sponge baths were to be used the other days. It was up to each resident to decide on a schedule. Rosemary decided to use one of her showers and go to bed. Someone had thoughtfully left towels, two changes of clothes, and a set of cotton pajamas in her room while she was at dinner. She liked the pajamas, which were light blue and had a motif of little strawberries hanging on tiny vines.

As the water hit her face and much neglected hair, Rosemary breathed a sigh of relief. She couldn't shake her feeling of anticipation—didn't really know if she wanted to—even though it was dreadful and exciting all at once. The only thing she could compare it to was the one time in junior high when she had been in a school play. The feeling, the butterflies in her stomach, was exactly what she remembered feeling before he teacher shoved her onstage. She felt watched. As she rubbed hotel shampoo through her hair, she shivered involuntarily.

Little bitch certainly had upgraded, Nate thought. The Brown Palace was something else. Gold colored carvings and red trimmed carpet that spread across the sidewalk. As Nate walked into the lobby, he sneered at the elaborate atrium. She was here somewhere; he knew it, and he heard Roman's voice urging him from the background.

"Action!"

The clap of the marker, and then:

"Take One"

Nate took a step forward feeling the weight of the work. He was stopped by Harry Hamlin, his gold and silver robes swept slightly back by the fan the gaffers had strategically placed.

"Welcome to the Brown Palace sir. The living quarters are for residents only. Do you have your key?"

Harry looked nervous. He was fidgeting with his robe. Nate expected Roman to call cut, but the camera kept running. Out of the corner of his eye, Nate saw a cue card, and as soon as he spied the first word, he knew his line.

"I'm meeting my wife. I've just arrived from out of town. Is there anyone who can assist me?"

Harry Hamlin stood up straight and pointed to the front desk before Nate even finished his line. The camera kept rolling, and Nate began to cross the lobby, conscious of the angle he was presenting to the camera he knew was following him. Roman was going for a one-shot scene, which meant three cameras followed him, each at a forty-five degree angle; no stops, no cutting away. Gaffers raced behind the cameramen, clearing the cable. You could hear a pin drop as the extras milled about the lobby, mouthing conversation to each other, silently laughing. The noise would be duplicated in the studio later; dubbed in. Right now, they needed to hear Nate.

He approached the desk and saw Mare Winningham behind the counter. She rose from a high stool when she saw him, and her voice was steady and metered. In this scene, it carried an edge of Katherine Hepburn wobble.

"Welcome. Can I help you, sir?'

Nate thought he saw Roman in the corner, waving at her. Her brown eyes brightened, and she seemed to relax her shoulders a bit.

"I'm looking for my wife, Rosemary McLeod. She arrived this morning. I believe she left a key for me at the desk."

Nate heard the rise of the C# scale in the background, the scratchy tone of a violin joined the piano and the scale picked up speed, but the volume remained low, but gained steadily in intensity.

Mare Winningham passed a key smoothly across the counter, and Nate smiled and nodded. A low drumbeat joined the scale, it's steady rhythm like a heartbeat. Nate turned to go, and the cameras narrowed onto his surprised face as Judd Hirsch appeared behind him, luggage cart in hand.

"Welcome to Denver, sir. Can I help you with your luggage?"
Nate shook his head, patted front pocket where the prop girl had placed the coiled piano wire right before the cameras started rolling.

"No thanks, I'm traveling light."
Judd Hirsch paused to obtain just the right effect. He leaned forward and delivered the line he had been practicing all day.

"I'm sure you are, sir. I'm sure you are."
As Nate started up the winding staircase, he looked back down at the lobby. Harry Hamlin, Mare Winningham, and Judd Hirsch all stood in a row, staring after him.

Rosemary stepped out the shower and wrapped herself in the white towel. As she began to pull a comb through her hair, she could swear she heard the faintest sounds of a violin. It was like the music she heard earlier in her dream; scratchy, discordant. She shivered again briefly, and then slipped on the blue pajamas. She glanced around the room again as she pulled her hair back into a long braid. Maybe Kevin had been right all along. Maybe this place was haunted. She tried her best to shake the butterflies in her stomach as she lay down in the big bed, but the music was growing louder, and gaining in strength. She heard tuneless piano chords and a djembe beat that was steady but intense. Some kind of metallic drum rang in like a shudder, and as the noise increased, so did Rosemary's fear. She wanted to bolt, wanted to run, but where? How do you run from something that's coming from inside you? She sat up in the bed, hugging her knees to her chest.

The cameras followed Nate up the staircase, desperate gaffers coiling so fast that their hands must have been burning. Nate took a left on the 6th floor according to Roman's excited hand directions. As he did, he nearly ran straight into Mary Elizabeth Mastrantonio, who was pushing a housekeeper's cart. She was wearing those white tights under her grey housekeeper's uniform. She considered him dramatically for a moment before she held out a stack of white towels.

"Does your room require housekeeping?"
Nate shook his head. "No. My room is all set."
Roman danced behind the monitor waving them forward. Mary Elizabeth parted from Nate after giving him a deep look. She swerved her cart expertly to the left, and let him pass. Finally in the clear, Roman waved him on

down the hall.

Room 617 was mid-way down the hall. When he found it, Nate paused before he slipped the card key in the sensor. As the green light flashed, Roman became still. He looked up at Nate. This was his scene; this was something not even he could write. Nate would do it alone. With a pale face, he collapsed against the back of his director's chair. His eyes narrowed, and he folded his hands. Nate pushed the door open just as the music swelled.

The click of the door made Rosemary slam back into the headboard. She instinctually scooted to the far side of the bed and accidentally slid off the side. The music was deafening. She had begun seeing lights from the periphery of her vision. Whenever she blinked, she saw an older man who sat with his hands folded in a director's chair and stared at her expressionlessly. She wanted to scream, but the sound caught in her throat.

She heard footsteps round the end of the bed and quickly slid under it and tried to slither to the other side. Maybe she could make a run for the door. Her scream finally escaped as the bed with its frame attached was suddenly hurled against the opposing wall. The sound of the violin pierced her ears as she looked up and saw Nate silhouetted in the window. The streetlights outside framed his face, which was torn and gouged. In the dim light, she saw that puss had started to form on the gashes near the base of his neck. He was wearing green hospital scrubs, and his hands and feet were puffy red; too dark, frostbite dark, the blackness of the dead tissue spreading from the extremities. He smelled like something already dead. His voice was too quiet, yet horribly raspy.

"Thought I wouldn't find you? Well I found you, bitch! No use trying to hide him, either. Where is he? In the closet? In the bathroom?" Nate stormed to the closet door and tore at it with his hands. Rosemary screamed again as he ripped the antique bureau door cleanly off its hinges. Never dropping his dead stare, he slammed his hand on the bathroom door, sending it flying as well. The wood splintered. Nate reached for the light switch.

"No use hiding him, dear. I know all about the game you've been playing."

The bathroom light highlighted the horror of Nate's injuries. His face was mottled red with dried blood, the gashes looked like tear marks, like he had torn at his face. His neck was swollen to twice its size, a milky puss forming a cocoon. Almost more frightening, his eyes held a detached and ravenous look. Blood oozed from the deadened, black flesh at the tips of his fingers. Rosemary tried to propel herself up, tried to run for the door, but Nate lunged.

The scene was all wrong. She wasn't in the bed, and her blond lover hadn't rushed forward to protect her. Nate was enraged. He circled the room, and in the dim light he saw the impression she'd left on the mattress. She was hiding. Damn little bitch was hiding. He fingered the piano wire in his pocket as he stared into the camera. He saw Roman, eyes blazing, hunched forward with tension. He would make it work. He would finish the scene.

The sharp pain radiated from Rosemary's head, down her neck and back. She couldn't focus on what happened, the overpowering foulness of Nate's rotting breath filled her senses and snapped her back. She gasped for the air that was being blocked by Nate's hand that now wrapped tightly around her throat. She flailed at him with every ounce of feral strength she could muster, but she only made him laugh. When had this happened? Who had be become? Rosemary didn't have time to react to the monster in front of her, didn't have time to mourn for the man she knew was still somewhere underneath. In the seconds she had, she used the only weapon she knew ever worked against this madness. She knew what she needed to say, but she had to force the words from her constricted throat. In gasps and fits, she snapped at him as loudly as she could:

"Cut this out! You'll ruin the shoot! We're on a schedule!"
Nate's eyes clouded for a minute and the intensity of his grip decreased slightly. For half a second, he looked scared.

Something was wrong. A voice was coming from behind Roman, telling him to stop the scene, to call a break. Nate faltered for the smallest second and looked to Roman for direction. Roman pushed his director's chair back so hard it slammed against the wall behind him. He pointed at Nate, his eyes black.

Rosemary saw the fire return to his eyes. His grip increased again, and she felt the pressure from the air trapped in her lungs. Her throat burned. With his free hand, Nate reached into his pocket and pulled out a thin silver wire. Rosemary's panic rose anew, and she thrashed back and forth under the viselike grip knowing what he intended. As the silver wire grew closer, she felt the tears streaming down her cheeks.

"Please...don't. Nate, please don't do...."
As Nate unfurled the wire, Rosemary was blinded. The air suddenly rushed back into her lungs and the pressure released. She dropped to the floor like a stone. She couldn't stop the hacking, her lungs burned, and for the first time, she heard the pounding on the other side of the door. Voices. Scared voices.

She looked up, but brilliant flashes blocked her vision. In between the moving blobs, she saw a signpost where Nate had been standing, where he'd been trying to kill her.

To Whom It May Concern:
The resident known as Nathan McLeod
Has been judged guilty of grievous violations
Of the new guidelines.
As a result, he has been permanently removed.
We apologize for the inconvenience.

Rosemary opened her mouth, and from the bottom of her soul came a sob that shook her entire body. The door flew open and a small crowd of   people tumbled in and rushed to her side. They glanced at the sign, and Rosemary felt their featherweight hands on her battered neck and shoulders. Someone switched on the lights, and Rosemary shook with the sobs that were as much for what had just happened as they were for all the memories and images that were flooding her mind. Nate's face in the moonlight, laughing at her stories as they sat on *Clementine*'s deck. The feel of Nate's hands on her hips, the sweet smell of his aftershave, the dark green of his eyes, his lips on her neck. It all flooded her senses. She felt hands supporting her, but the blackness was powerful, and it advanced steadily as the scratchy music abruptly cut out.

75

As the sun came up, Rosemary opened her eyes to see her mother leaning over her bed. She was confused. Had any of it happened? Was it all some weird dream? As she tried to raise her head, she felt the stabbing pain course from her neck down her back, and she knew it hadn't been a dream.

"Oh, baby. Just lay back, baby. We got here as soon as we could. We've been here all night. Don't worry, we're not going to leave you."
Rosemary recognized her mother's voice, and when she blinked her eyes into focus, she saw her standing close by. Being careful not to turn her head, she glanced around the room to find that Lilly and Chuck were sitting at the edge of her bed. Lilly's face was red and puffy. Rosemary's throat burned as she asked.

"But, what...what happened. Don't you have to work?"

Her family exchanged stunned looks for a moment before they erupted in laughter. It felt good; the tension washed away. Her mother smoothed her hair back.

"That's my little girl. Nearly gets killed overnight and the first question she asks is why we aren't all at work. Don't you worry about that. It's a break day, we all get them. We took ours together; just settle back. Don't worry about the details for once. The doctor said you needed some time to recover."

Rosemary felt her tears stick in her throat. "He's gone, Mom, he's gone."

"Shhhh, shhh, I know, honey. But from what I've heard, it wasn't him anymore, baby. People downstairs said he acted fairly normal until he got to staircase. They tried to get him a doctor, but he was speaking gibberish. He was also pretty torn up. I think he got hurt real bad before he got here, honey. It sounds like he wasn't in his right mind."

Despite the pain she knew would come, Rosemary shook her head.

"He's sick! He has a disorder. It's not his fault, he can't help it when he goes off the bridge like that. They didn't even give him a warning!" The last of her cry was muffled with a fresh sob.

"Oh, honey, they already had. I don't know how to tell you this, but I think the other guy must've been a friend of yours from California. He, well, there was a sign about it this morning; an explanation. Eli Wilkins, you know him?"

Rosemary nodded a little. Eli; that was the conspiracy theorist's name.

"Well, they found him, this morning, honey. Looks like he was beaten to death just outside Green River, Utah. Crazy story, according to the front desk. Evidently, there was some kind of hideout, underground cave or something. Anyway, they found a half-starved girl on the highway with your friend, but it was too late. He was gone. Guess the signmakers knew something had happened to him but couldn't figure it out. There was a car there too; it had run off the road. They found out that Nate did it, but they almost didn't find him soon enough. Some trucker out in the fertilizer fields sent a note into town today warning about a weirdo he'd left on the road the night before."

Rosemary shook her head a little. She felt dried up, drained. He was gone; she'd lost him days ago maybe. She hadn't been there to stop his voices, to order them back in line. Now, Eli was dead and Nate had been removed. And it was all her fault. The car she had seen, that had been Nate. Maybe she could have stopped him. But she might have ended up like Eli. She breathed out, empty.

"Hon, you just need to rest. You'll be all right now. Relax. You can't save everybody. Sometimes, people have problems bigger than what we can fix..."

Rosemary doubled over, the dry sobs draining into her hands. She felt her mom's tender touch on her shoulders and fought the urge to shrug them off. A cramp filled her gut, a stabbing pain shook her body. From inside her misery, she heard Lilly's voice.

"You guys have got to see this! Quick, get over here. It's crazy!"

Rosemary struggled up from the bed and with her mom's help limped to the window. A large sign had sprouted in the middle of the street, and it was quickly attracting attention. People were flocking to it, murmuring to each other. Lilly looked over her shoulder.

"I'm going down. C'mon, Rosemary, you could use some fresh air."

In her blue strawberry pajamas, Rosemary allowed Lilly and her parents to help her to the elevator and then out to the street. Stunned, they stared up at the sign.

To Whom It May Concern:
We kindly request that you refrain from
All future attempts to destroy or otherwise
damage us.
All weapons of mass destruction that were
Previously overlooked or undisclosed
Have now been located and permanently removed
Please remember, we are only here to help.
Thank you

Who knew which handwritten note had been correct, which city had been bombed, who had been blamed. All that mattered in the early morning light was that a great wrong had been made right. Rosemary watched the people around her acknowledge the sign and begin again on their paths. Unforeseeable consequences weighed heavy in the morning air. Still, time didn't stop, it didn't even acknowledge the change.

Standing in the middle of 17th Street with the wind blowing against the thin fabric of her pajamas, Rosemary felt the sum total of her experience bear down upon her. With dry eyes, she angled her head upward and pulled the crisp morning air into her burning lungs. Without a word, she turned from the warning sign and walked back to her room. There was much still to be done.